SINS
of the
PAST

SINS OF THE PAST

A ROMANTIC SUSPENSE NOVELLA COLLECTION

MISSING BY DEE HENDERSON

SHADOWED BY DANI PETTREY

BLACKOUT BY LYNETTE EASON

DISCARD

BETHANYHOUSE
a division of Baker Publishing Group
Minneapolis, Minnesota

Missing © 2016 by Dee Henderson
Shadowed © 2016 by Dani Pettrey
Blackout © 2016 by Lynette Eason

Published by Bethany House Publishers
11400 Hampshire Avenue South
Bloomington, Minnesota 55438
www.bethanyhouse.com

Bethany House Publishers is a division of
Baker Publishing Group, Grand Rapids, Michigan

Printed in the United States of America

ISBN 978-0-7642-1798-2 (cloth)
ISBN 978-0-7642-1797-5 (trade paper)

Library of Congress Control Number: 2016930533

These novellas are works of fiction. Names, characters, incidents, and dialogues are products of the author's imagination and are not to be construed as real. Any resemblance to actual events or persons, living or dead, is entirely coincidental.

Cover design by LOOK Design Studio

Dani Pettrey represented by Books & Such Literary Agency
Lynette Eason represented by The Steve Laube Agency

16 17 18 19 20 21 22   7 6 5 4 3 2 1

Contents

MISSING

DEE HENDERSON

ONE

John Graham, police chief for Cheyenne, Wyoming, knew the value of remaining calm in a crisis. He'd learned that during the early days of his career working undercover, when often it was his own life on the line. But he could feel that control slipping now as he strode down the O'Hare Airport concourse.

His mother was missing. The last confirmed sighting of her was Monday afternoon around 4:30 p.m. at the retirement village where she lived. It was now going on 9:00 p.m. Tuesday. That was too many hours for a son to take without it causing a great deal of internal turmoil.

People moved out of his way, either the grim set to his face or the pace of his stride making it clear he wasn't a man they wanted to slow down.

"Chief Graham."

He spotted a dark-haired slender woman in a police jacket aiming in his direction, and he moved across the traffic flow to meet her, accepting her handshake. Her fingers were chilled.

He wondered briefly where her gloves were on a cold December evening in Chicago.

"I'm Lieutenant Sharon Noble with the Riverside PD. I'm very sorry about your mother," she said, sounding genuinely concerned. "I'm primary on the case. I figured it would be faster to fill you in on the drive than have you face a fifty-person search and try to get an orderly sense of what is happening. Do you have checked bags?"

He tipped his head toward his carry-on. "This is it."

"I've got a squad car waiting."

She sounded competent, and he felt just a bit of the stress lift.

She aimed for the terminal entrance without more than a pause in her stride. "I've got a concealed-carry permit if you require it," she said over her shoulder.

She was skirting TSA flight regulations and indirectly asking if he'd brought a gun with him while smoothly indicating she wasn't going to slap his wrist for the infraction. He appreciated her even more. He'd left his duty weapon along with his badge with his deputy chief. "We don't have her back in a few hours, I'll take you up on that and will be carrying."

"With what I've already learned about Martha Graham, I'm guessing she raised a smart son."

"Smart enough."

"While you were in the air I confirmed your alibi for the last forty-eight hours."

He narrowed his eyes but nodded. "You didn't make lieutenant by not checking the obvious. Dad left her comfortably well-off. I'll inherit, but I don't plan on doing so for another twenty years."

"I got that impression when I saw the list of phone calls between Chicago and Cheyenne. I'm told you two are close. All right, continuing to rule out family, she has a sister in Boulder,

Colorado, and a cousin in Wichita, Kansas. Your late father has a younger brother and sister living in Boston, Massachusetts. Anybody significant I'm missing?"

"That's the list."

They stepped out into a below-freezing night, and a car's lights in the pick-up lane flashed. John wore a sheep's-wool-lined coat, heavy gloves, and boots that could handle whatever snow was on the ground. She was in a lined police jacket with freezing hands and uncovered hair, wearing tennis shoes and hoping for traction. He'd like to at least offer the gloves, but she was already headed toward the Riverside Police squad car. She opened the rear door for him, grabbed his duffel bag and dropped it into the trunk, then circled the car to the other side. He ducked his head and climbed in while she also settled into the backseat.

"Officer Jefferies," she said, leaning forward, "this is John Graham, the police chief for Cheyenne, Wyoming."

"Nice to meet you, sir." The driver handed back a drink carrier. Sharon accepted it and the sack that followed. "We have hot coffee and a mega sub sandwich for you, John, while you listen for the next twenty minutes."

Officer Jefferies turned on the overhead lights for the backseat and quickly cut through the airport traffic. Sharon handed over a hot coffee and took the other for herself, wrapping both hands around it. Though John wasn't hungry, he took the sandwich from the sack, knowing food made it possible to run longer and harder on this job. "I'll listen without interrupting."

"Appreciate it. Here's what I know, in contrast to what I suspect. Your mother played bridge Monday afternoon at the home of a Mrs. Emily Chestnut—a nice name for the Christmas season," she mentioned with a smile. "Martha left there shortly after 4:30 p.m. Your mother's car is presently in the parking lot of the Riverside Retirement Village, in her normal parking place in front of Building Number One. The security gate for the complex is closed at 10:00 p.m., and a guard clears traffic in after that hour. The man on the gate remembers your mom's car being parked there when he went on duty Monday night.

"Friends stopped by your mother's apartment this morning for their usual 'Tuesday Tea at Ten' gathering she hosts every week. Martha didn't answer their knock. They called her apartment phone, got no answer. They called her cell phone, could hear it ring inside, but also got no answer. They assumed your mother had stepped out momentarily to get something and would be right back.

"At 10:12 a.m., with growing concern, Mrs. Heather Jome—who states she's one of your mother's closest friends in the complex—called the staff desk."

He nodded, confirming the ladies' friendship.

"The manager for the Riverside Retirement Village, a lady named Theresa Herth, arrived and unlocked the apartment to conduct a wellness check on the resident. She found the apartment empty. Your mother's purse is sitting on the chair inside the door, cell phone inside, keys missing. It appears she stepped out of her apartment, keys in hand, assuming she would be gone no more than a moment. After that—" she paused—"we don't know."

And the son in him wanted to shudder at those words. He felt his muscles tighten, but only nodded.

Sharon paused to drink more coffee before flipping open a folder. She held out a stack of photos. "Photos of your mother's apartment. There are no obvious signs of a struggle or accident, a rug she might have tripped on, no smear of blood in the shower, nothing disorderly among things on a table, no noticeable items missing from the dresser or desk. The apartment is being printed so we can tell who's been inside. But to me it looks like she had her keys in her hand, stepped out, and whatever's occurred didn't happen there."

He sorted slowly through the photos—the purse on a chair, pillows neat on the couch, mail on the counter, hairbrush on the bathroom sink, jewelry box still full. His heart twisted at all the familiar items from his mother's life. Was this all he'd have left of her? He stopped the thought and wouldn't allow himself to go any further down that road.

Sharon was saying, "The women's bridge group agrees that on Monday afternoon Martha was wearing a red dress with small white dots, black leather shoes, open-circle one-inch earrings, long black dress coat, patterned scarf, and black gloves. I didn't find those items in the apartment."

That was useful information. John flipped rapidly through the photos again.

"It's possible Martha came home Monday and changed, that the dress is already at the dry cleaner," Sharon offered. "Or she may still be wearing the dress. One possibility suggests she stepped out of her apartment Monday evening, the other that she stepped out early this morning. The fact she grabbed her coat and keys suggests she wasn't just going down the hall."

He studied the photo of his mother's bedroom. "She makes her bed as soon as she rises. She always has."

"That's what her friends said. So . . . it could be this morning when she stepped out. I asked if she had a habit of walking over to the commons building to retrieve a newspaper, but the responses were mixed. I didn't find the dress in her closet or a dry-cleaner pickup stub in her purse, which pushes me toward her leaving the apartment Monday evening."

"If that's the case, she was gone twelve hours before someone noticed," he said heavily, wishing he had someone to blame for that so he would have somewhere to put this pain. Blame himself. He hadn't called to say good-night, which he sometimes did.

Sharon reached over and lightly rested a hand on his arm, extending a small slice of comfort for that pain. "Keys in her hand, she pulls on her coat, leaves her purse and phone, steps out thinking she'd be gone just a moment. And *something* happened. Nobody noticed her absence until midmorning tea."

He knew his mom. She would have returned, been in touch somehow, if it were in her ability to do so. He took a deep breath and let it out. "Keep going," he requested softly.

"My read on the Village manager, Theresa Herth—thirties, competent, organized, well-liked. She doesn't miss much among her staff or among those who live in the Village. Theresa doesn't know of any romantic interests in your mother's life—at least not within the Village community—or of any neighbor disputes, or even something where your mother was trying to mediate a concern among her friends. Affairs happen, there have been divorces in the complex, and a few residents don't speak to one another. But it seems your mother was remarkably free and clear of any social drama going on."

"She's more a live-and-let-live kind of lady," John said. "Well, that's not entirely true," he added. "She loves to help when someone will let her."

Sharon nodded. "That could be useful. Her friends checked your mother's phone for messages and calls, yet didn't see anything useful. I've been through them and agree. Still, I've got an officer re-creating message and phone traffic as far back as we can go for a deeper assessment. You want the tick-tock or the overview?"

"Give me the tick-tock."

"At 10:45 a.m. Theresa put out a 'locate resident' call to her staff. It sends a photo of your mom to every staff member, and they have assigned areas they are to visually check—the commons rooms, the bike path, the pool and garden, the parking lots. Staff weren't able to locate Martha and saw no signs of anything amiss. They then started a phone chain, calling her friends, people in her building, looking for someone who had last seen her.

"At 1:00 p.m. the staff began an official walk-through, working off blueprints, initialing where they checked. They called the hospitals in the area. Volunteers began to pass out her photo around the complex and at stores within walking distance of the Village.

"At 4:00 p.m., six hours after they knew Martha was missing, Theresa called the cops. That six-hour time window is the agreed protocol between the police department and the Village.

"We wouldn't normally work a missing adult in the first forty-eight hours unless there's evidence of suspicious circumstances. I don't like what I see here, but I don't have evidence that points to foul play. So officially we're treating this case as an elderly missing medical. It lets me bring in uniforms before those forty-eight hours have passed."

"I appreciate that. Just out of curiosity, why the six-hour protocol?"

"At under four hours we 'locate' too many seniors taking a nap. At eight hours we've probably lost whatever daylight is left, any eyewitnesses, and so forth. There aren't enough cops to handle all the alerts, but six hours tends to put us on the cases we should be working. This one is a suspicious missing, even if we're calling it something else. A cop's mom is a unique case. Not simply that you are one of us," she added, "but you're high profile in law enforcement. We'll get to that later."

"Having manpower on it early may be the difference."

"Let's hope that proves true. What we've done since the call came in: we're interviewing people, trying to fill in and tighten the timeline, and we're doing a systematic sweep of the property. The Riverside Retirement Village is a complex of six apartment buildings and has—" she pulled a sheet of notes from her folder—"two hundred forty-two residents, fifty-one full- and part-time staff, a commons building, spacious gardens, bike path, enclosed pool, and miscellaneous support buildings. All this spread across forty-one acres. We're not going to complete that sweep tonight. We've got fifty people working on the search—half are cops, half volunteers. I pulled in those from the community who have helped before, and I've got a number of cops on their own time since this is a cop's mom. But it's a lot of area to recheck."

"To do it right, it's going to take time," he agreed, already feeling that duration rest heavily on him.

"We have uniforms knocking on doors and asking for permission to do visual checks inside apartments, focusing first on your mother's building and the adjoining one. The residents are mostly mid-sixties to mid-eighties, and I've agreed to stop knocking on the oldest residents' doors at 9:00 p.m., 10:00 p.m. for the younger ones. We'll start again first thing in the morning.

"We're pulling security-camera footage—there's surprisingly little of it within the complex, I'm sorry to say—from the Village and from businesses within the immediate area. We've locked down the place for outgoing traffic, and cops are checking any vehicles before they exit. Background checks on staff and those we can identify who have been on the property are under way."

"You're really moving on this."

"I'm treating it like it's my mother."

He appreciated the sentiment. "Her car?"

"They moved from the apartment to the car for prints and photographs. I don't have those yet. We need to know who was in your mother's life, and the more prints, photos, phone calls and the like I can gather means that people we interview can't lie to me."

She was taking the right steps. He just wished for a solid lead, that he could be out there *doing something*.

"If we don't have her located by morning, we'll release her photo to the media in time for the 7:00 a.m. newscasts," Sharon continued. "Police will handle the early-morning interviews, but if we don't have solid info by noon, we'll talk about you doing interviews to increase media coverage."

"Agreed."

She nodded ahead at the snarled traffic. "We're about to arrive at the Village complex. Any questions at this point?"

"I can stick with you?"

She smiled. "I'm mostly accommodating. It's not often I get to direct around a chief of police. I'll employ you where I can."

"Thanks."

"If you need to go somewhere during the next forty-eight hours, Officer Jefferies here—or his partner—will be your driver. I want to be able to locate you quickly if necessary."

Jefferies cleared the front-gate security and parked. John started to get out when Sharon put her hand on his arm. "Give us a minute, Jefferies."

"Sure, Lieutenant." The officer stepped out and closed the door.

"You know the most logical answer to this, John. A cop's mother has disappeared. I'm going to assume you're willing to consider this a kidnapping for ransom, and you're prepared to get a phone call."

He'd made that assumption before he boarded the flight out of Cheyenne. "My phone is being tapped, traced, and recorded. Anything to my private line back in Cheyenne, home or office, they'll reroute to this cell. The phone in my mother's apartment is now being monitored?"

"Routed to me."

He sighed. "If that's what this is about, I should have gotten that call by now."

"Or they're waiting for your face to appear on screen." She pushed open her door. "Command center first, then I walk you around—to her car, her apartment, and put you to work. You know her better than any of us. Maybe you'll notice something we've missed."

■ ■ ■

The commotion was more than a low buzz. That was his first impression as he followed Sharon into the commons building. In the lobby, tables had been set up, and volunteers supervised by officers studied maps and marked them up, talking about locations where they had already given out flyers and places they had checked. The smell of coffee and hot chocolate mingled with woodsmoke from the fireplace now burning brightly to counter the chill from the constantly opening doors.

A woman barreled into John for a tight hug that stopped him in his tracks. He recognized her when he could see more than the top of her silvery head. "Annabelle, you know my mother well," he said. "We'll find her."

"We're mostly filling coffeepots for the searchers and calling people."

"It's help and it all matters," he assured with another hug.

He followed Sharon to the conference room where the police had set up shop. Sixteen people were working the room, a tight fit. The walls were taped with street maps, blueprints of the buildings, large sheets of butcher paper in place of a whiteboard, lists of names being marked off, checklists running down assignments. This room was about organizing what was happening in the lobby area and beyond.

But it was a cop-driven search center, and when John read *morgue, homicide desk, sex registry, accident calls,* he felt his chest tighten. But he would have put them on the list himself. He moved on to more positive items, such as the timeline. A snowflake sketch showing Martha's links to various people, including her friends here and a few from the past, neighbors, former co-workers. He didn't see anybody who was even close to being an enemy; he didn't think she had one. His snowflake would not be so tidy. Those who might harm her would come at her because of him.

He spotted an item written in blue marker on the lead board. "Gray van?"

An officer leaning over a table turned at the question. "Pulled through the parking lot Monday evening at dusk, slow-rolled, didn't stop. Noticed by two residents walking back from the commons building. They thought it was a delivery van, but there was no logo on its side."

Sharon nodded toward the officer. "John, this is Detective Bryon Slate. He's coordinating matters. Bryon, Martha's son, John Graham. Tell me you've got the van on some camera footage."

"We're looking. I don't think it's going to be our answer, Lieutenant. The couple who described it were walking to Martha's building. They swear no one exited or entered the van. It simply circled and left. They would have seen Martha if she'd been outside or just coming out. I've got two people looking for some other video on it, but the van didn't come around again that I can pinpoint. We'll nail this down. For right now though, it's an anomaly."

"Okay. What else?"

"Officer Martinez, run that video you found for the lieutenant."

A uniformed woman headed over to the laptop feeding the large wall screen. She typed, and soon grainy security-camera footage appeared on-screen. John walked with Sharon across the room to better see it.

"The Sonic Restaurant at the end of the block has a camera facing south," the officer explained. "This is today, 6:19 a.m." She pressed pause. "That stone pillar at the edge of the image, that's the front gate to this property. You can see the security gate arm is up—they open the drive at 6:00 a.m." She restarted the video. "Normal street traffic going by. That white van entering is the newspaper delivery truck. Next a smaller cargo van, that's the bakery delivery. Nothing for three minutes, then this." She stopped the video on a dark-blue sedan, its driver's door displaying a taxi logo.

"We called the company to see about the pickup. They had no pickup on the books for the Village. We can't see the cab medallion number from the angles we have. It could be a driver making some extra money off the books, but a 6:30 a.m. pickup seems like something scheduled. Cabs are a common sight here, since a third of the residents no longer drive. The thing is, we can't find a resident who's currently out of town, or one who left early this morning and came back later." She ran forward the tape. "The cab leaves twelve minutes later. It's an anomaly, like the gray van."

"If you're looking for inconspicuous, a taxi would do that for you," Sharon said.

"I'll find more footage, get a medallion number. They've got questions about taxis on the interview list. Hopefully we'll find someone who saw this one."

"Good. Any video of Martha's car returning from her bridge game on Monday?"

"Maybe."

"Explain."

Officer Martinez cued up another piece of video. "The same Sonic Restaurant security-camera footage. Unfortunately, that view frequently gets blocked. This is Monday at 4:30 p.m." They watched the street traffic. Cars regularly came and went through the Village gate. The image abruptly became gray metal with a sliver on the right of continuing street traffic. "A semitruck is unloading at the restaurant for twenty-two minutes," she said.

She fast-forwarded. The obstruction was gone, the image back to street traffic moving by, the occasional car entering or exiting the front gate.

"I've been through the footage between 4:30 and 10:00 p.m.," Officer Martinez said, "when the security guard says he knows Martha's car was in her parking space. Since I never see her car enter, I can assume she turned into the front gate during a period when this camera view was blocked. I can give you six windows of time, fifty-seven minutes total, when the view was blocked. That's a lot of traffic coming and going that I can't see. And once it gets past dusk, the lighting becomes a problem." Now on fast-forward again, the streetlights were coming on, and the ability to distinguish vehicles dwindled to shapes seen only by their headlights. "The most I can give you after dusk is that a car entered, and a rough idea of its model by the type of headlights."

"You have those blocked times written out?"

"I have them as Post-it notes on the timeline. We need to find another video source. Her car six blocks away coming this direction, something like that, will give us the correct time window for her return. I'll find something to tighten it down, Lieutenant."

"Anything that refines our timeline will be a great help." Sharon scanned the room and the boards. "Bryon, what do you want to work next?"

"Felons in the area. Turns out three with records work here on staff."

"I'll be back to help on that." Sharon turned to John. "We're good at this part of the job. I'd like to take you over to your mother's apartment. You'll be more useful to me there. You know her best, and that matters when assessing what's there and what's not."

"Let's go," he said.

She led the way out. He glanced at his watch and saw it was nearing 10:30 p.m. "Lieutenant, I'd like to speak briefly with Annabelle and the other friends of Mom's who are here—try to convince them to get some sleep for a few hours, if nothing else."

"Check the library down the hall on the left. They were holding vigil for her there earlier this evening."

He nodded, skirted the other volunteers, and went to locate Annabelle. Five of his mother's friends waited together. They turned his direction as he walked over. "Thanks for being here, ladies," he began as he sat down. "I understand Mom stood you up for Tuesday Tea at Ten." The lighthearted comment was just the right touch for the moment.

"Oh, she would have hated to be the center of all this attention," Annabelle told him, looking around the group at their nods of agreement. "Do they know anything, John? Anything they aren't telling us yet?"

"She came home from bridge. What happened after that is simply conjecture. She has her coat, so I don't think she's cold. She must have her keys since they haven't been found. In the next twenty-four hours the cops are going to cover a lot of ground, and that should answer some questions. I expect Mom will be

22

home by then." They blinked at that reassurance, and he saw a measure of hope return to their weary faces.

"Can we do anything to help?" several of them asked.

"Coffee for the searchers, prayers for my mother's safe return, a sympathetic smile when I sit down to wait with you awhile. It all matters. You keep us going; you remind the volunteers by the simple fact of your presence how important Martha is." He scanned the circle of faces and knew his mother had been right to stay in Chicago in the years since his father passed away. She had good friends here.

He saw Sharon in the doorway. "Please, head back to your apartments now," he suggested as he stood, "get some sleep, come back in the morning to help keep the volunteers organized. It's likely going to be double the number of volunteers tomorrow, and what might seem like small acts of service do matter. I'll be around until Mom is safely home. If you need me, a message at the front desk will get to me." He paused to hug Annabelle, said his goodbyes to the others.

Sharon handed him a coffee mug. "You called friends in to help before you left Wyoming?"

He wasn't expecting the question, and it took a second. He smiled. "It's what a smart man does when his mother goes missing."

"I've got two from FBI now in the conference room, and a Chicago PD captain who says you used to work for him unloading heat-detection equipment. He plans to sweep the bike path and surrounding landscape when the night is the coldest."

He hated the reality of it, but was glad that would be done. "It needs to be cleared off the list."

"Agreed. And I'm accepting all help," Sharon mentioned, "wherever it comes from. How many more friends should I expect?"

"By morning or in the next hour?"

She smiled. "I'll take them as surprises then when they arrive." She nodded to the side door. "Let's slip out this way."

She still didn't have any gloves. He held out his hand for the binder she carried and tucked it under his arm, and she shoved her hands in her pockets.

"How are you holding up?" she asked.

"A long plane ride with nothing to do but think the worst, followed by the reality of this—I'm glad I'm not in charge. It's different when it's personal. The assignment at her apartment will help. I've got a few good hours in me yet tonight."

Sharon nodded. "It's hard leaving family to others, but Bryon is good, and I've been doing missing-persons cases for seven years. We're going to make a lot more headway over the next hours."

She pointed out his mother's car as they approached Building One. "Would you like an officer to open the car for you to take a look?"

"Got photos of the interior?"

"Yes."

"It'll be easier to work from photos on a cold night."

He counted windows to the second floor, fourth window . . . the lights were on in his mother's apartment. "Do you think she's outside in this cold?" he asked.

Sharon removed her hand from her pocket to squeeze his arm. She didn't try to answer.

■ ■ ■

They bypassed the elevator and walked up the stairs to the second floor. Wide hallways, carpet barely showing wear, good lighting, neat apartment numbers and traditional doorbells—he'd approved when his mother decided to move here. The officer outside the apartment nodded to the lieutenant, then looked over at him. "I'm sorry about your mother, Chief Graham."

He heard the sincerity in the comment and nodded as he read the uniform tag. "Thank you, Stephens."

Sharon opened the apartment door and stepped back for him. All the lights were on, even the tiny canister lights shining down in the glass display cases. In preparation for Christmas, his mom had laced a strand of white lights around her kitchen window curtains, and they blinked off and on.

It was all so *normal*. His mother's purse still on the chair inside the door, its contents now neatly set out on the side table.

He walked slowly around. The pillows, magazines fanned neatly on the coffee table, her music selections. The faint smell of lilac, no doubt from the sachets she tucked in drawers to scent her world.

He saw the wall of photos, and a wave of emotion came over him. His father, family vacations, his own face looking back with a wide grin and a baseball bat slung over his shoulder, his mother with friends here in the retirement village—all capturing rich memories. He blinked hard, and his hand fisted. She'd had a good life here. And it seemed likely she'd never walk into this apartment again. . . .

Sharon silently stepped past him. A stray coil of red yarn from his mom's needlework lay half hidden beneath the couch. She bent, picked it up, set it on the desk. "Your mom loves life."

He nodded, not trusting his voice, but appreciating the present-tense statement.

"We're going to give this back to her, John. This place and her friends."

"Yes." He took a deep breath. "Where should I start?"

She came to stand beside him. "Give yourself a minute first."

"I'm okay. It caught me hard, but I'm okay."

She studied his face, and nodded. "Hang up your coat. I'll start some coffee."

He opened the closet and did so.

It was a spacious apartment, but not too large: a nice-sized living room, small kitchen, two bedrooms, bath, stacked laundry machines. His mother had filled the space with comfortable furniture, and everything he saw told him she enjoyed living here among her friends, her things. He walked into the kitchen and accepted the cup of coffee Sharon offered. "What do you need from me here?"

"What is here that doesn't fit your mom? She strikes me as a lady who loves to entertain. Tuesday Tea at Ten is like a calling card for her personality. Whomever she went to meet has likely been here as her guest. Find me a guest I can define by a type of flavored coffee they like, the type of candy they prefer, the type of cheese in the fridge, something that says 'not my mom.' I'm thinking if a woman as vibrant as your mother had a man in her life or wanted to have a male someone in her life, she would make him welcome here with what she kept on hand."

"She would have mentioned to me if she was seeing someone. Or considering it."

Sharon tilted her head and smiled. "Maybe she is the one woman who actually would confide in her son. But speaking as a female, I can dream and hope for a lot of things before I'm ready to tell family about it."

He smiled back. "Point taken. I'll look. She did have strong preferences for many things, so it shouldn't be hard to spot what doesn't fit."

"I also need you to build me a bio of your mom. I can read her calendar, look at names in her address book, but I don't have the context of *knowing her*. Look at her receipts, her checkbook, her credit-card bills, her phone records. That folder I brought over has the printout for her phone—the messages and calls for as far back as we could go, copies of her calendar and address book we've been working from. What was Martha doing, who was she talking with? We fill in enough of the blanks, we'll see the answer to why she went out."

John could see what she was after. "I'll dig and pull together that information."

Sharon finished her coffee, set aside the mug. "I'm going to leave you here and go work with Bryon on the felon list. Call me if you find something we can help you pursue."

"Got a card?"

She pulled out a business card, motioned him to turn, and used his shoulder to write a number on the back. "Don't lose that card. It's like the holy grail of private numbers around here."

He memorized the number, smiled at her, and slid the card into an inside pocket. "Thanks."

"We're going to find her, John."

"Yes, we will."

She patted his arm. "I'll be back in an hour plus."

Sharon closed the door behind her. John stood in his mother's apartment, alone for the first time since the call had come in to the Cheyenne Police Department telling him his mother was missing.

He felt cold, overwhelmed, and growing sadder with each hour that passed. He'd fall apart when this was finished, even if they found her, and that reality pressed on him like a mountain. But he wasn't going to break before it was over. "I'm coming, Mom," he whispered. "Wherever you are right now, hang on."

He'd tried to pray for her safety. It wasn't as though he had any doubt about how much God cared about his mother. Or himself, for that matter. It was that the emotions of this, the pain of this, was too deep for words. *"Though I walk through the valley of the shadow of death, thy rod and thy staff they comfort me."* The familiar refrain from the Psalm had been reassuring him since Cheyenne. He looked up with another heartfelt plea to God, then began to carefully look around.

All right, he thought, *this is doable*. His mom liked to keep ticket stubs from movies she had seen, restaurant menus marked with dishes she'd enjoyed, coupons for shops and businesses she frequented. He could figure out where she'd been, where she might go, if he studied the pieces closely enough.

John walked over to the desk, pulled out a pad and pen, walked back into the kitchen. He began with a systematic search through the cupboards. Sharon was right. His mother was a natural hostess, and a guest to her home would be treated to what they preferred in food and drink. What didn't fit with her own preferences? Who else has been here, and why?

■ ■ ■

John was comparing printouts of the phone calls and messages with his mother's calendar when he heard a soft knock at the door, and Sharon stepped in.

"Quiet in here," she noted. "I figured you would have found music to break the silence."

"My thoughts are busy enough to keep me occupied," he replied, setting aside the paperwork and swinging the desk chair around to face her.

"Finding anything?"

He rubbed tired eyes. "I didn't know she was singing in a choir, helping a florist make Christmas wreaths, going out to lunch regularly with Bobby Sail—a banker, according to his business card—and reading through all the mysteries of Sue

Grafton. My mother was an open book to me, and still I missed layers of these details."

"That's why a woman will always be a mystery to a man," Sharon said with a little smile. "We do too much to ever share it all."

"Well said." He picked up his notes. "She's happy," he said, looking at the page. "That's what a summary of her life looks like." He shook his head. "I haven't found any signs of her expenditures changing recently. What she was doing, who she was talking with, fit with this place and the people now around her. The phone logs show names that seem familiar to me, either from here or from our prior neighborhood. It's going to come down to her living her life when she stepped out of this apartment with her keys in her hand."

"A normal week."

"It feels like it. Maybe someone in the choir was dropping by sheet music, and she ran downstairs to get it; or she had borrowed a book and went out to return it and swap for another one; or Mom walked over to the commons building to mail a letter—she still writes letters by hand. It's going to be simple, Sharon. She left this apartment for a simple reason."

She considered that answer. "The trouble she ran into may be unrelated to what she intended to do. It came at her from another direction. Possibly the wrong place, wrong time."

"Or," he suggested, "trouble from me spilled over on to her."

Sharon nodded. "Tomorrow we'll get into the undercover work you did here in Chicago. Your FBI friends are already digging there."

"If someone went after my mother to get me back in Chicago . . ."

"Like I said, a topic for tomorrow," she said briskly. "It's too complex to move that rock tonight." She reached into her pocket, took out a key. "Cops will be in and out of here tonight. The manager has an empty furnished apartment one floor up, and it makes more sense than a hotel. I had your bag taken there. Bryon will call you if there's news. I'm heading out now for a few hours of shut-eye myself."

He didn't protest. He knew he needed about five hours' sleep before he tried to go another full day. Sharon without doubt also needed rest. He glanced at her left hand to see if there was a husband waiting for her.

She noticed the look. "A couple of dogs and my sister will likely be waiting up for me. If Kelly's on her normal schedule, she turns on the lights at the bakery around two a.m. and wakes me up with fresh croissants at seven. A nice arrangement."

"Sounds like it." He accepted the key. "Thanks for today, Sharon. For the priority you've put on this."

"You're welcome, John. I'll see you in a few hours."

She disappeared, he heard a few words with the cop outside, and then her footsteps faded down the hall. He looked once more at the paperwork of his mother's recent life and then closed the folder. He'd seen for himself the cops were good. Bryon and the others would be working through the night to find his mom.

He pushed to his feet. Her son had learned to be a good cop too. Tomorrow she'd be back to this life she loved. Another outcome didn't bear considering.

TWO

The clock read 5:12 a.m. John shoved back the blanket and swung to his feet. The dreams from the short night were, thankfully, not remembered. The phone hadn't rung yet—there hadn't been a ransom demand, telling him how much it was going to cost to end this nightmare.

He turned the bathroom sink water on cold, held his face under the water until he couldn't hold his breath any longer. For shock value, it fully woke him up. He toweled off and reached for the clean shirt he'd pulled from his bag.

He didn't bother to shave. If this whole thing was being orchestrated by someone to cause him distress, he'd let them see they were winning. *I want my mother back safely* was his message, every way it could get out there. After she was safe, he would find the person or persons responsible.

He gathered up his belongings, zipped the bag, and hoped he wouldn't need this apartment a second night. He walked across to the commons building through a morning brisk with the snap of winter. The snow needed to hold off for another forty-eight hours, because searching in a winter snowstorm would shred any hope he still had.

Some volunteers were already in the commons lobby, signing in for their assignments. John nodded his thanks as he passed, knowing he'd never remember the names of all the generous people giving their time.

The officer standing outside the conference room leaned in, spoke to someone, and cleared John in. The shift hadn't changed over yet to the day crew. Bryon was on the phone. It had been a long night for everyone, and John could see it on their faces.

He scanned the boards. *Gray van* had been marked off, so they had closed that item as a concern, as had *taxi*. Staff background checks had been completed, area hospitals contacted again. He then realized from the notations that the hospitals were being called every three hours, and the list of names for further inquiry were down to a dozen. Given the number of people the police would have sifted through overnight, it was real progress. John had been involved in enough investigations to appreciate what he was seeing. Detective Bryon Slate knew how to make work flow.

A question remained open: *Bobby Sail. Alibi for Monday night confirmed?* The banker Mom had lunch with on a regular basis was a definite lead to tug. John wanted to know where they were with that item.

His phone chimed. John read the message, replied with an affirmative, and pocketed the phone. Friends he'd called for help had been pulling an all-nighter on the question of his past cases being a trigger. The information they had collected would shape part of his day. The lists on the walls here would shape the rest of his priorities.

John wondered how many apartments were unoccupied like the one he'd stayed in the night before. He looked at the building blueprints and found the apartment he'd slept in had been marked as cleared. Someone else had had the same thought.

Officers would be focused on apartments today, knocking on doors, asking questions, requesting permission to make a visual check inside. If they were met with a negative, that unit would attract a great deal of focused interest. Clauses in each rental agreement allowed staff to access an apartment for routine maintenance needs. A day, two days, to give whatever notice was required by the agreement and every room and closet would be cleared. Leaving any portion of the property unsearched wasn't on the table.

John thought his mom would have been found by now if it was a medical problem or simply an accident. If she was on the property, the search under way would find her shortly. If that also came up blank . . . the planning needed to focus beyond the Village.

"John."

He turned, surprised to see Sharon heading his way. "Couldn't sleep, Lieutenant?"

"I got enough. Had breakfast?"

"Not yet."

"Let's find some food and talk for a bit." She caught Bryon's attention and indicated she was stepping out.

"I'll take that concealed-carry permit if it's still being offered," John mentioned as they crossed through the commons building.

Without comment she pulled her wallet out, removed the paperwork, and handed it to him. He'd have a word with a friend from his time in Chicago to secure himself a firearm.

Scrambled eggs, bacon, toast, hot coffee—the breakfast the Village staff had arranged was simple but sufficient to keep officers and volunteers well tended. He waved Sharon through the line, then filled a plate for himself. They found seats away from the others.

"A night of pondering. Speculate for me, Sharon."

She picked up her coffee. "She's not on the property. We need to confirm that, but my gut tells me Martha isn't here. It's too easy to get her into a car and drive her away."

John nodded. "If she *is* here, the search under way will find her. We need to think beyond here." He pushed warm eggs onto his fork with his toast.

"The timeline hasn't resolved itself. That bothers me," Sharon mentioned. "I'm hoping the interviews this morning will clarify matters. It would be perfect if someone saw your mother on a walk around the bike path early Tuesday morning."

"It's possible—she does walk for exercise and enjoys the outdoors. But early? In this cold?"

"It's wishful thinking. I need a tighter timeline for when she went missing. It would focus matters and not leave us so scattered." Sharon ate her eggs. "The number of volunteers distributing flyers will be roughly double yesterday's number. We'll go back to every resident in the complex, try to cover every business in the area. Your mom's photo will be on the 7:00 a.m. newscasts. We'll be able to see the calls here as notes are created downtown, so we can work them in real time. Officers will go out to follow up on any viable leads. But you and I"—she pointed her fork at him—"we'll start looking that other direction: that this isn't about your mother, but about you. Someone used your mother to get you back to Chicago."

John nodded. She was going where he knew they had to turn.

"It would take a serious enemy, John, to involve your mother this way."

"I've got a few, mostly from my days working undercover. Friends here are looking into it, Sharon, have been since I got the call Mom was missing. They didn't need to clutter up your search group by being on-site. I've been getting texts on their progress. So far they're in a similar position to you. A lot of names marked off the board, but no workable thread to pull. Being undercover for six years, I made some serious enemies."

"I didn't realize it was that extensive. I knew you were Chicago PD, worked undercover for part of it, got promoted up the ranks, then got offered the Cheyenne chief of police job."

"A good summary. I worked hate groups mostly when undercover. Anglo-pride types that went after Asians, Latinos, blacks. Harassment, threats to drive them out of neighborhoods, vandalism of their businesses and property—we broke the groups apart and sent their leaders and a good number of their members to prison."

"I'm trying to picture you as a biker type. I bet you were good at it."

"My cover held until the trials."

"Give me the top of the list."

"A group called *Just Whites*, with JSW tattoos, would be the most violent." He pushed back his plate. "What time is the morning briefing?"

"Seven."

"I've got some people I want to caucus with. Let me borrow the wide-screen monitor so I can video-connect with something larger than a laptop, and you can join us."

"Now?"

"As good a time as any."

"Sure. We can quiet things down enough to use the equipment."

They walked back to the conference room, Sharon talked briefly with Bryon, and Officer Martinez helped get things set up.

John opened the connection and entered the temporary password. "Lieutenant Sharon Noble," he announced, "some of the people I used to work with here in Chicago." Eight faces were looking back at them from the tiled screen. Two additional tiles were close-ups of whiteboards, one full of names. "Introductions can come later. That work list is pretty long, Scott."

"People you arrested, put in prison, old grudges. We're dividing them up, tracking down where people were on Monday and Tuesday. There are no rumors out on the street—that's either good or bad, depending on your perspective. If this was JSW getting together again, I think there'd be talk of payback and inquires about who'd be interested."

"It's not just that it's quiet, John," an older man in the left frame said, "it's that there are no conversations going on about much of anything with JSW. It feels dusty, broken, like a shattered network no one's bothered to pick up. I've been going back to your old confidential informants, looking for rumors, speculation. They're willing to talk; there just isn't much happening."

"I get that impression too," a young woman on the right remarked. "I mention people that used to generate some passion, and it's like they simply don't matter. It almost feels generational, that what was shattered is irrelevant to the way racial fights are carried on today. Still as racist, just a different expression. More about 'economic warfare' and 'oppressive government' kinds of rhetoric."

"I've been away from Chicago so long that this shift is hard for me to grasp. Bill, what's your opinion?" John asked.

"As soon as I heard your mother was missing, I thought 'Kelly Green' or the 'Kern brothers.' It's such a personal move, and not many are willing to go at a cop that directly. But I had them eliminated in the first hour. It would take someone with a deep, personal hatred to do this. But I agree with the others. This isn't an organized thing, like JSW re-upping its game. But someone from the old days, likely still in prison, who could hire outsiders—that's the option still open to explore."

"I admit, I'm surprised at what you're telling me," John said. "Back in the day, it felt like the gangs had the energy and hate to live forever. Okay. At least it eliminates this direction. If the street is quiet, what do we know about those in prison?"

"I can help with that answer, John," a man in a blazer and tie said. "The FBI is taking a look at phone traffic, visitors to the guys you helped put in prison. They've kept a lot of Chicago links active, but the majority of calls are to relatives. It's going to take some time to fully rule it out. So far, though, it's come up dry."

"What about that kid from Sweden, the one who liked to use a baseball bat on his victims?" someone from another of the squares asked.

"Jorge," another replied. "I tracked him down to New York. He's doing time for aggravated assault."

"The two brothers John tangled with just before their arrests—Christopher and Anthony—did we locate them?"

"They're doing time in Houston for robbing a motel," another individual answered.

John thought for a long moment. "The teenager who caught me in the side with a knife after his father was arrested . . . Abraham, Isaiah? It's a biblical name—"

"Elijah Abrahams. Yeah, we definitely need to track him down. I'll take that one."

Scott said, "We'll keep working names, John. If there's something to find, we should at least get a whiff of it. You can't arrange something like this without tipping your hand."

"I appreciate that, everyone, and what you've all done already. Sincerely. I know it's been a long night for most of you."

"If it's coming from your past, it's personal to all of us. Let's caucus again end of day if there's not something hot before then."

"Agreed."

"Wear a vest, John. Somebody got you back here to Chicago," Bill cautioned.

"Yeah." John nodded his goodbyes, cut the link, and rubbed the back of his neck. "Well, that was not as useful as I'd hoped."

"It was useful for me," Sharon assured him. "You've got my team mirrored with another that's exclusively digging into problems from your Chicago past. I couldn't begin to do what they've accomplished in a day if I had a week and the manpower."

"They're good friends," he commented. "I've had a similar group looking at matters in Cheyenne, but while I'm the public face there, having a case from Cheyenne link to locating my mother here—I just haven't been there that long to generate that kind of enemy."

"Ruling things out is progress, John. If something is back there, it sounds like they are the right people to find it."

"They are."

"Your friend was right about the vest," she said. "I'm going to dig one up for you. Bryon can do the seven a.m. briefing while we watch Martha's photo air on the newscasts, and then I'm cutting him free to get some sleep. You and I are going to work the phone calls that come in. If there aren't enough possible leads by eleven, we'll talk about putting you on camera at noon."

"Okay." He pushed back his chair and stood. "If she was mugged, robbed, dragged into a closet—" he paused, blew out a breath—"finding her requires someone only opening the right door. But if she's with someone, her fate depends on who it is and why. Maybe it's best if I put my face out there for the noon news-casts regardless. He's got to make a move, contact me, something."

"That's a decision for a couple hours from now. You want more coffee?"

"Can you IV it straight into my arm?"

"You can say hi to Annabelle, get a cup from her, then come watch the newscast."

■ ■ ■

John got the coffee, talked with Annabelle, watched the news-cast. He thought again how beautiful his mother was, and the image of her with MISSING in the caption broke his heart. He pushed away the sadness to go speak with some of the volunteers and was introduced to more of the staff. He followed Sharon back into the conference room.

He was growing accustomed to the lieutenant's working style. The room keyed off Bryon, because she had him directing mat-ters, and she backed him up on decisions. She was letting her team do their jobs. And it was the small things—the lieutenant fetching paperwork off the printer, taking the phone calls com-plaining about the police searching cars leaving the property, passing over her own just-filled coffee to someone else—that made the officers working this room give her the extra effort. John even saw her slip Bryon a roll of sweet-tarts.

The phones were ringing somewhere downtown, calls were being logged, and the notes were showing up on-screen as they were entered into the database.

Sharon scanned the room. "Martinez."

"Yes, Lieutenant."

"How long have you been in this room?"

"Oh, I don't know, 'bout thirteen hours."

"Can you give me two more?"

"Absolutely."

"Your youth is showing," Sharon remarked admiringly. "We need a dispatcher on the calls. Why don't you print them out, decide what is worth acting on, ignoring, what we should jump on. Hand me the latter, the rest can be worked by your favorite officers."

"Can do."

"Bryon—"

"I'm a walking zombie, and I want a month in Aruba," he said before she could ask.

"Maybe your wife will give you a welcome-home back rub. I'll take the next ten hours. Go get some sleep."

"I'll take you up on that, boss. How about giving Christopher the apartment search?"

Sharon gave Bryon a second look. "Really?"

"He's got something to prove."

"Good point. Send him my way. He's somewhere in the scrum of volunteers."

"I still want Aruba."

"When I get my captain's bars, I'm hauling you and your wife to Aruba to celebrate, then contemplating staying there while you come back to do both our jobs."

Bryon laughed. "Close this one, Lieutenant, before I have to even think about waking up and coming back to work."

"That's the plan." Sharon scanned the room. "Detective Carter."

The officer studying a screen with a frown started and half turned. "Ma'am."

"You're now Bryon. Watch the boards for me, keep everything moving, nag when necessary. Let me know when you want me to care about something."

"Yes, ma'am."

■ ■ ■

Officer Martinez slid a piece of paper to an officer, who read it, rose, and left. She read another one, turned it facedown on the table. She went to retrieve more pages from the printer. Another officer left, paper in hand. Two more pages went facedown in the stack.

"Wait for it," Sharon said.

"What?"

"Wait for it."

John realized he was drumming his fingers on the table and stopped, embarrassed.

Another page from the printer, this one to Sharon. She looked at it, slid it over to him, and he read it quickly. The lieutenant was already getting to her feet. "Carter? Okay here?"

Detective Carter scanned the boards. "We're good, Lieutenant. I'll call if I need you."

John caught up with her. "It's pretty small. A grocery checkout clerk remembers Martha in the store Monday night about 5:30 p.m."

"It narrows the timeline. There's video over the checkout aisles. I get to see her on the day she disappeared. I'll take it." She pushed through the outer doors of the commons building. "Officer Jefferies, I've got an address for you."

"This way, Lieutenant. The squad car is ready to go—warm even."

She flashed a grin. "I like a bit of coddling now and then."

"All in a day's service, LT."

"Let's see where this call leads."

"You have an interesting style, Sharon," John remarked, his voice low as Jefferies pulled out into traffic. "The conference room," he clarified.

"They like the work, they like the team. They humor the coach."

John smiled. "I could see that. Where did you get the sweet-tarts?"

"A private stash, compliments of Bryon's wife."

"How long before you can move him up from detective?"

"He's passed the test. He wants homicide. I move him up to lieutenant now he gets traffic. End of the year, we'll swap a retirement, his promotion, and a lateral move so Bryon gets homicide and I get Vincent from traffic. We'll all be pleased. If one of my missing-persons cases turns out to be a homicide, I'll have Bryon to tap on the shoulder and know I've got someone who understands the priority it should have."

"Smart. Populate the other departments with your own people."

"The best way to get anything done," Sharon replied with an easy smile.

He wondered how much he could be in on what was about to happen. "How do we handle the grocery-store interview?"

She studied him, clearly amused with the "we," yet she didn't push away the offer. "You're a good-looking guy whose mother is missing. I plan to introduce us, then look at you. Everything this clerk thinks she might remember about your mom is going to come tumbling out of her like white water down a river, and you're going to nod and say 'That's helpful' and an occasional 'Thank you.' It's going to be a thorough interview by the time it's done."

"If it wasn't my mom's case, I would really be enjoying this, Sharon. I could learn a thing or three from you."

With a grin, she said, "Go ahead and be amused. It's not disrespectful to your mother to find something in this day worth a smile." She tapped his knee with the binder. "Allow me to give you a piece of advice. Levity during a crisis is a good thing. It promotes good health, and I encourage lightening the load to get through the day."

He nodded. "Thanks for the advice. So, how many missing-persons cases in your portfolio?"

"Over the seven years? One hundred eighty-six at last tally. Not that many when you look at the calendar, but too many when you have lived with the intensity of each."

"How many have been closed?"

Sharon shook her head. "Most, but not nearly enough."

■ ■ ■

The grocery-store clerk was helpful, the store's security officer quick to locate the correct security-tape footage. They crowded into a small office to watch the monitor—Sharon, John, the clerk, security officer, and store manager. John swallowed hard as he watched his mother set a handful of items onto the conveyor belt. The clerk finished making change for the customer ahead of her.

"Who's she talking to?" John asked. His mom was speaking to someone in line behind her, at one point laughing. "Can we identify him?" The angle wasn't great, the camera was above and to the right, but they could make out part of his face.

"Depends if he pays by credit card," the store manager replied. "Do you know him, Tina?"

"No." The clerk shook her head. "But I'm normally on morning shift. He might be a regular customer later in the day."

The clerk rang up the items for his mother, and she handed over what looked like a single bill, probably a ten, accepted the receipt and the change.

"We can show the man's photo to other clerks and the pharmacist," the manager said. "What he just took out of his cart looks like . . . a cake box," he said, peering at the screen. "We'll pull receipts, see if it was a special order. Do you think he had something to do with her disappearance?"

"No," Sharon said. John watched as the man behind Martha paid for his groceries, also with cash. "But if she mentioned another errand, if she had plans, that helps us narrow the timeline. They talked long enough that it was more than just pleasantries. It seems she might have lingered while his groceries were bagged to finish the conversation. He's still speaking with someone off-camera."

"We'll do what we can to get you his name," the manager promised.

Sharon thanked the clerk, left her card with the security officer and manager, and they left.

John wondered if that would be the last image he ever had of his mother, her head tipped back slightly as she laughed. Happy. Living her life. *Then gone.*

■ ■ ■

The calls generated by the morning newscasts tapered off by 10:00 a.m. John got coffee and read quickly through the pages Martinez had tabled, then the reports officers filed who had followed up on less specific calls, and finally through the interviews since Tuesday afternoon. What could be followed-up on had already been noted and pursued.

The Village grounds had been thoroughly checked. Officers were visually clearing apartments at a good pace. Volunteers and cops were walking the area for a mile around, doing a ground search. Flyers had been distributed to residents in the Village for a second time, and volunteers were taking more to businesses and homes within the area.

There wasn't anything further he could do or think of to do.

This search was going cold in the slow-motion way that cases often did, like a frost creeping in.

"Would a reward help?" he wondered aloud. Sharon was settled back in a chair, idly turning a pen end to end, observing the progress around the room.

"Not yet. It clutters up the phone lines with creative fiction—callers hoping they can provide enough general information they'll get some cash."

Martinez added another television station to the list of interviews arranged for the noon hour. John didn't know yet what he would say, but he'd get in front of microphones and cameras if only to keep the photo of his mother prominent to the public.

John swiveled his chair to face Sharon. "Talk to me about Bobby Sail. The banker mom was having lunch with regularly. He's still on the board with a question mark."

"I think your mom is dating a nice guy."

"Sharon."

She smiled and silently apologized by rocking a hand back and forth. "He's still on the board because I can't rule him out, but I don't like him for this. Bobby had lunch with your mother a week ago Wednesday and said they had plans—which are in her schedule book—for lunch again this coming Friday. They hadn't moved their relationship beyond lunch, to a date in the evening yet. He didn't want to rush her. What Martha told her friends about Bobby and their relationship is consistent with that."

"They were still at the beginnings of something," John guessed.

Sharon nodded. "I've had two of my best guys interview Bobby twice now. The bottom line, John, is that Bobby genuinely cares about her. My gut tells me if Bobby saw your mom on Monday, or had plans with her for Monday, he would have said so. If he hurt your mom, accidentally or otherwise, he would have tried to get her help, not sought to cover it up. He's a banker, older than your mom by a few years. Not a physically strong or forceful man, he comes across as a gentleman. His statements stay consistent. There isn't a false note. It's plausible he's our guy until you get to who he is, and then it just doesn't hold together. But he could knock on her door, and she wouldn't think twice about it, she'd simply be pleased to see him. If he asked her to come down to the car for a moment, she wouldn't hesitate. She'd grab her keys and coat. So he stays on the board."

John leaned back in his chair, watching her face as she spoke. He was hearing instinct speaking, and he tended to trust it. But this case was his mom. "What's the problem with his alibi?"

Sharon reached over for the stack of police reports, found the one she wanted. "Bobby Sail left work at the bank on Monday at 6:22 p.m. according to the security camera footage. Monday evening he was home alone, reading and watching television. He spoke to his broker by phone about 7 p.m. and to his neighbor in person about 10 p.m. when he came over to borrow a plumber wrench. The broker and neighbor confirm the conversations. He was at work Tuesday morning at 7:55 a.m., again according to the security-camera footage."

"That's basically no alibi."

"Hence the problem. I've got people trying to tighten it down. So far no one in the neighborhood remembers seeing him leave the house on Monday evening or remembers your mom arriving there. But if Martha was going to go visit someone, Bobby would be on my short list. If she was going to have a date that Monday evening, Bobby would be the one on my list. He is the guy most involved with your mom socially, if not romantically."

"Something she hadn't gotten around to mentioning to her son," John said around a rueful smile.

"Which tells me he really was just a guy she liked and had lunch with on a regular basis, but who was not yet more than that in her thinking."

Sharon considered the board again, frowned slightly. "Circumstances change. You and I both know that, John. Maybe Monday night was when their relationship was going to turn a new page, and they were going to go out that evening for a first true date. But Martha didn't tell her friends, didn't arrange to get her hair done, didn't fuss about what to wear for a date that would be a significant step forward in her social life. Bobby is well-liked by her friends; an evening out with him would be noteworthy. It doesn't feel right that there aren't footprints in her schedule if a date was planned."

John tried to theorize around the problem. "What if after Mom left the bridge game Monday afternoon, she went by the bank to make a deposit and stopped in to see Bobby for a brief minute. He makes an impromptu 'How about we go out this evening after I get off work?' or 'How about coming over for an hour this evening?' suggestion. She's now got plans for Monday night without them showing up as a phone call or notation on her calendar. She leaves the bank, goes by the grocery store, she's finishing getting ready for Tuesday Tea, and then she's going to go meet Bobby for the evening."

Sharon slowly nodded. "Yes. I can see that kind of circumstance. We can pursue the idea—we should be able to rule in or out your mom visiting Sail's bank rather quickly. We can look at the footage here at the Village, see if Bobby's car pulls in, if he was picking up your mom. We can do a third interview. It takes some strong nerves to steadily lie to the cops. We can see what's there."

John was running the idea out further, then stopped abruptly and tapped his fist against the table. "What if it's not Bobby Sail, Sharon, but someone close to him? I'm going to inherit from my mom. If she gets married at this age, I'm going to be looking twice at the guy, wondering if he's after what my mom has, if he's looking for a 'purse and a nurse,' as the saying goes. Does Bobby have a son or daughter, someone not thrilled Bobby is romantically inclined toward a new lady named Martha Graham? Mom might have grabbed her coat and keys and gone downstairs on the spur of the moment to meet someone from Bobby's family. She'd have had no reason to feel defensive or on guard with one of them."

Sharon had stilled as he drew out the scenario, and now she visibly winced. "I missed that, John—you're absolutely right. We look deeper. And we do it fast. At Bobby Sail and, even more critically, at his family. That question—*what about his family?*—suddenly feels very plausible." She turned. "Detective Carter?"

"I've been following the conversation, Lieutenant. Five guys?"

She nodded. "Shift them on to this. We need a full bio, we need his family tree. We need to re-interview Bobby to ask him about who in his family knew about Martha. And we need to put a priority on getting alibis for anybody close to Bobby who could expect to inherit."

"All over it, LT," Carter promised, reaching for a phone.

"I want regular updates on what the guys are finding." Sharon pulled out some interview reports. "John, read the ones with Bobby over again, see if anything else catches your interest."

He could see her frustration with herself. "You kept him on the board, Sharon. This is just a question, a theory to push, to see what hits."

She nodded tersely. "We'll get busy on it, and we'll soon know more than we do now. But the painful thing for me is that it *could* fit. Not your mom's developing boyfriend, but someone in his family. That puts her in very dangerous crosscurrents."

"She's been there since she disappeared. We go through this door, see what's there, and we go through others we have yet to spot. One of them will pay off. We'll find her."

"Thanks for that. Coming from you, it matters." She stood. "I need coffee. You want some more?"

She had found an excuse to pace for a bit while getting it. He had to smile. "Sure."

"Lieutenant," Carter called over his shoulder, and Sharon paused. "Bobby Sail has three adult children—two sons and a daughter."

Sharon simply pointed to the board. "Let's get them up there and get officers working each of them. Thanks." She went to get their coffee.

She came back with coffee several minutes later. Sharon's phone rang as she set a mug down beside him, and John instinctively braced for bad news as she answered. He relaxed only when he saw her smile as she listened.

"I appreciate how quickly you were able to find the information," Sharon said. "It's helpful news. Thanks again." She clicked off and said, "We've got a name for the customer at the grocery store. Eric Holland, an address on Longbow Ave."

"Eric Holland?" John sat forward.

"What is it?"

"I know an Eric Holland. I saw his name on Mom's phone-call list, didn't think much about it. He's from our old neighborhood."

"How do you know him?"

"His mother and mine were good friends in high school. Martha and June drifted apart—I doubt they've spoken in years, not since June moved to Florida. But it's an old family acquaintance. Eric would have been entering college last time I saw him. I didn't recognize him in the video."

"That's the birthday cake he was picking up. *Happy Birthday, June*. Your mother's high school friend is back in town. Let's go see Eric. Or do you want to stay here and focus on Bobby?"

John pushed to his feet. "I'll go with you. An hour from now your guys will have a lot more information on the Sails. I want to hear what Eric and my mom talked about as they checked out their groceries."

Sharon nodded. "Let's go."

THREE

In an unmarked police car, Sharon drove them to a ranch-style house in a quiet suburb within a few miles of the grocery store. The front steps were marked by flowerpots, which probably would hold a variety of colorful blooms come spring.

John followed Sharon up the walk, and she rang the doorbell. The door opened a moment later. "Eric Holland?"

"Yes."

Sharon held up her badge. "I'm Lieutenant Sharon Noble. This is John Graham. May we have a few minutes of your time?"

"Of course." He looked puzzled and stepped back to let them enter, then it clicked. "Of course, John." He reached out his hand. "We're going back in time a few decades. I heard you were working out west somewhere—Colorado, South Dakota?"

"I've been in Wyoming for a few years. My mother is missing, Eric."

"What? When?" He looked startled and shot a glance into the living room, where they could see an elderly lady in a recliner, asleep with an afghan across her legs. He stepped farther into the hall and lowered his voice. "I just saw her at the grocery store. Like just two days ago. What's happened?"

"That's what we're trying to figure out."

"Oh, man. This makes me sick."

"We've been tracking down her movements for Monday. The checkout clerk remembered her. Tell me about your conversation with Martha."

"Ah, yeah. Sure." He ran his hand through his hair. "She found me at the grocery store bakery actually. I was picking up a cake for my mother's birthday. Martha stopped to ask the baker to box up an assortment of specialty cookies, said hello when she saw me.

"She asked how I was doing, asked about June, how she was doing. That took a few minutes. Mom's now in late-stage dementia, I moved her up here from Florida a year ago. She gave me a bad health scare this fall, but she's rallied enough to be home with me for her birthday, and I'm praying we can get to Christmas. Your mother sent me a box of photos some months ago, John, pictures from back when June and Martha were in high school together—items I could put up on Mom's 'memory wall,' I call it—and it was nice to be able to thank her for those in person."

"I'm glad to hear that," John said.

"What else did you two talk about?" Sharon asked.

"Let's see . . . I kidded Martha a bit about only buying a couple of items, and she said she had really just stopped in for the cookies. She hosts a Tuesday Tea at Ten, but you probably know that. She laughed about the name, although you could tell she gets a lot of pleasure in having that event on her schedule. We talked about June's birthday and how time was passing by so quickly. I had a cartful of groceries, but she stayed and chatted while they were bagged. I walked out with her, and she held the cake for me while I shifted groceries into the car. I took her cart back with mine. She was turning south on Wabash Avenue when I last saw her."

"You remember it all pretty well," John commented.

"I suppose. The lady who comes to watch my mother while I grocery-shop and run errands—Verna Buck—lives down the street. Verna and I talk about what era my mother has wandered into when she is awake and conversing. So a rational conversation with a lady my mother's age was a pleasure."

"Did you happen to invite my mother over to share a piece of birthday cake with June?" John asked.

"I did. It was the soft-touch 'if you would like to come over' kind of invite, and your mom apologized before I even finished that she had plans for the evening. I didn't press her. Mom wouldn't remember if Martha was here five minutes after the cake was eaten, and ladies from the church were planning to stop by, so I knew Mom would have a few guests. I was just happy to have bumped into Martha and to see how well she's doing. We'd talked on the phone a couple times about the photos, but it's not the same as saying hello in person. The way Mom's dementia has taken over, I sometimes fear this is how everyone, including me, is going to end up."

"Did Martha say what her plans were for the evening?" Sharon asked.

"No, I'm sorry. Sincerely. Now I wish I'd asked. I took it as a polite reason to decline and didn't want to put her on the spot. I've always liked your mother, John, and I shouldn't have sprung the invitation on her. Seeing a long-ago friend your own age in late-stage dementia . . . well, it takes some thinking, some mental preparation, before you just drop everything to say hi."

They heard something from the other room. June must have awakened.

"I'm sorry, Mrs. Holland. What did you say?" John stepped into the living room to better hear her.

"You're talking about Martha?" she asked, her voice quivering. "I had such a nice lunch with Martha just yesterday."

"You did?" John couldn't help his astonished query.

Her eyes brightened, and she turned her head toward him. "Yes. Grilled ham salad sandwiches, petite blueberry muffins, and some banana pudding."

"Mom, what year is it?" Eric asked.

"Why are you asking me that?"

"Humor me. I need to get this check written properly." Eric had pulled out his checkbook and pen, had it open, and was looking expectantly at his mother.

"'94, of course."

"Thanks." He slid the checkbook back and stepped over to her, leaned down and kissed the woman's forehead. "*Jeopardy* comes on soon. I know you don't like to miss the opening. It's on channel four." He found the remote in the folds of the afghan and handed it to her. Her attention diverted to the TV, and she began looking for the right button to push.

Eric stepped back into the hall. "I'm very sorry. She's lost her sense of time—she was probably remembering an event from back in the good old days. I wish she did have lunch with your mother yesterday, John. Is there any way I can help with the search? My nightmare is my mom wandering out of the house and getting lost. I can only imagine what you're going through right now. If I can help in any way, I'd like to do so."

"The details of what you spoke to Mom about are useful."

"Eric," June called out, "we should invite Martha and Harold for dinner. Wouldn't that be nice? We'll have my pot roast, and she can bring her meringue pie."

"That sounds nice, Mom." He looked over at the two of

them with a sad smile. "I'm sorry, John. For what it's worth, her friendship with Martha, those days in high school and the years after—these are some of the strongest memories she has left."

"Mom would be glad to know that. I'm sorry, Eric, that this is how it is for June now. Thanks for the time and the information."

Eric walked with them to the front door. "I'm only sorry I couldn't help more. I'm serious—please call me if there's anything else I can do."

■ ■ ■

"You were kind of quiet in there," John mentioned as they settled into the car.

Sharon turned the key, backed down the driveway. "Eric reminds me of you, John. He's close to his mom, careful of her. The photos in the living room, the memory wall he has put together of her and the family through the years. They likely reinforce the memories that do remain. He's a loving son."

John fastened his seat belt. "I remember Eric as being a good guy. His parents divorced, and Eric stepped in to be the man of the house. Even in high school he had a responsible streak related to his mother."

Sharon pulled into traffic. "Okay, so what did we learn?"

"Mom had plans for Monday night. The open question now is, were those plans with Bobby Sail?"

"*Maybe* she had plans. It could have been a courteous way to decline an invitation she didn't want to pursue. But for now, let's assume it's true." Sharon tapped her fingers on the steering wheel. "John, if your mother went out Monday night, she would have taken her purse with her, even if someone else was picking her up. Say she does go out, sees someone—maybe Bobby Sail—but she gets back home again. She puts her purse on the chair inside the door, though I doubt that's where she would usually leave it. Maybe she thought of something, turned around and left the apartment with just her keys. We are where we were before, only it's later in the evening, more like 9:00 p.m. than 6:00 p.m. on Monday night."

"If she did go to meet Bobby, then he's lying to us. That's a critical fact to know."

Sharon nodded. "It is. But I'm stuck on the fact her purse is in her apartment. She would have taken it with her if she was going out, even if Bobby was picking her up. Maybe he came inside with her when they got back?"

John thought about that. "It's risky to be set on Bobby," he finally replied, "when Mom might have had plans with anyone. Say one of his kids invites her out to coffee, wants to get to know her better. Something. Maybe Mom goes out for the evening, gets back home, they call her cell as she's getting in the door. 'I forgot to give you an envelope Dad asked me to drop off with you . . . ' she grabs her keys, goes down to meet them in the parking lot. Then trouble happens. . . ." he didn't want to finish that thought.

"That fits," Sharon agreed. A long pause. "Or," she said, "I'm going to chase a thought out on a limb, John. Let me play it out and just listen. Say Martha had plans Monday evening. She went out. She came back . . . or maybe she didn't. Her car came back, her purse. Maybe she did not. Someone else brought her car back, set her purse inside her apartment to direct attention away from what this really was. They need some time to get an alibi together, to clear away evidence, so they get her car back here and her purse in the apartment. They make sure it's the retirement village and vicinity where we first focus the search."

John turned to look at her. "We've been looking in the wrong place."

"Maybe," Sharon conceded after a long moment. "This is quite a limb I just walked out on."

"If something happened at Bobby Sail's," John said slowly, "he would have every incentive to get cops looking elsewhere. Same goes if it were his kids. Wait till dark—most residents are in for the night—drive her car back, leave the purse inside her apartment, keep the keys. Walk out and slip away. It explains why there's no one interviewed who remarked 'I saw your mom Monday night.' She simply wasn't around to see."

"It's a theory, John. One with no supporting facts. Before we assume she didn't make it back to the Village, before we create someone out of whole cloth who drives back her car, returns her purse, it would be nice to have even a sliver of evidence pointing in that direction."

"It feels right, though. Something went wrong, someone's desperately trying to cover up that Mom was with him. Or her. If not Bobby Sail, maybe someone from his family. Or it's someone else she knows. She may well have had plans for Monday night and something went very badly wrong." His voice trailed off.

Sharon was quiet for a while, then said, "I'm the one who's come up with this theory, but we need a supporting fact. We are nowhere near having probable cause to search Bobby Sail's home—or anyone else's for that matter."

"We go back to her bridge friends, what she was talking about during those four hours," John suggested. "If she had plans for her evening, she surely mentioned them to someone besides Eric. If she went by the bank to see Bobby, there should be camera footage of her. Even if her plans consisted mostly of errands—grocery store, dry cleaning, a fancy cheese shop—we should be able to locate *someone* who saw her. We have to figure out where she went Monday night to have a chance of figuring out where to aim the search."

"Let me shoot down my own theory. Bobby Sail probably knows enough about your mom to know where she parks, the number of her apartment. But if not him, a stranger wouldn't manage to drive her car back and park it in the spot your mom normally uses."

"Maybe it was the only open spot in front of Building One, because residents think of it as Martha's parking spot."

Sharon inclined her head. "Got me there. But that doesn't give them the apartment number." She tapped her fingers once more on the steering wheel. "But I bet it's on her driver's license. Okay," she began, "so in this theory I created, your mother is out somewhere Monday evening, trouble happens, and someone drives your mother's car back to the Village, places her purse in her apartment to misdirect our search."

She held up one finger. "First, we have to figure out where your mother went Monday evening." She added a second finger. "We have to come up with some evidence it was not your mother who drove her car back or put her purse in her own apartment. And third, we have to target our search at the location the trouble actually happened."

John thought she had summed it up nicely. "Exactly. And in our favor, if this theory is correct, that evidence exists because it's what actually happened. We just haven't found it yet."

Sharon chuckled. "You're absolutely right." She glanced over. "Will you agree that sometimes flights of fancy that head into the deep end are useful if only because they lighten the weight of the work?"

"You're convincing, Sharon. But I actually like your theory."

"*Evidence*. We need it before I stand in the conference room and suggest we work the idea with actual resources."

■ ■ ■

Christmas shoppers were out in force, and traffic was tangled. They were not moving more than a car length or two with each signal change. John felt his frustration growing, an impatience with the world, and forced himself to take a couple of deep breaths. It really didn't matter in the long run how much time it took—there were phones in both their pockets if something came up they needed to know about that minute.

He rested his head back and wondered when—or if—his life would be normal again. Mom would have enjoyed being out on a day like this, running her errands, probably doing some Christmas shopping.

"Where are the groceries?" he asked abruptly, sitting up straight just as abruptly.

Sharon turned to look at him.

"Mom bought a box of specialty cookies for the Tuesday Tea at Ten," he reminded her. "Plus peaches. Apples. A handful of items like that. Where are the groceries, specifically the cookies?"

"They weren't in the car," Sharon remarked slowly. "They should be in the apartment."

"I need to see her apartment again. I don't think they were there. In fact, I'm very certain they were *not* there."

"John . . ."

He offered a grim smile. "We've got our evidence. Mom didn't carry her groceries up to the apartment. They aren't in her car. Mom never came home Monday night. We now have a piece of evidence that confirms it."

■ ■ ■

John searched his mother's kitchen, looking for signs of the cookies, of the fruit she had bought. "If Mom had been fussing around the apartment Tuesday morning getting ready for her guests, those cookies would have been neatly displayed on a serving dish, most likely that glass one"—John pointed it out for Sharon—"as it's one of Mom's favorites. So, again, push this back to Monday night. Mom arrives home with groceries, the box of cookies. She puts them on the counter, maybe in a cupboard, which I've now checked thoroughly and they're not here."

"Maybe one of the ladies saw the box of cookies, knows they'll go stale before the next tea gathering, and takes them to pass out to the searchers."

John considered that and nodded. "That's possible. The box could have been taken without the intent to cause us great confusion right now."

"I'll track down Heather Jome and the Village manager, Theresa Herth," Sharon said. "If there's an innocent explanation for the disappearing cookie box, they probably can ferret it out. I'll approach the subject low-key—'No harm, no foul, we just need to know.'"

"But stress it's urgent that we get this answered quickly."

She nodded and made the calls while he repeated the search, pulling open refrigerator drawers, pulling out the trash can, looking for the other groceries. No apples, peaches, no fruit of any kind. It wasn't just cookies that were missing.

"This case is beginning to shift directions over a missing box of cookies and a few groceries," Sharon said after clicking off her phone. "I accept that all kinds of twists happen in cases, but this is a first. Neither lady remembers seeing any cookies when Theresa came into the apartment to do the wellness check. Heather thinks she would have remembered if the box was here, because it's normally on the counter next to the tray and the tea caddy. None of the tea items, in fact, had been set out for the Tuesday Tea the next morning."

"Again it points to Monday evening," John agreed. He felt a bitter emotion surge in like a wave. "We've been looking in the wrong place, Sharon. Mom is somewhere, but the one place she *isn't* is the Village." He thought about all the time they'd wasted checking apartments and searching the grounds, all the time they couldn't get back, and felt literally sick. His hand came down hard on the counter as the frustration snapped his control. "She's not here, was never here, and we're just now realizing that fact." He spun away and considered kicking the cabinet base.

"Then we'll start looking in the right place now," Sharon replied quietly. "Get angry very often?" she asked, sounding more fascinated by the display of temper than bothered.

He rubbed his sore hand and blew out a breath. "Mostly only at myself."

"It's warranted to a degree, but pull it in. Her groceries are missing," Sharon said. "We should have realized this twelve hours ago, but we missed it. Now that we've spotted it, we'll work it, John. We've got an anomaly that could point to something small or something big. It doesn't mean for certain someone else drove her car back here. It means someone took those groceries and those cookies. She could have had her car broken into when she stopped at another store."

"Yeah, maybe. Mom wouldn't tolerate much from anyone. She could have seen someone breaking into her car and yelled at him, not thinking it through. A shoving match happens, she gets hurt, shoved into an alley, the car and purse are returned here to try to divert attention from what really happened."

Sharon was shaking her head. "If it's random violence, we likely will find her in the area between the grocery store and here. But no street thief is going to go to the trouble of bringing back her car or returning the purse and leaving cash in the wallet. If a person drove her car back, returned the purse, it's someone who knows her, who is working hard to misdirect us." She patted his sore hand. "Let's go run this by the guys. Her groceries and cookies are not here. That's a fact. I like facts. I want more of them."

He found himself smiling back as she smiled at him, aware his temper had just been defused. "Yeah." He sighed and pushed away from the counter. "Where were we before we took this walk out on a limb?"

"According to Eric, your mom had plans for Monday evening."

"Right. Back to the core question. Where did Mom go Monday after the grocery store?"

"That's the right question."

■ ■ ■

Sharon assembled as many of her team in the conference room as she could round up. "The search is taking a turn," she announced.

"Someone holler 'hurray' because I'm too hoarse," Carter said, pulling out a chair at the table.

"Not that big a turn," Sharon cautioned. "Guys, we're missing groceries. Martha Graham bought a specialty box of cookies, some peaches and apples, at the grocery store late Monday afternoon. They aren't in her apartment, and not in her car."

The detectives around the room glanced at each other, sat forward, and one of them whispered, "Interesting."

"Maybe she forgot to lock the car when she did other errands and the groceries were stolen. To test that idea, let's see if any other car break-ins were reported Monday evening—say, in a three-mile radius of the grocery store."

A detective found a marker and wrote the item on the board.

"She would have reported a robbery, don't you think? A cop's mom?" one of the officers asked.

"She would have reported it," John replied. "Or if she didn't report it because it was minor in dollar value, she would have at least mentioned it to a friend—'I forgot to lock the car door and my groceries disappeared.' Plus she would have gone back to buy more cookies for her Tuesday Tea. She would have replaced them."

Sharon nodded. "Which leads us to a theory that's not so simple or elegant. Her purse is in her apartment, wallet intact, her car is in the parking lot, but the groceries are missing. Not-so-simple theory Number Two says she never got home Monday night. Someone else brought her car back, returned her purse to the apartment, to redirect our search away from where something happened."

A collective wince went around the room. "It's a reach, I know," Sharon agreed, "but it could be an answer. Whatever happened, they've been trying to cover their tracks by returning her car and purse."

She nodded toward the boards. "So here's how we're going to work it. Our first priority remains the Village—we confirm beyond any doubt she is not on the grounds. We continue the check of every apartment and interview every resident. Remaining high on the probability list is a confrontation with another resident and Martha leaves here in another car not by her own choice. So keep pushing the interviews for anyone who saw something, or someone who seems nervous at the questions. I want to make sure we understand the dynamics of what has been going on in the Village before we move on from that possibility.

"We open a new priority. I want forensics to look at her car again. Has someone else driven it?

"I've already raised the possibility it was Bobby Sail or one of his family who Martha went to see Monday night. As we get more information about him and his family, it should lead to some new locations we'll then take a look at in more detail.

"Until we can identify those new areas and refocus the search, let's get her photo out more broadly around the community. I want patrols to start checking alleys and parking lots between the grocery store and the Village. As volunteers finish up here, we send them out in groups of three and take it street by street. Questions?" Sharon looked around the room and nodded. "Thanks, guys. Let's get this done."

■■■

John helped with the volunteer maps, marking streets off by sections, finding the work useful simply to keep his mind occupied. He saw Bryon Slate enter the lobby, skirt past volunteers, and discreetly motion for the lieutenant. John rose to join them. He could see in Bryon's face and stance that he had something significant to share. Sharon's face went unusually impassive as she listened.

Sharon stepped toward him as John got close, wrapped a hand over his arm. "There's a body in Glenwood, about four miles north of here. A woman who fits the age and description."

Fear slammed into his heart. "Let me come along."

"You're with me," she promised. "Bryon, let them know we're coming. Then put three of Martha's friends in front of reporters, keep the press focused here while we check it out."

"Will do, boss. I'm sorry, John."

■■■

The roadway rose gradually to cross over another one. John forced himself to concentrate on identifying vehicles: the medical examiner, squad cars from the Glenwood Police and State

Police. He could see a group clustered at the base of a brush-covered embankment below the overpass. A city utility truck blocked in by police vehicles suggested who had discovered the body. Jefferies pulled in among the other cop vehicles.

"Stay here with Jefferies, John," Sharon instructed as they stepped out.

He didn't protest as she ducked under the crime-scene tape. He was glad he couldn't see much from this angle. He'd worked enough homicides to know what would be there. The fact the medical examiner was still here told him the body had yet to be transported from the scene.

Time passed in agonizing slowness.

Sharon came back into view. As soon as she saw him, she shook her head. His muscles quivered, and his rigid control let go. She rejoined them and slipped under the crime-scene tape.

"Not your mother, John. She's the right age, the right features, but it's not Martha. A woman's been missing from Malmora. I think they just found her."

He had to absorb his relief, along with the reality someone else was going to be feeling the pain he had just experienced. Sharon shared a look that said she understood his mix of emotions. "Let's get back, keep on the search. That's the priority now."

He nodded, didn't try to speak. His immediate relief was overshadowed by the realization it could have been his mom's body and she was still missing. The next call like this one might be her. As Jefferies turned the car and took them back the way they came, John leaned his head back. *God, I can't whip back and forth between hope and horror like this. I just can't carry this. I can't.* He felt a numbness through body and soul.

He made no further plea—he hadn't even prayed for his mother's safe return today. After nearly a lifetime with God, he would have thought this was a moment when he leaned most heavily into his faith. But he stood back as though observing himself and saw . . . what? His belief in God hadn't changed. His expectation that God would help hadn't wavered. He was simply standing in a storm so ferocious he couldn't find words to form a prayer. He could only look up with *Oh, God. My God. Have mercy on my mother, on me.* It was the one cry of his heart he could put into words.

Then, *"Though I walk through the valley of the shadow of death, I will fear no evil. Thy rod and thy staff comfort me. . . ."* The words shimmered like a faint melody, unsought, just there. John shuddered out a long breath.

He coped by mostly staying in cop mode, asking questions, pushing along conversations, not letting similar moments overcome him. To think beyond the job was dangerous, to know and feel and absorb that it was *Mom* this was all about, and that, short of a miracle, it was *Mom* he would not see again alive. Force of will could not change what might have already occurred, but his emotions couldn't catch up with that.

He felt Sharon's hand cover his, and he wordlessly accepted the comfort. A fellow cop made it particularly meaningful. He could tell she wasn't holding to the professional reserve, the distance it required not to get personally involved. And he appreciated that more than he could ever express. He wasn't walking this alone.

FOUR

No longer needed as a work area for volunteers, the lobby of the Village commons area was being cleared, folding tables were being collapsed for storage, chairs stacked, and a woman was running a vacuum. Night had fallen. The only lights outside now were those from a few lampposts and the floodlights for the television cameras. John watched a reporter head his direction, saw Jefferies step in and cut the woman off. He had already given nine interviews to be aired during the evening newscasts. He was weary, numb with the stress of dealing with the press—providing just enough information but not too much, plus the fact of it being his mother they were asking about had him feeling absolutely undone.

The good-news-bad-news was that his mom wasn't on the property. There was no place that hadn't been searched. The Riverside Retirement Village would return to normalcy soon, without his mother here. He wondered if the police would remain on-site another day or if they would shift to the precinct. The search was now focusing away from here. Tomorrow would be more alleys and parking lots, more poking behind garages, hoping to find *something* that might be a clue.

The light scent of Sharon's perfume alerted him to her presence, but he didn't turn. She'd been nearby during every part of this horrendous day.

"We're going to call an all-hands at 9:00 p.m.," she said quietly, "go back over the interviews, calls, search grids, make certain nothing has been missed. Calls are still coming in from the evening newscasts."

John nodded. With no idea where trouble had begun, they could only keep going over the existing ground. Maybe a call would add another detail to the timeline for Monday evening. "Tell me something, Sharon."

"If I can."

"No ransom call. She's not on the Village property. Whatever occurred likely happened Monday evening, and happened fast. It's been over and done with for forty-eight hours."

She hesitated as if she would like to argue with where this was going, but she simply sighed with a soft, "Yes."

"What do families do when Christmas comes and there aren't any answers to give them?" Without consciously realizing it, he'd arrived at the all-but-certain conclusion his mother was dead. "It seems wrong to keep hope alive, to let Annabelle and the others believe Martha is coming home again."

Sharon turned him to face her. "We'll find her, John."

They would, he thought. He supposed it was one benefit of a city rather than a rural area, they probably *would* locate her—the body behind a dumpster somewhere, the victim of a robbery or the like, and forensics might collect enough to point to her assailant. The winter ground meant even a shallow grave would be difficult.

"You let people hope," Sharon said firmly, "because hope is

the very strong thread between earth and heaven. We still get miracles even after forty-eight hours." He felt her arm slide through his. "We'll re-interview tomorrow, pursue further that another person drove her car back. Her photo will go to more media, and we'll look at the option of a post-office distribution of flyers to all the addresses in this zip code."

"You're hoping for something to break open, for a lead to show up."

"It always does." She tugged him away from the wall. "Come on, walk with me. The fresh air will do us both good."

He let her lead him toward the doors. They walked outside into the brisk air. He handed her his gloves this time so that he wouldn't have to see her with ice-cold hands. She slipped them on with a small smile.

"Nothing further from your friends?" she asked while they trudged across the parking lot toward a paved pathway.

He shook his head. "More names to pursue, but no hint as to why or who. It's going to be a random act of violence, Sharon. Someone managed to cover it up well enough to buy two full days of time to disappear. We still don't have a thread to pull him or her in."

"The end of the race is what matters here, not the journey. And we need to change the subject. Tell me about your mom, not from today, from back when you were a boy."

She asked the right question to open a flood of memories. John had to relax to let himself go there. "She understood boys—their battles and adventures and competitions and challenges. My friends all loved hanging out at our house. The reward for getting chores done—and sometimes I talked the guys into helping me finish—were battlefield soldiers, and cardboard coffins for fallen soldiers, and cookies iced as medals for the heroes. Or we'd find a stack of planed wood pieces delivered to the side of the driveway, and she'd hand us a drawing or a photo of what she wanted us to build—picnic tables and bookshelves, derby cars. She bought an old junker car when I was thirteen, suggested we take it apart and put it back together. She was always giving us fun stuff to do."

"She was keeping you and your friends out of trouble by giving you those projects."

John smiled. "Sure. We occasionally acknowledged how sneaky she was, but the simple truth is we all loved her for it. She believed we could figure out how to do something, and she'd let us learn without interfering. She wanted us to grow up to become good men. She'd talk that way. About us growing up to be men she'd be proud to know."

"Why a cop?"

"A childhood filled with old westerns, where the sheriff always did what was right, even if it took a fight to enforce it. It was a role model that just kind of clicked with a boy's imagination."

"You haven't mentioned your dad."

He paused, then said, "I respected my dad. He gave me that safe neighborhood, college when it was time, the freedom to follow my dream and not his. He was a general contractor and busy most of my life—long hours at work, not so many hours with his son, though I knew he was proud of me. I missed him growing up, even though he was around. It's complicated, a boy and his father. I had his approval. And I loved and respected the man. But it wasn't like with my mom. She was always there to share my daily life. Dad passed away some years ago, and it left a hole, someone missing from the table, someone who would enjoy hearing about my life. But I could go on without him. Mom has always been closer to my day-to-day."

"That's why you and your mom talk so often, the phone calls to and from Cheyenne, even when they're brief."

"She wanted to stay in Chicago and enjoy life with her friends. She encouraged me to take the job, and I wanted the challenge of it, but we would stay family, stay in touch. I was the son who expected to know how his mom was doing, and she'd call to say 'I love you' in case trouble found me on the job that day. She would worry, though in her own way. She pushed me to do the job as it should best be done, despite the risks."

"I like your mom. I'm going to enjoy meeting her, John. Hang on to the hope for a good ending."

He looked at her, noting the confidence she could still express. "That's not so easy to do . . . I can see the train lights barreling down the tracks at me, Sharon. I'm afraid I know how this will end."

"Maybe that's why I still work missing-persons cases. You need an optimist in charge. I still am one." Sharon turned them back the way they came. "I'll get you some hot chocolate before the all-hands meeting," she said briskly. "You're probably drowning in coffee by now."

He slipped a hand out of his pocket to squeeze her gloved one. "I'd appreciate that. Thanks. For all of this, Sharon. I'm more grateful than I can express."

"I'm going to get you through this, John. And we are going to find your mom."

FIVE

The all-hands meeting paused to watch the 10:00 p.m. newscasts. Those monitoring the phone traffic shifted to see what notes were being logged in. Bryon dispatched officers to follow up on some calls, tabled others. Officers came into the conference room carrying plates of food and drink, and the discussion among those not rereading interviews shifted to theories.

"I think we can rule out Bobby Sail," Bryon said. "I walked through his place after this last interview, looked at his security system, the captured video, compared it with his neighbors. There are no glitches. I'm convinced he didn't leave his home Monday evening, and Martha didn't arrive."

"What about his family?" Sharon asked.

"As you know, he has two sons and a daughter. They have stable marriages and okay credit ratings, comfortable careers. They'll all appreciate their father's wealth in future years, since they haven't been saving as their father has."

"How did they seem in the interviews?" John asked.

"They each looked surprised at the questions. They were aware their father had found a lady he liked, had all been introduced to Martha. The two sons didn't see any future in it. The daughter did, but thought her dad would take the relationship slow—that he wasn't ready to replace their mom yet in his affections. None has a decent alibi for Monday night. If we can place one of them here at the Village, that will move matters along. We'll show around their photos tomorrow, try to trace their cars."

Sharon nodded, making notes. "Bobby's children sit at the top of the list for people we focus on. What else? Who has a theory or idea to put on the table?"

"I'm looking at that timeline," Detective Carter remarked, studying the board. "The last person to see Mrs. Graham is Eric Holland. I think he has to stay a viable person of interest."

"I'm fine with interviewing him again tomorrow," Sharon agreed. "And to tie things off, we should talk to the lady who was sitting with June while Eric was grocery shopping, confirm his arrival back home about 5:30 p.m. with loads of groceries and that birthday cake. He said ladies from his church were coming over, so let's see if we can get names, confirm they were there. I've got in the back of my mind that Martha maybe changed her mind, did stop in to see June and have a piece of that cake. So let's tie that off with a good solid bow."

"I'll pursue it, Lieutenant," Carter volunteered.

"Thanks." Sharon nodded to the timeline. "The fact the timeline hasn't narrowed further does raise a question. We don't know anything solid past the grocery store. How often do we get absolutely shut down when following someone's movements? Someone *always* remembers seeing a person *someplace*. So I've got a theory number three to propose."

Good-natured groans erupted around the table. Sharon smiled. "Hear me out, guys. We know Martha went to the grocery store, so she's out running errands. A stop to pick up a prescription at the pharmacy, a stop to drop off dry cleaning, could easily be on her list. The people we expect to hear from when we ask for information are people like the grocery-store clerk who *did* call us. Maybe the reason we're not getting those calls is that Martha walked into a robbery in progress. A wrong-place-wrong-time possibility that I thought about early on and didn't actively pursue. Maybe everyone's locked in a storeroom. Those we expect to be calling us simply can't."

She looked around the table. No one spoke. "Okay, too far out there."

"Too much time has passed," Bryon finally volunteered. "After two days, someone notices a business isn't open when it should be. It's a good theory, but it should have already surfaced by now."

Sharon pointed to the package of Oreos to be sent her way. "That's a good point," she admitted around an Oreo. "So . . . back to the car. Who drove it here Monday night? Martha? Or someone trying to redirect our search?" She tapped the edge of a second cookie against the table. "I want a photo of her car going or coming. Even better, I want a photo of Martha's car with someone else driving it. Tomorrow we should widen the scope of the traffic cam search to include any ATM and business within fifteen blocks of the Village. There's video out there with Martha's car. Let's find it."

"I've got a thought," Officer Bernardo offered.

Sharon slid him the package of cookies. "Let's hear it."

"Start with the premise Martha ran into trouble here at the Village Monday night. She stepped out of the apartment with her keys in her hand, took her coat, so she was going to the parking lot or across to another building. Trouble happens. It likely involved another resident, given no one is reporting a stranger hanging around. We can't find Mrs. Graham on

74

the property. So she was taken off the property, most likely by car. We need to look at people who returned to the Village after 10:00 p.m. Monday evening, residents the security guard checked in through the closed gate. They would be back into their normal routine as soon as they could do so. But could they have left the property with Martha and returned before the security gate closes at 10:00 p.m.?"

"That's an interesting idea," Bryon said. "We need the security gate logs."

"I'll get them," Bernardo said, pushing back from the table.

"Extend it," Sharon instructed. "Who was away from the property Monday night—residents or staff? Someone whose absence was out of the ordinary? This has never felt like something planned, but rather a random event. Someone has a block of missing time in their routine."

"We can re-interview with that question," Bryon suggested. "'Did you see your neighbor go out?' Maybe get some back-and-forth gossiping going on."

"I'm for whatever works," Sharon said.

John's phone rang. He tugged it out of his pocket and saw a number he didn't recognize with a prefix for this area. His gaze shot to Sharon's. Those around him stopped talking and the rest of the room began to quiet. Sharon picked up a phone, asked a question, and she nodded to him that the trace-and-record was active. He answered the call. "This is John Graham."

"Come get me, John."

"Mom! Where are you?" Several notepads and pens slid across the table as he frantically looked for something to write with.

A long pause. "The main library, by the museum gift shop entrance."

John relayed it to the room. Before he had finished the words, a street map of the area was up on the wide-screen monitor and zooming in on the location. Martinez put a finger on the screen—lots of one-way traffic, direct flow out to major avenues heading away from downtown. "Stay on the line, Mom. Stay with me. I'm coming."

"It's a public pay phone, limited time." Another pause. "I'll be here at the bench out of the wind." She sounded . . . He closed his eyes.

"I'm on my way," he repeated, moving toward the door, wishing he could reach through the phone connection and wrap that reassurance around her.

"Bryon, we'll go in on Cypress, you in the lead car," Sharon directed, swiftly putting it together. "No lights, no sirens. Carter—close off State, Cook, and Beach two blocks out, drop a net at six blocks. I want license plates for everything that moves. Martinez, position EMS at Elm and Oak, contact Riverside Hospital, secure our arrival. Nelson, block in what press vehicles are here, buy us a few minutes before they catch on." She and John were out the door as she gave the last order.

Someone tossed his own coat around his shoulders as John headed out through the lobby.

"Still have her, John?" Sharon asked, holding the door for him.

He shook his head. He could hear only traffic noise, not his mom. The pay phone wasn't back on the hook, but she was no longer holding it.

"It's three minutes from here."

He knew without having to ask that they'd try to make it two.

■■■

The illuminated sign on the corner turned a slow circle, announcing Riverside Public Library and Museum. Trees and huge, empty flowerpots made ghostly shadows along the brick-paved sidewalk. The upper floors of the library were dark, while security lights from the main floor spilled out through oversized windows. John could see an entrance hall, interior glass doors, caught a brief glimpse of a bench inside and someone sitting on it.

"John, you have to let me do my job," Sharon said, her tone firm. "You have to stay back. I will pass her to you just as soon as I can."

"Go, Sharon. I get it."

Jefferies swung the squad car to a stop in front of the building behind Bryon. She was out of the car, following Bryon, who had a few steps' lead on her, his attention directed everywhere but toward the entrance glass doors and bench inside.

The UNSUB might well still be in the area, John knew. He should have thought to grab the vest. If this was a setup designed to catch him in the open, a rifle shot could come out of the darkness without warning. He searched for any sign of movement in the block around them.

Sharon disappeared through the doors as Bryon stepped into shadows at the side of the door, still scanning the area for any movement.

■ ■ ■

Sharon recognized her on sight. "Mrs. Graham. Martha. I'm Lieutenant Sharon Noble." The woman looked like a faded version of her picture. Elderly now, not simply older. Sharon felt relief and sympathy meld together. "It's very good to see you," she said gently, slowing her steps.

Their surroundings were more secure than she had expected. This hall between the entrances to the library and museum was fifteen feet of polished tile and anti-skid carpet runners designed to catch melting snow from footwear. The bench was metal without a cushion. They were alone at the moment where often the homeless would seek shelter from the weather. In fact, the library board had voted to leave the outer doors unlocked during November through March for that very reason.

Martha was wearing her winter coat, buttoned, her scarf in place. Sharon discovered Martha's hands were icy cold, even under the gloves she carefully removed. She found a steady pulse. "Can you tell me where you've been? Who did this to you, Martha?"

The briefest shake of her head, the woman was starting to cry now, silently.

The coat's sleeves covered her arms, the rest of it most of her legs. Sharon eased open a couple of buttons. Martha was wearing the red dress from Monday afternoon. It looked neat, as though pressed. No signs of blood. No bruises on her face, her hands, nothing immediately obvious on her lower legs. Sharon gently ran a hand along her ribs, watching for any sign of pain, but there was no wince on Martha's face. The shoes were not scuffed. Her hair was neat, almost artfully so. If there had been makeup, Sharon would have instinctively stiffened even more than she had to what she was finding. This wasn't fitting together. Shock had a grip on Martha, the cold was obvious, and the aging this woman had undergone in two days was striking. Sharon wished for a clean ending that might spare John a nightmare, but she wasn't going to be able to give him that. Not given the car, the purse, and what she was now observing.

"I'd like to see my son," Martha said quietly.

"John's going to join us now, and we'll get you to the hospital," Sharon replied with a reassuring smile. "When we're done there, tonight or in a few days, we will get you to where you'll feel safe so you can rest, not have to worry about friends dropping by until you're ready for that."

"Thank you."

Sharon tightened her hand over the woman's and reached for her radio.

■ ■ ■

John heard the calm in Sharon's voice. "John. Then EMS. Try to stay in the shadows as you move."

He nodded to Jefferies that he'd heard the direction and headed to the library entrance at a fast jog. Bryon had the door open for him before he reached it.

Sharon. The bench. Martha.

"Mom."

His world righted itself when her eyes met his. He took the bench beside her, wrapped his arms around her, tucked her head in against his shoulder, and rocked with her.

"I'm okay, John." He heard the faint words, the strength coming back into her voice as she repeated, "I'm okay."

Sharon stepped away, and John let the emotions and adrenaline find release in tears. He heard a small sob against his chest, and his mom's hand found his and held on. "Cry it out, Mom. You've got a big shoulder to weep on now." His mind overflowed with questions, but he knew she didn't need them at this moment.

He looked over her head to Sharon. *Who?* he mouthed silently. Sharon shook her head.

■ ■ ■

The paramedics—both of them women—were careful with Martha, no hurried movements as they worked: easing the coat off, moving her onto the gurney, covering her with her own coat, layering on blankets. They were working through a list, checking her breathing and her pupils and her pulse, looking for broken bones and pain, making light conversation to keep her engaged.

John sat on the bench beside the gurney, his hand holding his mother's. He was aware of the police officers coming and going, reporting in to Bryon or Sharon, sharing information regarding security video, cars in the area, reports from patrols.

When the paramedics said they were ready to go, John stood as the gurney was raised, walked to the ambulance, his mom's hand safely tucked in his. More officers had pulled into the street to block further traffic.

"Go with her to the hospital," Sharon said. "I'll meet you there."

He nodded and climbed into the ambulance beside his mother. This case wasn't over, not by a long shot, but he had his mother back. He brushed her hair away from her face with gentle fingers, wondering how many of the lines in her face had been hiding there for years or were new in the last few months—even in the last two days. His mother had grown old on him while he was in Cheyenne. Her smile wasn't there tonight to hide the changes that time had wrought. He lifted her cold hand and kissed the back of it, saw a small smile cross her face. Okay. That fleeting small smile was good. His mother was still in there, under the explosion of all that had happened.

He couldn't get warmth into her hand, even when he held it with both of his. The thin skin and fragile bones couldn't seem to draw from his heat and strength. His world had changed in ways he didn't know how to clarify, but the core of it was solid again. *Thank you, God.* The heartfelt prayer relaxed the tension inside him coiled tight since that first call to Cheyenne.

■ ■ ■

Hospitals sounded like life and death, the equipment beeping, the instructions between doctors and nurses, stifled tears and serious conversation of family members, the groans and whispers of patients. John hated the sounds of a hospital.

"How is she?"

John turned his head. The wall he was leaning against was holding up his body so he didn't try to get a true look at Sharon, instead just put a moving person into his periphery and realized it was her. "The doctor is in with her. My adrenaline began to crash a few minutes ago," he mentioned, knowing she would understand what every cop encountered. He'd hit a wall where his body was done taking on more stress.

"You need this more than I do." Sharon handed him a coffee, the kind that costs real money and came in layers of foam and flavors.

He hesitated, but reality was he did need it more than she did—she was still moving. He tasted nutmeg and cinnamon and drank because it was hot, felt the caffeine hit and the warmth spread through his body. "Mom's doctor, a woman, has a nice bedside manner and she's taking things slow. She kicked me out so she and the nurse could get Mom comfortable. I'm guessing you know the doctor."

Sharon nodded.

John had seen Sharon's handiwork in what had been arranged before they arrived. They hadn't remained in the emergency room, had instead been whisked through the hospital and up an elevator to this private room on the third floor. "Mom isn't ever this quiet. Besides a whisper that she was glad I was here and that she was cold, she hasn't said anything. What's the scene look like?"

"It's going to take some time. It's a public place, so I'm hopeful," Sharon replied. "Cameras at the library show your mother approaching the pay phone, making one call, moving to sit on the bench. She's alone. She's doesn't appear to be looking over her shoulder, checking someone watching her. She looks to have walked straight from the street, as though dropped off there. We're pulling cam footage in a five-block radius. Her call gives us the two minutes when the car we're looking for was on that street."

"Good." He leaned his head against the wall again. "She hasn't said man or woman—one, two . . . or more. She hasn't given me anything."

"She knows you'll go hurt whoever did this to her."

He half smiled. "Under the fatigue, that sentiment is running strong."

Sharon's hand gripped his, reassuring. "She'll talk when she's ready."

"Yeah. I called Annabelle and Heather. They're spreading the word she's been located and is now at the hospital. Apparently there's a phone tree for those who wanted to be awakened with news. Fortunately it's good news."

"I understand," Sharon replied. "Life matters to the elderly perhaps the most of all."

The doctor stepped out of his mother's room. John tried to read her face as she came to join them. She nodded a greeting to Sharon.

"Mr. Graham, I'm pleasantly surprised. Your mother is in overall stable health. I'm going to give you the details now, but don't worry if you don't take it all in tonight—we'll be talking several times in the next few days. There are no major signs of physical or sexual trauma. Some light bruising on her arms, strained muscles in her shoulders, some mild trouble breathing. She's dehydrated, exhausted, a little disoriented—not unlike a surgical patient in the recovery room four hours after anesthesia. She's not fully reacting to sounds and lights. Acute stress would be my core diagnosis. Those symptoms are going to clear.

"Her blood pressure is high, her pulse elevated. Both are going to settle as her world gets quiet and safe again. She's a little hungry and that's a very good sign. I'm having a meal sent up—soup, some thin-sliced turkey and fresh rolls, cottage cheese. You should sit with her while she eats, talk to her about her friends, about Christmas. She needs to see you relaxing. She'll begin to mirror you and do the same."

"I can do that," John agreed.

"It would be good if you could stay with her tonight when she drifts in and out of sleep," the doctor continued. "You can expect she'll be doing some serious dreaming the next few nights, and if her anxiety gets high I'll give her something. But I'd rather not introduce more meds unless necessary. I've drawn blood for a full work-up, and I want to do another complete exam tomorrow when she's more responsive. But all in all, I think you've both been spared what this could have been."

"I'll be with her tonight," John assured the doctor. "She's not had trouble breathing in the past—no history of asthma or respiratory problems, never a smoker."

"What I'm seeing reminds me of stress-induced asthma. We most often see it in young adults. I'm not overly concerned. I expect it to resolve itself overnight. Any other questions I can answer for you?"

"She's been inside," Sharon confirmed.

The doctor nodded. "I'm certain of that. Exposure to cold for an extended period of time for a woman her age would show up quickly: hypothermia, circulation problems in her hands, her feet, mild frostbite. Even as little as half an hour, I would have seen signs of it. She's feeling cold right now, but her core body temperature hasn't dropped."

"Has she said anything at all regarding the last two days?" John asked.

"No, she's not even answering innocuous questions like 'Have you eaten today?' I would have thought she's afraid to talk about what happened, but normally a victim who is actively scared has an anxiousness that's quite palpable. Your mom isn't giving me that impression. She's made a decision not to say anything. That may be a first reaction to being found. She feels a need to turn away from what happened, push it aside for a few hours or a day in order to get her bearings. If so, it's a normal defense mechanism and nothing to worry about. If she continues to deflect even the easiest of questions a few days from now, I'll likely give you a different answer."

"Will she be staying in the hospital a few days?" John asked.

"If she improves significantly overnight, as I expect, she can be treated as an outpatient for any lingering concerns. But given the circumstances, it's appropriate for her to spend the next week here if she feels comfortable with the care. I'm going to leave that decision up to you, John, after your conversations with her. Some patients need familiar surroundings before they can accept a situation is over. Others want an environment that feels more secure than home if that's where the problem began. I'd like her to be comfortable with talking to doctors about what happened. But inpatient or outpatient, we can work with what you both prefer."

"Thanks, Doc."

She nodded and walked over to speak with the nurses by his mother's doorway.

John turned to Sharon. "I'll sit with Mom through her meal and until she's asleep, then maybe touch base with you. I know it's getting late and you've got to get some sleep too. I can call you at home if that's okay."

"Let's play it by ear for another few hours. She may suddenly tell you a great deal while you're holding her hand and she's heading toward sleep. Martha strikes me as a strong woman, well able to deal with whatever has happened. She just needs to decide what she wants to say. Right now is probably the first moments she's been alone to gather her own thoughts since this began."

John was startled by the astute observation. "A very good point. Would you stay with her while I go down to the gift shop, talk someone into opening it so I can get her some flowers?"

Sharon smiled. "I'll be glad to."

John opted for the stairs rather than the elevator and went to see what he could arrange.

■ ■ ■

Sharon tapped lightly on the hospital room door before stepping inside. Martha lay with her eyes closed, the light over the bed on its lowest setting, the soft glow directed up toward the ceiling. Martha had the remote beside her to call for a nurse.

"It's Lieutenant Sharon Noble again, Mrs. Graham." She took the chair by the bed, leaned forward but didn't try to take the woman's hand. "John just went to get you some flowers. He might have to take a side trip to Florida to find a florist open at this hour of night, so if he ends up bringing you a ceramic mug with a painted rose, you might want to be amused with him." The woman cracked the faintest of smiles, even though her eyes didn't open.

"How about I have Heather Jome pack a bag for you. If there's anything specific you'd like, just make a list and I'll make sure she gets it. I'm leaving a pad and pen on the bedside table," Sharon said, leaving the notepad where Martha could easily reach it.

"A nightgown would be nice," Martha whispered.

"Aren't hospital gowns the worst? When your son gets back

from the gift shop, I'll sneak down and see if there's one there you might like for tonight."

"Thanks."

"I like being useful." Sharon leaned over and checked that the water pitcher was filled. "There are options after the hospital, such as returning to your apartment if you wish, to a hotel, or I know a private home within a short drive that's open for guests. If you would like a few days there for you and John—an anonymous place, not a hospital room, and better than a hotel—I could arrange that for you."

There was little reaction, but Sharon wasn't expecting one. Martha was listening and that was enough. Sharon had more experience than John might realize with the second part of working a missing-persons case, with what needed to be done in the days after a victim was found. "I like your son, Martha. He's showing the stress of the last two days, just as you are. He needs twenty hours of sleep. He needs to hear you say good morning to him, have you nag him about needing a decent shave."

Martha opened her eyes, blinked, tried to focus. Sharon smiled at her, moved to the edge of the bed. "He's a good man, your son. A smart cop. And he's worried that something from his past is what made this happen to you. He's not going to rest easy until that is answered." Sharon let Martha absorb that piece of information. "If there's anything you think you should tell me but don't want to mention to your son, write it down toward the back of that pad of paper, and I'll keep it between us."

"All right."

Sharon smoothed the woman's hair gently away from her face. "He thought he'd lost you, and he looked as broken as any man I've ever seen. He loves you, but I bet you already know that."

86

"I love him too."

Sharon smiled. "It's going to be fine, for both of you. Let me do my job now and help you."

"Tomorrow," Martha whispered.

"Tomorrow," Sharon agreed. She heard the door opening behind her and didn't turn. "What do you think, Martha, a ceramic mug or actual flowers?"

She didn't require an answer. Martha's eyes filled with tears, and Sharon moved from the bedside as a massive vase of flowers was placed on the movable table. The professional arrangement was so fresh the baby roses still had moisture on the buds. John drew one of them out and put it in his mother's hand. "The perfect welcome-home flowers for a pretty lady."

"Promise me you didn't steal them from somebody?"

John chuckled as he eased onto the side of the bed. "Fresh flowers are being delivered around the hospital at this hour. The hospital administrator let me have the display intended for his reception room."

Martha chuckled briefly, and there was no sadness in the sound. "I shall enjoy them even more knowing their story."

Sharon turned as an orderly brought in Martha's dinner. "I'll let you two get settled in. John, you have my number?"

He patted his shirt pocket. "I do."

"Call me whenever you like. Good night, Martha. If I'm successful in the gift shop, you shall have a package forthwith."

Martha smiled and nodded. "Thank you, Sharon."

The stress was leaving Martha's voice and demeanor, Sharon could see the change happening. The woman needed family now, not cops. Sharon nodded to them both and slipped out of the room.

■ ■ ■

Officer Dell had drawn the hospital security assignment for the night, and Sharon paused to speak with him after she left Martha. The press would be trying every trick in the book to gain access to Martha. Sharon knew John would forcefully evict anyone who managed to locate Martha's room, but she wanted a buffer of her own in place so that John wouldn't be faced with the problem.

She made a call while she walked down the stairs. "Bryon, I'm leaving the hospital. We're settled here. She isn't talking about matters yet."

"That isn't good."

"I know. Where are you?"

"At the precinct scanning traffic footage. I've got thirteen license plates that look promising for the time and the street they were on. I've already cleared a third of them. Ask me in an hour about the others. I've got officers wrapping up our presence at the Village, boxing up what's in the conference room and transferring it here. The police presence will be gone from the Village by sunrise."

"You're making this easy on me. Thanks, Bryon."

"We both know what comes next is the hard part of the case. How's John holding together?"

She thought back to the man she'd seen resting against the wall, weary beyond words, but also his expression as he sat on the library bench holding his mother's hand.

"He's the most dangerous man I've seen," Sharon replied, startled at her own realization. "The gloves are off. He's got his mother back. Now he gets to track down who did this with no worry about her getting hurt in the cross fire. We'd better be prepared to manage some real fury."

"Yeah. Thanks for saying what I've been thinking. I spoke with the friends he has running the search related to his past cases. The fact she shows up like this, dropped off in a public place—they think whoever had her got paid a visit or heard from someone who got paid a visit. They're going back over the list of who's been interviewed. Someone must have gotten his cage rattled, realized it wasn't worth holding her."

"An old grudge triggers it, but new blood from the present hierarchy shuts it down," Sharon guessed.

"It could be that simple, boss. You've got to admit, it's sudden, her abrupt reappearance."

"I agree. The media coverage may have contributed to it. It's too hot to hold her any longer, and too dangerous to cause her any harm. Cops put out word this is personal, being she's the mother of a cop."

"Exactly," Bryon agreed. "His friends are going to fold us in on what they've been reviewing, send copies of the materials over."

"Good. We'll poke at that idea in the morning. Depending on how matters go, I'll be at the hospital, then at the precinct. Come in after you've had enough sleep your wife thinks you'll live another day."

Bryon laughed. "Will do, Lieutenant, as long as you'll take your own advice."

"I'm heading home momentarily," she promised, then ended the call. She was well known around the hospital. She headed to the night check-in desk. A janitor with keys was summoned, and she found a nightgown in the gift shop that Martha would like, clipped off the tags, chose a gift box covered with hearts, left full payment and a Post-it note on the manager's desk and had an orderly deliver the package upstairs for John to give to his mom.

Sharon went home satisfied. It wasn't a full win—they didn't have the persons responsible yet—but still a good day.

SIX

Sharon tapped lightly on the hospital door and eased it open, not wanting to disturb Martha if she was asleep. She wouldn't be surprised to find John asleep in a chair as well. The television was on low, a movie playing. John turned his head her direction as she came in. He needed a shave, some serious sleep, but he looked more relaxed than she had ever seen him before. He looked good, a solid man, protecting his mother.

"She's drifting in and out," he said softly.

She took the chair beside him and slid a box from her sister's bakery onto the movable table. "Has she said anything?"

"No, I would have called. How about you? Any success?"

"Traffic around the library didn't lead anywhere, but the timeline for Monday has tightened. We found an ATM photo with your mom's car in the background, parked on the street two blocks over from the grocery store, outside a florist at 5:53 p.m. Maybe she stopped to pick up flowers for the Tuesday Tea. The next ATM photo was at 7:52 p.m. and the car was gone. I've got officers on that block conducting interviews."

"You found another step in her evening, maybe even where it all began."

"It looks promising." She studied his mom. The stress was leaving her face, her sleep looked peaceful. "You haven't left this room. Why don't you walk down to the cafeteria, have a real meal, make a few calls to your friends. I'll sit with Martha and call if I need you back here."

He hesitated.

"I won't ask her about it in detail, if at all. Today your mom needs mostly to sleep, eat, and think about Christmas."

John nodded. "Thanks. I won't be gone long." He slipped out of the room.

Sharon picked up the pad she'd left, saw three items listed for Heather to bring from the apartment—nothing was written at the back. She hadn't expected it, but she had hoped. She settled in to watch the movie, wondering how long it would be before she nodded off herself. She was tired in a way that reached down to even how her heart beat. She needed rest, the kind that came with days off work, time with her sister, laughter.

It would be a week, she thought, before Martha trusted the process enough to face what had occurred and talk about it. John's mom was a strong woman. This stage simply took time.

Martha was drifting to consciousness, as the elderly did at times, a drowsy awakening that slowly registered. "Hello, Martha," she whispered, "its Sharon Noble again. John is downstairs at the cafeteria—probably eating a man-size quantity of food after being here through the night."

Martha turned her head on the pillow, and Sharon offered a kind smile. "I thought we might talk for a minute while he's out."

"No."

"It's not so hard, the questions I'm curious about. What happened to the cookies?"

Martha blinked. Sharon leaned over and refilled the water glass, handed it to Martha with the straw bent. Martha drank thirstily, then nodded her thanks. "I ate them. The fruit too."

"Were they good?"

Martha gave a glimmer of a smile. "Very good."

"I nearly brought you a box of cookies, but my sister thought you'd enjoy her finger-food selections. She makes really good quiches and puff-ball pastries and miniature croissants." Sharon nodded to the box. "You can share with John, then tell him to stop by the bakery and pick up another dozen of your favorites. My sister loves to bake all kinds of things. There are days I watch her humming as she works and wonder why I didn't choose a career like that. Food makes people happy."

"I like to bake too. Pies mostly, some candies."

"Christmas is the time for it." Sharon leaned back in the chair and relaxed. "I can help you if you let me. I want to help you. And I don't need all that much information to accomplish a lot. Will you let me?"

Martha looked toward the door. "I won't hurt my son any further. He looks very worn out."

"You are the love of his life, Martha—until he has a wife and then has two loves of his life. This scared him, Martha, as it has to have scared you. Please help me end this for both of you. It can be over and finished before Christmas."

Sharon saw expressions she couldn't identify cross the woman's face. "You stopped at the grocery store. You stopped for flowers next? Then something happened. Two days later you were able to call your son. I think one of the reasons you were free to call your son is that you were very convincing in whatever you said to the one who did this. You've been brave for two days, holding yourself together and getting back to your life. Be brave and tell me about who did this."

"One person. A man," Martha whispered.

Sharon waited. "Can you tell me his name? How old he is? Was he a stranger to you?"

Martha didn't respond for a while. "A mother wants several things for her son," she finally said. "John's done dangerous things, working undercover, taking the public role of leading a police department. He doesn't tell me about death threats and attempts on his life and the stalker he once had fixated on him—a mother has ways of learning these things. He's a man of courage and conviction, and he handles whatever needs doing with fairness. For John, the job is personal. But now it's a different kind of personal. What I tell you, John will act on. He can't be my son and sit on his hands."

Sharon tried to grasp the layers of what Martha was trying to tell her, and thread the needle with her reply. "He's a civilian here, Martha. He can and will sit on his hands if I tell him to." Her slight smile as she made the promise didn't include that she'd possibly have to cuff those hands to keep John out of it. But the man would follow the law, and Sharon could trust him for that much.

"This is personal for me, Martha," Sharon said, "because I like you, I like your son. You mattered to me the moment your photo went up on my board. But I can keep the emotional distance required to be sure the outcome is the correct one. Was it someone from John's past? Is that what now worries you most, a vengeance reaction on the part of your son?"

Martha twisted a fold of the blanket around her fingers before she looked over. "Sharon, you want something from me I can't provide. One person. A young man. He knew me, knew John. He let me go because he was ashamed . . . he had interrupted my evening."

Sharon's eyes narrowed. "Ashamed he had interrupted . . ."

Martha simply held her gaze.

"I'm confused," Sharon responded, "which is what I think you want right now. True statements, as far as you've said, because a cop's mom won't lie to the cops, but you're hoping I don't resolve this."

"For my son's sake, no, I can't help you find answers. I won't hurt my son, Sharon."

"How will the truth hurt your son?"

"This wasn't from John's work, didn't happen because of something he's done or not done. But the answer will hurt my son, and as his mother I will not let that happen."

"You could give me info for a sketch, identify the man in a photo array?"

"I could, but in this circumstance, I won't."

"You're protecting who did this."

"I'm protecting my son," she said with a firm shake of her head, "and accepting that means not helping you further find who did this."

Sharon took a big step back mentally. This didn't make sense, and the need to keep Martha talking was critical. "Were you in a house, an apartment, a basement, a warehouse?"

"I *want* to help you, Sharon. It doesn't feel good pushing back against your questions, but I can't answer that."

Sharon searched for a way around the impasse. "Mrs. Graham, I promise, I will do everything in my power to protect your son as you want to do. But you know it's my job to solve it. Please, don't hold that against me."

"You should keep calling me Martha. My son likes you, Sharon—I can hear it in his voice when he mentions you, the respect he has for what you've done the last few days. All that tells me you're a good cop. I can understand when it's the job behind the questions."

"Would you answer this question so I know how much protection is needed to keep you safe? Are you worried about any person from John's past causing you trouble? Are you concerned about being in your home if this man knows you and your son?"

"There's not a soul I am afraid of right now, not even the man who did this. Sharon, tell John this has nothing to do with him—not in any way. I will be fine at home. I'm looking forward to getting back there."

"I don't understand, Martha," Sharon said, tilting her head, "and you're being deliberate about that, but I've worked on puzzles before."

"Now what?" Martha asked.

Sharon smiled and turned off any further cop questions, which was what Martha needed now. "Have you finished your Christmas shopping yet?"

"Mostly."

"I haven't even started. My sister is the main gift I need to find. She's a baker, a lover of lace and color and music. She's normally easy to buy for, but I have to see it, so my Christmas shopping means a lot of wandering around interesting stores. And I want to pick up some small things for the people who work with me. Have you found your gifts for your friends?"

"I'm always on the lookout for items they will enjoy. The pleasure of giving a gift never fades."

"How about Christmas shopping with me, Martha? I'd like the company. And your help."

"I'd enjoy that."

A tap on the door and John entered with a small suitcase and another bouquet of flowers. He set them down, moved over to kiss his mom. "What are my favorite ladies talking about now?"

"Martha's joining me for Christmas shopping," Sharon answered. "I see Mrs. Jome found you to deliver Martha's case."

"Heather and Annabelle are both downstairs, hoping you might feel up to visitors today, Mom."

"After I change, and for a few minutes. They'll chatter like magpies. I'll enjoy that."

John laughed. "I'll let them know."

Sharon caught his glance over his mother's head and simply shook her head, nodding toward the hall. She stood. "Martha, I'll leave you to your son and your friends, probably come back to see you this evening if you're up to it."

Martha nodded. John followed Sharon out into the hall.

"The one-minute summary," Sharon said swiftly. "I think she'll talk with me, but it's best if she doesn't feel like we're both asking her questions. So for now, you're the safe zone, I'm the incident. She's going to sleep a lot the next couple of days. When she's resting, you and I will talk."

"She gave you something?"

"Yes. A bit. She gave me what she's feeling, thinking. Seriously, John, divert her attention from this as much as you can. She needs ninety percent normal with you, and with me, ten percent what happened. It's going to move slowly because she needs it to, but I think we'll have all this behind us before the New Year."

"All right, Sharon. I trust you."

"I'll be back tonight. We'll talk," she promised.

She headed for the elevator. She would tell John tonight what his mother had said and maybe he'd be able to interpret it, because it did no good to put a wedge between them where he felt like she was withholding information.

Sharon pushed the down button. Martha felt sorry for the person who had done this. Sharon had seen that reaction when an infant was missing and the woman taking the baby was a grieving mother who had lost her own. But to have that kind of reaction toward a young man . . . maybe a homeless person. Martha was hiding the truth so as not to hurt her son—that felt real. It didn't make sense, but it was true from Martha's perspective. She spent most of her work time puzzling about all kinds of things. She'd figure this out.

■ ■ ■

At 10:00 p.m., the hospital guest lounge on the third floor was empty. Sharon settled there with John, passing back and forth a large order of spicy beef with rice, another of garlic chicken with asparagus. "One person. A young man. He knows Martha, knows you. She's adamant about it not being anything related to your work, nothing you did or didn't do."

"Implying it was something from hers?"

"John, she somehow feels a certain identification with this young man. Maybe we're looking for a homeless person. She dodged the question of where she had been held."

"She was neat, presentable," John commented. "That doesn't say 'homeless' to me. She wasn't outside."

"I admit I'm reaching here to sort through what she said. She's worried about the truth hurting you. She refused to tell me why it happened, what the young man wanted."

"How could the truth hurt me? Someone I know did this?"

"I think someone . . . saw your mother, and she meant something to him—either for who Martha is or what she represents. A young man to your mother could mean someone in his twenties or thirties now. Doesn't have to be homeless, simply . . . mentally lost? Does that description ring any bells?"

He thought a moment, then shook his head.

"Someone from your old neighborhood perhaps, before you

moved out west and your mom moved to the Village? A troubled young man. It would have been an impulse, to have seen her and made her come with him."

"Seriously, I'm drawing a total blank. I can give you irrational people associated with my work, but none of them would know my mother. The demarcation between my undercover life and my personal life was a solid barrier. When I was a cop in the Chicago ranks, some of my friends would meet my mother when I hosted a holiday gathering, but most of those were the people you've met in that video conversation. Mom wasn't part of my life as a cop."

"Then we need to think further outside the box. I think it's clear someone moved her car and returned it to the Village. So it's someone who could drive, who could blend in well enough not to be noticed. A young man who knew your mom, knew you. I'm going to keep coming back to that statement because it's the key. When we put his picture up on the board at the end of this, you're going to say, 'Of course, that fits.'"

John considered that, but shook his head. "There's no name or idea coming to mind. I'll be pondering that question for hours tonight. Did the canvass around the florist turn up anything?"

"Not what I had hoped. We showed your mother's photo, we pulled work orders checking for her name, and no one remembers assisting your mother Monday evening. If she paid with cash, bought something already made up, a clerk might not remember her. I've spoken with the patrol officers who work the area. There were no other crime reports from those blocks in the last week—something that might be random, a crime of opportunity. There's no homeless man or other transient who's in that area on a regular basis."

"So we've got the vague facts Mom is willing to say: one person, a young man, and her explanation she won't say more because she doesn't want to hurt me. The big mystery is the question of where she was for the two days."

"Yes."

John leaned his head back to stare at the ceiling. "Don't take this wrong, Sharon, but I'd like to go shake my mother right now and yell, 'Tell me! Please!'" He looked over and saw Sharon's smile.

"As if you have ever in your life raised your voice to your mother. Martha's trying to protect you, John. I don't know from what. But she's a mother protecting the son she loves."

"It's someone I know. It has to be."

"As good an interpretation as any. Someone not related to your work."

"Did you ever finish tracking down that question about Eric Holland?"

"An officer stopped by to do a follow-up, then paid a visit to the lady who sits with his mother. She confirmed Eric arrived home Monday around 5:30 p.m. The news was still on. He had multiple sacks of groceries and a cake. The officer talked to two of the three women who stopped by to see June for her birthday and confirms they were having cake and talking with June about people in the photos on the memory wall until around 6:45 p.m. when June began to nod off. Eric said the last time he saw your mother was at the grocery store. He could be lying, but I don't know why. Neighbors of Eric remember cars coming and going from his place Monday evening, but didn't mention a car that sounds like your mother's. It doesn't seem like your mom changed her mind and went by for a piece of cake."

"So cross Eric Holland off the list of people from my past."

"I'm not crossing anyone off the list until we get something that is evidence to work with. But he's probably low priority right now."

"I don't know Bobby Sail or his children," John mused. "I've looked at their DMV photos and their bios. We didn't cross at school or church years ago. So if this is someone who knows me, they go to the bottom of the list as well."

"It's really frustrating," Sharon agreed. "But we've made progress. We know another point on the timeline. We have a possible area where this might have happened around the florist shop. We know we're looking for a young man. It's someone who knows both your mom and you. So we create a long list of names and look at where they were Monday evening. And I still want to find a photo of your mother's car with someone else behind the wheel. I haven't given up on that."

"Okay." John passed over the Chinese carton he held. "I do think you've got this well in hand, Sharon, as much as it can be worked. Mom wants to go home tomorrow, so that's where I'm going to put my focus. I'm tired. But I will start making a list of names. I want answers. I want this thing over with."

"Ditto." She pushed to her feet, picked up the dinner cartons. "I'll be in touch tomorrow."

"Thanks."

"Don't mention it. Two days ago we would have been thrilled to be at this point, John. Remember that in the middle of the night."

■ ■ ■

John took his mother back to the Village shortly before noon on Friday, relieved to be escorting her out of the hospital with a clean bill of health. As he helped her out of the car, her friends lined the walkway, wanting to welcome her home. Martha was feeling steady and strong enough to pause and speak with most of those gathered, occasionally laughing, reassuring with a smile and a few words that she was fine and glad to be home. The few unthinking questions about where she had been simply got a friendly wave as Martha walked on.

It felt nice being mostly a background presence to the home-coming. John carried her one bag, offered his arm to help where the walkway was slick, held the door for her. She tired very quickly, but her color was coming back. She wasn't as frail in her movements today.

"I'd like you to rest for an hour now," he encouraged as they entered her apartment. He'd brought the flowers from the hospital over earlier, taken the time to do a quick cleanup of the apartment to remove fingerprint dust. He turned the door locks behind them. A security guard would keep reporters away from her door for a few days, and he had switched her phones to an answering service.

"I'm heading for a nap soon," she said, "but first I want to sit on the couch and enjoy being home. Put on some music, get us ice water to drink, and let's sit for a few minutes."

She had something on her mind. It was simple enough to do as she requested. He brought her the drink, sat on the couch beside her, relieved to have her here. "What's on your mind, Mom?"

"Sharon convinced you not to be asking me questions."

"Good cop, bad cop." He grinned. "I get to be the good one this time, not nagging you for answers."

She chuckled. "Then I like her even more than I do now. But we need to talk."

He took her hand. "I'd like to listen."

"I've told her what I can about what happened, and that will have to do for now. For your sake—for a few days—let this go. I'm home, unharmed. Let's enjoy Christmas."

"I need to know, Mom, if I'm ever going to have peace again."

"If I promise you this will not be a mystery forever, will you let it go for now?"

He leaned back with a long sigh. "I'm trying to decide if I need a bodyguard outside your door here, a chauffeur for when you go out, if I should move in here with you on a permanent basis. I need you to be safe, Mom. I lost you for two days. Please understand that. I need you to trust me and tell me about what you went through so I can help you. You know I love you. Nothing you could say is going to rock that. I need to know we have the person responsible for this before I'm ever going to breathe easy again."

She reached to rest her hand against his face. "I know that, John, absolutely know it. And I simply need you to trust me. I'm not being silent for sheer stubbornness—I love you too much to be that callous. But I've said all I can for now." Her hand lowered to her lap and she smiled at him. "You can have my second bedroom for the holidays if you like, and we'll talk about the rest. I'm not likely to go anywhere without you for now. I'm tired. I want my place, my music, my friends coming over for tea. I want Christmas on my terms."

He recognized an impasse when it stared him in the face. He leaned over and kissed her cheek. "What sounds good to you for lunch?"

"Your grilled cheese sandwiches, maybe some tomato soup, and ice cream if there is any left in the freezer."

He rose to move into the kitchen. "I'm going to enjoy taking care of you, Mom."

"You know we're going to drive each other crazy within a week."

He laughed as he started pulling items from the refrigerator. The last time he'd lived with his mom, he was seventeen. She was probably right.

■ ■ ■

John stepped into the commons building and saw Sharon sitting in one of the guest chairs across the lobby. He wasn't surprised to see her working, jotting down notes. "Thanks for coming."

She looked up from her notepad, closed the portfolio. "How's your mom?"

"Peacefully asleep. Annabelle is watching a movie in the living room so someone is there if she wakes. Let's talk in the library—it's normally empty this time of night."

It was a lovely room, full of books and places to sit. The fireplace was closed for the night, but the flames were slowly flickering above a still-glowing bed of coals. John settled on the first couch, feeling a deep sense of relief that the day was about over. "Sorry to drag you out on a weekend."

Sharon settled on the facing couch. "It's no problem, John."

He leaned over to hand her some stapled pages. "My list. Every name I can remember in my entire life here in Chicago. I even went back to grade school when mom was a homeroom teacher's aide."

Sharon's eyebrows lifted as she thumbed quickly through the sheets. "It's what, five hundred names?"

"Five hundred seventeen. I separated out those I don't particularly know but I could connect with my mom. That's the first fifty names. The next two hundred fifty are people I know for certain are acquainted with both of us. The rest are ones I know, but she doesn't. I tried to stay with 'young man' as the screen."

"I'll work your list in with mine."

"I'll email you the file, but I figured the list was a good excuse to see you." He smiled when she glanced up, and she smiled back. "So I hear you and Mom are going Christmas shopping Wednesday," he mentioned.

"I won't let her get too tired. Mostly browsing, with an excuse to sit and watch people. She wants a small gift for Bobby Sail, something to apologize for him having been caught in our spotlight."

"He came by to see her. Mom enjoys his company. He seems genuine, but I'm withholding judgment. He's not someone I would have selected for her. Not that she's asked my opinion."

"She might if it comes to be something serious."

John simply nodded. "I've missed you the last twenty-some hours. I had become accustomed to being in the circle of what's happening."

"It's been mostly conversations around the conference table, trying to figure out how to get traction on the guy who did this. You're welcome to sit in, but I assumed you would elect to be here with Martha for now."

"Here is where I need to be."

"Frankly I don't know how we find him, John. Thursday I thought we had enough to make a list and narrow it down. Now . . . it turns out Martha told me just enough to *sound* helpful, yet not enough to actually *be* helpful."

"Mom can identify who it is and pick his photo out of a picture array."

"Yes."

"Then don't beat your head against the wall," John said. "We'll figure out another way for her to safely tell us what happened. She's the real key—the rest of this, the lists of names, are just a scattered hope that we can find something and solve it ourselves."

"All right." Sharon set aside the list.

John studied the coals in the fire for a while. Then he glanced

back at Sharon to see her relaxed and watching him. He told
her the real reason he'd asked her to come by this evening. "I'm
thinking of resigning and moving back here."

"I wondered if you might take that step."

"Mom wants to stay here, and it's easy enough for me to find
work." He shrugged. "I have her for another five years, maybe
ten. There will be twenty years or more after that of the job,
plenty of time to climb the ladder again. I won't waste what is
most precious to me by thinking calls and visits are the same
as being here."

"You don't need to convince me, John. I hang out with my
sister, share a house with her, because it does matter, being
with family."

"Could I ask a favor?" he asked.

"Sure."

"Spend an evening with us, as my guest. Not work."

"A guy taking me home to meet his mother?" she asked lightly.

"Shades of that," he agreed with a smile.

"If you'll do me a favor in return."

"What's that?"

"You and your mom visit my place for dinner, meet my sister."

"We'd like that, Sharon."

"Good. I'll talk with Martha for dates. I'm always willing to
make room for a friend if you're moving back this way. I enjoy
your company, and I like your mother."

"No interest in more than that?"

"I have no idea. I'd say that's why we might have the coming
year to discover that answer."

"Thanks."

She shrugged. "I'm a cop. It's tough on relationships, you
know."

"Tell me about it."

"Seriously, I'd marry a cop, but Bryon is taken, so is Jack. A real opportunity hasn't come up. Dating civilians works fine up until I cancel plans and pull a marathon on a case for the third or fourth time. They don't believe me when I say the job isn't more important to me than they are, it just looks that way. Then the question becomes, 'Why don't you do something other than missing-persons cases?' and before long we've agreed to go our separate ways with no hard feelings."

"You're telling me something with that answer."

"What's important to me matters for a reason. I like working missing-persons cases."

"I can relate. I like being the boss."

She grinned. "Yeah. I can see how that might appeal. I bet the Chief of Police badge is a rather impressive thing to hold."

"It has its weight," John agreed.

"Will you miss it?"

"Enormously. Doesn't mean I won't be trading it in for something worth more."

"It's a big decision."

"I lost her. For two days. And it felt like I had lost my life. It was an eye-opening look at what really matters to me. It's family."

"You're lucky to have had that moment while there's still time to enjoy more years with her."

"I am." He studied the fire for a moment, then looked over at her, his expression reflective. "Sharon, I was dating a woman in Cheyenne for a couple of years, not that I told Mom it was that serious. It didn't work out mostly because I was a cop—the hours involved, the work itself. It reached the point I considered giving up the job so the relationship could have more room, and I found I couldn't take that step. I'm a cop. It's what I'm good at, where I can make a difference. We ended up parting on friendly terms, much as you have in your relationships. It was interesting to go through the experience. I'll make a shift about *where* I work for family reasons, but I'm better off in a relationship with a cop than a civilian, someone who understands the job." He gave her a quick smile. "I mention it only because it will save you asking me that question sooner or later."

"I probably would have asked, eventually. I'm sorry it didn't work out for you with her."

"Actually, I'm not, but thanks. We both have our histories, Sharon." He looked at the clock on the wall. "You're going to be very late getting home. I should have driven out your direction."

"It's not a problem. I don't live far."

"Come on. I'll walk you to your car." He held her coat for her. "Where are your gloves?"

"Umm, probably on my desk at the precinct," she said, sounding a bit sheepish.

"It was one of the first things I noticed about you at O'Hare— you weren't wearing any gloves and your hands were chilled." He walked with her to her car, stood back as she fastened her seat belt.

"I'll be in touch, John."

"Drive carefully, Sharon."

He watched her leave. She would be a good friend to have. If he was rebuilding his life here in Chicago, he'd put her at the top of the list of those he would like in his life. He understood her. And he thought she just might understand him too.

SEVEN

John followed the directions the desk sergeant had given him, went to the second floor, took a left after the elevators. The open room full of desks, the sound of people on the phones, of keyboards clicking, the occasional slam of a metal drawer, all sounded like a police precinct. He spotted Sharon easily enough—her build, the light-brown hair, the hands gesturing to pass on paperwork even as she was on the phone.

He glanced around the area, scanning whiteboards, desks, nodding to detectives he recognized. It had the comfortable feel of a good working group. He waited until Sharon finished the call before he crossed to join her. "So this is where you work."

She turned, and he was relieved to see the immediate smile. "John. Hi."

"Mom is having Tuesday Tea with her friends, so I decided to go out. There are too many females hoping to gossip about me for it to be wise to stick around."

Sharon laughed. "I can see that."

He loved her smile, the way it lit up her face. "Lieutenant, could I buy you a cup of coffee?"

"Sure." She rose, picked up her coat. "Guys, I'll be back."

John was pleased to see the gloves she pulled out of a pocket. "You've caught another case," he mentioned as they waited for the elevator. The whiteboards had several photos of a smiling teenage girl and long lists of names.

"There's always another case. We've already located this one. She's on her way to San Francisco at the moment, the plane ticket bought with money she earned waitressing after school."

"Who's at the other end?"

"A college boy, we think, and her aunt. Plainclothes cops will be there to answer that for us. She ran because home life here is not good. She needs to talk to us, but she's of the age that if she wants to stay in California, we're not going to force her to come back. Seventeen is a lot different from fifteen when it comes to how we handle cases like this."

"I'm glad you've got it in hand. Especially at this time of year. I didn't notice a lot of festive garland and tree ornaments tucked around your desks."

"Our group's Christmas spirit would be captured by the never-ending plate of cookies beside the coffeepot."

"That works."

He directed her north toward the coffee shop near a bookstore. They passed a Santa ringing a bell, standing next to a red kettle. Sharon slipped a folded bill inside the kettle. "Have you finished your Christmas shopping?" she asked.

"There are a few items to ship back to Cheyenne for friends there, but I'm mostly done. I made a couple of stops this morning. But if you could help me with something more for Mom, I'd appreciate it."

"I'd love that—I'll keep an eye out when she and I shop."

They ordered coffee and chose a table. Sharon settled across from him, took a first sip and nodded her pleasure.

He had tracked her down at work for a reason and decided it was best to dive right into the subject. "I've been looking at real estate listings for a house," he began, "something I like that also has a bedroom and bath on the main floor, so if Mom should wish to move from her apartment one day the house would work for her as well. I noticed a listing over on Cherry Lane that looks like a possibility."

"You're moving fast."

"I need to be here. And this way Mom won't have as long to feel guilty about my coming back because of her."

Sharon shook her head. "She'll be glad to have you here, John. But I'm guessing she'll always feel a bit of that guilt."

"Then I'll simply have to make sure she sees I'm happy here," John replied with a smile. "I've informed the Cheyenne city council I am resigning," he continued. "Due to the circumstances, they're making the transition easy so I won't need to return. My deputy chief is covering my job, and I think the city council is smart enough to keep him there. He's qualified, if a bit more cautious than I might be. Selling my house out there may take some of time, but it's not an immediate problem."

"What about the roots you had formed there, the friendships?"

"I'll be back in Cheyenne for a day or two after the New Year to say goodbye to friends, but I won't look back. I'll rebuild a life here because it's necessary." He nodded to the waitress coming around. "Would you like lunch to go with that coffee?"

"Thanks, but I need to get back. Bryon's promotion at the end of the year is going to leave a giant-size hole that's going to take about three people to cover. I'm moving people around today, doing some promotions internally."

"You like being a lieutenant."

"I like getting the work done. I like watching a team work together smoothly. Sometimes I even like being the one in charge."

He laughed. "Sharon, is it going to feel out of bounds if I look for work at Riverside?"

"I don't think the chief plans to retire anytime soon."

"I'm thinking deputy chief."

"Wow. Nothing like burying the lead item in your news."

"Would it bother you?"

She wrinkled her forehead for a long moment, then shook her head and smiled. "It might look like favoritism if they moved me while we were . . . well, dating," she said with an easy smile. "So I could stay with missing-persons for as long as we might be seeing each other. That would be an extra benefit."

He chuckled. "Not the reason I'd hope to have a woman agree to a date, but I can work with it." He held her coat for her to slip on. "One reason this transition isn't so hard to make is the fact I've met you, Sharon. There's something good here I'd like to pursue in the coming year."

She slid her arm through his for the walk back. "I can agree with that, John."

■ ■ ■

John liked the routine of fixing breakfast—the oatmeal his mother preferred, bacon and eggs for himself. He set glasses of orange juice on the table. "What time is Sharon coming over for Christmas shopping?"

"Around 9:00 a.m."

He glanced at the clock. "You'll need to wrap up this morning, Mom, the temperature is only thirty degrees. And if you happen to see women's gloves, buy a couple pairs for Sharon. She must lose or misplace multiple pairs. She's constantly out and about without them."

"I'll do that. You should buy her something more personal than gloves, though, John."

"I've already picked something out."

"Good."

He ignored the twinkle in his mother's eyes. He got up to get strawberry jelly for his toast and offered her half. "Mom, talk to Sharon some more today. A quiet conversation over tea after you go shopping. Please."

She reached over to cover his hand with hers. "I do love you so."

"I'm serious."

"So am I." The doorbell rang.

John pushed back from the table and went to meet Sharon. "Welcome to the chaos."

She glanced around the perfectly neat apartment, saw the breakfast items on the table. "Are you two getting on each other's nerves already?"

Martha just laughed as she got up. "My son is trying to shepherd my life like a good son does." She opened the closet and took out her coat.

John helped her into it, dropped a kiss on her forehead. "Be good, Mom."

She hugged him. "We're off, to spend money and enjoy the crowds. I leave the breakfast dishes to you."

"Mom's in a good mood," John said to Sharon. "Either that or we've been living a little too close together the last few days."

Sharon smiled. "I'll call before I bring her home, if you want to take off and do some errands of your own."

"I'll take you up on that. Have fun, ladies."

He watched the two walk to the elevator, already chatting about which stores to explore, and had to smile. This was the Mom he remembered. In the last few days her spirit had revived.

He had no doubt she would come back with bags of Christmas presents for him to carry upstairs. It meant a lot to him that Sharon was taking the time to make such a personal connection with his mom. He knew part of it was work, but most of it was personal. He liked seeing them together.

■ ■ ■

Sharon bought the last gift on her list and turned to watch Martha studying a display of costume bracelets, deep in serious consultation with a young girl maybe eight years old. The child made her choice, and Martha selected hers. They both arrived at the cashier's desk and consulted again about which gift box was the prettiest. The girl went with roses in all colors, while Martha chose an elegant black satin with a painted white bow.

The girl's mother was watching the two of them, enjoying the moment as much as they were. Sharon suspected the girl was buying a Christmas gift for her mother. Martha might not be a grandmother yet, but she had the heart to be a good one.

Sharon and Martha exchanged smiles as the mother and daughter departed. Words weren't needed to explain what made Christmas shopping special.

"I'm thinking about tea as our next stop. We can sit and enjoy a cup while I select an assortment for my next Tuesday Tea," Martha suggested.

"I'd love that," Sharon agreed.

The tea room was mostly empty. They found a table, and Sharon went to the counter to place their orders, browsed the lovely teapot selections until the waitress arrived with china cups. "They have such elegant style, a teapot. I can see why your gatherings are popular, Martha."

"It's a chance for ladies to sit and gossip is what it is, but there's a time in life where you don't mind that, just for the pleasure of hearing a friend's laughter and see a blush when another friend tells a good story about the man in her life. It's good to have friends."

"It is." Sharon sampled the tea and thought it refreshing. She'd never be likely to switch from coffee to tea, but an occasional change would be nice.

"My son has been silently nagging at me," Martha mentioned. "I can tell it in the care he's taking not to ask his questions."

Sharon put down her cup. This was going somewhere beyond a shopping trip.

"I will not hurt my son," Martha said once again. "If I tell John what happened, I will hurt him. Therefore, I'm not going to say anything more."

"Martha, you must realize your silence is hurting him," Sharon said carefully. "For a man who loves the law, has sworn to uphold it, it hurts him that you can't trust him with what happened. He is failing you, because he can't get you to trust him enough to talk about it. Further, he feels he's failed at being a good son."

Martha stared into her cup without responding, but Sharon could see her indecision, could see the pain she was feeling.

"I think despite what you've said," Sharon continued, "that John believes his past is why this happened to you. That someone from his days working undercover in Chicago located you, abducted you, and caused this."

His mother looked up from her tea. "I was with Eric and June for the two days."

"With . . . I don't understand." *Eric Holland, his mother, June . . . they had looked and it hadn't fit.*

"June had an affair with my husband. It's what shattered our friendship. It's why she moved to Florida." Martha twisted a sugar packet, tore it open. "I forgave my husband. And that wasn't easy. We had a separation of sorts while John was in college. A lot of marriage counseling." She sighed and sipped her tea. "June was very lonely after her divorce. Eric had left for college. My Harold had always liked her. He would handle small repair projects around the house for her, and they let it become something more.

"I didn't tell John at the time because he would have viewed his father differently had he known. I won't tell him now for the same reason. I won't destroy his good memory of his father."

Martha turned her cup round and round on its saucer. Sharon didn't interrupt the silence. She didn't know yet what to safely say. But her heart ached at the words Martha had said thus far.

"Eric didn't know about the affair until June spoke about it recently, in her dementia not realizing what she was saying. June had no peace, was living with the guilt of what she had done. Eric wanted me to let his mom apologize before she was no longer able to do so. And knowing the truth, he realized I wasn't likely to accept an invitation to see her. He politely asked again if I would come over when I saw him at the grocery store. I just as politely told him no, that I had plans for the evening, and I left to go purchase flowers for the tea. But something—" she paused, gave a deep sigh—"maybe the weight of years, the need to forgive, the fact it was her birthday, and likely her last . . . well, I changed my mind. I drove around for a while, gathering my courage, and then I went over to see June.

"Eric was relieved to see me, but it didn't go well. June was nodding off when I got there and woke disoriented, which rather set the stage for trouble. She got . . . very agitated. June was going on about Harold and where was he and she needed to see him, that I was keeping him from her, screaming really. I'm afraid I started shouting back—he was my husband, not hers, and I'm crying too, and poor Eric is standing there horrified, trying to calm us both down. And then rather abruptly June switched to the present, that God has cursed her with the dementia because of the affair. I'm not saying it, but I'm thinking, *good*." Martha stopped, put her hands to her face, and shook her head. She let out another sigh and collected herself, looked over briefly before turning her attention back to her tea.

"I thought it best to leave, and Eric's trying to convince me to wait, explaining he just needs another hour of my time, that June will have a coherent moment after the drama settles down, that his mom wants to apologize, needs to apologize, that she's not going to live much longer, and if I walk out she's going to lose any hope of dying at peace. But June's back to shouting about Harold and she needs to see him and . . . and I never loved him like she did."

Sharon reached across the table and took hold of Martha's shaking hands.

"I cannot tell you how angry I was," she said, tears pooling in her eyes as her voice shook. "I gathered my things and keys, but Eric begged me to stay, insisted I stay. That if we would just calm down and talk like rational people . . ." Martha's voice trailed off, and she looked over to Sharon. "I confess I wanted to strike him at that moment. June did. She hit him upside the head, yelling at him to get out of her way. The next thing I remember I awakened in the guest bedroom about midnight. He'd used some kind of spray medication to calm his mom down and accidentally got me too. I believed him when he said he hadn't intended to catch me with it. But what a mess."

Martha finished her tea. "Eric made it impossible for me to leave. He was apologetic, but firm. As long as I had come, he insisted I wait until June was able to do what she really needed—confess and ask forgiveness. I was with Eric and June for the two days. She eventually apologized for the affair. June and I made our peace. And when she passes away, Eric will do what's right and come forward, admit to what he did."

"Martha, do you realize—?"

The woman held up her hand and shook her head. "Let me say my piece, Sharon. Until his mother is gone, Eric will deny any part of what I've just said. He can't leave June and be charged, imprisoned. If you find my fingerprints in his house, I'll say I went to visit an old friend on her birthday. Let this rest until June is gone—it's only a matter of time now."

Martha's look turned distant. "During those two days I had to relive the most painful part of my personal history. I don't want to go through it for a third time with John. I don't want to deal with his questions and why I didn't tell him when it happened. I don't want to watch his respect for his father crumble. I had put what happened in the past. I will do the same with these two days. It's my choice not to speak of it, for the good of my son.

"Eric will do the right thing because he's a man of conscience. After June dies, he'll admit to what he did and plead guilty. But what is history regarding his mom is not going to be mentioned by either of us. I can understand his reasons for forcing me to stay. And I forgive him. He loves his mom, just like I love my son."

Sharon was still holding Martha's hand. Tears slipped down her cheeks, mirroring those of Martha. She reached for Kleenex from her purse for them both. "I know you love John."

"That is why I won't speak of it, Sharon. I won't hurt my son by revealing this truth about his father. Justice doesn't need these dark facts, only a guilty plea, and Eric will take that step. This will be closed without damaging more people. That's what I want."

Sharon understood more than Martha realized. A victim

reclaiming her life happened in many ways, and it was Martha's decision. "All right. With minor conditions, so that Eric doesn't disappear on us."

"This stays between us," Martha insisted.

"John won't hear about it from me," Sharon promised.

■ ■ ■

John said a quiet good night to his mother, as she had elected to watch a Bette Davis movie until she fell asleep. He turned off lights in the hall, detoured to the kitchen to refill coffee cups. He hadn't convinced Sharon to stay for a meal after the ladies' shopping was done, but he had talked her into coming back over for dessert. He returned to the living room, saw Sharon's face in repose as she rested her head back with her eyes closed, listening to the music.

"Everything all right?"

She sat up and took the mug he offered. "A long day, and things on my mind."

"Anything I can do?"

"No. It was an enjoyable morning, shopping with your mother."

Sharon diverting the subject . . . not a good sign. He settled on the couch beside her. "She's already wrapped the gifts she had me carry up for her."

"Mine are done too."

"Mine are still in sacks in the closet." His remark got a brief smile from her that faded again.

"Your mother told me a few things," she said slowly.

"Good. I'm glad."

"You're not surprised."

He shook his head. "I pushed pretty hard. I'm glad she could talk to you."

"She said you nagged at her with your silence."

He considered that comment and smiled. "I suppose I did."

She paused, then said, "What happened had nothing to do with your previous undercover work."

John studied her face with interest. "Then what?"

"Which would you rather have, the truth at the price of me breaking trust with your mom, or your mother continuing to talk with me?"

"It's that serious."

"Yes. I basically know what happened. Can't prove it, but know it."

"Would I be able to help you in the investigation if you told me?"

"Yes and no. It would go faster with you fully aware, but I don't know that's such a good thing right now. Martha needs this Christmas with you. Enjoy the holidays. Leave the rest of it to me. Trust me enough to do that."

"You're asking more than you realize."

"I'm very aware of how much I'm asking. She was abducted for two days. That fury you feel, that need for justice, is there because it has to be satisfied. Society can't survive without justice. You were born to be a cop. So was I."

He was hearing the tone under the words. "You don't like knowing what you do."

"Let's just say I'll enjoy putting the handcuffs on when the day arrives." She set her mug on the end table. "Give me some time. I'll either convince your mother to tell you more or be in a position to act on what she's told me."

John leaned over and kissed her cheek. "Thank you."

"It's not solved yet."

"It will be." He trusted her. "Want another slice of pie?"

"Maybe. If it's small."

"We could pretend this wasn't an evening with you basically on the job and me standing guard for my mom . . . maybe edge it toward a date? Watch a movie. Sigh at appropriate times. See if you happen to giggle at something funny."

She smiled. "We could, John, but I need to get home."

"Another time?"

"I would like that. But, sorry, I don't giggle."

"Ever?"

"Mostly ever."

"My fantasy is shattered." He set aside his coffee, got to his feet. "We'll do a movie another night."

He helped her slip on her coat, drew her into a hug, resting his chin against her hair. "It matters that you got Mom to trust you. More than I can put into words."

"My job."

"Hmm. And more than that." He drew back. "I'll walk you to your car."

■ ■ ■

"So are you going over to see his new house, Sharon?"

"I'm thinking on it, Martha," Sharon replied, pouring herself a mug of hot cider from the pan on the stove. She was their guest for the evening meal, and enjoying herself. "John's talking built-in bookshelves and storage units. I think I might appreciate it more after he has finished his remodeling plans. Since he gets to move out of your apartment when the work is done, he's got some incentive not to be idle once closing day arrives."

"I heard that," John called from the living room.

Sharon laughed. She hoped he enjoyed the Christmas gift she'd bought for his new backyard.

There was a knock on the door, and John went to answer it.

"I came to pay my respects to your mother—I mean, if it's okay with you. I heard she was back home safely."

"Come on in, Eric."

Martha tensed, and Sharon stiffened. The two women shared a look. Martha left the kitchen. Sharon set down her mug of cider before she followed.

"Eric." Martha's expression faltered. "I didn't realize you would be stopping by. How's June this Christmas?"

"Martha, it's okay to tell them now. My mother passed away two nights ago in her sleep. It was a peaceful passing, thanks to you."

John stared at him, then at his mother. Martha carefully wiped her hands on the kitchen towel she held.

"Tell us what, Mom?"

Eric answered, "Your mother was with me, with June, the two days she was gone."

Sharon saw the glance John gave his mother, and then he was moving. Sharon quickly stepped between them before a fist could get thrown, more for Martha's sake than Eric's.

"You knew."

"Yes," Sharon said quietly. "Let him finish."

Eric gave her a brief nod and warily watched John. "I wanted my mother to be at least at peace, if not happy, in her last days. I've spent years watching her slip away. I could tell the rift between your mother and mine mattered deeply. I arranged for Martha and June to have two lunches together, to have time to talk in private."

Sharon could feel the fury in John and understood it. She'd been battling her own anger since Martha told her what had happened.

Eric said, "I drove Martha to the library Wednesday. I waited and watched until the police came. I had asked Martha not to tell anyone until Mom passed away. It was obvious to me, to her doctors, that it was going to be soon. If I was arraigned and jailed before Mom passed, she'd be put in a nursing-home care facility, be frantic without me around, and I asked Martha not to do that to my mom. I'd confess to what I'd done once she passed away. Martha honored that request, and now I'm honoring mine. I'll plead guilty to whatever the DA wants to charge—aggravated kidnapping, whatever—and do the time."

Martha moved over to John and laid a hand on his other arm as if apologizing to him for her silence of the last weeks. Sharon could feel the tremor as John absorbed the gesture. John didn't take his eyes from his mom as he said one quiet word. "Sharon."

This was her jurisdiction. She did what he would most want to do himself. "Eric Holland, you're under arrest for the kidnapping of Martha Graham." She pulled handcuffs from her bag and cuffed him while she finished reading him his rights. Then she opened the door and led him out of the apartment, made a call to a patrol unit in the area.

"Will you tell me the rest of it, Mom?" she heard John ask.

"No. What he said was truthful and enough for me, enough for the justice that you and I need. Forgive him, John. I already have."

Sharon pulled the apartment door closed behind her. John and his mom deserved privacy for their conversation. "Eric, you and I are going to walk through a very detailed confession in the next hours, and you're going to sign it so they can have a decent Christmas."

The man simply nodded, and she directed him toward the stairs. She was sorry his mother had died, but right now there wasn't much sympathy in her, given what he had done.

■ ■ ■

John pulled out a chair at the table in the precinct annex interview room, next to the city jail, nodded his thanks to Bryon. Ten minutes later, Eric was led in. He looked diminished in the jail shirt and pants, the polished nature of the man already wearing off.

"I need details, Eric, every last one of them."

"My statement is written. Everything is there."

"I want to hear it from you."

Eric ran a weary hand across his face, then nodded. "It wasn't planned, John. It was my mother's birthday. I pressed Martha to come over for a few minutes when I saw her at the store, because Martha and June needed to talk. She said no, but then changed her mind and came over to see June. Mom got . . . very upset. Martha wanted to leave, and I needed her to stay. It wasn't planned. But once it went south, I didn't give your mom a choice."

"How?" John demanded.

"I didn't hurt her, John. I swear. There's a spray, approved in Europe, but not yet by the FDA. You breathe it in, it puts you to sleep. I paid to get a prescription of it from France for when my mother got really agitated and might hurt herself. It would put her to sleep and she'd wake up past the crisis. I had to use the spray on my mom that night, and I didn't realize Martha breathed in enough of it to also go to sleep. I put her in the guest bedroom till the effects wore off.

"I knew people would soon be looking for her, and I didn't think I could have her home that soon. Your mom's car couldn't sit in my driveway when the search began. So I drove your mom's car back to the Village and put her purse in her apartment. I left, walked to the corner store, and caught a taxi to a house two blocks from mine, then walked home. Both our mothers were still sleeping.

"John, you have to understand how it was," Eric pleaded. "While she was alive, I couldn't leave my mother alone. She would wake at odd times and wander. I had to lock doors with keys or she would have wandered out of the house, gotten lost at night. I use the cell phone I carry with me rather than have a house line. This wasn't planned, but the situation made it possible. I suppose your mother could have tried climbing out a window, but short of seriously hurting me, it wasn't going to be possible for her to easily get away.

"Your mother woke up about midnight. We talked for two hours, I fixed her something to eat, I explained what I needed, and I assured her I'd take her home afterward. Martha and June had lunch together on Tuesday and again on Wednesday. I used the spray again on Mother to make certain she would stay asleep while I delivered Martha to the library Wednesday evening.

"I've apologized to Martha for what I did and how I did it. I know what I did was wrong. I told her I would turn myself in, and I have. I won't disagree with what the DA charges as my crimes. I'll plead guilty."

"Why did you have to keep her the second day?" John asked.

Eric sighed. "Monday night had been a disaster, and the first lunch on Tuesday didn't go well. Tears on both sides, more raised voices. It would have made me sick to leave it like that, worse than it was before. I insisted Martha stay one more day, one more lunch, and I promised I'd then take her home. The second lunch . . . it was better than I had hoped, whatever they said to one another. It was more than just your mom humoring mine—there was genuine calm between the two women when the meal ended. I told Martha I would take her home as soon as it was dark, and she spent the last hours before I took her to the library taking a nap."

"Was this all worth it?"

"My mother died at peace."

"What you did . . ."

"I know, John."

"What was the rift about? What did your mother need to say to mine?"

"I can't answer that. Their conversations were private."

"You know. You didn't go to these elaborate lengths because they drifted apart over some disagreement."

"I can't say, John. It's not my place."

John wanted to slam his fist on the table. He needed to hear the answer to the last piece of this awful puzzle. "You'll tell me, Eric. Because at the core it's why you did this. You'll tell me, not my mother."

Eric told him.

■ ■ ■

"Are you okay?"

John stirred as Sharon joined him on the couch. "I will be." She'd stayed with Martha while he went to hear Eric out.

He'd been staring at the crystal ornaments on the tree, the faint sparkles they sent dancing around the walls and ceiling in reflections from the tree lights. "I didn't see this coming. Of everything I had imagined, it didn't look like this."

"A son's love for his mother. A mother's love for her son."

"Yeah. I see those parallels."

"Do you wish Martha had told you about your father?"

He didn't answer for a while. "No. Not knowing was easier than the truth."

Sharon rested her head against his shoulder. "Is this a date?"

He half smiled. "I didn't want to put it in words in case you took exception to it." He settled his arm around her.

"I think that allows me to make a personal observation."

"All right."

"Your mom loved your father, forgave him. Your mother loved you, protected you. She did those hard things because her love is strong and resilient. She's got backbone, that mom of yours. And good judgment. She did what she believed was right as this unfolded. You have to respect that." She lifted her head and looked at him. "Don't tell her you know."

"I won't. I love my mom. She needs my silence. She'll have it."

They sat quietly for a moment. Everything had been said on the subject.

"It's all tied up before Christmas," she finally offered. "That's a good outcome, John."

"It is."

Sharon rubbed his arm. "Come see me out. I've got a busy day tomorrow."

"You caught a case?"

"My California runaway is coming home for a visit. I'm meeting her at the airport in the morning."

"I could give you a lift if you like."

"Let me think about that."

He helped her with her coat. "I'll find my shoes and come down with you."

"I'm good for tonight. I'm still armed."

He'd step on her cop's pride if he insisted. He shook his head as he held out his gloves. She was without hers again.

She took them with a laugh and put them on. "A little big, but thanks." She paused at the door to hug him. "Be happy," she said.

He smiled and rested his head briefly on hers. "I'm finding that happiness right now, right here."

She pushed him half a step back, and he saw the blush. "Good night, John."

"Good night, Sharon."

He watched from the window as moments later she started her car and backed out. The year was coming to a close, a new one ahead. It was peaceful here in the shadow of the blinking lights on the tree, the festive decorations, and the reminder of the reason for the season. He felt like truly praying, for the first time since this had begun. "You walked with me, with Mom, through the valley of the shadow of death, and we both came out okay on the other side." He felt God's comfort, His understanding, when he finished.

Next year would bring a different job, a different home, an awareness of how much family meant to him, and a woman in his life he was looking forward to knowing better. God had fashioned something good out of a dark valley.

John took his mug into the kitchen and refilled it. He returned to sit on the couch and pick up his Bible. Another dark valley and a very hard three days had ended with a resurrection. He found the section in Luke and read the Christmas story for when it had begun. The night outside was quiet with a dusting of snow. His mother slept safely in the next room. *Thank you, Father.* He relaxed and let himself be the son he was, safe in the care of his heavenly Father.

SHADOWED

DANI PETTREY

Libby sliced through the frigid water, her limbs burning and weak . . . so weak after a dozen miles. Two to go.

One, two, three. Rolling her head to the side, she inhaled and then back into the deep, dark blue water, bubbles fizzing around her on the exhale.

Her wet suit clung to her like a second skin, but the forty-two-degree water seeped through, burrowing into her bones.

Just swim.

They can't catch you if you keep moving.

Her lungs burned—ice shards stabbing her chest, each breath torturous, but she had to keep going.

She was surrounded by swimmers, but had one of them been sent to kill her?

ONE

Libby's sunflower-patterned rain boots sloshed through the deepening puddles as she made her way down the pier to the *I>Waves*.

Who named their ship using a mathematical symbol, let alone calling it *I Greater Than Waves*?

She couldn't wait to meet *this* guy.

Rain pattered about her, her yellow raincoat hood shielding her hair and new Sony Walkman as Blondie's "Heart of Glass" played over the headphones. It was a rather extravagant gift, but one her parents sent after she won her last tournament.

Unfortunately the hood blocked her view, and the only time she appreciated tunnel vision was when she swam—just her and the sea, rhythmic strokes and breaths, singular focus. Today she wanted to see the world—well, the *wildlife*—around her.

Flipping back her hood, she let the cool Alaskan summer rain wash over her and slipped her Walkman and headphones into her jean coverall pocket, the melody still dancing through her mind.

She cast her gaze to the end of the pier and found it devoid of people. Just two moored boats. One a small eighteen-foot sailboat. The other craft—white with teak railings and a gorgeous cobalt blue stripe along its sides—was closer to thirty feet, and what she assumed would be her touring vessel for the afternoon.

She glanced at her waterproof Seiko. *3:00*. Where was everyone?

"You lost?" a man asked.

Following the direction of the deep timbre of his voice, she blinked up through the rain at a stunningly handsome man. Dark hair fell beneath his white baseball cap. The hat had *UNM Lobos* scrolled across it in red lettering—and a grey wolf. A smattering of auburn-tinged scruff covered his cheeks. He had to be at least an inch or two over six feet, with broad shoulders. A navy slicker draped open revealed a forest green thermal Henley hugging his defined torso. With crinkled lines at the edge of his eyes and wind-kissed skin he looked every bit the seafaring sailor.

"Are you lost?" He enunciated the phrase—probably a reaction to her ridiculous gaping stare.

She shielded her eyes to better meet his gaze, his eyes Confederate grey, with a tinge of blue. Or perhaps it was just the silvery sky reflecting in them.

She found her voice. "I'm here for the whale-watching tour."

He rested his booted foot on the rail, his hand clasping the top rung, towering over her from his perch on his ship. "If you haven't noticed, it's raining."

Yeah? "I doubt the whales mind the rain."

Bemusement flitted across his lips. "No, but people do. You're the only show."

"Oh." She slid her hands in her pockets, the rain slicker material cool against her already chilled skin. So this was Alaska's idea of summer. "Then I guess it'll just be you and me."

He arched a dark brow barely visible beneath the brim of his cap. "You still want to go?"

She shrugged. "Why not?" Her coach had given her the afternoon off, and she was taking advantage of it.

His wide eyes lit with curiosity. He lifted his chin as rain drizzled off the brim of his cap. "What's your name?"

"Libby. Jennings."

"Well, Miss Jennings, everyone else has rescheduled for tomorrow. Same place. Same time." He dropped his foot to the deck and turned to go.

"Good for them," she called.

He paused, shaking his head, and turned back around. "You wouldn't rather go when it's *not* raining?"

"I'm here. Might as well go." She tilted her head, fixing a smile on her face. "Don't tell me a big strapping Alaskan fisherman is afraid of a little rain?"

Okay, it was a pathetic route to take, but was the guy serious? She wasn't wasting her afternoon off just because of some rain.

"Hey, I'm good if you're good," he said.

"Great."

He reached out a hand to help her aboard, but she did it on her own. Just as she did everything.

"I'm Ben McKenna," he said. "Welcome aboard the *Waves*."

"Thanks." Maybe she'd ask him about the story behind the name later. It had pricked her curiosity.

"By the way . . ." he said, glancing over his shoulder at her as he started the engine. "No need for the mocking flattery, but I appreciate the strapping part." He chuckled.

She bit her lip. Yeah, it had been beneath her, but she liked that he'd called her on it. She moved to the bow as Ben piloted them out of the marina. Her gaze should have been fixed on the gorgeous mountains surrounding Yancey or on the expansive Gulf of Alaska before them, but instead she was drawn to the man at the helm.

There was something intriguing there. But as always, she was in town for the competition and the competition only. It wasn't worth the effort to try to get to know him. In less than a week she'd be gone and Ben McKenna would be a forgotten memory.

Forcing herself to fully turn around, she faced the gulf and the boat entering the marina as they exited.

A man dressed in a red shirt and rainbow suspenders. The silly accessory that had been all the rage back in Cali five years ago had apparently finally made its way up to Alaska. The only other person she ever saw still wearing them was Robin Williams on *Mork and Mindy*. Perhaps that's where he'd gotten the idea, missing the intended comedic value of it.

The man smiled—or rather *leered*—at her across the white-capped gap and then turned to Ben. "Private tour, ay, McKenna?"

She rolled her eyes as the spray of the sea mixed with the rain splattering her face. Like she hadn't heard that one before.

"Looks like you had a disappointing day, Karl," Ben called. "What'd you catch—a pity handful? Seems even the fish know to avoid you."

Karl coughed up a guffaw. "Funny, McKenna. Real funny." He winked at Libby before he turned back to his wheel. "We'll see who gets the bigger catch."

Ben waved him off and opened the throttles.

She set her JanSport backpack—way more comfortable and sensible than carrying around a purse—on the ground and wrapped her arms tighter around her as the wind billowed over the bow.

Rain lashed even harder as Ben idled the boat nearly an hour later, an island on their port side, nothing but the sea and wind on the starboard.

Chilled to the bone didn't begin to describe how she felt. Water was one thing. The bite of the Alaskan air, even in July, quite another. Everyone in town said they'd been having record lows—figured on her first trip so far north—but this tropical island girl was hurting.

"Here." Ben handed her a steaming mug of coffee. "It'll help."

She took it, cupping her hands around the blue metal mug. "Thanks." Maybe it'd help to settle her jittering jaw.

Growing up in the Caribbean, she was most definitely warm-blooded. Even Santa Barbara, where she was currently based, got cooler than she preferred, but cold-water competitions were for the elite of her sport, and she liked being at the top of it—even if it meant freezing now and again.

Ben hopped up to sit or rather impressively balance atop the starboard rail. "Sorry about Karl back there. He's Yancey's resident jerk. Keep your distance and you'll be fine."

"Thanks, but I know how to take care of myself." Guys like Karl hardly fazed her.

"Got it." Ben nodded.

She took a sip of the coffee, and the first sensation of warmth in nearly an hour sparked inside. She glanced over at Ben. He most certainly was handsome, but she'd lose the scruff. Seemed nice enough, but why was he still sitting there? She wasn't interested in anything beyond the tour. Wasn't interested in men period since the train wrecks of two attempted relationships and her coach's insistence on singular focus during the tournament season.

"There," he said, pointing over the starboard side, excitement tinging his baritone voice.

She looked, saw nothing and frowned.

"Wait for it," he said. "Any minute . . . now . . . ." An enormous humpback whale surged out of the water twenty feet off their starboard side. It flipped, twisting on its side in the air before crashing back into the gulf with a gigantic plume of water jetting up, the spray dousing them.

"Oh . . . my . . . goodness." She jumped up and down, unable to contain her enthusiasm as coffee sprayed across the deck, though fortunately not burning either of them. "That was incredible. How did you know? Where to look, I mean?"

"I caught sight of the tail. Figured she'd be popping up soon enough."

"Will it come again?"

"We can wait and see."

"Do we have time?" It'd been advertised as a two-hour whale-watching tour. They were more than halfway through and still had the return trip to make.

He shrugged his broad shoulders. "I'm not in any hurry. Are you?"

She shook her head, watching as another whale surfaced and then a third. The trio surging out of the water, gliding toward the sky and then flopping back in with gigantic splashes, waves of seawater gushing across the ship's bow.

"There," Ben said, shifting and pointing to the port side.

She followed his gaze and spotted the shafts of water spurting into the air—five, ten, close to a dozen.

"Orca feeding pod," he said.

One surfaced, its dorsal fin dipping back under. Another surfacing, bouncing something across the bridge of its black nose.

"What's it got?"

"Maybe a seal, but they don't usually play with their food or bring it to the surface."

138

Ben moved back to the helm, slowly inching the boat closer to take a better look.

Whatever it was, they weren't so much interested in eating it as nudging it to the surface.

"Shoot," Ben said, rushing to the stern of the ship.

She followed as he grabbed a silver pole with a hook on the end. He climbed into the red kayak fastened at the stern and used the pulley ropes to lower himself down into the gulf.

Libby grasped the wet railing, peering down at him. "What are you doing?"

"It's a body."

Shock radiated through her. "What?" She looked back to the whales.

"Surf must have washed it into the lagoon," he hollered, paddling toward the pod.

She grabbed the binoculars, wiping the lashing rain off the front in a futile attempt to dry them long enough to see what he saw. To her horror, Ben was right. A long clump of hair clung to the person's back. Libby squinted. Was that a swimmer's cap?

"Get on the radio," Ben hollered. "Channel sixteen. Tell the coast guard we're on the south side of Tingit Island and we've got a floater in the lagoon. Coordinates are on the display panel."

■ ■ ■

Ben approached the orca pod, knowing he could be flipped any instant, praying they didn't view him as a threat.

The lagoon was teaming with shoals of herring this time of year and most of the pod was feeding on them below the surface.

If he could just maneuver close enough, he could grab hold with the hook next time they nudged the body off one of their noses.

They spotted him, several circling the kayak. He'd spent

enough time in these waters that the kayak shouldn't be an unfamiliar sight to them.

With great patience he waited until the opportune moment presented itself, and then he scooped, tugging the body to him—a woman—still intact for the most part.

Laying her across his lap, he eased back and paddled for the boat.

Libby greeted him at the stern, concern etched across her furrowed brow.

"You reach the coast guard?" he asked.

"Yeah, but they want to talk to you."

That was never a good sign.

"Okay, help me lift her up."

Libby's eyes widened, but she did as he instructed, grabbing hold of the woman's torso and pulling as he hefted her onto the ship.

Libby lost her balance on the slippery surface, tumbling back, the body's dead weight collapsing on top of her.

A surprised yelp escaped her lips, but not the horrified shriek he'd expect from most in the situation. "Hang on."

Securing the kayak, he scrambled up to assist, rolling the body off of her.

He helped Libby to a seated position, and her eyes widened in horror at the sight of the woman's partially nibbled face.

"Kat?" her voice squeaked.

Shock rooted him in place. "You *know* her?"

Libby nodded grimly.

■ ■ ■

Libby stared at the woman she'd known, and not known, for the past dozen years, remembering the first time they met and the last—just this morning.

Ben returned from talking with the coast guard, his jaw and expression tight.

"What's wrong?" In addition to Kat being dead, of course.

"An underwater earthquake was detected ninety miles south of here."

"Okay."

"Last time that happened the nearest island was struck by a hundred-foot tsunami within the hour, followed by massive storm surges."

"So we should get going?"

"We don't have time to make it safely back to Yancey."

"What are you suggesting?" Certainly not riding out a hundred-foot wave in his fishing vessel.

"We need to get to high ground."

"What?"

"Tingit." He nodded toward the island. "We need to anchor and get to the highest ground possible."

"And Kat?"

"We'll secure her below deck."

"A hundred-foot wave could crush your boat. We can't just leave her there."

"We can't carry the extra weight. We have to bring supplies and move fast."

"What kind of supplies?"

"Whatever we can carry to make it through the night."

"I don't understand. Can't someone help us with shelter?"

"Tingit is uninhabited except for wildlife."

"Then what was Kat doing way out here?"

He answered as he started making preparations. "I have no idea. Maybe she was on a boat and fell overboard, but the coast guard hasn't received any distress calls."

"She's in her wet suit and cap so I'd say she was training, but no swimmer goes this far out without a support vessel."

"Swimmer? You're here for the tournament?"

She nodded. "And so was Kat. She's one of my fellow competitors. My toughest one."

"Coast guard and Yancey police will have to sort out what happened to her later. Right now we need to brace for the tsunami."

Libby helped Ben carry Kat's body below deck, a hundred thoughts and one massive regret sifting through her uneasy mind.

Ben laid Kat on the floor of the storage compartment and covered her with a tarp.

"Wait," Libby said, reaching for Kat's cap and watch. "Just in case the wave hits your boat, just in case the worst happens, her family back in Russia might want these." Her goggles no doubt had been lost at sea.

Ben nodded as she stuffed both in her backpack.

"Do you have room for some more supplies in there?" he asked.

"Yeah." She opened it, and he shoved a few items inside, testing the weight before handing it back to her.

"Is not too heavy is it?" he asked.

She was a champion open-water swimmer. She trained hard. Pushed herself. Doug, her coach, pushed even harder. She could take the weight. "It's fine." She fastened it in place and waited while he filled a huge pack of his own, placing it over his broad shoulders.

He checked his watch. "We've got to move."

Rain poured down as they trudged up the slope of the island's southern face.

Birds screeched, flocking high in the sky, away from the island. That was not a good sign.

She looked down at the sea churning violently, the waves growing in height, hitting higher and higher against the island's rocky shore, battering his ship like a toy boat in a bathtub.

"Don't look back," Ben said. "Just keep moving."

She increased her pace, focusing on the task at hand. Shutting all else out. She lived that mentality every day in the water. She could do it here.

But Kat . . . ? Her lifeless face kept flashing before Libby's eyes, and a plague of questions assaulted her.

They reached the highest point of the island in under an hour; the echoing holler of waves slamming the tiny island shook her repeatedly. There were no caves, only copses of tall, slender trees scattered across the otherwise sparse tundra.

"We'll set up camp here," he said, standing inside an alcove as the treetops swayed in the burgeoning winds.

It didn't take long with them working together before they were hunkered in the two-person dome tent, only partially protected by the slender trunks surrounding them.

"It's smart," she said, "keeping camping gear on your ship."

"Ship's my home," he said, lighting the small battery lantern. "For now. I keep everything on it."

She thought about the tiny galley kitchen and miniscule bathroom they'd passed on their way down to the lower deck. She wondered if he lived there by choice or necessity. Though her loft wasn't much bigger. Then again, with the swim-tournament schedule, she was rarely home other than winter. Even then she most often flew to Nevis to spend a prolonged holiday with her folks.

She wondered how Kat's folks would take the news. Having never met them, it was hard to say. She retrieved Kat's cap and watch from her pack as driving rain pelted the nylon material, the wind surges testing Ben's skill at grounding the tent.

The soft lantern glow was soothing amidst the unknown surrounding her, surrounding *them*. Who was this man she was stranded with?

He draped his arm across his bent knee, lifting his chin at Kat's belongings. "How well did you know her?"

She ran her fingers across the watch face.

"That's the crucial question."

TWO

Ben studied the resilient woman sitting beside him. Despite the roaring waves and winds battering the island and their tent, she hadn't complained or freaked out once. Her strength was impressive and refreshing.

Swimming the fourteen-mile stretch between Yancey and its nearest barrier island for the Yancey Open Water Invitational was no small feat. It was a competition he'd never undertake. He was a strong swimmer, growing up in and surrounded by Alaskan water, but his heart lived either standing in it fly fishing, as he'd learned alongside his dad, or gliding over its surface in the *Waves*, which, again, he'd inherited from his dad. He came from a long line of Alaskan fishermen on his dad's side and a long line of teachers on his mom's. His dad had instilled a love of water, his mom a love of learning.

He missed his dad, though he doubted as much as his mom must after thirty-five years of marriage. If ever there was a couple in love . . .

He raked a hand through his tousled hair. It was hard to believe it'd been four years since Dad headed Home.

So much had happened—both good and bad. So much he could have used his dad's advice about.

Libby shifted beside him, drawing his attention. She, on the other hand, clearly lived *in* the water, an endurance athlete to the extreme. He'd caught a practice session the other day as he'd piloted out of the marina. He was highly impressed at the determination, persistence and sheer will required of all the participants.

It made him wonder what had happened to Libby's friend and why she had been all the way out by Tingit.

He was pretty sure about her cause of death, but there was no sense startling Libby. He'd leave that determination up to the coroner, Doc Graham, when they returned to Yancey.

"That's strange," Libby said.

"What's that?"

"The back of Kat's watch is gone, all the mechanics too." She held up the empty cavity for him to examine.

"Probably knocked against a rock or fell apart in the surf."

"Yeah. Would have been nice to have it intact to send to her folks."

"That is unfortunate." He shifted to study her better in the soft lantern light as it danced along her long blond hair, leaving elongated shadows on the tent's domed walls. "You said earlier that your friend wouldn't have swam this far out without a support vessel?"

"I mean, we often do our daily swims alone." She set the watch aside. "It's important to swim without someone pushing you. We need to learn to push ourselves."

He doubted she had any problem in that area.

"Had Kat learned to push herself?"

"Abundantly. She was the ultimate competitor. Russia's open-water sweetheart. Practically a national hero."

"So why was it surprising she was on her own, if you all do solo swims?"

"We must be at least twenty miles from Yancey. The max an open-water swimmer will traverse on their own is five miles, maybe six."

"Let me guess? You've mastered that?"

She nodded.

She *was* one strong woman, but something was clouding her thoughts. Something beyond the death of a fellow competitor. There was something much more personal there. He didn't know her well enough to ask—and he, of all people, respected privacy—but she'd piqued his curiosity, and that wasn't something easily done.

He exhaled. "I'd say the currents could have carried her out here, but they're flowing east. If anything she would have been carried back toward Yancey if that's where she'd started from."

"I saw her leaving practice as I arrived. I think she got an early practice in."

"Did she mention an upcoming solo swim after practice?"

"We didn't exactly chitchat."

He arched a brow. "But I thought you knew her?" Her reaction to the woman's death had been one of friendship or at least familiarity rather than just one competitor to another.

She clutched the woman's cap in her hand. "We used to be friends."

He was about to respond when she cocked her head, clutching the material tighter.

"What?" he asked at her perplexed expression.

She shifted the cap, moving it around, running her fingers over the rubber surface. "There's something in here—something sewn inside. Can I see your knife?"

He pulled it out and handed it to her.

She carefully cut the length of material and pulled out a slip of paper. It was mostly dry, having been sealed in, and the small amount of dampness that had permeated hadn't smeared the writing, which was surprising. She smoothed the fortune cookie–sized slip out and read the passage scribbled across, "*Out of your vulnerability will come your strength.*"

"Freud," Ben said.

Libby arched a brow. "Impressive."

He shifted as the tent shook, praying he'd staked it deeply enough. "You mean for a strapping Alaskan fisherman?" That was the phrase she'd used, or at least the sentiment.

"No." She bit back a smile. "For a man in general."

"Of course. Let me guess, you're one of those feminists." He should have seen that coming. It was 1979, after all. A woman had just become Britain's prime minister. If ever there was a time of women's empowerment propelling forward, it was now.

"No. Just . . . *enlightened.*"

He kicked his boots closer to the front of the tent, stretching out his socked feet. This could end up being a *long* night. "I suppose that's one way to view Freud." Most did.

"And your view?"

He crossed his legs, bracing his weight on his elbow. "There's one source of truth in this world, and Freud isn't it."

"Ah. Let me guess now. You're a . . . *tree hugger?*"

He laughed. "I respect creation, but, no, I'm talking about the Creator."

Her beautiful green eyes narrowed. "Creator?"

"God."

She sat cross-legged, facing him. "There are a lot of different views on God."

"Perhaps," he said, before she could continue with some philosophical debate, "but there is only one God."

"I see, and who's that?"

"The God of the Bible."

"And Jesus?" she asked.

"My savior."

"So," she said, clearly appraising him, "you're born again?"

"Yes."

"Hmm." She set the cap aside. "I wouldn't have pegged that."

He chuckled. "So you have me pegged? That doesn't sound very enlightened."

"Please. You think you have me pegged too. I can see it in your eyes."

"Is that so?"

"Yes." She squared her shoulders. "So, let's hear it. Who do you think I am?"

"Okay." If she wanted to play . . . "You went to Brown or. . . . No . . ." He snapped. "I got it, Berkeley. Philosophy major, perhaps?"

"Yes on Berkeley."

He knew it.

"No on philosophy."

"Women's studies, then? I hear it's all the rage at select colleges."

"Double major, actually. Comparative Literature and Math."

He had not seen that coming. "That's quite the combination."

She shrugged. "I have diverse interests."

And yet she swam competitively. *Intriguing.* He wondered how she got on that path. He wondered about a lot of things about her. She'd burrowed into his mind, his thoughts, even his senses. It was difficult to ignore how good she smelled in such small quarters. Tropical and intoxicating, despite the hike and the rain. Her shampoo, perhaps.

"My turn," she said, her face scrunched as if deep in thought. He found the twinkle in her eye adorable. "College was a waste of your time," she began. "Real men already know all they need to know. Am I right?"

"Not even close. Atomic Physics from Princeton." He wasn't trying to brag, but she'd asked.

She tried to remain still, but he could see he'd rocked her back on that one. "Then why are you—?"

"Running an excursion business?"

"Yes."

He'd been asked that a hundred times. "Because it's what I love to do."

"But don't you—?"

"Think I'm wasting my life, talents, and degree?" Yep. He'd heard it all. But this was home. This was where he belonged. He'd learned the hard way, but at least he'd learned. Some folks spent their entire life searching, restless, but he was at peace. Well, as much at peace as possible while knowing what might be out there waiting to return to haunt him and the country he loved.

"Well, yes."

"Are you a mathematician or literature teacher?"

"No. I'm a professional athlete."

"But your degrees . . ."

"That's—"

"Different?" He smirked. "How? I assume you compete because you love it, or is it because you have something to prove?"

"Prove to who?"

"You tell me."

She shook her head, a faint flush creeping over her cheeks. Pulling what looked to be a journal and a pen from her backpack, she said, "I'm not trying to prove anything."

He'd seen that look, the hunger dancing in her eyes. The need to please, to prove. "Keep telling yourself that."

"You don't know me at all."

He stretched his hands behind his head. "I bet I know you better than you think."

She shifted away from him on an exhale, opened to a fresh page in her notebook, and began scribbling—no doubt venting about him.

Thunder cracked, vibrating in his chest, tremoring the earth beneath them.

THREE

Libby spent the night stewing, pouring her thoughts, questions, and frustrations onto her journal pages. She was thankful to find the sun shining when she awoke from the short stretch she'd managed to actually sleep. Ben was gone, probably seeing to his boat, so she took time to pull her hair back in a bun and her *The Way* Bible from her pack—turning to Habakkuk 2. Anxious to hear God's answer to the questioning prophet. She was full of questions herself. The Bible had been given to her by her RA her senior year on campus, a Christian revival of sorts sweeping the nation with its distribution.

"Morning," Ben said, stepping inside the tent, a thermos and two blue metal cups in hand.

"Coffee?" she asked, the aroma a welcome scent.

He kicked off his boots by the entrance. "I checked out the *Waves* as soon as the surge settled. The damage isn't too bad. She's a sturdy ship. Made a thermos of coffee." He lifted a mug. "Would you like some?"

She *could* use something. His comment about needing to prove herself still stung, but why? He didn't know her. Didn't know what drove her. Or at least she'd kept telling herself that all night long.

"Coffee?" he asked again.

"Fine," she grunted, wondering why was she letting him or his comment get to her. She barely knew the man.

"So"—he filled her cup—"you're a peach in the morning."

Something about him rubbed her wrong. He had far too much insight into her for a man she'd just met, and it irked her. "You know, for a man running a tourism business you really should learn better people skills."

"I think you have it the other way around." He poured himself a cup.

"Excuse me?" He was right. She *was* being rude, but he wasn't exactly putting on the charm. Who talked like that? Said things exactly as he saw them? Heat flushed her cheeks. *She* did.

"What I mean is *people* need to learn better *people* skills. Too many folks have forgotten basic courtesies such as please and *thank you*." He nodded toward the cup of coffee he'd just poured her.

Remove foot from mouth. She'd just been schooled. "You're right. Thank you for the coffee, but are you always so vexatious first thing in the morning?"

"See. Right there," he said with a smirk, clearly finding the interchange amusing. "People skills. Why use a big fancy word to insult me instead of just saying annoying. Is that so difficult?"

"Fine. You're annoying," she blurted, realizing she was being equally so, but unwilling to admit it. She always was a bear before her coffee.

He nudged his chin at her Bible still open on her lap. "That's something I didn't expect to see, Miss *Enlightened*. Why'd you grill me so hard if you're a believer?" He cocked his head. "*Are* you a believer?"

She smiled and nodded. "One. I grilled you because I wanted to see how serious you were about your faith. A lot of guys say they're Christians . . ."

"But they don't live like it?"

"Yeah."

"And two?"

"I was giving you a hard time because . . ."

"I was being a jerk," he said to her surprise.

A smile tugged the corner of her mouth. He certainly was honest. "I wouldn't exactly say jerk, but you definitely riled me up."

He grinned as he hunkered down on the sleeping bag beside her. "I tend to have that effect."

She reached over and slapped his cheek.

"What the heck?" He cupped his face.

"I see you're exuding your usual McKenna charm," a woman dressed in orange coveralls said from the tent's entrance.

Libby looked to Ben. "You had a big black bug on your cheek."

He rubbed his skin. "You could have just told me."

"Sorry." She gave an awkward smile. "Instinct kicked in."

"Uh-huh."

"I'm serious." She was.

"Should we come back later?" the woman at the tent door asked.

"Sorry, Nat." He climbed out of the tent, and Libby followed to find a man standing beside the woman.

"Libby, this is Nat and Greg with the coast guard."

They took a moment to exchange pleasantries, and then Nat said, "Gus insisted you should have been back by now, demanded we come check on you."

Libby frowned. "Gus?"

"He's a friend who worries way too much," Ben said.

"Also Yancey's mayor and a royal pain in the tush," Nat added.

Libby narrowed her eyes. "You aren't here for Kat's body?" That's why they'd called the coast guard in the first place.

"Ben could have brought her in," Greg said. "Does it several times a year."

"What?" Why did a fisherman bring in dead bodies?

"You didn't tell her?" Greg asked.

Ben shrugged. "Didn't see the point."

What was going on?

"What happened?" Greg asked.

"Doc Graham will have to take a look." Ben shoved his hands into his cargo pants pockets, clearly trying to keep his voice low, but she heard him all the same. He hesitated, looking at Libby, then back at Greg. "But I think her neck was snapped."

"What?" Libby sputtered. Why would he even think . . . ?

"Doc can take a look, but we both know you've got more experience than a transplant straight out of med school," Greg said.

"You okay taking the body in despite having a client on board?" Nat asked. "We've got a disabled trawler not far from here."

Ben rubbed the back of his neck and looked briefly toward Libby. "All right."

Libby shook her head. "Why would you have a charter guy transport a body? You're the coast guard." And why would he have more medical experience than a doctor?

"Ben's head of Yancey Search and Rescue," Greg said.

"And EMT certified," Nat added.

The man was one jolting surprise after another.

"So why do you think someone"—she swallowed the brutal word as they climbed back on his ship, Nat and Greg's vessel already fading in the distance—"*snapped* Kat's neck? And why didn't you say anything earlier?"

"I didn't want to alarm you."

"Well, I'm *alarmed* now. You really think someone snapped her neck?"

"I do."

She ran a trembling hand through her hair. "What if . . . ?" she murmured more to herself than to him.

"What if, what?" he asked.

Everything started spinning.

"Whoa! You don't look so good." He placed a steadying hand on her shoulder. "Why don't you sit down." He directed her to the bench. "I could be wrong. Doc Graham—Emmanuel—will make the final ruling. It's possible—"

"It's not that. It's just . . ."

"Just?"

"I was thinking of something Kat told me a long time ago." What if she'd been telling the truth? What if . . . ?

Ben sank down next to her. "Tell me what's going on."

She might as well. She had no one else to talk to, and he certainly wouldn't hold back on what *he* thought. "Kat and I attended Berkeley together for a while. She was a Russian exchange student. We were roommates because we both swam. It was weird, because we were competitors. I tried becoming her friend, but she really kept to herself. Almost spookily so." Libby rubbed the back of her neck. "I always had the feeling something was off with Kat, and one day not long into our sophomore year I caught her rifling through our physics professor's files."

"Really? What happened?"

"I confronted her."

"And?"

"She made up some lame excuse, but while we were talking Professor's Wagner's secretary came in and questioned what was going on, so I told her the truth."

"And?"

"Kat said I had no idea what I'd done. She claimed Professor Wagner was a communist spy, and she was trying to get proof so she could defect."

"But she was already in the country. If she was telling the truth and wanted to defect, why not just stay?" he asked.

"You don't understand. Kat was their star athlete. If she defected it'd be a huge embarrassment to her motherland. Besides she claimed she was always being watched. Before the school board could even attempt to take action against her, she was gone. Two men came and took her and all her stuff."

"And she never came back?"

"Not to school. I continued to see her each competition season, but she'd never speak to me. Wouldn't even look at me."

"So you don't believe she was trying to defect?"

"I didn't. I thought she was trying to cheat on our upcoming exam. She had to maintain a really high GPA to remain in the exchange program, and she was struggling."

"So she was probably lying. Just trying to cover her tracks."

"That's what I thought, but right before I graduated rumors spread that Professor Wagner was in fact a communist sympathizer and a possible spy. Apparently the government was investigating him."

"You think he really was? Or were they just running with what Kat had told you?"

"I never told anyone what Kat said to me. Wagner was let go, and I never heard anything more about him."

"So you think maybe Kat *was* telling the truth?"

She swallowed. She'd wrestled with that thought ever since Wagner's removal from Berkeley. What if she'd sent Kat back to the country she'd been trying to defect from? "I thought she'd made up a crazy story to cover her cheating, but what if she was telling the truth? What if that past just caught up with her?"

FOUR

He sank into a booth at the only diner in town, Gus's, and perused the menu. *American* food. How did they eat like this and dare compete against *them*?

The sheriff strode in and moved to join the mayor at the table behind him.

"Gus," the sheriff greeted the man.

"Jim." The mayor set his coffee cup aside. "Is he back yet?"

"No?"

"He should have been back by now. That's why I called the coast guard this morning. Greg and Nat said they'd head out to Tingit to check on him."

"And the lady," the sheriff added.

"Lady?" Gus asked.

"Greg said a woman radioed in from Ben's boat about the body."

Gooseflesh straightened on his neck, and he set his mug down.

The sheriff continued, "When Ben called back in he mentioned he had a female tourist on board. Seemed concerned

159

about protecting her from the body. It's why he wanted the coast guard to bring her in."

He swallowed, put on his most sincere expression and best English accent, and turned to face the two men—both in their thirties. The mayor had brown hair and eyes, while the sheriff was blond with blue. "Please excuse my interruption, but I couldn't help but overhear. Did you say a *body* was found?"

The sheriff nodded, his expression grim. "Afraid so."

"How awful. Any idea who it is?"

"I can't comment on that."

"No. Of course not. I understand. I only ask because I'm here to watch a relative compete in the swim tournament, and I'd hate to think . . ."

"I'm sorry, but I can't comment. Not until an official ID has been made."

"Of course." Which meant they'd be bringing the body back in. He swallowed. What were the chances it was someone else?

After waiting a reasonable amount of time, he exited the diner and moved to the pay phone at the end of the street, placing a call.

"I think we may have a serious problem," he began. "They are bringing a body found off the coast of Tingit back to the marina."

"When?"

"Shortly, I anticipate."

"Get over there. Figure out who found her and what they know."

FIVE

en piloted his ship into the marina. Two men stood at his slip, waiting. The rain had ceased and the sun shone, but to Libby it felt wrong—devoid of warmth.

Winds and the tsunami's surge had left their imprint on the busted pier boards and frayed sails, but the damage looked nowhere near what Tingit's terrain had suffered.

Libby's gaze shifted beyond the pier to the top of the marina where a crowd buzzed. Her and Kat's fellow competitors and most of the coaches angled to see what was happening, along with a throng of locals—or who Libby assumed to be locals, as she didn't recognize any of them. Her coach's eyes shifted from being tight with concern to softening with relief. No doubt he'd worried it might have been her—understandable considering she'd missed morning practice. She never missed practice. Neither did Kat.

An ambulance had reversed up to the top edge of the pier and the sheriff had the pier between Ben's slip and the vehicle cordoned off, but she doubted it would be long before they figured out whose body it was.

She wondered how Kat's stoic coach would respond, whether he'd even show any emotion.

Pulling into the slip, Ben hopped down and tossed the mooring line to a man she could only assume by the brown uniform was the sheriff. Blue eyes, blond hair, hair swept to the side. A handsome man, but not nearly as breathtaking as Ben McKenna.

"Ben," the sheriff greeted him.

"Jim. Looks like the storm didn't hit Yancey too hard."

"Tingit shielded us. Just some high winds and rough seas."

"Glad to hear it." He turned to Libby. "Jim Dalton, this is Libby Jennings. She was with me when . . . we discovered the body."

Jim extended his hand as he climbed on board and Libby shook it.

"Ben radioed this morning. Said you knew the victim?"

Her gaze instinctually shifted to Kat's coach. He had to know, had to have guessed.

"Miss Jennings?" Jim said softly. "I know this is difficult."

Libby rubbed her arms. "Sorry. I was . . ."

"No apologies required. I'm sorry for your loss."

Her loss? She'd lost Kat years ago. "Her name was Kat. Katarina Stanic. She is . . . was an open-water swimmer from Russia."

Jim noted the information. "Do you know how I can get in contact with her family?"

"Last I heard they lived in Vladivostok." But that was before Kat had left Berkeley. She'd track them down, though. See that Kat's cap and watch were returned to them. Who knew what her coach would do with them. "You could check with her coach," she said. Though again she highly doubted how helpful he'd be.

The other man, who'd been standing silent through the conversation cleared his throat. "You mentioned the woman's neck may have sustained an injury?"

"Yeah. Sorry. Libby, this is Doctor Graham."

The young man, probably a few years younger than her, extended his hand. Average height and build with brushed-back light brown hair and subtle green eyes, he wore a light blue turtleneck sweater and tan trousers. "I'm also sorry for your loss."

She nodded, feeling awkward accepting sympathies when she'd let Kat down all those years ago. Or perhaps hadn't. She needed to know for sure. Needed to know if Kat's death tied to her actions in any way. "You were inquiring about Kat's neck?" she prompted.

"Right." He cleared his throat. "Ben?"

"Follow me. I have her below deck."

The men followed Ben down the narrow steps through the tiny galley and down the second shorter set of steps to the lowest deck. Libby brought up the rear. She was a part of this whether they'd welcome her or not. Kat had been her friend or at least she'd been Kat's at one point in time. She needed to know what happened, needed for her own peace of mind and out of respect for Kat's memory.

Ben knelt by Kat's body, gripping the tarp. As if sensing her presence at the edge of the stairs, he glanced over his shoulder, making direct eye contact with her. "You may want to look away."

Swallowing, she did so, though she highly doubted she'd ever be able to forget the memory of Kat's face when he'd rolled her dead body off of her.

"The bruising on her neck looks like finger marks, and her head flails unsupported—plus, run your hand over her throat," Ben said. "Feel that?"

"Feels like a transected tear between C4 and C5, but I'll need to confirm at the morgue."

Libby swung around at the doctor's words, instantly regretting it. Death had taken further toll on Kat's body overnight. She looked away. "So her neck *was* snapped?" she asked. Kat had been murdered?

"I'll need to confirm with an autopsy, but she definitely suffered damage to her cervical spinal cord." Doc Graham stood. "Let's get her out to the stretcher and back to the morgue so I can make a substantiated finding."

Ben lifted Kat's shoulders while Doc Graham took hold of her feet. Jim led the way back topside. They placed her on the stretcher and covered her with an additional layer—a grey wool blanket.

The lone deputy at the top of the ramp struggled to hold back the crowd. They pressed forward as Ben and Doc Graham wheeled the stretcher to the waiting ambulance.

"Who is it, Libby?" Ashley, one of her fellow swimmers called from the crowd.

"Is it a swimmer?" one of the townsfolk asked. "Or one of our own? Steve didn't come home last night."

"I heard it's a woman," another townsperson said. "Steve's probably sleeping one off somewhere, as usual."

"Don't talk about my Stevie like that," the woman snapped.

The mass of people surged forward as they neared the ambulance.

"Kat and you weren't at practice this morning," Ashley said. "But you're here now. Where's Kat?"

"Is it Kat?" Sasha, one of Kat's younger compatriots asked, urgency flooding her tone.

Ben and Doc Graham hefted the stretcher into the back of the ambulance, and the doc climbed in with Kat's body.

"See you at the morgue," Jim said before shutting the ambulance doors.

The ambulance sirens wailed, and people slowly cleared a path allowing it to pull out of the marina lot.

"Can I give you a lift back to your hotel?" Ben asked.

"Hotel? I'm not going to the hotel," Libby said. "I'm going to the morgue."

His brows dipped. "What?"

Sasha pushed her way through the crowd and grasped Libby's arm. "Is it Kat?"

Libby swallowed. "I can't say."

Sasha's jaw tightened, her eyes squinting. "I'd say you just did. What . . . you decide you were tired of getting beat so you killed her?"

"I didn't kill Kat." How could Sasha even suggest something like that, especially if she knew the brutal way that Kat had died?

Ashley gasped. "So it was Kat?" And the crowd erupted.

"Time to go." Ben protectively wrapped his arm around Libby's shoulder, and sheltering her as much as possible, moved her through the questioning and hollering crowd. Reaching a grey Jeep, he opened the driver's-side door, scooted her over to the passenger seat, and climbed in beside her.

He reversed out of the lot, Kat's coach staring her down the entire way.

Ben turned the wheel forty-five degrees and shifted into drive, pulling out onto the dirt road leading from the marina. "That was intense."

"I can't believe anyone would think I'd kill Kat."

"Usually the ones casting blame and making such accusations are the ones responsible or at least capable of doing it."

Sasha kill Kat? How could one woman snap another's neck? The entire situation was surreal.

He turned right, taking the small road up to Main Street.

"Where are you going?" Was this the way to the morgue?

"To the Yancey Bed-and-Breakfast."

"How do you know that's where I'm staying?"

"There are only two places to stay in town. I took a guess. Heard most of the swimmers are staying at Milli's. She makes the better breakfast."

"Milli?"

"The B&B's owner."

"Oh. Yeah. Most of the swimmers are staying there."

He glanced over. "But not Kat?"

"No. The swimmers from communist countries always stay somewhere else."

Ben shifted gears, banking right onto Main Street. "The Cold War is alive and well right in our small town, even over hotel choices."

"Please. Yancey's, what, fifty-some miles from Russia's coast? Living that close to the enemy must keep the Cold War very real for you all."

"Trust me." He downshifted as they approached the only stop sign on Main Street. "It got extremely real for me a few years back."

That piqued her curiosity but not enough to dissuade her from her task. "Where's the morgue?"

"In the hospital basement." He pulled to a full stop. "But Doc Graham certainly isn't going to let you—"

She hopped out of the Jeep and raced across the street.

"Hey," he hollered. "What are you doing?"

"Thanks for the lift." She'd find the hospital and hopefully some essential answers.

■ ■ ■

He watched her climb from the vehicle. Watched her striding with purpose toward the cross street, which led where?

She was the one who'd found Kat.

Knew Kat. Though he doubted anyone truly *knew* Kat.

She was going to be a problem. *Again.*

SIX

Libby paced the cold cinderblock-lined hall on the lowest level of the newly built Yancey Regional Medical Center.

From what she had seen, the floor was mostly used for storage and laundry facilities, but when she'd stopped at the door labeled *Morgue*, through the small glass window she saw what she assumed was Kat's covered body on the exam table. She was in the right place, but where was Doctor Graham?

It'd been nearly a half hour and he had yet to appear.

The hall was silent save for the chugging of the washing machines. She'd never felt quite so alone. The stairwell door opened at the far end of the hall, a shadow appearing across the freshly scrubbed linoleum.

"Doc Graham?"

A man stepped out dressed in a dark hooded sweatshirt and jeans. Definitely not Doc Graham.

She stilled. "Can I help you?"

"I hope so." His voice was oddly familiar, tugging at something in her memory.

The elevator dinged, and the doors slid open across from her. Ben McKenna stepped out.

She looked back to the stairwell, but the man was gone.

"What are you looking at?" Ben asked.

She shook her head. "Never mind. What are you doing here?"

He held up two paper vending machine cups, pop-out handles and all. "Thought you could use something warm."

She ignored how his presence alone provided that.

"Seriously, what are you doing here?" As thoughtful as his attention was, she didn't need it, and she certainly didn't want to grow dependent on it. That would be the worst possible thing.

"I'm making sure you're safe," he said, stepping in front of her.

"Thanks, but I told you, I can take care of myself."

"And also to keep you out of trouble." He winked.

"Trouble? Not like I'm breaking any laws."

"Laws, no. Hospital policy . . . ummm." He shrugged.

"It's against hospital policy to stand in a hallway?"

"On this floor it is."

"Well, as soon as Doctor Graham can manage to find time to perform Kat's autopsy"—and give her some answers—"I'll leave."

He handed her a cup of what looked like brown-tinged water.

"Thanks, I think."

"It's not as bad as it looks. Just cover the taste." He pulled a handful of creamer and sugar packets out of his jean jacket pocket.

She arched a brow.

"Go on. You may be waiting a while."

"And why is that?"

"Because Doc Graham is stuck in his office being barraged by Kat's coach to release her body to him."

"He's doing *what*?"

"Doc's sorting it out."

"Sorting what out? For all we know it was her coach that murdered her."

"And why would he do that?"

"If she was telling the truth all those years ago, Saturday was supposed to be her last race. She probably knew it'd be her last chance to defect while in the States, and he never would allow that." Exhaling an exasperated huff, she dumped the coffee in the trash and raced for the stairwell.

"She's a Russian citizen," he called, running after her.

She shoved open the door and took the concrete steps two at a time.

"She was killed here. If Doc Graham gives up custody, they'll take her back to Russia and we'll never know what happened."

"Emmanuel is handling it. He has Jim calling the federal office up in Anchorage. They'll know the right diplomatic agency to handle this."

Libby rounded the stairs, took the last four, and crashed through the door, heading for the heightened voices at the end of the hall.

The door read *Doctor E. Graham*.

She burst through and all four men stared at her. Kat's coach, Yuri Yesnavich, assistant coach Arshavan Barinov, Sheriff Jim Dalton, and Doc Graham—now wearing a white medical coat over pea-soup green scrubs.

"You," Coach Yesnavich said. "You couldn't beat her, so you killed her."

"I didn't kill Kat. I . . . we"—she pointed to Ben—"found her."

"*Hmph*. Likely alibi." He glanced at his assistant coach, who nodded in agreement. "Now," Yesnavich said, addressing Doc Graham, his voice cold and stern as always, "give us our athlete."

"That's all Kat was to you, wasn't she. Just an athlete," Libby said. "Someone who brought *you* glory?"

He ignored her with a flick of his hand.

"Someone from the State Department will be here as soon as possible," Doc Graham said. "I've already placed the call. In the meantime Miss Stanic's body remains with us."

Yesnavich's usually pale complexion reddened, matching the cherry red of his velour tracksuit. "Very well. You can shortly expect a Russian ambassador too. Miss Stanic's body *will be* returned to the motherland, where she belongs."

He glared at Libby before turning and practically marching from the room, Arshavan, dressed in matching attire, following suit.

Panic seared inside. If they took Kat, they'd never find answers. She looked to Doc Graham. "You'll perform the autopsy in the meantime?"

"I've been told to assess what I can without going invasive."

"Meaning?"

"He can't cut her open," Jim said.

"Jim," Ben scolded, gesturing in Libby's direction. "A little delicacy."

Jim winced. "Sorry, ma'am."

"Will you be able to tell if her neck was snapped noninvasively?"

Doc Graham nodded. "Imaging will tell us."

"Then get to it," Jim said. "I doubt you have much time."

Knowing the Russians, after Kat failed to appear for practice, they'd probably placed the call as soon as word of a body spread. As they walked down to the basement, Libby prayed Doc Graham would work fast. She needed to know if Kat had, in fact, been murdered.

Forty-five minutes later, Doc Graham entered the dismal hall.

"Well?" Libby said, setting the journal she'd been scribbling in aside.

"It's my conclusion her neck was snapped premortem."

"Which means *before* death?"

"Yes. Her injury wasn't sustained after death. Bobbing around the ocean or among the orcas didn't cause it. It is my professional opinion her neck being snapped occurred at the time of death—and that death was not accidental."

"So she *was* murdered?" Libby tried to process that, but how did one process such a thing?

Doc Graham nodded. "I'm afraid so."

■ ■ ■

Libby stepped out into the cool, pale sunshine barely breaking through the clouds, her head spinning.

Kat had been murdered. At least they knew *that* truth. They still needed to find the person or persons responsible.

"What will you do now?" she asked Jim.

"Start with questioning her coaches and the other competitors."

"I highly doubt you'll get anything out of the Russians, but the other competitors maybe . . . It's possible. If I go with you, you'd probably get a warmer reception."

Jim frowned. "Why's that?"

"Just as the locals asked if the body belonged to one of theirs. Swimmers are still a community, even if we are competitors. I'm one of them. You're an outsider."

Jim looked at Ben, who agreed with a tilt of his head, and then back to Libby. "If you think it'll help, I'm willing to give it a try."

"I'm coming too," Ben said.

"Look, I appreciate all you've done, but I don't need to be

babysat." She was already coming to enjoy his company far too much.

He lifted his chin at Jim. "I don't like how one of her own accused her of murdering Kat. I want to make sure she's treated right. Humor me, bud?"

Jim exhaled. "Fine." He looked to Libby as she grunted in frustration. "It's best not to fight it when a McKenna sets his mind to something."

She rolled her eyes. "I'm quickly coming to see that."

SEVEN

Ben climbed the steps of the Yancey B&B, where Libby and the majority of her competitors were staying. Jim had suggested they start with the friendlier of the two locations and then move to the Alaska Inn, where the communist swimmers were housed.

"Anyone in particular I should be looking at?" Jim asked as they entered the two-story mansion converted into an inn with nearly twenty rooms.

The house had once belonged to a wealthy Russian fur trader and was passed down through the generations until Milli Bentner and her husband, Al, purchased the property several years back in 1974, refurbishing the aging home and opening it as a bed-and-breakfast.

Ben hoped for their sake it drew tourists and for his sake too, as it was how they made their living. Alaska was becoming the new hot spot for travelers—the last frontier to explore. Even the dozens of missing women from Anchorage and surrounding area over the past decade hadn't appeared to deter visitors, at least not from the Kodiak archipelago where he lived. In the back of his mind, he couldn't help but wonder if the Anchorage killer had made his way farther southeast than usual, but Libby seemed sold on the Russians being behind Kat's murder. Either way, he didn't feel comfortable leaving Libby on her own until matters simmered down. He didn't know why. She clearly was a strong woman, but something deep inside told him to stick fast to her.

"Monika Juergen," Libby said answering Jim's question. "West German swimmer. She's my and was Kat's stiffest competition, though she always comes in third. It's no secret she hates us both. I'd start with her."

"Hate strong enough to kill?" Jim asked, pausing in the lobby.

"She gives new meaning to German stout."

"Jim," Milli said, as she entered the lobby. "I have to tell you I'm not real keen on you turning my dining hall into an interrogation room."

Anne Murray's latest, "Shadows in the Moonlight," played over the lobby speakers. She had a good voice, but Ben preferred Eddie Rabbitt when it came to country singers.

"Don't worry." Jim smiled. "I'm just grouping them there. I'll interrogate in your library."

Milli frowned. "Yeah, that makes it loads better." She looked past Jim. "McKenna, heard you were the one who found her."

"Found who?" Ben asked, curious about exactly how much everyone in town knew.

"That poor Russian swimmer. Thelma Jenkins overheard her coach ranting on the pay phone. In Russian, of course, but he'd just come from the morgue and his swimmer is missing. Doesn't take much to put two and two together."

At least not when it came to Thelma Jenkins, the burgeoning town gossip.

Ben followed Jim into the dining area, Libby stepping close

behind. A number of women and a handful of male coaches sat around the various tables. Doug stood and stepped toward her. "You okay, kid?"

She nodded, and after a moment's concerned assessment her coach retook his seat.

One of the young women rushed forward. "What's going on? We heard it was Kat."

Libby shouldered Ashley's weight as she lunged into her crying, her tube top and Jordache jeans as skintight as her wet suit. Most guys stammered in her presence, but Ben didn't seem the least bit interested. "Was it really Kat?" she asked, sniffing. Ashley had never had a nice word to say about Kat, and suddenly, here she was, overwrought at Kat's death?

Libby looked back at Jim, unsure what or how much she was allowed to share.

He nodded his go-ahead.

She swallowed, slipping her hair behind her ear. "I'm afraid it was."

A murmur buzzed through the room.

"What happened?" Sylvia, the one Australian swimmer at the tournament, asked as Ashley sat again.

Jim hitched up his pants. "I'm afraid all I'm able to confirm is Miss Stanic's identity at this point. But I'm hoping you all will be able to help me put the pieces of her last days together."

"How?" Sylvia frowned.

"By answering a few short questions."

"What kind of questions?" Monika asked, her German accent thick.

"Just the basics. Miss Jennings here has kindly offered to assist me, so we'll call you into the library one by one. I thank you for your cooperation in advance. This shouldn't take long."

Wearing brown corduroy coveralls and a yellow T-shirt,

Monika slumped back in her chair. "Why aren't you questioning the Russians? They were closest to Kat. Not us."

"We're planning to, Miss . . . ?"

"Juergen."

"Well, Miss Juergen, why don't we start with you." He held out his hand, gesturing to the library at the far end of the dining hall. "This way, please."

Monika eyed him warily.

Libby crossed her arms. "Unless you have something to hide?"

"Me?" Monika stood, her shoulders broad, her arms muscular, her blond hair cropped short. "Look who's talking. You were Kat's number-one enemy. You conveniently happen to find her body. *Please*. If anybody should be questioned, it should be you."

"We have," Ben said before Jim could even respond. Always so quick to jump to her defense and protection. While she greatly appreciated that, among other things about him, it didn't change the fact she'd be gone soon and there was no room for a man in her life. Even a stellar one, as she was coming to view Ben McKenna.

"Correct," Jim said, following up on Ben's statement. "Miss Jennings has already been questioned."

Libby hadn't realized he'd viewed their conversations as official questioning.

"Are we going to do this," Monika asked, standing in front of Libby, shifting her gaze between her and Ben. "Or are you two going to gawk at each other all day?"

Heat rushed to Libby's cheeks. She had been staring at Ben. *Again*. Ignoring the smirks spreading across the room, she turned and followed Jim and Monika into the library. Two brown leather wing chairs sat in front of an ornate fireplace, the walls covered with bookshelves from floor to ceiling.

Monika plopped down on one of the chairs and rested her

foot over her bent knee, her white Nike tennis shoes bouncing up and down as she jiggled her foot. "So, what do inquiring minds want to know?" She swiped her nose. "Isn't that what you all say in the States when you're looking for juicy gossip?"

"We're not looking for gossip, ma'am," Jim said. "We're looking for facts."

"Facts. Right. Well, the fact is you're standing next to Kat's enemy. Not looking at her."

"As I've said, I've already questioned Miss Jennings. Now it's your turn."

"Fine." She exhaled, blowing her fringed bangs from her forehead. "Let's get this over with. I'm ready for a hot shower and my rubdown. Trained hard this morning."

"How well did you know Miss Stanic?" Jim asked.

"Not well at all."

"How many competitions have you been in together?"

"We've competed against each other maybe twenty times."

"Over how many years?" Jim asked.

She shrugged a shoulder. "A decade, maybe."

"And in all those years how many times did you beat Miss Stanic?"

Libby bit back a smile. Jim was good. Getting right to the heart of the reason for the animosity that existed between Monika and Kat.

Monika's jaw clenched. "None," she gritted out.

"None." Jim strode forward, squatting in front of her. "That must have made you angry?"

Disgust rippled across Monika's face. "I see what you are doing here."

"What am I doing?" he asked.

"Trying to make me look like the bad guy, but I'm tired of playing along." She got to her feet. "I'm done here."

"Sit down, Miss Juergen. Please," Jim said, polite but firm. "Only two questions to go."

"Fine." She retook her seat. "Two."

"Did you see Kat at practice yesterday?"

"Yes. We both swam early."

"Why?"

She glanced over at Libby. "Less distractions. Better focus."

"And then what did you both do?"

"No clue what Kat did, but I came back here and changed, then went for a long run."

"A run after swimming? Why the extra exercise?"

"Part of my training regimen."

"So you run every day?" Jim asked.

"Not every day."

"Where'd you run?"

"I don't know the names of places. Back off in the wilderness somewhere."

"See anyone on your run?"

"I was focused on the run. Not my surroundings."

"And then?"

"And *now* I'm leaving. I've answered far more than two questions. If you want to talk to me more, you can go through my coach." She strode from the room.

"You're just going to let her leave like that?" Libby asked, outraged.

Monika always liked to be in control, calling the shots, but this was Jim's arena. Why'd he let her walk like that?

"She's not a U.S. citizen. As far as I know she's committed no crime. I have no right to force her to answer any of my questions. What she did was a courtesy."

"I'd hardly call that a courtesy."

"She told us both she and Kat practiced early."

"Yeah. I saw Kat leaving practice yesterday as I arrived."

"And Monika?"

"Can't say I recall seeing her at all, come to think of it."

"Then we should speak with her coach next."

"He's only going to back up what she's said."

"Only if it's the truth, or if she told him what she told us."

"And how will we know which is the case?" Libby asked.

He smiled. "Ben's out there listening."

Right. Ben. What had he heard?

A few minutes passed before Monika's coach, Claus Dieter, entered. Libby looked past him to Ben before Jim shut the door. They'd have to learn what Ben had overheard, if anything.

"Mr. Dieter, please have a seat."

The man, balding though only in his early forties, sat. He was the stereotypical, overbearing, hard-nosed coach, and Libby doubted they'd get more than a grunted one-word answer or two out of him.

"Did you see Kat Stanic at practice yesterday morning?" Jim began.

"Yes. She and Monika practiced before the rest of the girls."

"Why?"

"Because Monika had other training she wanted to do, and the two of them practicing alone makes them drive one another. It's good for Monika to go against her stiffest competition." He offered a slide glance in Libby's direction along with the jab. Monika had yet to beat her either.

"What time did she finish practice?" Jim asked.

"Seven thirty."

"And then?"

"I told you, she trained."

"How?"

"A run, I believe."

"You believe? Aren't you in charge of her fitness?"

"Yes, but she keeps her own log and I oversee."

Interesting, she hadn't offered to share her log.

"Did you see her running?" Jim asked.

"No, I had another swimmer practicing at regular time."

"So you can't verify Monika was running?" Libby said.

"If Monika said she ran, she ran. She's my most dedicated athlete. You can check her log."

Logs could easily be forged.

"We'll do that," Jim said.

"Any idea what Kat did after finishing her practice?"

He shook his head. "It's not my business to keep an eye on the competition."

That was a flat-out lie. All coaches kept an eye on the competition.

"Thank you, Mr. Dieter. I appreciate your cooperation. If you think of anything that might be helpful, here's my card."

Dieter slipped it into the pocket of his green tracksuit.

Jim turned to Libby after Dieter left. "Sounds like we may want to start asking if anyone actually saw Monika on her run, and when we are done here we need to speak with Kat's coach and see where she headed after her run."

"I doubt he'll tell you anything."

"If he wants to find her killer, he will."

"You're assuming he's not her killer," Libby said.

"You really think her own coach would kill her?" Jim asked.

"You've got to understand. Russia works very differently than we do."

Ben popped his head in. "How's it going?"

"Okay. How's it going out there?"

"Good. I'll catch you up when you're done."

Time passed, and they finally reached the last competitor—Sylvia Mollet, from Australia.

"Thanks for your patience, Miss Mollet," Jim said, shutting the door behind her.

"No problem. If I can be of any help."

They ran through the typical questions—how well she knew Kat, if she saw Kat after practice, when she saw her last. But Libby moved forward with the question burning on her mind. She'd asked every competitor, but no one had seen Monika between seven thirty a.m. and four p.m. the day Kat turned up dead. "Any chance you saw Monika after yesterday's practice?"

"Actually, yeah."

Libby's heart lightened. *Finally.*

"Where?"

"Heading off toward the old marina."

"The *old* marina?" She turned to Ben, who had joined them in the room.

"No one uses it anymore," he explained. "It's become a boat junkyard. We needed a nice new-looking marina for all the cruise tourists."

"Well, I was curious, so I followed her for a bit."

"And?" Libby asked.

"I saw her meeting with a man."

"Recognize him?"

"He had a baseball hat and sunglasses on and I was a distance away, so I couldn't say, but he was carrying a bag in his hand and the two of them headed up over the hill together."

"And then?" Libby asked.

"I turned back around. I was meeting the Canadian girls for lunch."

So Monika was lying. Libby knew it. They'd have to talk to her again.

"Anything else you think might be helpful?" Jim asked.

"There was this guy."

"With Monika?"

"No, hanging around the tournaments. I saw him in Cali and then again here. Seemed to always be watching Kat from a distance."

"Did you report him to anyone?" Libby asked.

"Yeah, I told Kat."

"And?"

"She just brushed it off. Said he was probably some shy fan. Nothing to worry about."

That didn't sound like Kat.

"Can you describe him?" Jim asked.

"Tall, lean. I think he had dark hair, but it was hard to tell. He always wore a hooded sweatshirt and sunglasses—even on cloudy or rainy days. Weird, huh?"

Libby leaned forward. "Did you say a hooded sweatshirt?"

"Yeah. A black knit one."

Just like she'd seen at the hospital earlier today.

EIGHT

What now?" Ben asked as Sylvia left the room. He wondered about Libby's interest in Sylvia's hooded mystery man.

"We ask Monika what she was doing by the old marina and why she lied to us," Jim said.

It took a bit of searching, but they found Monika out by the old marina, of all places, her back to them, deep in conversation with a man. The man caught sight of them, and she turned, her eyes full of fear.

"Jakob?" Libby asked.

"You know him?" Ben said.

"He's an assistant trainer for Kat and Sasha."

"So for the two Russian swimmers in this race?" And Monika's main competition.

"Yes."

Interesting.

"What are you two doing out here anyway? Trying to get your stories straight?" Libby said, approaching. "It's already too late. We know you lied to us, Monika. What? Did the two of you conspire to kill Kat, knock the competition out of the way? You couldn't wait another week? You know this was her last season." Rage and indignation for Kat and how she'd been murdered in cold blood boiled in her veins.

Monika stepped toward her. "It's not like that."

"Monika," Jakob cautioned.

"We don't have a choice. We have to tell them."

"I'll get fired, and you'll get pulled out of the competition."

"It's better than them thinking we murdered Kat."

Libby's face scrunched. She looked as confused as Ben felt. "What's going on here?"

Monika reached back and took hold of Jakob's hand. "We're in love."

Libby's head bobbed. "Seriously?"

Monika looked at Jakob with eyes full of affection. "Yes. We know it's against the rules, which is why we were meeting in secret, which is why I couldn't tell you the truth."

Ben looked at Libby, curious if she was buying it.

"You could have told me," she said.

"Like you wouldn't have ratted me out to get me out of the way."

"If I beat you, I want it to be fair and square," Libby said. "Not because I busted you for dating the competition's coaching staff. But how do we know you two didn't do anything to Kat?"

"Because we saw her leave on a boat with another man."

Libby's eyes widened. "What?"

"Why didn't you say something before?" Jim asked.

"Because I would have had to explain me and Jakob."

"You could have just said you saw them while jogging," Ben said.

"I thought it better not to open any possibility of you finding out."

"So this boat, this man. What can you tell us?" And why did they leave from the old marina? Because they didn't want to be seen together either, perhaps? Had Kat gone willing? So many questions raced through his mind, and no doubt Libby's. He wondered where Jim would start.

"Not a lot," Jakob said.

"Let's start from the beginning," Jim said. "You came here and . . ."

"Waited for Monika to show," Jakob said.

"I heard footsteps down on the rocks below the hill and thought it was her. I looked down, but it was Kat."

"Did she see you?"

"No. I ducked back as quickly as I could. I couldn't risk her seeing me with Monika."

"So then what?"

"I crouched back behind a tree and saw Monika coming over the hill. I waved her to me, signaling for her to hurry and stay quiet. A few minutes later we saw a boat leaving the marina. Peering around the tree we saw Kat still in her practice gear, standing near the stern talking with a man."

"Can you describe the boat?"

"White boat. Decent size. Maybe a twenty-eight-footer."

"And the man?"

"Average size and build. Brown hair. Nice suit."

"Suit, as in dress suit or swimsuit?"

"Dress suit and tie, which I thought was odd for a day at sea."

"How did Kat seem? Nervous? Happy?" Libby asked.

"She was intent on what he was saying but kept looking around too. Like she wanted to make sure they weren't seen."

"And then?"

"They sailed out of the marina and we went on our picnic."

"Did you see the boat or Kat come back?"

Monika and Jakob shook their heads.

"When she wasn't at practice this morning . . ." Monika began.

"You should have said something," Libby said. "It could have meant saving her life."

Ben stiffened. Or at least identifying her killer sooner.

"I'm sorry. I didn't want to get Jakob fired."

"We're talking about a woman's life," Libby said, frustration clear.

"We had no idea she was going to die," Jakob said.

"What happened?" Monika asked. "No one has said what happened to her. Did she fall overboard? Did she drown?"

"She was murdered," Jim said.

"Murdered?" Monika choked. "I know I suggested Libby might have done her in, but I didn't really think . . ."

"We can do it discreetly, but I need you both to work with a sketch artist, see what you can remember about the boat and the man you saw."

They both nodded like scolded schoolchildren, and rightly so.

"I'll go ask around the docks," Ben said.

"I can send Tom," Jim offered.

"I know Tom's your deputy, but he's so new and he doesn't know the guys at the docks like I do," Ben said. "Let me help you out with this."

Jim nodded. "Okay. I'll drop these two off with Marge for the drawings and then head over to the Russians' lodgings and question them." He looked at Libby. "You want to come?"

"Actually, I think I'll go with Ben."

Ben arched a brow. Not that he minded time with Libby, but . . . why did she want to come with him? He ignored the thrill that shot through him at the ludicrous thought it might be because she liked his company and wanted to spend more time in it.

"The Russians won't speak with me around. They loathe me. And I'm not just going to sit this one out, so I'll go with Ben."

He swallowed. Of course it was a sensible reason.

Jim nodded to Ben. "Keep me updated."

"Will do."

NINE

Why do you assume they rented the boat?" Libby asked, following Ben down to the marina, not wanting to think about how much she enjoyed his company.

"Most do," he said, offering her a hand to step over the bowed dock board, and she took it—from his expression, surprising him

"What if they didn't?" she asked, not wanting to let go of his hold just yet.

He exhaled. "Then this will be a dead end." His thumb caressed the top of her hand before he finally pulled back.

She shoved her hands in her pockets, her skin still alive with his touch. "Let's pray that's not the case." She'd made it her personal mission to see her onetime friend's killer found and to determine whether or not it had anything to do with her actions at Berkeley so many years ago.

Ben started with the harbormaster, who pointed them in Willy Craig's direction.

"Willy has the biggest rental operation, which affords a nice level of anonymity," Ben said as they approached the man with the clipboard, directing a handful of teens how to better scrub down his ships. "Hopefully not too much anonymity, in our case."

"Hey, Will," Ben began.

"Ben." He looked over his shoulder. "And?"

He was old enough to be Libby's father but was certainly not looking at her like one. She took a step closer to Ben. *Him* she trusted, which was amazing given the short amount of time she'd known him. But given the circumstances they'd endured and the fact he'd basically saved her life on Tingit, it only made sense.

"Libby Jennings," Ben said, introducing her to Willy while taking his own step closer to her. The scent of seawater and fresh air lingered around him.

"What can I do for you two?"

"We're looking for a boat you may have rented out late yesterday morning."

He laughed. "Well, that narrows it down."

"It was to a man in a suit."

"Oh, that dude. Hard to forget Mr. Businessman."

"Was he with anyone?"

"Not that I saw, but he assured me he could handle the boat. Paid cash up front. Brought it back in pristine condition."

"You remember his name?"

"Can't say that I do."

"Remember which boat?"

"Maybe *Killing Time*, but I can't be certain."

Well, that would be ironic.

"Mind if we take a look at your logs?"

His brown eyes narrowed. "What's this about? Don't tell me you think it has something to do with that body you brought in."

"Witnesses put her on a boat with the suit yesterday."

"Great." He exhaled. "Go on ahead." He pointed to his largest boat, which as Ben explained also served as Willy's home and office. "Place is yours."

"Thanks."

"Too bad about that lady. But she was probably a Commie."

Libby halted, heat radiating up her neck. Yes they were the enemy, but Kat was a person. She wasn't the politicians running her country.

More importantly, she was a human being and had been murdered in cold blood.

Libby understood the hatred and fear between countries. She'd succumbed to it herself, assuming the worst of Kat simply because of where she came from. And being this close to Russia had to be unnerving, but Willy's antagonism toward Kat, a woman he didn't even know, gnawed at her.

Maybe Kat had been trying to defect. Libby prayed that was the case and it wasn't that Kat was a spy using her profession and the time it allowed her in the States to gather intel for Russia.

Ben took Libby's hand, leading her into Willy's office before she or he said anything to Willy that would get them kicked out.

"Remember the bigger picture," Ben said, giving her hand a soft squeeze. "We need to find her killer. Willy's just . . ."

"I understand." She exhaled. "They are our enemy. We are at war with them. But Kat . . ."

He cupped his hand over hers, warmth spreading through her limbs. "I understand too."

Her gaze locked on his, and something powerful shifted between them. She swallowed, knowing she should pull back, but oh so wanting to lean in. . . . She shook her head, attempting to clear her brain. "What exactly are we looking for?" she finally managed to say.

Ben cleared his throat, taking a step back as he shook out

his hands. He grabbed Willy's most recent rental logbook and flipped it open. He cleared his throat again. "Names we recognize, so we can rule them out. Willy would have recognized a local."

"And names we don't recognize?" she asked.

"We give them to Jim to track them down." Ben scanned the names. "I see our typical fishing charters."

"I recognize several names too," she said. "Trainers who probably wanted to take out a boat on their afternoon off. Coaches control the competition rentals."

"Gotcha, but they are still suspects, as Willy wouldn't have recognized them."

"I hardly doubt any of them would get dressed up in a suit to take a boat out."

"Perhaps if they were trying to impress a beautiful lady."

She cocked a brow. "So you thought Kat was beautiful?"

"Well, I didn't meet Kat when she was alive, but I think she was beautiful, in a generic sort of way."

She was curious to see where he was going with this. "Generic?"

"Tall, brunette, big eyes, high cheekbones. You see it often."

"Uh-huh. I can see how model-like qualities must get redundant."

"That's not what I meant."

"Then what did you mean?"

He exhaled. "I prefer a more natural beauty."

She narrowed her eyes. "So . . . plain?"

He stepped to her, standing but a breath away. "I'd hardly call fair skin"—his gaze followed the curves of her face—"soft, round cheeks, full lips, and sultry eyes the green of the Aegean Sea plain."

She opened her mouth, but no words came.

Ben swooped in and kissed her, cupping her face, splaying his fingers through her hair.

Her mind temporarily shut down, and her heart took over. His kiss deepened and—

Willy cleared his throat. "Find what you were looking for?" he asked with a gigantic smile.

Maybe she had after all these years.

Gathering their list of names and excusing themselves, her cheeks aflame with embarrassment, they stepped past Willy in the narrow passage and headed for the sheriff's station, where Jim hopefully had some answers.

■ ■ ■

He watched the two leave the marina. So they'd made the connection to the boat. No matter. It'd been scrubbed down. Brought back cleaner than when they'd left. Question was, why were they digging so hard?

TEN

So what did you find?" Jim asked as Ben and Libby entered Yancey's sheriff's station.

Ben handed Jim the list they'd compiled from Willy's log. "The names highlighted in yellow are locals, in green are with the tournament—"

"And blue?" he asked.

"Neither of us recognized them. They could be tourists."

Jim exhaled. "I count three unknowns."

Ben nodded.

"I'll have Tom track them down, find out where they're staying. Maybe they are visiting a local or watching someone in the tournament." He took a bite out of his sandwich. Smelled like bologna. "Sorry. Way past lunch," he said, wiping the mustard from the corner of his mouth.

"Lunch? It's more like dinnertime." Which meant he and Libby needed to grab a bite too.

"They all paid cash," Jim said, scanning the notes Ben had made.

"That's not at all unusual," Ben said. Most folks did.

"I suppose not. Just makes them harder to track." Jim took another bite.

"How did it go with the Russians?" Libby asked.

He swallowed before speaking. "About as good as you anticipated."

"Did you learn *anything*?"

"Nothing useful, I'm afraid. Other than you are their top suspect."

"I can't even be a suspect," she said with irritation. "I was at regular practice and then with the team until I met Ben for the tour."

Jim exhaled. "Try reasoning with them." He added some salt to his sandwich before putting the top slice of bread back on.

"When will the officials arrive?" Ben asked.

"The man from the State Department will be here tomorrow, hopefully before the Russian ambassador shows. I'd hate to have to try and hold him off until the U.S. official arrives."

"And in the meantime?" Libby asked.

"I'll get started on these names." Jim tapped the paper.

"And us?" she asked.

Ben liked the sound of that. "We eat."

Libby frowned. "Not exactly the riveting mystery angle I was hoping to track down."

"Even cops need to eat." Ben lifted his chin at Jim chomping down on his bologna sandwich, the Oscar Mayer song running through his head—the jingle was contagious.

■ ■ ■

Libby bit into the juicy burger at Gus's Diner. "Mmm."

"Told you they were great," he said, across the red vinyl booth from her. The place was packed, the scent of burgers and milkshakes swirling in the air.

195

"You weren't kidding." If she was going to cheat on her training diet, this was the way to go.

He smiled, watching her.

"What?" She swiped at her chin. "Do I have sauce on my mouth?"

"No. I was just . . . Never mind."

"Come on. You, shy? *Please*, I've never met anybody more blunt."

He shrugged. "I tend to call it like I see it, but I have to say you hold your own very well."

"Thanks. How about girlfriends?" She was assuming he didn't have one after their kiss but needed to make sure. She wasn't that kind of girl, despite the crazy decade she lived in. Hopefully the '80s would be better. "Do they like your bluntness?"

"No girlfriend." He bit into his burger. "Not for a while."

Pleasure filled her. "No?"

"No." He shook his head. "How about you? How do your boyfriends handle your superior wit?"

"No boyfriend. Not for a while." She watched the smile spread across his lips—lips so soft she wished they were still pressed to hers.

"No?" He arched a brow.

"Too much travel. Makes relationships difficult at best," she said. As much as she had enjoyed their kiss it was time she got the realities of her profession out in the open. She was developing strong feelings for Ben McKenna, rapidly, and it was time he got a little insight into how her life really worked.

She had a loft in Cali but barely spent any time in it. Her waitressing job allowed her to work in the off-season, but her sponsorships covered the bulk of her necessities. It wasn't a bad way to live, but at thirty the yearning for something more occasionally reared its head. Then again, competition was all she knew.

Ben took a sip of his Coke before speaking. "I imagine it's hard to maintain relationships with all that travel."

It was for all the competitors.

"What about Kat?" he asked.

She frowned. "What about her?"

"You didn't mention a boyfriend."

"I don't believe she had one. Not since Berkeley. At least not that I'm aware of." Rick, her college sweetheart, had been so heartbroken at Kat's departure he'd left Berkeley too, transferring somewhere. But then again, she and Kat hadn't truly talked in years, so maybe Kat did have someone special in her life.

"Are you going to send the quote you found back to Kat's family with her cap?"

She dabbed the barbeque sauce off her mouth with a napkin, still shocked that Ben's western burger suggestion—BBQ sauce, sharp cheddar and an onion ring—had actually turned out to be so tasty. Go figure. "I hadn't thought about it, but yeah, I suppose so. It had been in her cap for a reason. Maybe it'll have importance to her folks."

"Makes sense. Probably something sentimental." He popped a fry in his mouth. "Kind of like that journal you're always writing in."

"I don't write quotes, but yeah, I suppose it's similar."

"So . . ." He dipped his fry in ketchup. "What do you write in there?"

Her eyes narrowed. "Are you fishing to see if I wrote about our kiss?" He'd caught her scribbling in it not long after.

He gazed up at her, his eyes so easy to get lost in. "Maybe."

She smirked, remembering the tingling intensity of his lips pressed to hers. "Well, it most certainly was noteworthy."

What *was* she doing? Playing with fire. She'd told him in the nicest way possible that relationships didn't work with her career, but somehow she knew deep inside saying good-bye to Ben McKenna was going to be brutally painful. How had she let herself get attached so quickly?

■ ■ ■

So Kat had hid something in her cap. That—

He bit back the vulgar word as the waitress topped off his coffee.

He nodded his appreciation and exhaled. His superior would not be pleased with this revelation.

No. This was something he needed to take care of himself, and there was no better time then the present.

He lifted his arm, catching the waitress's attention. "Check, please."

ELEVEN

Ben walked Libby back to the bed-and-breakfast. It was a gorgeous night—low sixties, gentle breeze riffling through the summer leaves.

"You sure you're okay?" he asked. "You've been quiet since I asked about the kiss."

"I'm fine, really."

He lifted his brows, not buying it.

She exhaled. "It's just. Traveling for my job . . . my life . . . It makes attachments difficult."

"You said it wasn't easy to maintain relationships."

"It's nearly impossible and makes it all the harder when I say good-bye."

He scuffed his boot on the concrete landing of Milli's front walk as they reached the Yancey Bed-and-Breakfast. "You *always* say good-bye?" he asked.

Her heart ached at the disappointment radiating in his deep voice. "I don't have a choice."

He tucked his chin in. "We all have a choice."

"Not if I want to compete professionally."

"But surely the other competitors have people in their lives—family, friends . . ." He lifted her hand, tracing her palm with his thumb. "More than friends . . . ?"

"For a time and at a distance."

He frowned. "For a time?"

"I've seen more relationships fizzle, fade . . . implode than I can count."

He nodded. "You sound pretty firm on that."

"I have to be." The sooner she cut off these emotions, her feelings for Ben, the better. She'd already let it go too far. She needed to pull back before the pain stabbed too deep.

He pulled his hand back and slid it into his jean jacket pocket. "If that's where you are, that's where you are."

"It's not where I am. It's *who* I am."

He cocked his head. How did he see right through her? "You sure about that?"

Seriously? One kiss and he was questioning her? The fact that he was right was beside the point.

"Hey, Libby. Still with your friend, I see." Ashley winked, passing them on the walk wearing a long blue T-shirt over a pair of black leggings and black ballet-style flats. It was the new trend among the younger competitors.

Libby shoved her hands in her pockets, still more comfortable wearing jeans.

"Hey, you two." Sylvia waggled two fingers as she climbed up the steps past them, also wearing leggings, but in a black-and-white abstract pattern.

Great. Libby sighed. Everyone's gawking would only get worse if Ben escorted her inside. "You should probably go," she said.

"After I see you in."

"I'm a big girl."

"And there's a killer on the loose. Humor me."

She shook her head, Jim's words echoing in her mind. *"When a McKenna sets his mind to something . . ."*

Ben flashed his adorable, addictive smile. How she wished things were different—that she was definitely ready for more, brave enough to try—but the circuit made such an easy excuse, and it was the only life she knew.

Ben walked her down the west hall to her room—the last one on the bottom floor.

She exhaled a stream of pent-up frustration, yearning to be back in his arms, his warm lips against hers. Somewhere in the last twenty-four hours *easy* had gone out the window. All that was left was painful, and she hated it.

"Good night, Libby Jennings." He offered her his hand.

She smiled despite herself. It was his way of saying good-bye. "Good night, Ben McKenna." She shook his hand, ignoring the giggling of girls peeking their heads into the hall to watch. What was this? High school?

"It's been a pleasure," he said.

"You'll still keep me updated on the case?" She was committed to seeing it solved, but for her heart's sake, just not at Ben McKenna's side.

"Yep. As Jim keeps me updated."

"Thanks. I appreciate it." She should go now, but she desperately wanted to remain in his company. She pulled the room key from her pocket, the red plastic key fob clammy in her hand. Unlocking her door, she turned and leaned against the frame. One last good-bye. "See ya."

Tomorrow she'd go back to regular tournament training and he'd go back to his life—their short, intense time together a passionate, pleasurable memory. The sheriff was on the case, and Ben promised to keep her updated, but their time of partnering up was over.

Ben nodded and stepped back. "See you."

Before she did something stupid, she quickly turned, entered her room, shut the door, and fell against it.

She squinted in the darkness, taking a moment for her eyes to adjust.

Her throat constricted.

Had someone been in her room?

Fear danced up her spine.

Was someone in her room?

Chills skittered along her skin, raising gooseflesh.

"Ben," she hollered, reaching for the doorknob.

■ ■ ■

Libby's scream vibrated in his ears, his heart pounding in his chest as he raced back to her, pulling his .44.

She opened the door as he pushed in.

He took in the disarray and pushed her into the hall and toward safety. "Wait here." He moved through the ransacked room, clearing the space. Once done, he yanked Libby back inside, shut the door, and locked it behind them.

Her gaze fixed on his hand. "Is that a gun?" She shook her head, clearly flustered. "Of course it's a gun. Why do you have a gun?"

He put it back in his holster, the threat of danger gone, at least in her room for the moment. "I live in Alaska."

"So, what? Everyone in Alaska owns a gun?"

"In Yancey. Yeah, pretty much."

"Okay then . . . Bypassing that." She knelt, gathering her garments strewn across the navy-and-rose floral carpet. "You don't think . . . ?"

She didn't need to finish the thought.

"Yeah, I do." *Kat's belongings.* Crazy how he could already follow her thoughts. "Are they gone?"

"No." Libby shook her head, shoving her clothes back into the antique bureau drawers. "I still have them in my pack."

"That quote or those items clearly hold some importance. Something we're missing."

"So what do we do?"

"Figure out the secret they hold."

"How?"

He extended a hand. "Come with me."

She frowned. "Where are we going?"

"To visit a friend."

"What sort of friend?"

"One who specializes in Russian-Alaskan history."

"But how will that help? This isn't history. It's present day."

"Trust me."

She did, placing her hand in his and loving the enveloping warmth that tracked through her.

They headed back out of the B&B hand in hand, much to the amused expressions of her fellow swimmers. It's not like she'd *never* had a guy around, though it had been a long while and most of the girls were much younger than she was—newer to the circuit.

With Kat's planned retirement this year, Libby had already started considering making next season *her* last, but giving up something she'd worked for practically her whole life and needed so badly . . .

She wasn't sure she could let go, but thankfully, she didn't need to ponder that right now. She had plenty of other things to worry about—like who killed Kat, who had ransacked *her* room, and what somebody would possibly want with what appeared to be Kat's innocuous belongings.

"Where does your friend live?" she asked, following Ben across Main Street. She glanced up at the library, which Ben explained was housed in a historic refurbished Russian farm-house. The building was exquisite. A park bench and a freshly planted sapling sat out front.

"Above the shop she just opened last year," he answered.

"Shop?" There were only a few lining Main Street—Gus's Diner, Baranov Books, a hardware store, flower shop, and . . . ,

"The Russian-American Trading Post," he said, pointing at the two-story white-paneled building. "She's still waiting to get the sign up. Something about the color not being right."

Russian-American shop? She frowned. "Why, *exactly*, do you think this friend will be helpful?"

He held the shop door for her, and she stepped inside, a bell announcing their arrival.

"Either our questions ticked someone off and they wanted to scare you, or much more likely someone figured out you have Kat's belongings."

"But what would anyone want with a cap or a broken watch?"

"Maybe it's neither of those."

She frowned. "The quote?"

He nodded.

"But why would anyone care about a quote scribbled on a slip of material?"

"Maybe it's more than it seems."

Still a bit confused as to how helpful this visit would be, Libby couldn't help but admire the amazing collection of antiques surrounding her. While her knowledge of antiques wasn't vast, she certainly recognized a Fabergé egg when she saw one. "Is that real?" she sputtered.

"Oh yes," a woman said, entering the gallery behind her. "It's the pride of my collection." The woman was her age or a bit younger. Petite in height and stature. Dark brown hair cut and styled in Audrey Hepburn fashion. A classic look, but out of date. With almond-shaped brown eyes and soft pink, pouty lips the woman had quite the striking yet soft appearance.

"Agnes Grey, this is Libby Jennings. She's one of the open-water competitors."

"Is that so? I can't imagine the endurance you must possess."

"It takes a lot of practice and hard work." And aching muscles and burning lungs.

"Well, it's a pleasure to meet you. What brings you and Benjamin into my shop?"

Benjamin? Libby bit back a smirk. It seemed too formal for the rugged, outdoor man she was getting to know surprisingly well.

"We have something we'd appreciate you taking a look at," Ben said.

"Oh?"

Ben dipped his head, and Libby pulled the quote from her pocket, handing it over, with a bit of hesitation, to Agnes.

Agnes took it, moving to what looked like a drafting table. "What do we have here?" She clicked on the overhead lamp, swiveling its metal arm to position it where she wanted it.

"I figured if it was important enough for someone to ransack your room over, there was more to it than you or I are seeing," he whispered to Libby, his breath tickling her ear.

"Come," Agnes said with a waggle of her fingers, not bothering to look up from the light, which was probably a very good thing since Libby couldn't manage to smother her smile. All Ben had to do was whisper in her ear and she was a bouncy frenzy of pleasurable emotions—a giddy teenager when she was typically anything *but* giddy.

They hovered behind Agnes, glancing over her shoulder at the quote.

"The material is silk," Agnes said, splashing water from her cup on it, nearly stealing Libby's breath in horror.

"Waterproof." Agnes smiled. "An old sailor's trick."

"Well, it makes sense that Kat would want it waterproof in case the seal in her cap ever ripped," Libby said.

"Yes, but that doesn't explain why someone would break into your room to find it," Ben added.

"Someone broke into your room for this?" Agnes asked, taken aback.

Libby nodded.

"I was hoping you might have some idea why," Ben said.

Agnes studied it under a magnifying glass. "I'm afraid beyond the material it's made from and the type of ink used, you've come to the wrong person. I'm sorry I'm not of much use, but I know who might be."

Ben raked a hand through his hair. "I was really hoping to avoid that."

"If you want to see if this holds any secrets, he's your man," Agnes said.

Why were they talking in code? "*He* who?" Libby asked.

"Elliot," they both said with a sigh.

Libby frowned. "Who's Elliot?"

"A crazy old kook who lives out in the woods and also happens to be a friend of mine," Ben explained.

"And this kook is supposed to help us?"

"You'd be surprised," Agnes said with a smile.

Ben moved for the door. "We'll have to get a message to him."

"Message? Why don't you just call him?"

"He doesn't have a phone."

"It's 1979. Who doesn't have a phone?"

"Elliot." Ben held the door for Libby. "Thanks, Agnes." He waved.

"My pleasure. Nice to meet you, Libby."

"You too," she said before stepping outside and turning to look up at Ben. "So how do we get a message to this Elliot?"

"You'll see." He winked.

TWELVE

Libby settled in by the campfire Ben had made somewhere in the middle of the Alaskan wilderness. She felt as if she were in an extreme Alaskan cloak-and-dagger documentary. They'd actually left a chalk X on a mailbox in town to get Elliot Hargrove's attention. *Seriously?* How crazy was this guy?

The crackling wood, dancing flames, and warmth of the fire on her face was soothing. The pine scent of the trees surrounding them and the vast number of stars shining down made it a magical setting for a date, but it wasn't a date. She had to keep reminding herself of that, despite the fact she was in the company of a man she was coming to believe was perfect—handsome, intelligent, resourceful, honest . . .

She exhaled in frustration, needing to distract her thoughts from Ben. "Okay, so what's the deal with super spy guy?"

"Elliot?" Ben smiled. "He's paranoid, but given his background, he has reason to be."

"His background?"

"Let's just say he's witnessed backstabbing firsthand."

"As in literal or figurative?" Apparently everyone in Yancey owned a gun, and most she'd seen carrying a knife as well.

Ben chuckled, but there was heartache in it. "Figurative, but, trust me, it's no less painful."

She eyed him curiously. What weight was *he* carrying? "If you don't mind me asking, what happened?"

"That's for Elliot to say, if he chooses."

"No." She shook her head. "I meant with you."

He stopped stoking the fire. "That obvious, huh?"

"Apparently I'm not the only one who's easy to read." She smiled softly wanting to know more about what made the man who'd hijacked her heart tick. What was at the center of Ben McKenna's soul, bumps, bruises, and all?

He sat back, rubbing his hands together—sturdy yet gentle hands she loved holding hers. "Remember you asked why I run fishing excursions?" he said.

"Yeah, you said because you love doing it."

"Yeah. And that's true . . ."

"But . . . ?"

"There's another reason. After receiving my doctorate in Atomic Physics I started at Los Alamos labs."

Her brow pinched. "In New Mexico? The crazy one the atomic bomb guys used to fly in and out of secretly?"

Curiosity danced across his brow. "Don't tell me you're a conspiracy theorist?"

"No. I just read a lot of newspapers while traveling. Some more scandalous in nature than others."

"No . . ." He drew out the word as amusement tinged his lips. Lips that she ached to have pressed again to hers. "Don't tell me."

She leaned back with a bashful shrug. "Enquiring minds."

He laughed, hard.

"All right, Chuckles," she said. "Back to Los Alamos."

"Right." He moved to sit closer to her. His strong, broad shoulder nestled against hers. She certainly wasn't complaining as she leaned into his strength.

"I worked there two years," he continued. "On a team under the tutelage of a man whom I greatly admired, Randolph Hess. He was a father figure to me, especially after my own father passed."

"I sense a *but* coming. . . ."

Ben swiped his nose with a sigh. "One day he stole our team's work and disappeared."

"What?" Her eyes widened.

Ben shook his head, pain etched on his brow. "Rumor was he sold the Soviets our designs and defected to Russia."

"What work? What designs?"

"I specialized in particle physics and worked with the team on a magnetically confined fusion weapon. It had never been done. We were so close to succeeding, but couldn't quite get it to work. The government viewed it as a side project and never gave us the funding we required. If we'd had more time, more resources, maybe, just maybe . . ."

Libby shifted sideways, her knee brushing his muscular thighs. "I don't understand. If your team didn't succeed, then why did he bother stealing the work?"

Ben exhaled. "Randolph once told me it was the closest he'd ever seen a team come. I think when he realized our funding and program was being shut down to shift full focus on nuclear weapons he decided to find someplace else where they'd let him continue with the work."

"And did he?"

"I have no idea, but I've had to live with the fear that he or whomever he sold our designs to in Russia put the funding into it and one day they—if they haven't already—will succeed in making a compact fusion weapon."

"What exactly is the threat of a fusion weapon versus a nuclear one?" Having grown up in the midst of the Cold War, she knew all about the nuclear threat. Air-raid drills during school when they had to climb under their desks and brace for impact. As if a three-by-three desk would provide any protection from a nuclear attack.

"Fusion weapons would be undetectable to our surveillance systems. That's what makes them so dangerous." Ben swallowed, his Adam's apple bobbing in the firelight. "I believed our team was working on something that would help protect our country. Just the threat of a functional fusion weapon would instill a gigantic layer of protection, but after Randolph stole our work . . ."

He shook his head. "His motives don't really matter, but in a weird way, I hope he stole the designs out of love for the project—no matter how horribly misguided—rather than simply for the money. But the entire thing made me sit back and take in the magnitude of what I had been part of, what we had been trying to create. All along a part of me had been terrified we'd become Oppenheimer, but after he disappeared, I finally grasped how disastrous the work could be if placed in the wrong hands. I started to doubt if I'd ever be able to tell who had the wrong hands after how Randolph deceived us all."

"So you left the profession?"

He nodded. "I left and came back to Yancey, where I know folks can be trusted and relied on."

"Have you considered the possibility Randolph didn't steal the project? Maybe someone else did and killed him because he got in the way?" Maybe his mentor hadn't betrayed him and his team.

"Security records indicate Randolph swiped in that night and then out again in fifteen minutes. Neither he nor our team's work have never been found."

"Oh, Ben, I'm so sorry." She wrapped her arms around his sturdy shoulders, embracing him. He leaned into her hold, cupping her face and . . .

A stick cracked behind them.

"Elliot?" Ben turned. "You're usually much more careful. I never hear you coming."

"Please, Benjamin." The man stepped into the clearing. "You're too good and the only one I can't sneak up on, but the stick . . . Just wanted to give you a heads-up to my impending interruption."

Ben smiled softly at Libby. "We appreciate it." He helped her to her feet.

She turned to face the small man—five-six or so, maybe one hundred and forty pounds, silver-streaked brown hair, and round spectacles.

"Elliot, this is—"

"Libby Jennings. I know."

She frowned. "How did . . . ?"

"He knows everyone in town," Ben said.

"Then maybe we should have asked him about the blue highlighted names on Willy's logs."

"Jim already did," Elliot said. "Knew two."

"But the third?" she asked.

"An alias. Haven't heard it around here before. Will take some more digging, but that's not why I'm here."

"No," Ben said, indicating for Libby to hand over Kat's items.

She did. Cap, then watch, then quote.

He studied them for a moment and turned to leave. "I'll be in touch."

"That's it?" Libby said, looking at Ben in confusion.

"Trust me." He took her hand in his. She exhaled, amazed at how quickly Elliot disappeared, blending back in with the night.

■ ■ ■

Libby shut her room door and locked it behind her. Ben checked it was in fact locked from the other side before she heard his footsteps move away. She didn't want him to leave. *Ever.* And while it was exhilarating to experience feelings on such a deep and passionate level so mind-blowingly fast, it was also terrifying—because it would mean taking a gigantic risk. One she wasn't sure her heart was ready to take. She grabbed her journal and hopped on the bed. Ben had tried convincing her to change rooms or to at least bunk with one of her teammates, but since her room had already been ransacked, it seemed highly unlikely it would happen again.

Grabbing a pen, she flipped to the first empty page in her journal and poured out everything stirring inside her heart, along with the events of the day.

The worn leather journal had been everywhere with her this past year. And when she returned to Nevis for Christmas, her parents would no doubt continue the tradition and give her a new one for the coming year.

She lay back wondering what the new year might hold and what role, if any, Ben McKenna would have in it.

■ ■ ■

Libby's eyes fluttered open.

A shadow stood over her—dark and looming.

She struggled to move but couldn't, to scream but only a whimper squeezed through.

Panic set her heart aflame as a sharp pinch pierced her neck, heat flooding through her veins. Everything . . . faded . . . awa—

THIRTEEN

What had she done with it? He'd searched her room again after drugging her to make sure he wasn't interrupted, but nothing.

He shook out his hands, anger flooding his body, surging through him with a mixture of adrenaline and pain. She'd left him no choice but to call it in. Stupid broad.

He lifted the pay phone receiver, gazing at the empty Yancey streets. What a nosy group of people in this little nothing town.

His superior answered on the third ring, and he swallowed hard, praying this didn't get him whacked.

"It wasn't there."

"Are you certain?"

He shifted, hearing something. Once again, he surveyed the streets, but again he found them empty. "Positive," he said, turning his attention back to the call.

"Then where is it?"

He swallowed, his throat constricting. "I don't know."

"She must have stashed it somewhere."

"I already checked the fisherman's boat."

His superior inhaled and released his breath slowly. "Go back. See if the swimmer left any clue where she may have hidden *it*."

"And if not?"

"It may be time to take her."

■ ■ ■

Ben sat on the dock, his feet hovering over the water's edge as the sun rose in the east, the early morning air brisk. He set his coffee mug on the pier beside him and grabbed his Bible, opening to Psalms. He always found solace in David's life. A life full of joys, betrayals, pain, and love. Not a perfect life or a perfect man, but a full life and a man after God's own heart. He longed to be that man.

Please, Father, there is so much to distract. Let this time with you be my solace. Be my and Libby's shelter. I don't know the depths of what's happening here, but it's triggering memories, uncovering old wounds. I pray Kat knew you. And I pray you'll guide Jim through the investigation.

After last night's good-bye, the thought of actually saying a forever good-bye to Libby Jennings hollowed him. It was ridiculous after such short a time. The woman didn't just cross his mind once and again—she'd taken up residence in it.

He couldn't shake her and he had no desire to do so. Thankfully, circumstances aside, they'd be spending more time together. He was counting down the minutes before he could see her. He'd drop by with coffee before her practice, and afterward they could follow up with Elliot. Hopefully his friend would have something. Hopefully there was more to the quote than just words.

FOURTEEN

Libby woke, her lids unbearably heavy, her neck tender. She sat and the room spun. She grabbed her head, closing her eyes and taking a deep breath.

The spinning finally settled—*barely*. She glanced down at the clothes she'd fallen asleep in, shoes and all. Clearly she'd been more exhausted than she'd realized.

She got to her feet, her mind and body woozy.

What a strange nightmare.

A knock thudded on her door, reverberating through her head in pulsating waves.

"Yeah." She swallowed, mouth and throat dry. "Just a sec."

Swaying to the door, she opened it to find Ben.

"Hey," he said, holding up a drink tray with two Styrofoam cups.

"Hey." She braced her weight against the doorframe to stabilize herself.

He frowned. "You okay?"

"Yeah." She turned, moving back into her room. "Just not fully awake yet."

"I brought coffee."

The smell rubbed her wrong.

"You sure you're okay?"

"Yeah, just feeling dizzy."

He studied her carefully. "What happened to your neck?"

"My neck?" She grabbed it to feel and winced at the bruised sensation.

"Yeah." He examined her more closely. "Looks like something bit or *punctured* you."

"Punctured?" Her mind cleared. *No. It couldn't be.*

"What?"

"Nothing. It's just I had this weird dream."

"What kind of dream?"

"Like something stung my neck."

"Maybe we should have Doc Graham take a look."

"It's probably just a bug bite, but . . ." There'd been a shadow of a man standing over her.

"What's going on in that beautiful head of yours?"

That caught her off guard. "You think I'm beautiful?"

"Come on, you know you are. Now, let's go." He took her hand. He was making a habit of that.

"Where?" She grabbed her backpack, never going anywhere without her journal and pen tucked inside.

"Doc Graham's. Something isn't right."

■ ■ ■

Doc Graham finished examining Libby and handed her a cup.

She frowned. "What's this for?"

"Bathroom is that way."

"Are you kidding?"

"Not at all. We need to be certain you haven't been drugged.

SHADOWED

I'm running a blood test, but those take time. Urine will tell us right away."

"Lovely." She hopped down and trudged to the bathroom, leaving the sample with Doc Graham while she got dressed.

She stepped out of the exam room to find Ben waiting in the hall. He was furious at the thought someone might have broken back into her room and drugged her. Concern was still etched on his handsome face. "Doc said to meet him in his office."

"Okay. You coming?"

"You don't mind me being in there?"

"Of course not." She wanted him there.

He smiled and she did the same.

They moved into Doc Graham's office.

"Take a seat," he said, shutting the door.

"Well, Doc?" Ben said before the man could even sit.

"Everyone is so impatient this morning, but in your case I understand. The Russian ambassador acted as if the world was going to end if we didn't release Miss Stanic's body instantly."

"Wait." Libby shook her head, regretting the sudden motion. "The ambassador was already here?"

Ben looked at his watch. "That was quick."

"Like I said, impatient, but the man from the State Department . . ." Doc Graham pulled a card from his pocket and handed it to Libby.

Brandt Dawson.

"He showed up soon after," Doc Graham finished saying.

"And?" Libby asked, clutching the card.

"And he released Miss Stanic's body to the Russians."

"Of course he did." But at least they didn't get Kat's stuff.

"The ambassador inquired about belongings on Kat's person at the time of her death. I told him you'd taken them to send to

218

her family. He said he'd be in touch. If he gives you any trouble, call Mr. Dawson."

Great. She tucked his card in her bag.

"Now to the more important matter at hand. The urine test confirmed my suspicion. You were drugged." He looked at Libby, his eyes brimming with concern and compassion.

"With what?" she asked.

"Rohypnol."

"Someone really *was* in my room last night?" They'd *drugged* her. "They already searched my room once, why come back?"

"Probably thought you had Kat's possessions in your pack," Ben said, clasping her hand, his sturdy fingers engulfing hers in an envelope of protection.

"Thankfully we left them with Elliot," she said.

"Elliot." Ben swallowed. "You didn't happen to write anything about meeting Elliot in your journal, did you?"

"I . . ." *She had.* She wrote everything in it. "But I just said how we met him. You don't think . . . ?"

Had the men who drugged her left a chalk X and gone to the meeting spot pretending to be them?

"We gotta go, Doc." Ben tugged her toward the door, and they raced out of the hospital toward his Jeep.

"I'm so sorry. I didn't think . . ." she said, climbing inside.

"There was no way for you to know." He started the engine, peeling out of the parking lot.

"But Elliot?" she said, fear gripping her. If anything had happened to him because of her. . . .

FIFTEEN

Ben steered his Jeep down the paths that Elliot deemed close enough to roads that led to his cabin deep in the Yancey wilderness.

He'd had the honor of being invited into Elliot's home once and prayed he remembered the right paths of the numerous options to take.

More importantly, he hoped he'd find and overstep any recent booby traps. According to Elliot he switched them out regularly.

Ben slammed to a stop in front of the foliage-covered gate leading to Elliot's property. He got out to open the camouflaged barrier and found the lock busted.

His pulse hitching, Ben swung the gate open and drove over the cattle guard, no doubt triggering the silent alert system he knew Elliot had in place.

Finally reaching the house after a number of switchbacks and hidden drives he pulled to a stop before the silent cabin, an eagle rising from its nest in the tree overhead.

"What's wrong?" Libby asked.

"Elliot greets visitors on the porch with his Remington 700."

Exhaling a steadying breath, concern for his friend's safety surging, he climbed from his Jeep, pulled his .44, and positioned Libby behind his right shoulder.

Moving cautiously toward the door, he stepped over a series of trip wires, indicating for Libby to follow him move by move. She did so, mimicking him perfectly—the two of them so in sync in the strangest of circumstances.

"Elliot," he called, wanting to give his friend a heads-up just in case everything was okay, but he knew in his gut it was far from it. "It's Ben and Libby."

Nothing.

"Elliot?" He rapped on the door and glanced through the front window—what little was visible through the askew shade. The place had been tossed.

Kicking in the door, he wasn't surprised that Elliot's advanced alarm system didn't trigger.

They moved, Ben clearing each room until they reached the kitchen. Elliot lay on the floor, puddles of blood surrounding him.

"Dear God," Libby said.

"Elliot." Ben rushed to his friend's side, kneeling, feeling for a pulse, praying for one.

Thank you, Lord.

"He's alive. Barely. His pulse is very weak. We need to get him to the hospital ASAP."

"Should I call an ambulance?"

He arched a brow.

"Right. No phone. You're an EMT, and there's no way an ambulance is getting back here."

Using supplies from his first-aid kit along with items scavenged from Elliot's, Ben bandaged Elliot's head, arm, and chest wounds. He'd been sliced up. Tortured.

221

Elliot. He shook his head. *Why didn't you just give them what they were looking for?* This was on him. He'd brought his friend into it.

Transporting Elliot to his Jeep and securing him in the backseat with Libby cradling his head, Ben tore back through the woods to the hospital.

■■■

Sitting beside Libby in the waiting room of Yancey Regional Medical Center Elliot's blood still smeared across his clothes, Ben clenched his fists tight. What was so vitally important in Kat's meager belongings they were worth a man's life? It made no sense, but then again, most of the world didn't.

Please, Father, don't let Elliot die.

His prayer was short, but it came from the depths of his soul—a plea God would spare his friend's life.

Doc Graham rounded the corner, and Ben lurched to his feet, Libby doing so beside him.

"We've got the bleeding to stop and have begun transfusions. He lost a lot of blood." Doc Graham shook his head. "It's a miracle he survived."

Thank you, Jesus.

"So he'll be okay?" Libby asked.

"I believe so, but we can't be certain until he regains consciousness."

Libby sank back in the chair. "I'm so sorry. I never should have written . . ." She shook her head, tears tumbling down her cheeks.

"Hey." Ben sat beside her, pulling her into his arms. "You couldn't have known. They"—whoever *they* were—"did this to Elliot. Not you." *He* was the one who'd brought Elliot into this. Not her.

222

"I suppose they got what they wanted," she said as Agnes Grey rounded the corner.

"I just heard about Elliot." Agnes shook her head. "I can't believe it. We just spoke last night."

Ben frowned. "Last night?"

"Yes. He showed up banging on my door at midnight. Highly improper, but that's Elliot."

"What did he say? What did he want?"

She looked around the waiting room, empty save for the three of them, now that Doc had departed. She closed the door and sat, lowering her voice. "He said he figured out the quote was actually a microdot communication."

Libby frowned. "What's a microdot communication?"

"It's a method spies use to convey information through text or an image substantially reduced in size." Ben explained. "Like the size of a period at the end of the quote, for example. The recipient then needs to use a special microdot reader to detect the hidden information."

So Kat *had* been spying. Question was, for which side?

"Elliot said it was an older version of microdot communication. He needed a Russian WWII reader and asked if I could call on my antique contacts and suppliers in Russia. Told me to say it was for a buyer who'd come in the shop. I made some calls this morning. I went to leave Elliot a message but heard on the way to the mailbox that you'd brought him here." She smiled and shrugged. "Thelma Jenkins."

Ben grimaced. "No surprise there, but I am glad she sent you to us."

"They may have Kat's quote, but it doesn't mean they know what it is," Libby said.

"If we're dealing with the kind of people I believe we are, trust me, they know." Ben raked a hand through his hair.

"*They*, whoever *they* are," Agnes said, "don't have the quote."

"What?"

"Elliot gave me the watch to return to you. He didn't believe it was damaged in the ocean. He thinks whoever killed Kat thought whatever information is on that coded slip of paper was actually being stored on a microchip in the watch. He believes it was a decoy in case Kat felt threatened."

"So, they thought they had what they needed and killed her?"

"Yeah, probably learning after it was too late that she'd faked them out," Ben said. *Good for Kat.*

"And the quote?" Libby asked.

"Elliot put it in the cap, had me sew it back in, and said he was going to hide it someplace safe," she explained.

"Did he say where?"

"Not outright. We both know that's not Elliot's style."

"Of course not. That would make it easy."

"He did, however, say that it was at one of your coffee spots. That way if anything happened to him, you'd know where to look."

"How did he know someone might come after him?" Libby asked. "He couldn't know I'd write it in my journal, could he?"

"Nah. He knew because he understood what he was dealing with."

"A spy communication?" she asked.

"Yes." Ben nodded.

Libby rubbed her arms. "Now the question is, which side was she spying for?"

His thoughts exactly.

Doc Graham ducked his head around the corner. "Elliot's still unconscious, but I wanted to let you know that his vitals are improving."

"Thanks, Doc," Ben said.

Agnes set her bag on the side table, taking a seat. "I'd say you two should get started with coffee spots. I put some supplies in the back of your Jeep on my way in."

"But Elliot . . ." Ben said, not wanting to leave his friend.

"I'll stay here," Agnes assured him.

"But—"

"You know he'd want you protecting the communication, not sitting here worrying about him."

She had him there.

SIXTEEN

Libby nearly skipped behind Ben as they moved for the rock formation overlooking Yancey's western shore where, according to Ben, he and Elliot shared coffee occasionally. They'd already checked the diner, much to everyone's amusement, ducking under their "usual booth" to look. It'd been closed when Elliot would have stashed it, but a locked door was no deterrent to a man of Elliot's skills. They'd checked Ben's boat, but Ben would have heard Elliot board last night. Then the park bench in town. According to Ben's recollection this was the final coffee location.

While reverently keeping Elliot in prayer, she still couldn't help but enjoy the thrill of the hunt. She'd never been on an adventure like this nor shared one with a man like Ben.

What was it about him that pulled her to love him so? He drew her as the ocean did—on a primal, inexplicable level that she attributed fully to God's innate makeup of her. Was Ben the man God had planned for her? The idea she would feel so close to him after so short a time together was ludicrous, yet it anchored in her and held fast.

I'm gonna look fully to you on this one, Lord. It makes no sense to me, but your ways are not my ways, nor are your thoughts my thoughts. Maybe I'm just overcome by the depth of all that's happened, maybe I'm just caught up in the intensity of the moment, but I've never felt more at home, not even in the water. What does that mean?

Ben examined the perimeter of the boulder where he and Elliot had sometimes sat, searching crevices, and then moved a second time around more impatiently, and then a third time in flat-out frustration.

"It's not here," he finally said.

She hated to say it, but . . . "Do you think the men who tortured Elliot got the location out of him and beat us here?"

"Elliot wouldn't talk."

"How do you know?"

"I know Elliot. Know his background. He'd never talk. Trust me."

"Even under torture?"

"Even under torture. I'm confident."

"I need to have a chat with Elliot when he wakes. Sounds like he has an intriguing past."

"If you only knew the half of it. Actually, that's probably all I know. He's a man of many secrets and one great heart."

"Okay, then we're missing a place."

"I'm telling you those are our spots."

"You never met anywhere else? Not once? Not someplace for a special occasion or something?"

Ben snapped. "Ahh. I can't believe I forgot. You," he said, bracing a hand on either of her shoulders, "are a genius." He bent in and kissed her until she went goofy in the knees, then pulled back with a smile and stepped back to the trail they'd taken to the overlook. "You coming?"

"Dare I ask where?"

"You'll see." His smile broadened. "And I'm so glad I get to show you."

Intrigue flickered inside, among other things. Ben McKenna was unlike any man she'd ever met. Not so much his individual traits, but the unique combination of them, along with his thirst for adventure and soulful depth. He was a man of character, and if the '70s had taught her anything, it was that men of substance were rare.

She held on to the Jeep's grip handle, bracing herself as they bounced through woods, across rushing riverbeds and along marshes with reeds taller than his vehicle. Where was he taking her, and would she be able to contain the joyful laughter bubbling to erupt from her throat? She hadn't had this much fun since . . . she couldn't remember when. If only she knew with certainty Elliot would pull through, but God's soft voice whispered His assurance to her that Elliot would be okay. She relaxed in that.

Ben crashed through another stream, cool water spraying across the Jeep's hood in a fanlike pattern. He looked over with a playful grin, and she broke out laughing, unable to suppress the joy of the moment any longer. He burst out laughing in chorus with her.

■ ■ ■

"Where are they?"

He cleared his throat. "I lost them."

"We're on a bloody island. How exactly could you *lose* them?"

"They took off in his Jeep on terrain I couldn't maneuver in the rental car. Not without the risk of getting stuck and drawing unwanted attention."

"Why did they head off road? Do you think they spotted you?"

"No. I'm sure they didn't. They've been driving all over the island, clearly with a purpose in mind."

"You think that crazy man hid it out in the Alaskan wilderness? Is that why we couldn't find Kat's things at his place?"

"Yes. It's looking that way."

"All right. Hang back where you lost them and pick up their trail when they appear. They've got to exit the woods at some point. Intercept if it's remote enough not to draw attention. This has gone on long enough. We need to find out if they have it on them."

"And if not? I'll have blown my cover."

"Then kill them, but try to make this one actually look like an accident."

"How was I supposed to know anyone would find her body all the way out there or that anyone in this joke of a town wouldn't simply assume the stupid woman had drowned."

"You know I'm not a man for excuses. Just get it taken care of, once and for all."

■ ■ ■

Ben pulled to a stop a hundred yards from the southwest coast of the island.

Libby jumped down from the Jeep before Ben could offer his hand.

She surveyed the white-sand-and-rock-strewn beach, dune grass swaying in the warming afternoon breeze. Evergreen trees surrounded an open parcel of land with four stakes marking a perimeter—but of what?

"What is this place?" she asked as the scent of salt water drifted on the breeze, ruffling her hair, soothing her senses, as it always did.

Ben rested his hand on his hips, his eyes gazing over the land. "My home."

She frowned. "I thought you lived on your boat?"

"I do, for now. But I purchased this acreage and plan to build a house right there." He indicated the staked-out area.

So that's where Ben McKenna's future home would sit. She wondered what it would look like and who would one day share it with him, and her heart ached in a way it never had before.

"Let me show you." He guided her along the property, or at least a portion of the acreage, pointing out what he loved about it and what he envisioned.

"Aren't you going to miss the *Waves*?" He loved his boat.

"I'm not leaving her behind. Building her a slip and dock right there." He pointed to a spot he'd picked out on the deeper end of the shore.

"It's beautiful."

"Thanks, but I suppose we better get back to the task at hand."

"Right. Where did you and Elliot sit when you had coffee here?"

"He helped me stake out the house, and then we toasted over it with coffee square in the center of the pegs, talking about the day the work would be finished, the house built and the view we'd have from the porch for our future coffee meet-ups."

They moved to the staked-out area.

"Cozy house size."

"It's just me," he said, examining the ground for signs of disturbance, then looked up at her with eyes tinged with hope, "for now."

Somehow she knew he wasn't talking in general terms, not with how he held her gaze, not with the hope and longing lingering there. Excitement and terror danced a jig in her gut.

Being the chicken that she was when it came to relationships, she indicated the ground. "Anything?"

"You tell me?"

Were they really about to have *this* conversation? Her mouth went dry, the moisture shifting to her clammy palms.

He moved toward her, but his gaze momentarily flickered to the far right peg.

"What?"

"We staked these nearly a month ago." He spun, examining the other three. "But this one . . ." He strode toward the peg, kneeling beside it. "The ground's been recently disturbed." He pulled the trowel he'd been carrying in his jacket pocket in case any digging was required and set to work. A foot down the tip of his trowel dinged off something metal. Digging around the edges of the object and using the trowel as a lever, he lifted a metal box from the hole.

"It's got a combination lock. Elliot . . ." He shook his head with a sigh. "Why would I expect anything less?"

"Agnes said he purposely hid Kat's items someplace you'd know how to find so it stands to reason he made the combination something you'd be able to figure out."

"It's got four numbers."

"An address?"

He shook his head. "I don't think so. Yancey's addresses consist of three numbers, at least for now."

"The year?"

He tried 1979. "Nope."

"Okay, how about a date? Your birthday, perhaps. Month, day, last two digits of the year?" she suggested.

"May 31st, 1943."

They tried various combinations of the date, but no luck.

"What's your birthday?" he asked.

"How could Elliot possibly know my birthday?"

"You'd be amazed what Elliot knows."

"July 16th, 1948."

"Ah, a younger woman. Nice."

"Yeah, a whole whopping five years."

"We'll have to celebrate your birthday if you're still in town."

The comment hung heavy between them. She was supposed to be gone, but she didn't have another tournament until mid-August, so technically she could stay, but was this worth taking a chance on and spending more time to see where it would lead? Her heart and soul abundantly replied *yes*. But how did Ben feel?

She watched again as he tried various combinations, but again no luck.

"What about something to do with the place Elliot hid the box?"

"My home site?"

"Do you remember the date you toasted with coffee?"

"Yeah, it was the day I became the legal owner of the land. Elliot met me out here and helped me stake out the house. 6-7-7-9."

The box opened, and there sat Kat's cap, resewn. She ran her hand over it, feeling the quote tucked back inside, just as Agnes had said.

"Thank you, Elliot," Ben said.

"Ready to go?" she asked, standing.

"We haven't eaten all day. Agnes said she put a basket of food in the back of my Jeep on her way into the hospital. Something to tide us over on our hunt. I'm going to grab it. We're going to eat and then we'll head back."

She should have known he wouldn't let her off that easy.

She nodded, famished, but unsure of where the conversation might lead.

Ben pulled a picnic basket complete with wool plaid blanket from his Jeep.

She helped him spread out the blanket and squatted on it, him doing the same.

He opened the basket and doled out the food. Ham and Swiss sandwiches with mustard on Wonder Bread, Charles Chips, grapes, and Oreos. Along with a thermos of Tang and two cups.

"She thought of everything," Libby said, taking a sip of the orange beverage.

"She usually does. Just like my mom."

"You said your dad passed. Your mom still living?"

"Going strong. She's an amazing lady."

"Does she live nearby?"

"In the home I grew up in, just north of downtown."

"So you get to see her often?"

"Every Sunday at church and afterwards for supper. Plus I drop by once in a while during the week. Just to check in on her."

"That's sweet."

"She deserves the best." He brushed her hair over her shoulder, cupping her neck. "So do you."

She swallowed, her natural instinct to squash the intensity of the emotions swelling inside. "It's really beautiful here," she sputtered. "I'm sure the *Waves* will like its new home." She shifted to sit cross-legged, trying to settle the overwhelming rush coursing through her from his statement, from the depth of love in his eyes. What was she doing? Why was she so afraid to admit she'd fallen in love with him? "You never explained the meaning behind its name."

He smiled at her less than subtle diversion to change the subject and said, "Matthew 14:28–31."

She thought for a moment. "Peter walking on the water to Jesus?"

"Correct. If he'd kept his eyes on his Savior . . ."

"He'd have walked on the waves." Was God calling her to take that first step? Her soul cried "Yes!"

"Right," Ben said, draping his arm over his bent knee. "This world has tossed some pretty ugly things and giant waves at me, and yet God has given me the sea to soothe my soul. It's where He brings me peace. I glide over it, keeping my eyes on Him, and everything that matters comes into focus. How about you?"

"How about me, what?"

"Why do you love the water so? How'd you get started swimming?"

"My dad's a tennis pro, so we moved around a lot when I was a kid. From resort to resort, in the Caribbean, mostly."

"Sounds exciting and hard."

"Yes, it was both. When I was seven we moved from Jamaica to a small—and I mean small—Caribbean island off St. Kitts called Nevis."

"Nevis. I haven't heard of it."

"Most people haven't. I'm an only child; my dad was busy with work, my mom living the resort lifestyle, as they housed us on resort property. She spent her days at the pool and helping keep all the visitors happy."

"Sounds like it could get pretty lonely for a kid."

"It did, but the resort swim instructor took pity on me and gave me a lesson one day. After that, I was hooked. She started training me. I was in the water more than I was out, shifting from the pool to the ocean quickly. I began competing in island competitions when I was ten and internationally at twelve. Been going strong ever since."

"That's been the majority of your life. How will you feel when it's time to stop competing?"

"I've been thinking a lot about that since Kat announced her retirement. We are the same age. Were. Competing at this level takes its toll, and competing against sixteen-year-olds is becoming tougher and tougher. I think next season will be my last."

"Then what?"

"I don't know." She smiled, suddenly not so afraid. "Maybe I'll just have to keep coming back here so we can continue our verbal jousts."

He looked her in the eye, the depth of his heart wading in them. "I'd like that very much."

So would she. "Maybe it's time I pick one sea to settle in." Take that leap of faith.

Hope he hadn't felt in years flickered in Ben's heart. "What would it take for that to happen? For a mermaid with wings to settle in one sea?"

"God's leading."

He couldn't argue with that. "Could you ever see yourself in a place like Yancey?" *With a man like me?*

"Yancey seems like a great place to live, with great people." She looked around. "I could see this being a great home."

He told himself she was probably talking in generalities, that she may have no leading from God yet. He knew she might never return to Yancey, but the hope her words inspired welled inside.

She blinked as he stared at her, realizing how badly he wanted her to stay. The thought of never seeing her again stole his breath away.

He cupped her face, caressing her cheek, and pressed his lips to hers, letting his kiss say it all.

All thought vaporized as she kissed him back just as passionately, near desperation binding them together, molding them into this single moment where their futures teetered on what choices would be made next.

The rain that had been threatening for the last half hour let loose. With massive restraint Ben pulled back, his breath heavy. "I better get you in the Jeep."

She yanked him back, her full, soft lips a breath from his. "I live in the water. A little rain isn't going to bother me."

Man, I love this woman.

Time passed, but eventually he managed to draw back. "Please let me get you someplace dry. I don't want you catching a chill."

"Okay." She clutched the metal box in one hand and his hand in the other as they raced for the Jeep, pools of water littering their path.

He situated her in the Jeep and walked around, climbing in his side, drenched.

He grabbed the blanket he always kept in the Jeep, wrapping it snugly around her, and cranked up the heat. "Buckle up tight. We have to go back a different route. The riverbeds are no doubt flooded by now."

■ ■ ■

He waited in the pouring rain, impatiently searching for headlights, his plan fixed and ready to execute. He'd had Alexi run him the necessary supplies.

Finally, after what seemed like hours of waiting, headlights appeared in the blurry distance. He watched the Jeep curving down the winding road, wrapping around the trees rather than through them. They'd taken the road back. All the better.

He rolled down the window, set up his shot, and waited for the perfect moment, firing twice.

The Jeep swerved, flipped across the road in front of him, and careened over the edge of the ravine.

Making sure the coast was clear, he stepped out and peered over the edge to be certain there was no movement.

Now time to ensure it looked like an accident. He grabbed his knife, gas container, and lighter. There was about to be an unfortunate explosion. If they had the code it would burn with them.

SEVENTEEN

Ben and Libby had just crossed back into Yancey proper when a search and rescue call came in over Ben's portable shortwave radio.

"It's Jim. We've got a bad one off Gentry Road."

"Be there in ten." Ben pulled a U-turn, heading back toward the city's outer limits.

"Gentry Road." Libby frowned. "Isn't that where we headed off road to your property?"

He swallowed. "Yeah."

"I guess it's good we came back another way. That could have been us."

His thoughts exactly.

Jim was already on site when they arrived, smoke funneling up the ravine in the now misting rain.

"It's a bad one," Jim said as Ben and Libby approached. He tilted his head at the older gentleman standing beside his patrol car—the man who'd be Ben's closest neighbor once he moved. "Wilkinson heard the explosion, and he and Ellen came out to check. He sent her back to the house to call it in."

"Speaking of . . ." Ben tilted *his* head at the approaching car with Miss Ellen inside.

"Darling," Fred Wilkinson said, moving toward his wife as she approached. "I told you I'd get a ride back. I don't want you to see this."

"I want to help if I can."

"Thanks, ma'am, but we've got it," Jim said.

"The rest of SAR are on their way," Ben said, having called the two men he'd trained—Tony and Jason.

"Fire truck and ambulance are en route," Jim added.

"Come on, Ellen." Fred wrapped his arm around her shoulder. "Let's get out of their way so they can do their job."

"You call if you need anything, Jimmy, you hear?" Ellen said as Fred opened the car door for her.

"Thanks, Miss Ellen. Will do."

"What do we got?" Ben asked, looking over the ravine at the Jeep on its topside, a fire still ablaze despite the rain.

"We need to get the fire out. Then we'll send you down."

"The fire hasn't reached the passenger compartment yet. You know it'll be too late if we wait."

"It's skirting it."

Ben moved for his Jeep and his harness.

"What are you doing?" Libby asked.

"Going down."

"But Jim just said—"

"If anyone managed to survive that wreck, I'm not going to let them burn to death when I can intervene."

"Take this," Jim said, helping him latch a fire extinguisher to his pack.

Ben's SAR crew arrived, and they and Deputy Tom Miller lowered him down.

The fire-truck sirens whirred in the distance.

The flames danced closer to the front cabin.

"Faster," he hollered up.

His feet touched the outcrop the Jeep had landed on.

Unsnapping the harness he moved to the driver's side and blinked in horror at the gunshot wound to the driver's head.

■ ■ ■

"I can't believe someone shot them," Libby said.

"We'd never have known if the fire had spread faster. We need to thank God for the rain," Ben said.

"Why would someone shoot the—?" Libby's question died as the realization hit. A Jeep similar in color to Ben's, two people up front, coming around the road right by where they'd entered the woods. Her limbs trembled. "That was meant for us."

Ben pulled her in his arms, holding her tight—as close to his heart as possible. She could feel it thudding through his still-soaked T-shirt.

EIGHTEEN

Libby couldn't stop shivering—not from the rain, as Ben kept scolding himself for not getting her out of the elements sooner, but rather from the stark realization they were the intended targets.

If they hadn't taken a different way back . . .

And it broke her heart to think of the poor tourists who'd been in the wrong rental Jeep, on the wrong road, at the wrong time.

Her heart squeezed, choking the breath from her lungs. Everything was so far out of control she struggled for purchase, for an anchor despite the raging waves crashing over them. And thanks to Ben's earlier words, she knew exactly Whom to go to.

Ben reached over, clasping her hand as they drove back to town and to the hospital.

She closed her eyes seeking, desperately needing, her Savior.

Father, I can only look to you. I don't understand why all this happened, but I thank you for sparing us from death today. I pray for the souls of the couple who died, pray they knew you.

She gripped Ben's hand tightly.

And I thank you for this man you have blessed me with to help carry me through deeper waters than I could have ever imagined battling.

■ ■ ■

Reaching the hospital, they learned Elliot was improving but still hadn't woken for more than a few seconds of fluttering eyes and jerky movements at a time. Doc Graham said it was a good sign, but Ben would only breathe a sigh of relief when his friend fully awakened.

He and Libby were set for the night in a room down the hall. Two beds and a privacy curtain between them. His gun handy and Deputy Tom stationed outside the door.

Libby thought it overkill and had expressed as much, but when it came to her safety Ben wasn't taking any chances. He'd keep her safe or die trying.

She paced the tile floor, back and forth past the beds, desk, and small faux leather green sofa. At least the hospital administration had given them the biggest room available upon Doc Graham's request.

"How soon did Agnes say she'd have the reader?"

"Tomorrow evening at the latest. She'll call as soon as she does. In the meantime we sit tight."

"I hate sitting tight."

He hopped back on the bed, kicking off his shoes and stretching his arms behind his head. "It's the safest thing, so you might as well get comfortable."

"Fine." She took her shoes off. "But I'm not missing the race tomorrow morning."

Ben sat stock straight. "You can't seriously be considering going out there. Someone is trying to kill us."

"I didn't come all this way to quit. Besides I highly doubt

they'll do anything in front of dozens of swimmers, all the coaching staff and support vessels."

"You can't take that risk."

"I'm not letting them cage me up when they are the monsters." She shook out her hands. "I need to get in the water. It's my home."

He exhaled. It was her grounding. Boy, how he got that, but her safety was too important.

"'When a McKenna sets his mind to something,'" she said. "You're not the only one people say that about."

NINETEEN

Libby sliced through the frigid water, her limbs burning and weak . . . so weak after a dozen miles. Two to go.

One, two, three. Rolling her head to the side, she inhaled and then back into the deep, dark blue water, bubbles fizzing around her on the exhale.

Her wet suit clung to her like a second skin, but the forty-two-degree water seeped through, burrowing into her bones.

Just swim.

They can't catch you if you keep moving.

Her lungs burned—ice shards stabbing her chest, each breath torturous, but she had to keep going.

She was surrounded by swimmers, but had one of them been sent to kill her?

■■■

From her training boat, Ben watched every stroke Libby took, his heart in his throat. He understood her desire to race, to be back in the water, but if anything happened to her . . .

He gripped the boat rail, watching as she rhythmically turned her head every three strokes to inhale, and then back in the water. She was a thing of beauty to watch. He'd fallen in love with a mermaid.

Deputy Tom had joined him on the boat to watch everyone else while he focused on Libby, Sheriff Jim remaining with the crowd on shore.

The killer was here. He felt it as sure as the breath in his lungs. Anticipation riddled through him. When would he strike and from where? The water, one of the boats, or from land?

■ ■ ■

Breathing through the regulator he moved under the water, his target fixed twenty feet above and slightly ahead.

He'd maintain his distance until the shoals, where the training boats had to maneuver around rather than through. Another ten feet and he'd have her.

■ ■ ■

Libby wove her way through the shallow depths of the shoals gliding over shadows of rocks beneath.

It was the most direct path for the swimmers and a beautiful section before they reached the last two-mile stretch of the race.

The shoals being too shallow for the support vessels, they maneuvered around the outskirts, passing through the deeper waters a hundred or so feet to her starboard.

She knew Ben had to be panicking at the distance but with binoculars he could still see her clearly, and the sequestered section of the shallow waters and narrow swimming field made her feel safer than she had in the wide open.

One, two, three. She rolled her head as something clamped hard around her ankle, tugging her down, the motion too swift for her to utter a scream before plunging beneath the surface.

Down into the blue.

She flailed, fighting whatever or whomever was dragging her down.

Water swooshed around her, the person's hands grabbing higher up along her waist.

He pulled her down, her back to him, his strong arms engulfing her in a bear hug, pinning her arms to her side.

Panic set in.

Please, Father, don't let me die.

She kicked, fighting the urge to take in air, but he held her down, his arms clamped tightly around her.

■ ■ ■

Where is she? Panic seared through Ben as he lost visual on Libby.

One moment she was gliding through the water, the next she was gone.

"There are so many swimmers, how can you tell?" Tom asked as Ben yanked his shirt over his head and kicked off his shoes. "What are you doing?"

Ben handed him his .44. At least he still had his knife. "Hold this for me. I'm going in." Before Tom could argue, Ben grabbed a spare pair of goggles from the deck, climbed over the rail, and dropped in. The water was cold, his limbs searing with adrenaline. He fitted the goggles in place, clearing out the water, and swam with all his might toward where he'd last seen Libby.

Please, God, I know something is wrong. Protect her.

■ ■ ■

Libby squirmed. Fought. Kicked. But she couldn't break free. She was suffocating.

She needed air, needed to breathe, needed to surface, but he held her fast as darkness closed in around her.

Her limbs grew heavy, her movements slowing. All she could think was she'd never see Ben again.

She slipped away.

TWENTY

Ben frantically searched the shoals, fear and despair choke-holding him. Finally he spotted her, limp beneath the surface, a scuba diver's arms locked around her.

He approached from behind, knife in hand, and sliced the diver's regulator hose, then jammed his knife into the back of the man's thigh. Air bubbles and blood pooled in the water, and the man released Libby. Ben grabbed hold of her; wrapping his arm around her waist, cradling her back against his chest as he swam toward the light.

Breaching the surface, he hollered, waving frantically for help.

Getting Tom's attention, he lay back, focusing on Libby. Moving the hair from her face, he cleared her airway. Her cheeks were cold, her lips blue. He started mouth-to-mouth as rescue rafts lowered from the support vessels, moving quickly for them.

"Come on, baby," Ben said.

Hauling her into the raft, he began full CPR, sending Tom and one of the trainers into the water after the man.

Please, God, don't take her from me.

"Come on, Lib." He pumped her chest. "Come on."

She coughed, spurting up water, and he rolled her onto her side, helping clear the water from her lungs.

Thank you, Jesus.

He pulled her into his arms.

Tom and the trainer surfaced, the man wrestling in their hold.

Ben aimed the .44 Tom had brought in the raft with him at the man. "Get in the boat or I shoot you *now*."

They pulled him on board, his thigh bleeding.

The trainer moved to bind it as Tom bound the man's hands, then removed his mask.

Libby's eyes widened. "Rick?"

Shock raked through Ben. "You know him?"

She squinted, shaking her head in dismay. "He was Kat's college boyfriend."

■ ■ ■

Refusing to answer any questions, he was taken back to shore, where he would no doubt meet his death.

He'd screwed up one too many times—losing Ben and Libby in the woods, shooting the wrong Jeep, and now failing to kill Libby and exposing his identity, or at least one of his aliases.

He was a dead man. It was only a matter of time.

"I don't understand," Libby kept saying. "Why are you here? Did *you* kill Kat? Were you her lurker?"

She didn't get it. Being Kat's boyfriend was his cover, or it had been until Kat screwed up and got pulled out of Berkeley and the States.

He'd been part of the team that had extracted. The way Kat looked at him when she realized the truth of his role . . . If he'd had a heart, that would have broken it.

He was still her watcher, still had to follow her around, but she ignored him, even with her dying breath had refused to look at him.

"Who do we have here?" the sheriff asked as the deputy handed him over.

A *thwack* sounded and everything disappeared.

■ ■ ■

"Get down," Ben hollered, dropping to the ground, covering Libby as the shot killed Rick, or whoever he was, instantly.

"Sniper," Tom called, and panic ensued, everyone screaming and racing for cover.

Ben shuffled Libby behind the boathouse, shielding her from the direction the initial shot had come.

They waited, breaths labored, hands clutching.

He spotted Jim making a wide sweep of the perimeter, Tom moving in from the other side.

Twenty anxious, silent minutes later Jim and Tom returned.

"No sign of the shooter. No shells left behind. Nothing," Jim said.

■ ■ ■

Libby sat numbly in the chair at the sheriff's station as Ben handed her a cup of tea.

Her thoughts were so tangled. Why had Rick been there? Who'd killed him? And who'd killed Kat?

Agnes Grey bounded inside. "It's here."

They hunkered in Jim's office as Agnes pulled out the microdot reader and Ben pulled the quote from Jim's safe, where they'd stashed it before the race.

"Do you know how to use one of those?" Ben asked Agnes.

"No, but I know who can."

"But Elliot—"

"Woke up this morning," Agnes said with a smile.

Ten minutes later they were huddled in Elliot's room with Tom stationed outside the door.

Elliot placed the slip of silk in the reader. "It's a set of numbers," he said.

"Numbers?" Libby frowned.

"5779261473941," Elliot read.

"A phone number?" she asked.

Ben shook his head. "I think it's too long."

"Even with an international exchange?" Libby asked.

"Russia's exchange is 7," Elliot said.

"Whose is 5?" she asked.

Elliot thought a moment. "Colombia."

"Okay, so probably not a phone number," she said.

"Bank routing number?" Ben suggested.

"Perhaps," Elliot said.

"Let's write them out." Libby grabbed her journal from her pack. "I always think better when I can see something."

Elliot read off the numbers again and Libby wrote them down, separating the two sections where Elliot denoted a brief pause this time.

It took a little while, but then it hit her. "What about coordinates?"

Ben smiled. "Brilliant. I can't believe I didn't see that sooner." He studied them, working out latitude and longitude, and discovered it led them to Yancey's post office.

Within minutes they stood out front—Ben, Libby, and Jim.

Ben shook his head. "You've got to be kidding."

"You have Kat's picture?" Libby asked Jim.

"Yep."

Jim showed Kat's photo to the postmaster, and he recognized her as having rented a P.O. box upon arriving in town. Fortunately he had a master key.

Opening the box they found a file.

Ben flipped through it.

"Please explain what I'm seeing?" Libby asked.

"Back at the station," he said, realizing the horrific scope of what he was looking at.

Once there, he interpreted the files. "It's evidence the Soviets have accomplished constructing what appears to be a vast number of suitcase bombs, they are planning to smuggle into the U.S. and detonate at key strategic locations."

"Planning?" Libby said. "So they aren't already here?"

"I pray not, or we're looking at a terrorist attack beyond imagining."

"What do we do?"

"Call the State Department."

Libby pulled the card Doc Graham had given her from the State Department for Brandt Dawson, the agent who'd arrived in town after Kat's death.

"I'll call him," Ben said.

"So Kat was trying to defect to the U.S. and brought intel so vital that the U.S. would have risked upsetting the Russians by letting one of their star athletes defect," Libby said. "I can't believe Brezhnev just signed the SALT II treaty with Carter when all the while they had this planned."

"Politics and spies—both nasty," Ben said.

TWENTY-ONE

The meet was set with Brandt Dawson from the State Department at the Yancey airstrip.

Ben couldn't help but feel his past had come back to haunt him as they approached the airstrip. The suitcase bombs weren't made of fusion weapons, but the compact size and theory behind them was frighteningly similar to the nature of what he'd worked on.

He thanked God that Kat had managed to get ahold of the Russians' plans and that they'd be turned over to the authorities. He prayed they'd be able to thwart the plans and nothing so disastrous would ever be launched against the country he loved. He might not love the politics at play, but he loved his country.

The sun was full and bright, the air reaching a warm seventy degrees as the plane touched down.

They waited as it taxied to a stop, the cabin door opened, and the stairs folded down.

A man ducked his head out and signaled for them to come aboard.

Jim entered first, then Ben, and finally Libby.

The twelve-seater plane was impressive—leather seats, cocktail tables between the various groupings, a lavatory and rear compartment. Seemed too nice a plane for a government official to travel in, but maybe he had special ties. Or maybe the government had determined this handoff to be important enough they'd given him whatever he needed to get there as fast as possible.

"Please, take a seat," Brandt said. "I owe you a great debt."

The cabin door shut, and Ben looked up to find a second man standing beside it, gun in hand. "As does my country," he said with a thick Russian accent.

"This is Alexi," Brandt said, gesturing toward the man. "My Russian counterpart."

Libby's eyes narrowed. "I don't understand."

"I'll take those." Brandt pulled the file from Jim's hand as Alexi aimed the gun at Libby's head.

A turncoat agent. Disgust burned through Ben's veins. How on earth was he going to get Libby safely out of this scenario? He tried the best play he had. "You have what you want, so we'll be leaving now."

"So you can tell the world what you uncovered and expose my identity," Brandt said, pulling a gun of his own. "I think not. Kat tried that, and look where it got her."

"She called you for help in defecting and you turned on her," Libby said, outrage burning in her voice.

"I killed her. I *turned*, as you call it, decades ago."

"And now?" Libby swallowed, her panicked gaze flashing to Ben.

"Now," Brandt said. "We need you three to disappear."

Libby scooted forward on the leather seat. "People know we are here."

"So what? They'll assume the big, bad Russians got you before you could reach me," Brandt said. "I'll play the sorrowful American agent mourning your loss."

Ben inched his hand toward his weapon.

"Uh-uh," Alexi said, yanking Libby from her seat and pressing the muzzle to her temple. "Hand it over." He looked to Jim. "You too."

Brandt collected their guns. "Let's get this bird in the air," he said to Alexi. "We'll drop them off over the ocean somewhere. Unlike Kat whose death Dmitri screwed up, you three will never be found."

"Dmitri?" Libby said. "Oh, you mean Rick?"

Brandt chuckled. "So you figured that out, but as you saw, 'Rick' outlived his usefulness."

"You're a monster," Libby spat.

"Perhaps, but I'm a very well-paid one." He indicated for Alexi to release Libby and head to the cockpit. "I've got it from here."

Alexi shoved Libby toward her seat as he moved for the cockpit. Ben kicked his leg out, tripping her. Brandt's gaze shifted momentarily, but long enough for Ben to lunge forward, knife drawn, stabbing Brandt in the chest.

Ben used Brandt as a shield, wrestling his weapon from him, aiming and firing at Alexi as he turned.

Alexi stumbled back and his gun fired, the bullet hitting Jim in the shoulder as he pulled Libby behind the seat in front of him.

Ben fired again, and Alexi dropped.

■ ■ ■

Libby sat on the back of the open ambulance, a blanket draped over her despite the warmer temps, her mind still scrambling to process everything that had happened.

Ben stashed the folder in the back of his pants, flipping his shirt over it until they could hand it over to the proper authorities.

"How will we know who we can trust?" She shook her head. "So many people weren't who they seemed. So many let Kat down, me included. How am I going to live with that?"

"You didn't know. You couldn't have."

"But I—"

"If this entire crazy situation has taught me anything, it's that you can't wade in the past. If you do you'll eventually drown. I didn't realize it, but I was drowning until I met you. Letting the past consume and jade me. I can't control the outcome of what happened in the past, and I certainly can't control the future. That's God's place." He cupped her face in his hands. "God has reminded me again that while there are bad people, there are plenty of good ones. Yancey is full of them. People you can trust with your life. And you can trust me with yours. You know that, right?"

She leaned into his hold. "I do."

"Ah, Libby . . ." He caressed her cheek. "I meant what I said. I was drowning until you came. You reminded me to keep my gaze above the waves. Now, give this burden you're carrying to Jesus, let Him carry it so you can walk on the water."

She clutched his hand in hers. "Only if you're by my side."

Epilogue

B en sat by Libby at the fire pit he'd built for them to enjoy while he continued working on his house. It was framed, paneled, and shingled. The only remaining work was on the inside. By spring it would be ready to move in to.

Libby had remained in Yancey until her next tournament and then returned at the end of September when her season was over. They'd spent the last three months inseparable, and he never wanted that to end.

He reached in his pocket and hooked his finger around the ring.

Libby lay against his chest, a thick wool blanket beneath them and another above as the fire crackled at their feet. It was too cold to remain out long, but this was where he wanted to propose—her curled up in his arms, the flames dancing along her skin, illuminating her blond hair much as the lantern had their first night together in the storm.

God had brought them through more than one gigantic

storm, and he'd face a thousand more as long as she was at his side.

He pulled the ring out and her eyes widened. "I guess I better be on one knee for this."

"I think you better forget the one knee and put that ring on my finger this instant."

He chuckled. Only Libby. "I take that as a yes?"

She kissed her reply.

"Feel free to answer like that anytime you like."

"I'll keep that in mind." She smiled, staring at the ring on her finger. "I can't wait to show my parents."

"My and Mom's first trip to the Caribbean." Libby had invited them both for Christmas with her family.

"You guys will love it, but this, *here* . . ." she said gazing at the house and the land surrounding them. "This is home. *You*"—she rubbed his chest—"are my home."

"And to think how it all started. One obstinate lady in sunflower rain boots."

"And one strapping Alaskan fisherman afraid of a little rain."

He laughed. "It's hard to believe all we've been through."

"Crazy." She nestled against him, intertwining her fingers with his.

"Too bad we were sworn to silence and our kids will never get to hear the real story of how we met."

She rolled on her stomach, facing him. "You think about our kids?"

"Of course." He brushed her hair back. "Don't you?"

She smiled. "Guilty."

"Well, let's hope we've gotten our fill of crazy and our kids can enjoy a nice, quiet, peaceful life."

"I don't know that I wish a quiet life for them," she said.

He arched a brow. "You don't?"

"No. I hope they have the heart of adventurers, like their parents."

"Ah." He smiled, kissing her. "Of course."

"And deep love for one another and for the Lord."

"Sounds like a great prayer for a great life."

She rolled back around, lying against him. "I can't wait to meet them."

"Them?" He chuckled. "How many are there in that mind of yours?"

"Three . . . maybe. No. I don't want to have a middle child. That can't be any fun."

"So four?"

"Four . . . or"—she held up their joined fingers—"maybe five, a full handful."

"We have five adventurous kids who take after us, and we're definitely going to have our hands full."

She smiled, lowering her lips to his. "I can't wait. It'll be the best adventure yet."

He couldn't agree more.

BLACKOUT

LYNETTE EASON

ONE

Macey Adams wished she could remember the sins that haunted her. Because if she could remember, then maybe she would be able to figure out who was trying to kill her—or drive her mad.

She stood with her back against the wall, a butcher knife clutched in her right hand, facing the kitchen door. Could he get in? She'd locked the doors and checked the windows. Just like she did every night. Tremors wracked her slight frame, and she wished she'd thrown a coat on over her sweatshirt. Anger surged through her along with the adrenaline. It was two in the morning. She shouldn't have to be worried about someone trying to get into her house.

Her eyes landed on the windowsill above the sink, where she'd left her phone after talking to her sister almost four hours ago. A conversation that had brought on the nightmare that had awakened her. Or had it been the noise under her bedroom window that had interrupted her restless doze? She didn't know. It didn't matter.

All that mattered was that she'd come into the kitchen to

get her phone, and now it wasn't where she'd left it. And the window was open, letting in the freezing night air.

The phone's glaring absence mocked her, but that didn't shake her nearly as much as the black hole of the open window. Had he been able to climb in? Was he in her house even now? Hiding? Waiting? She shuddered. Did she dare go outside and run? Or was he out there?

Desperation choked her. She moved to the cordless phone on the counter and turned it on. Held it to her ear.

Dead silence.

Fear now had a stranglehold around her throat. No cell phone, no landline, no alarm. And a possible intruder in her home. A whimper escaped her lips, and one unsteady step at a time, she walked to the open window. Tremors shook her, but she had to close and lock it. She couldn't leave it open. He could come in that way. If he wasn't already inside.

Close the window, close the window. Two more steps. She stood in front of the sink, staring at the window, bracing herself for someone to reach in and grab her. She almost couldn't do it. Almost couldn't lift her arms.

Do it!

She forced her arms up, grasped the window, and slammed it shut. She twisted the lock and let out a shuddering breath. No one had grabbed her, and the featureless face she saw so often in her dreams hadn't appeared. She pressed a hand over her racing heart.

Without taking her eyes from the window, she backed from the kitchen into the foyer. The hair on the back of her neck prickled and she spun. No one behind her. But what about in the hall closet? She pressed a hand to her mouth to stifle a sob.

Her wooden front porch creaked, and Macey stiffened, her blood renewing its rapid surge through her veins. She whirled to stare at the front door, at the knob. It gave a slight turn to the left then stopped. It jiggled to the right then again to the left.

Terror clamped down on her lungs, and she struggled to breathe even as she stayed still, her mind racing, flipping through escape scenarios and discarding each one. But the wiggling doorknob told her one thing: he wasn't inside.

She tried to envision how she could protect herself. The knife in her hand would require close contact, and that was the last thing she wanted. If she went out the kitchen door and through the garage, he could see her. Could she climb out of her bedroom window? Maybe.

Her head pulsed and a bright light flashed behind her eyes. *Woods, trees . . . the feel of the rain . . . the pain of the gunshot wound in her shoulder, the smell of the freshly turned earth that was supposed to be her grave.*

She blinked fast, wondering at the images forcing themselves to the forefront of her mind even while she listened for the intruder. She knew she'd been shot six years ago, she had just never been able to remember the details.

Her breathing now came in short, gasping pants and a fine sheen of sweat broke out across her forehead. Her fingers, clenched around the knife's handle, protested the tight grip. She loosened them slightly.

Silence slithered over her. Had he left? Her ears strained in the dark quiet. Or was he just waiting? Or perhaps looking for another way in?

Minutes passed without another sound. Finally she dared to move to the front door, just to check the lock one more time. Then back into the kitchen to check that door. Also locked. But the top half of it was glass. Easily broken should he decide to smash through it.

She turned away and let her gaze bounce from shadow to shadow. Did she dare turn on a light?

Her spine tingled, and the hair on her neck stood up straight. She spun back toward the kitchen door.

Saw the black face that had no eyes, no nose, no lips.

She dropped to the floor and screamed.

And screamed.

And screamed.

■ ■ ■

Chad Latham sat straight up in his lounge chair at the first terrifying cry. His blanket fell away from his shoulders and he shivered in the cold November night air as he tried to discern where the cry had come from. What was it? An animal?

When the second scream came, he bolted from his deck toward Macey Adams' house. By the third chilling screech, he'd already used his pile of firewood to enable him to vault over the fence that separated the two small yards. The roar of a car engine registered, but it was the direction the screams had come from that he focused on. Macey.

He raced up the front porch and pounded on the door. "Macey, it's Chad. Are you okay?" Sobbing reached his ears. Was she inside or outside? "Macey?"

"Chad? Is anyone else out there?"

He looked around. "No, it's just me. Open up." He heard rustling, shuffling, the click of the door unlocking. The door opened a crack.

Concern for the fragile sound in her voice made him step toward her. "Hey, what's wrong? What happened?"

"Someone tried to break in." She backed up and let him in. He shut the door and faced her as she paced the small foyer. "I—I couldn't find my phone even though I left it on the windowsill in the kitchen and the window was open, but I know I closed it and the alarm didn't go off and then he looked in my door and he didn't have a face and—" She pressed her hands against her temples. "Ugh! Why can't I remember?"

"Whoa, hang on." She wasn't exactly hysterical, but she wasn't making any sense either. He took her hand and led her from the small foyer into the open-concept living area. He gestured to the couch. "Sit down. I'm going to check everything, then you can tell me what happened."

"No!" She grasped his hand. "Don't leave me."

The frantic fear in her voice stopped him. "Fine. Fine, I won't go anywhere, but I need to call it in. The guy could still be in the area, looking to hit another house."

She ran a shaky hand over her face. "Right. Of course."

Chad stayed right next to her while he reported the attempted break-in. While he talked, she seemed to calm slightly, but shivers still shook her thin frame every so often. He went to the thermostat and adjusted it then lowered himself into the chair opposite her.

"I'm sorry," she said. "I probably woke you up with my screams."

"I heard the screams, but they didn't wake me." At her raised brow, he shrugged. "I was sitting outside on my deck."

She blinked. "Oh."

His lips flattened. "I have my own memories that keep me awake. Probably not as bad as your nightmares, though."

"I hate nightmares," she whispered. "Especially when I'm not even asleep."

"Tell me what happened."

She shuddered and goose bumps pebbled her bare arms. Her cheeks reddened. "You'll think—"

"What? I'll think what?"

"That I'm . . . that . . ." She lifted her hands in a hopeless gesture. "I've tried to leave the past behind, Chad, but it won't let me."

"Then tell me."

"I can't," she whispered.

He pulled her against him and she let her forehead drop against his chest.

Chad blew out a soft breath. He'd met Macey when she'd moved in almost two years ago. In those two years they'd spoken on a regular basis, shared a few late-night talks when they'd been iced in last winter. He'd even borrowed the clichéd cup of sugar two or three times, but he'd never scratched the surface of the shell she'd built around herself. If she'd shown an inkling of interest, he'd have asked her out long ago. But she hadn't.

It had been a bit of a blow to his healthy ego, but he'd survived and committed himself to just being her friend.

For now. He'd noticed her withdrawing even more in the last two months, and she'd avoided him any time he tried to bring up the subject. It was frustrating. Maddening. Because he did care about her. But he'd left her alone and now realized he probably shouldn't have given her quite so much space.

He grasped her hand and tilted her chin to look into her eyes. They looked tired, weary. Scared. And much too old. And she'd lost weight. Something had happened recently.

"I think you need to tell me."

She leaned away from him, pulled her hands from his, and rubbed them on her sweatpants.

"Macey, I've known you for two years. We're friends. Or at least I thought we were."

"Yes, we're friends. Of course we are. But I . . ."

"Then tell me." He cupped her soft pale cheek, and for a brief moment, she leaned into his touch.

She opened her mouth then shut it. "Let me think first. I need to make sure it's the right thing to do."

"How could talking to me be the wrong thing to do? I just want to help."

"I know, and that's the problem." She stood. "I want to see if I can find my phone. I know it was on the windowsill. If it's not there, then he took it."

"Macey—"

She walked into the kitchen and flipped on the light. Chad came up behind her. "It's not there," she said. She walked to the sink and braced herself against the stainless steel then reached up to check the lock on the window. Her hand shook.

"What is it, Macey? Why are you so scared?"

"Because my window was open and my phone isn't where I put it."

He frowned.

Her gaze dropped to the sink and she gasped. "My phone." She picked it up.

Chad plucked it from her fingers before she had a chance to drop it—or contaminate it. "Sit down before you fall down."

She plopped into the nearest chair. "What's around it?"

"A note."

He walked across to the small built-in desk and picked a pen from the cup holder in the corner. He met her gaze for a brief second before using the pen to loosen the rubber band that held the note to the phone. It popped off, and the letter fluttered to the table faceup.

He leaned over. "'Remembrance of things past is not necessarily the remembrance of things as they were.'"

She shook her head. "I don't understand."

"I don't either, but someone's sending you a message. The

question is . . . what kind?" He pulled out his phone and snapped a picture of the note.

"Who said the quote?"

"Let's find out." He tapped the Internet button on his screen and typed the quote into the search box. "A Marcel Proust. He's an author."

"Of what?"

"Books."

She huffed a small laugh that held no humor. "I figured that."

Chad continued to scan the words. "He's a French novelist. Was born in Auteuil, France, in 1871."

"Why is someone quoting a dead French author to me? What does that have to do with anything?"

"I would say that whoever it is, they're using the quote to get a point across."

"What kind of point? That what I remember isn't what happened? That's stupid. I don't remember much, period."

She pressed a hand to her right temple and gave a low groan as she dropped her forehead to the table.

TWO

She felt Chad's hand on her shoulder. The pulsing pain in her head slowly eased, but the flash of the Jeep remained. Tyler's Jeep. The memory came again, more clear this time.

The Jeep. Two teens. A figure with no face. A gun. Blood. The crack of the shot. Pain . . . so much pain . . .

She shuddered and rubbed her eyes. She knew Tyler and Collin. She couldn't forget them even as much as she had tried. But the person with no face . . . who was it?

Chad was saying something. Finally, she was able to tune into him. ". . . need a doctor?"

"What? No." She shook her head and was relieved when it didn't start to pound all over again. "I'm all right. It'll pass."

"What happened?"

"A memory, I think. I . . . was involved in something as a teenager. Sometimes the memories come back to haunt me."

He glanced at the open window. "That was no memory."

She swallowed. "No. That was the real thing."

Goose bumps rose on her skin, and she rubbed her arms and bit her lip. Should she trust him? Ask him for help?

Her gaze dropped to the floor. "You're a police officer," she said.

"A detective, yes. You know what I do. You know I can help."

She lifted her head and met his gaze. "I . . . I want to tell you what's going on, maybe you *could* help, but . . ."

"But what?"

"I don't want you to—"

Flashing blue lights penetrated the living area's blinds. He stood. "Hold that thought."

She followed him to the door. He opened it and greeted the uniformed officers who approached. "Barry, Nick, thanks for getting here so fast."

"Sure thing," Barry said. "What's going on?"

On some peripheral scale, Macey registered Chad explaining the situation to the officers while the rest of her brain tried to process the events of the last thirty minutes.

Someone had tried to break in. Someone had bypassed her security system and stolen her phone. Someone had wrapped a cryptic message around that phone and tossed it through the open window and into her sink. It didn't compute.

"Did you see the intruder?"

She looked up and realized the officer Chad had called Barry was speaking to her.

"No. I didn't. I saw a face—or what should have been a face. He didn't have any eyes, or a nose or mouth." At his frown, she rubbed her head. "Now that I've calmed down, I realize he had some sort of covering over his face, a ski mask probably. He was in my carport, looking in the window of my kitchen door."

Barry nodded. "We'll take a look around."

"Thank you."

They left, and Macey returned to the sofa in her den. Chad followed her. She pressed shaky fingers to her eyes. This had been going on long enough. It was time to either run or take a stand and fight back.

She looked at her neighbor. He was a good man. He'd never given her reason to think otherwise, as he'd been nothing but kind. When he'd found out she had the flu about six months ago, chicken soup and crackers and a loaf of French bread had appeared on her front porch, along with a box of Tamiflu and the latest DiAnn Mills novel. It had touched her, reached into that deep place she kept so closed off and cracked the wall—a deep crevice she'd never been able to fully repair when it came to keeping Chad Latham away. As a thank-you, once she was well, she'd fixed him a full-course meal complete with a case of his favorite soda, Dr. Pepper.

She knew he was interested in her, had even hinted at the possibility of dating. She'd made sure to discourage him, not because she wasn't interested or attracted to the idea of dating him, but because simply put, she was toxic. Trouble followed her everywhere. She couldn't allow that to spill over into his life.

Only now it had. And it looked like she was going to have to tell him what was going on in order to protect him. Because if she didn't . . .

"Macey?"

She looked up and snagged his gaze. "I'm sorry I'm being so spacey. I'm just trying to figure out what to do."

"Trying to decide whether to trust me or not?"

She felt the heat sweep over her but ignored it and gave a small shrug. "I already trust you, Chad. It's not just that."

"Then what?"

She sighed. "I'm trying to figure out the best way to protect you because the last person who tried to help me died."

■ ■ ■

Chad blinked. Okay, that hadn't been what he'd expected her to say.

A knock on the door pulled his attention from her and her startling last sentence. He answered it without asking permission. The two uniformed officers stepped inside and he shut the door behind them.

"Well? You find anything?"

Nick nodded. "Her phone line was definitely cut, but that doesn't explain why the alarm didn't sound."

She held a hand to her forehead. "I'm not thinking straight. Of course the alarm wouldn't sound. My windows aren't wired, just my doors." She fidgeted with the hem of her T-shirt. "I couldn't afford to do the windows too, but I figured something was better than nothing when I got the system."

"What about the note?" Chad asked.

Nick held up a paper bag. "I've got it in here. If the guy used gloves, it's a lost cause."

"Macey touched it briefly so you'll find her prints on there," Chad said. He looked at her. "They'll need to take your prints to compare with the lab." She nodded and he turned back to Nick. "Maybe we can figure out where the paper was bought or something."

Nick lifted a brow. "We?"

"Yeah. I'm claiming lead on this one."

"This isn't a homicide, detective."

"Exactly. I'm planning on keeping it that way." He gave the officer a tight smile. "I'll discuss it with my sergeant, but I don't think it'll be a problem."

Barry shrugged and hitched his belt. "Fine with me." He nodded at the bag. "We'll get this to the lab and see if they find anything." He looked at Macey. "In the meantime, I'd get my windows wired. The fact that someone cut the phone line is not a good indication. If he didn't get what he wanted this time, whether it was just to throw a good scare into you and be done with it, or actually break in and steal something—or worse—you can better believe he'll be back."

"Yes, I know." She sounded tired. Resigned.

Chad wanted to offer reassurances, comfort. Something. But she held herself rigid. Like she was standing behind an invisible wall and no one was going to penetrate it.

■ ■ ■

Once the officers were gone, Macey came to a decision. "All right."

"All right what?"

"Maybe you'll be different."

"Depends on what you mean by that."

She motioned to the couch. "Sit down and I'll tell you my story."

He sat without a word, but his gentle expression encouraged her.

"Six years ago, I was involved in a serious car wreck. I was barely conscious when the rescue workers found me."

His brow creased. "I'm sorry. Sounds like a rough time."

"Yes, it was, but it goes beyond that." She rubbed her eyes. "I'm not explaining this well."

"Just keep going. I'll make sense of it."

"Let me start at the beginning. I was seventeen years old and in love. His name was Tyler Norwood. My parents didn't like him, said he was nothing but trouble and I was to stay away from him. I argued and continued to see him secretly. Then we moved to Myrtle Beach the summer before my senior year and

I was convinced my parents had ruined my life." She pressed her palms to her cheeks. Why was this so hard? It had been six years. "Tyler's eighteenth birthday fell during Christmas break. I wanted to do something special for him so I hopped a bus and came back to Greenville. From the bus station, I took a cab to where he worked. At first I was just going to walk into the restaurant where he was bussing tables, but I found his car unlocked, so I climbed inside the backseat and waited."

"Thinking you'd surprise him when he got in the car."

"Yes. He drove one of those big four-door Jeeps. I wasn't thinking it might scare him to death to find someone in his backseat. I was just thinking about how happy he'd be to see me and how cool he'd think I was for being able to pull off the trip. He even had a blanket in the back, and I pulled it over me and waited."

"So what happened?"

She rose to pace the small area, stopping at the mantel to straighten the one picture of her and her sister. Then she turned back. "When he came out of the restaurant, he had someone with him. A guy we went to high school with." She frowned. "His name was Collin Hart. He was pretty bad news. I'd never really liked him or understood why Tyler was friends with him." She shrugged. "But he was and frankly, Collin never paid me much attention. He would acknowledge me, then it was like he forgot I even took up space in the universe."

"Sounds like a stand-up guy," Chad murmured.

She grimaced. "I think he resented the time Tyler spent with me. Anyway, they got into the front seat, and I didn't want to surprise Tyler with Collin right there, so I just kept quiet. I figured if they found me, they found me, but maybe if I waited, Tyler would drop Collin at home and then I could reveal my presence and we would have the fairy-tale evening I'd planned.

My older sister lived and worked in town, and I knew she'd let me crash at her place once I'd had my fun. She'd be mad at me, but she'd get over it and give me a place to stay. And money for the bus ride home." She drew in a deep breath. "Only Tyler didn't drop Collin off. He drove to the home of a wealthy couple named George and Patricia Benjamin, who lived in an exclusive neighborhood."

Chad's eyes widened and he pursed his lips. "I think I remember this case. George was killed in the home invasion, wasn't he?"

"Yes."

"Okay, keep talking."

"Tyler and Collin got out of the car, and I was getting frustrated. I hadn't planned for this. I sat up and watched them walk up the front walk then go around to the back of the house. I tried to figure out what they were doing there. Tyler had said that Collin had started dating a girl from a wealthy family, so I came to the conclusion that this was her home and that maybe they were going to see her. Or pick her up. Or whatever."

"But they weren't?"

"No. They were there to rob the place."

He breathed in and leaned back, gave a short nod. "And?"

"And then I heard a gunshot and the boys were running back to the Jeep and I was terrified. I didn't know what—"

Her front window exploded, sending shards of glass scattering across the room. A burning rag in a bottle spun like a top in the middle of her den floor.

THREE

A Molotov cocktail.

"Out through the kitchen!" Chad hollered. His hand gripped Macey's and he shoved her toward the kitchen door.

The explosion rocked the house. He felt something slam into the back of his head, and for a moment his vision faded. He felt her shoulder jam up under his and her arm wrap around his waist.

At six feet two inches, he towered over her, and there was no way she could hold his two-hundred-twenty-pound weight. Although he had to admit she was doing a pretty good job at the moment.

The smoke was already rolling into the room. Chad coughed and smelled the pungent odor of gasoline. He blinked and moved toward the door, forcing his feet to obey his brain. They reached the door and she opened it. His head had cleared enough for him to guide her out into the carport. Because the area wasn't closed in, the cold air was fresh, reviving him even more.

But they were also sitting ducks.

Had the makeshift bomb been to smoke them out so a sniper could pick them off? He kept her tucked up under him, determined to use himself as a shield. No one was going to get a bead on her.

She tugged him toward the back of the carport. "Let's go this way." She coughed and shuddered. "The door leads out to the backyard. If we go out the front way, someone might shoot at us."

So she was smart too.

"We can go over the fence to my house," he said. "We've got to get the trucks out here before the fire spreads."

She followed him without a word, but he could feel the tremble in her hand. They made it out the carport door and into the backyard. As far as Chad could tell, there was no one waiting to shoot them. "Ready?"

"Yes."

He pulled her from the relative safety of the back of the house and to the fence that he'd vaulted over just a short time before. Sirens reached his ears. "Someone called for help."

"Good."

He pulled her trash can over and helped her up on top of it. "Over you go. Be careful when you land."

Chad heard her drop then hauled himself over and found her waiting. He took her hand again and led her to the sliding glass door off the deck, pushed it open and they slipped inside. He locked the door behind them.

"Hang on a sec while I call reinforcements on this one." She nodded and he saw the tears standing in her eyes. A pang shot through him. "I'm sorry about your house."

She shrugged and turned away. "It's just a house."

FOUR

But it had been hers. And someone had destroyed it just as surely as they were trying to destroy her. She raised a hand to her head, heard the sirens scream to the curb of her house next door. Why was she remembering now? Six years after that awful night. Who was the faceless man who'd been looking in her kitchen?

Hands settled on her shoulders, and she flinched then realized it was just Chad. He turned her to face him, and while she thought she was pretty tall at five feet seven inches, she still had to look up a good distance. She frowned and reached up to touch his neck. Her fingers came away red.

She gasped. "You're bleeding."

He blinked and reached up to feel the back of his head. Blood covered his fingers. "I got hit with something in the blast."

"Come into the kitchen. Let me clean that up for you. Do you have a first aid kit?"

"I'm more worried about what's going on at your place." He grabbed several tissues from an end table and wiped the blood from his hand. He strode to the window and peered out. She followed him and did the same.

Fire trucks lined the street. Police cars with their blue lights lit up the neighborhood. Her neighbors had been pulled from their warm beds to gawk at the commotion. Streams of water flowed from the hoses and she tried to think of any possessions she would miss. The picture of her sister on the mantel. The one of her parents in her bedroom. That was pretty much it.

She walked into the kitchen and rummaged in the drawers until she found a dish towel. She ran it under cold water and returned to find Chad on the phone.

"Yes, it was deliberate. Someone tossed it through her window. See if there are any security cams on the street." He frowned. "I don't think there are, not in this neighborhood, but see if there's one at the entrance." He listened for a moment. "Okay, let me know what you find out."

"Who was that?" She handed him the wet towel.

He took it, cleaned his hand with it, then placed it at the base of his neck, winced, and closed his eyes. "My partner. Lilly Johnson. She's going to be working this with me." He swiped at the wound on his head.

She took the cloth from his hand. "Let me take a look at that, will you?"

"It's fine."

"I'll be the judge of that." She pressed the cloth against the cut. "You don't have any communicable diseases, do you?"

"What? No."

She almost smiled at his indignation. "Don't be insulted. It's a routine question when dealing with blood."

He glowered at her. "I know that. I can take care of this myself."

Macey lifted a brow. "I doubt it. Let me look." She led him to the nearest chair and gave him a gentle shove. "Sit."

He pursed his lips and sat. "You don't seem very concerned about the fact that your house is burning."

She scowled. "I'm concerned. But I have insurance." She paused to look into his eyes. There was a righteous anger there. Anger on her behalf. She let her gaze stay connected with his. "And I'm trying not to think about it."

"And I'm the distraction?"

"Something like that." She focused back on the wound. "Do you have a flashlight?"

"In that drawer."

She opened the one he indicated and found the light. She shined it on the back of his head and winced at the sight. "It's a pretty deep cut and could probably use a couple of stitches. If I had my paramedic kit, I could do it for you."

He looked at her when she shut the light off. "Always on the job?"

"Of course."

"Can I tell you a secret?"

"A secret?" She laughed. "I don't know that I need to know any more secrets."

"Well, it might sound creepy to you."

She paused. "Oookay."

"I didn't mean it that way, of course, but I have a buddy who's a paramedic. He lets me know your shift schedule so I can watch for you to come home, make sure you get home safe."

She gaped then snapped her lips shut. "You're right, that could come across as creepy. Why would you do that?"

"Because I care about you."

"You don't know me."

He gave her a gentle smile. "Come on, Macey, we've known each other for two years. As much as you've tried to keep me at arm's length, you've still let me in whether you thought you were or not. I know you pretty well. We may not verbally share a lot, but sometimes things don't need words. Think about the things you've picked up about me just because you've paid attention."

She'd known he was a cop because of the unmarked SUV he drove, but she'd never asked him any personal questions, had kept everything on the surface. What *had* they talked about? Things like:

Hey, how are you? It sure is cold today, isn't it? Do you have plans for Thanksgiving?

Casual conversations about nothing. She blinked. And yet he was right. She did feel like she knew him. At least a little. She remembered him talking about his brother only wanting a tree house for his birthday one year. His mother said no, so Chad, in typical big-brother fashion, went out and built it anyway. Only to have said tree house collapse, which resulted in a visit to the ER and thirty stitches in his thigh. Thankfully his brother hadn't been hurt.

Which led her to know that he was adventurous, a risk-taker, and could be a tad disobedient to authority when it suited his purposes. Which didn't seem to be very often, as he still had a job.

He had told her about the little nine-year-old girl he'd found abandoned in the crack house just outside of the city. The child had latched on to him like a leech, making him her security. The one time he'd tried to leave, she'd wailed and begged him not to go. Chad had confessed he'd been unable to do it. So he'd stayed with her, holding her, feeding her, and making sure she felt completely safe until her grandmother could come get her.

She'd talked about the last family vacation the summer between her junior and senior year, her relationship with her sister. But all on a surface level, she had thought. Never a word about her feelings or anything that would allow him to know her on a deeper level.

But he'd gone there anyway. He knew her. And he'd looked out for her with no ulterior motives, but just because he cared. It wasn't creepy. It was incredibly sweet. And it made her heart hurt because now he was possibly in danger because of her. Which brought her back to his head wound.

She felt the stickiness and looked at the blood on her hand. Lights flashed behind her eyes. *She saw blood, a lot of it. He'd rolled out of the car, and his blood . . . everywhere. In the car, on the ground. She smelled the coppery scent. So very still. She touched his head and the warm liquid flowed over her fingers . . .*

"Macey? Macey? You all right?"

She looked up from her hand and realized she'd shifted back into the past, to the memories that never seemed too far away, yet never close enough to fully grasp.

The knock on his door distracted her. He ignored it, and she realized he was waiting for her answer. She sucked in a deep breath. "Yes. Yes. Sorry."

She pressed a hand to her forehead. What was wrong with her? She was used to tense situations. She was used to life-and-death trauma. She'd seen blood before. Why the flash of memory now? She just wasn't used to being the target.

"You want to answer that?" she asked.

"Yeah. Why don't you go into the kitchen and wash your hands?" He rose. "And that spot on your forehead you just touched."

She grimaced but didn't lose eye contact with him. "You're right."

"What?"

"You're right. I hadn't realized it until you just pointed it out to me, but I do know you."

He trailed a finger down her cheek. "Yeah."

She drew in a deep breath and headed for the kitchen, his touch igniting a flame inside of her. One that wanted to have it all. With Chad. The thought terrified her. Not that she might not get it, but that she might. That he was still interested in her and a future with him was a real possibility.

If they lived long enough to explore those possibilities. She kept an eye on him as he went to the door.

After a glance out the window, he opened it. "Lilly, thanks for coming."

"Of course. You're hurt?" His partner gestured to the bloody rag in his hand.

"I'm fine. Just a knock on the head."

"That's a relief. If it's your head, I doubt there's much damage."

"Always the comedian. Come in."

Macey had to smile at the banter. She and her fellow paramedics often engaged in it themselves. Sometimes for fun, sometimes as a coping mechanism.

Lilly stepped inside and Chad turned to Macey, who had just finished drying her hands. "Lilly, this is Macey Adams. She's my neighbor. It's her house that was targeted."

Macey walked over and shook hands with the other detective. The woman was about the same height as Macey with green eyes and brown hair with red highlights. She was pretty in an understated way. Macey thought if she smiled, she'd be beautiful. "Thanks for getting here so fast."

Smiling didn't seem to be on the woman's agenda. Lilly scowled. "Throwing a homemade bomb into someone's home is serious stuff. Now tell me, who do you think would have a reason to do it?"

Macey shook her head. "I don't know."

"Wait, what?" Chad said. "Surely you have some idea."

"No. I don't." She blinked up at him, refusing to let him see the turmoil raging inside her. And while her answer wasn't the complete truth, it wasn't a lie either. She truly didn't know who was threatening her—she could guess, but she didn't know for sure.

"If you're not saying something that could help us catch the person responsible, you're impeding an investigation," Lilly said.

Macey's head pounded. Nausea swirled inside her. "I can't talk about it right now."

She pressed a hand to her right temple. Images swirled in her mind, but she couldn't nail them down, make sense out of them. She had to figure out how much she could say without endangering anyone else. Because while she wasn't a hundred percent sure who had tossed the bomb into her house, she could make an educated guess.

And until she figured out if she wanted to let Chad in on the whole sordid mess—not because she didn't think he could help, but because she didn't want to put him in any more danger than she already had—she was keeping that to herself.

■ ■ ■

Chad wasn't sure he believed Macey, but it was obvious she didn't want to talk in front of Lilly. "Do you have a place you can stay while your house is repaired?"

Macey blanched, hesitated. Then shook her head. "No."

"What about your sister?" Chad asked.

She hesitated. "No, I don't want to involve her."

"Parents?"

"Ah . . . no. We're not exactly on the best of terms. And besides, they're in Myrtle Beach. My job is here."

"A friend?" Lilly asked.

Macey rubbed her temples. "Yes, I'll call one of the girls I work with. My partner, Chelsea, has a spare room. Or a couch. I don't need much. She'll let me stay with her."

"How long has it been since you've had a good night's sleep?" Chad asked.

Macey shot him a wary look then grimaced. "A while."

He looked at Lilly. "You mind hanging around?"

His partner lifted a brow. "I don't mind."

"Good." He turned to Macey. "You can stay here for the rest of the night. It's only a couple of hours until morning. Sleep in, and we'll talk more when you get up. You also need to supply your prints to compare to the note from your phone. I'll take you by the station in the morning to do that."

She studied him, weariness and a sad resignation written on her face.

"Please. Let me do this for you," he said. "There's a toothbrush in the top right-hand drawer in the bathroom still in the wrapper. Clean towels in the cabinet next to the shower. Help yourself."

She finally nodded. "Thanks. I appreciate that."

He showed her to the guest room. "We'll talk when you get up." He squeezed her fingers and then wished he'd kept his hand to himself. The softness of her skin, the vulnerability in her eyes all combined to make him want to hold her and keep the real world at bay for her.

But he couldn't.

She let her eyes linger on his then turned and walked into the bathroom. Before she shut the door, she looked back. "Really. Thank you."

He nodded. "Of course."

"I'll tell you everything in a couple of hours, okay?"

He hesitated. "Good enough."

He returned to the den to find his partner sitting on the couch with her phone pressed to her ear. She glanced up at him. "Yeah, yeah, I understand. Okay, thanks." She hung up.

"Who was that?"

"The fire chief. Said they got here in time to keep the flames under control and most of the damage would be smoke and water."

Chad nodded. "Thanks."

"Uniforms are also going door to door, asking if anyone saw anything, like someone watching her house or something."

"Let's hope they turn up something useful."

Lilly nodded. "She tell you why someone would do this to her?"

"Not yet, but she promised me we would talk when she woke up."

She tilted her head toward his. "You need a doc to look at that?"

"No. I'll be all right. I've had worse knocks."

She shrugged. "If you say so."

"How's Charlie?" Charlie was Lilly's ten-year-old son.

"He's fine. Sleeping like a rock when I left. I woke Mom and let her know where I was going and that I'd be back when she saw me."

"You've got a saint for a mother."

"Tell me about it." When her husband had walked out on them four years ago, Lilly's mother had moved in to help care for Charlie. Lilly yawned and leaned her head back. "Wake me when it's time to eat breakfast."

Chad laughed. "Sure." Her ability to fall asleep anywhere, anytime, never failed to amaze him.

"You sure your head's all right? Has the bleeding stopped?"

"It's fine." He tossed her a blanket and a pillow and headed down the hall to his room. He needed some Ibuprofen and a couple hours of sleep. With his aching head and spinning thoughts, he doubted he'd get much sleep.

Which might not be a bad thing. At least he'd be awake if Macey needed him.

FIVE

Macey lay on top of the comforter with a heavy blanket pulled over her. She'd showered and shampooed and pulled on the T-shirt and sweatpants Chad had laid out for her. They were only slightly large and she wondered who they belonged to. A girlfriend? Sister?

Sister! She groaned. When Valerie heard about this, she'd flip. Since the incident six years ago, Valerie had become overprotective and obsessive about Macey's safety. Not to mention the fact that after her husband had been killed, she'd been able to focus every ounce of energy on Macey. As a result, her overprotectiveness had intensified over the past two months to the point of suffocation.

Macey figured it was denial or some kind of coping mechanism. Two months a widow, Valerie was still deep in the process of grieving. So Macey had become the object of her attention. The person who could distract her from her pain, if only for a short while.

It was sweet that Valerie cared so much, but honestly it got old sometimes. Only now, Macey had to admit, her sister's concerns were valid.

Her eyes grew heavy, but to sleep meant she'd dream. But she was safe here. For the first time in almost two months, she actually felt safe.

But she couldn't sleep because she was afraid. Not that the person who was causing havoc in her life would be able to get at her, but that she'd wake screaming. She shuddered at the thought. What would Chad think about that? She had a feeling he'd be understanding and nonjudgmental. He would come to her rescue as quickly as he had when he'd heard her scream just a few hours earlier.

But she didn't want him to have to be the white knight once again. Not tonight. She glanced at the clock and rolled out of the bed.

She walked to the window and peered out. 4:40 in the morning. The police and fire trucks were still at her house, but it looked like things were winding down. Police officers, firefighters, even an ambulance crew congregated on the curb. She probably knew half the people who'd been called out but didn't think anyone would realize it was her place. She socialized only on occasion, was friendly but never had anyone in her home. Simply because she was afraid to get too close.

Because when she got too close, people ended up hurt—or dead.

She walked back to the bed. Then back to the window.

A knock on the door shifted her attention from the scene at her house. "Come in."

The door opened and Chad's dark head appeared. "Hi."

"Hi."

"I can hear you pacing. Can't sleep?"

She shrugged.

He frowned. "Okay, you either can't sleep because your adrenaline is rushing too fast or you're afraid to sleep because you'll have nightmares."

Her jaw dropped. "What are you, psychic?"

He gave a low laugh. "No. Just more aware than the average person." He turned serious. "And because I've been there. Pacing and depriving yourself physically won't help the situation." He nodded to the bed. "Try to sleep. You're going to need it."

She nodded. He was right. "I'll try. I just—" She wrapped her arms around her middle and shivered.

He walked over and engulfed her in a hug. The act surprised her. She wasn't a particularly "huggy" person but decided she quite liked being in Chad's arms. Slowly, she let her arms slide around his waist. He just held her, and she could almost feel her blood pressure lowering as a sense of security slowly invaded her. She drew in a deep breath, smelling the lingering scents of soap and smoke. Fatigue washed over her. Her eyelids grew heavy.

He stepped back and she wanted to protest. Instead she bit her lip and stared up at him.

His gaze dropped to her lips then moved back up to her eyes. One side of his mouth lifted in a half smile. "I'll be here if you need anything."

She nodded. "Thank you."

He lifted a hand to push a lock of hair behind her ear. "Sleep, okay?"

"Sure."

With one last lingering look, he left, and she crawled back onto the bed.

Sleep. She nearly laughed. Not with humor, but with disbelief. Sleep. Right. It would be impossible with everything going on outside—and with the attraction she felt zinging between her and Chad in spite of the danger that stalked her. But she shut her eyes.

And remembered.

The gunshot echoed in the night air. Seventeen-year-old Macey stilled in her spot in the back of the vehicle. She sat up and reached for the handle. The two boys raced from the front door, one of them carrying a small bag, the black strap with the silver buckle banging against his leg. Tyler.

He froze when he saw her, his eyes wide, mouth a perfect O. Then he was clamoring into the passenger seat, his buddy taking the driver's side.

"What are you doing here?" Tyler yelled as the tires squealed from the curb.

"What are you doing here? Robbing houses? I heard a gunshot! Did you kill someone?" She barely managed to contain her hysteria.

Collin cursed and pressed the gas. The Jeep surged, and he headed away from the neighborhood. A left, a right, a left, squealing tires. She lost track of the twists and turns.

"What are you doing?" she screamed.

"Shut up!" Collin ordered. He grabbed his phone and dialed a number while he continued to drive. She heard him talking to someone about meeting him.

Then they were on the curve. On the one road her parents forbade her to drive on because of the steep drop-off. She wanted to put her seat belt on but didn't dare let go of the door handle to do so. She refused to look out the window.

A loud pop sounded, and Collin cursed when the car jerked. "A tire blew, hold on!" He fought with the wheel but lost control, and they spun in a one-eighty.

Macey slammed against the door, heard Tyler scream, felt the impact against the guardrail, and then they were airborne, upside down. She crashed against the top of the vehicle, felt a searing pain in shoulder.

She heard her cries of terror mingled with theirs. Then they were upright once more for a mere second before the vehicle jolted to a sudden stop. The collision dislodged her once again and her head bounced off the window.

Then darkness.

SIX

Chad blinked when the sun hit him full in the face. He squinted and saw Lilly pushing back the curtains to his sliding glass doors.

He sat up and rubbed his cheeks. His head pounded a harsh rhythm from the knock it had taken a few hours earlier, and all he wanted was coffee and some Ibuprofen. In that order.

Lilly stared down at him. "Rise and shine, beautiful."

He groaned. "You're mean."

"You're a baby."

He rubbed his eyes. "What time is it?"

"Time for you to either start cooking or make a biscuit run."

"I'll cook," a new voice said.

Chad turned to see Macey standing in the hallway, still dressed in his sister's sweats and T-shirt. She had her blond hair pulled up in a ponytail and her feet were bare. "Naw, you don't have to do that. Besides, I can't remember the last time I went to the grocery store so I doubt there's anything edible in the fridge. Lilly'll go get us something, won't you?"

Lilly rolled her eyes then shrugged. "Sure. What do you want?"

"I'm not picky," Macey said.

"I want a chicken biscuit."

Macey nodded. "That sounds good. Make it two."

Chad sniffed and turned a sour look on Lilly. "You couldn't start the coffee?"

"You really want me messing with your coffee pot?"

"Good point." He looked at Macey. "She blew up my other one."

Lilly clicked her tongue. "You really do have the gift of exaggeration." She looked at Macey. "It was really just a fault in the coffee maker, but he blames me because I was the one making the coffee at the time of its demise. I can't help that the plate got too hot and caused the glass to . . . ah . . . break."

"Break? It exploded. I'm still cleaning coffee off my ceiling."

"Like I said, you have a gift." Lilly smirked and tossed him a pill bottle. "I called the boss and told him what happened and that you got conked on the head. He said for you to take the day off. I'll be back."

Once she was out the door, Chad decided the Ibuprofen could come before the coffee. He downed three dry then walked into the kitchen, Macey following slowly. She settled herself into one of the kitchen chairs while he got the coffee started.

"Could I use your phone to send my sister a text that I'm going to be out of pocket for a while?" she asked. "At least until I get a new phone?"

"I might have a phone you can use. Who's your carrier?" She named a popular one and he smiled. "Hold on a sec." He finished pouring the water into the coffee maker then walked down the short hallway to his bedroom. He rummaged in his nightstand drawer and found his old phone. When he returned, he showed it to her. "We'll program it with your number for now."

"Thanks, I'll put in an order for a new one and give yours back when it comes."

Chad nodded and pulled out his own phone, already dialing the station. "Give me your information and I'll have our tech guy at the station program it for us."

Once finished, he handed her the phone, and she slipped it into the pocket of her sweatpants. "That was easy."

"It comes in handy to have friends in high places sometimes." He poured a cup of coffee then glanced at her. "You sleep okay?"

"I actually did."

"You look better."

"Thanks?"

He smiled. "It was a compliment."

"Well, I can't remember the last time I had five consecutive hours, so I imagine anything would be an improvement."

"You want to finish telling me your story now?"

She rubbed a hand down her face. "I'll tell you. I don't know that it will do anything but put your life in danger, but—"

"Look, I'm a cop. I can take care of myself. Who died trying to help you before?"

"My brother-in-law, David Chastain. He was killed two months ago."

He leaned against the counter with a sigh. "Oh wow. How did he die?"

"Someone ran his car off the road. At least that's what I think. I can't prove it." She clasped her hands together on the table. "The police ruled it an accident, but I don't believe it was. Neither does my sister."

"I see."

She gave him a sad smile. "No. You don't."

"Then make me see."

She pursed her lips and looked past him, but he had a feeling she wasn't seeing anything in the kitchen, she was gathering her thoughts. "David was a psychiatrist," she finally said. "He and my sister, Valerie, were married three years ago. They lived here in Greenville. Valerie is seven years older than I and was already working as a nurse when my parents moved me to Myrtle Beach my junior year of high school. When David heard about my issues with being unable to remember anything after the crash the night of the wreck, he insisted he could help me."

"And did he?"

She shrugged. "For a while, nothing seemed to happen. But then about six months ago, I started getting flashes of memory. David was really excited. He said he thought in time I'd remember everything."

"But you haven't."

"No. But I do seem to be having more 'flashes,' if you will."

"And when did all of your troubles start?"

"When I defied my parents and caught a bus to surprise my boyfriend." She grimaced. "But if you mean lately, everything bad started happening when I started remembering."

"And you don't think it's coincidence that the man who was helping you remember was killed in a car wreck."

"Would you?"

He rubbed his chin. "Probably not, but if the police ruled it an accident . . ."

"I suppose it could have been. I mean, accidents happen all the time, right? I should know, I've worked enough of them." She pulled at her lower lip then frowned. "But shortly after David died, someone tried to run *me* off the road. It was that incident that made me think maybe David's accident . . . wasn't."

"What else has happened?"

"Well, after that, I got a little more cautious, started watching my back. I noticed someone following me a couple of times, but before I could do anything about it, like go up and confront him or snap a picture, he would disappear."

"Did you recognize him?"

"Maybe."

Chad lifted a brow. "Okay, who?"

"My ex-boyfriend. Tyler Norwood."

"The one who broke into the Benjamin house. Why him? Why come after you now?"

She shrugged. "The only thing I can come up with is because he knows my memory is coming back, and for some reason he doesn't want that to happen."

"So what is it that he doesn't want you to remember? And how would he even know you're starting to remember things?"

She pinched the bridge of her nose and shut her eyes for a moment. When she opened them, there was a depth of sadness there that he could only imagine feeling. "I don't know. He went to prison six years ago when he was convicted of being an accessory to the murder of George Benjamin. But three months ago, just before David was killed in the car accident, Tyler was released."

"Well, the timing certainly fits."

"Tell me about it."

"What about Collin? What happened to him?"

"I don't remember the details, but he died the night of the accident."

Chad nodded. "I'm sorry." He fell silent while he thought, then asked, "Has Tyler tried to contact you?"

She nodded and looked down at her fingers. They'd twisted the edge of her shirt into a knot. "He tried to call me from prison but I wouldn't take his calls after the first one. He was very rude and blamed me for everything, so I hung up on him.

He kept calling and I would just disconnect the call when I saw it was him. Every time I thought about talking to him, I got sick to my stomach and a migraine would lay me out for a couple of days. So I finally wised up, changed my number, and the calls stopped." She drew in a deep breath. "The day he got out of prison, he showed up at my work. I wasn't there, but I got word that he'd come around asking about me. He didn't give his name, but the security cameras caught a guy that looked like him. At least the *him* that I remember."

"You checked the cameras?"

She rubbed her eyes. "When I heard someone was asking about me, I figured it could only be one person. I asked my boss if he would look and see for sure. He's a great guy and was happy to check it out for me. I couldn't be one hundred percent positive, but it sure looked like him."

"He have on a mask?"

"No, a hoodie. I caught a flash of a goatee or a beard. I don't remember Tyler ever having facial hair as a teen, but in prison? Who knows? All that to say, I warned my boss and my partner about him and told them to keep an eye out for him. I got a restraining order on Tyler the next day and haven't heard from him since."

"When was this?"

"About three weeks ago."

"That's enough to make someone mad, furious even, but is it enough to kill for?" He shrugged. "Maybe. I've certainly seen people killed for less."

Her eyes met his. "Well, it was also my testimony that sent him to prison."

Chad lifted a brow and poured himself another cup of coffee. "Ah yes. That would probably do it."

SEVEN

Lilly returned with the food, and they ate while Chad and Lilly planned their day, Lilly continuously fussing at Chad for working when he should be resting. Macey had to smile at their rapport. They were like brother and sister. Which was good. She sure didn't want them to be like a couple.

She frowned. Why would that idea make her stomach twist? She knew exactly why, she just didn't want to admit it.

"I'm fine," Chad said. "I don't need to take the day off. I want to hit this case while it's hot and the trail is still warm." He grimaced. "No pun intended."

Chad had convinced Macey to bring Lilly up to speed on what was going on. "She can help. She needs to know." Macey had finally agreed, and Chad had filled Lilly in. He glanced at Macey. "Anything else you want to add?"

"Just one thing."

"Go for it."

She paused then shook her head. "Right before Tyler was released on parole, his parents demanded the case be reopened."

"Reopened? Why?"

She rubbed her forehead. "They wanted to blame the entire thing on Collin and me. Said they had new evidence that I was involved in everything, that it was my idea to rob the house."

"What kind of evidence?"

"A voice mail from me. Apparently, they were cleaning out their basement to donate some of their stuff to a charity auction and they came across an old answering machine. They plugged it in to make sure it worked, and a message was on there from me to Tyler."

"What did it say?" Lilly asked.

"That I had a special plan to make his birthday a day to remember. That he didn't need any money, I would take care of that. All he had to do was be ready for some fun."

Chad snorted. "That could mean anything."

"Yes, but they wanted to twist it to mean that I coerced him into participating in a robbery, that I lied on the witness stand, and that their son should have his name cleared."

Chad raised a brow. "Obviously he never got the message, though."

"Or he got it and just didn't delete it." Macey shrugged. "But I don't think so. His surprise that night was genuine. I don't believe he'd heard it."

Lilly nodded. "So are they going to reopen it?"

"No. At least I don't think so. Now that he's made parole, I don't see any reason for them to reopen it, do you?"

"Not unless, like you said, it was an attempt to clear his name."

Macey nodded. "I'm sure that's probably it. His parents aren't wealthy, but they are considered 'good people,' and to have their only child incarcerated for a crime . . ." She shook her head. "They couldn't handle it. They went to church every Sunday, and both of his parents worked, his mother as a nurse and his dad was in sales—pharmaceuticals—so Tyler's actions really sent them over the edge. His dad especially."

"Why his dad?" Chad asked.

Macey glanced away. "I had a bit of a reputation in high school. A party girl, wild and out of control. Tyler's father and the principal were best friends. He turned Tyler's parents against me before they even met me. One night when Tyler and I were at the bowling alley with a group of his friends, his father came in and made Tyler leave. He pointed at me and told me to stay away from Tyler."

"Wow." Chad took another bite of his biscuit and brushed the crumbs from the table onto his napkin. "So his dad wasn't happy with you."

"Right."

Lilly leaned forward and clasped her hands in front of her. "Do you think he would do something like this? Try to get even for sending his son to prison?"

Macey blew out a low breath. "I don't know. Truthfully, he seemed so broken when the verdict was read. He just broke down and wept. They had to get paramedics to give him something to calm him down."

Chad exchanged a glance with Lilly. "Sometimes brokenness can morph into a desire for revenge."

Macey shrugged. "Maybe."

"I can check into it for you if you want."

Macey nodded and rubbed her temples. "Okay. Thanks." Her borrowed phone buzzed. She glanced at it then sighed. "It's my sister. Do you mind if I take this real quick?"

"Of course not."

She pressed the button to accept the call then lifted the phone to her ear as she stood and walked into the den. "Hey, Valerie."

"Hey, have you seen the news?"

"This morning? No. Why?" Although she had a sinking feeling she knew.

"I just saw something on the news about a fire in your neighborhood. Caused by a bomb! Are you all right?"

She grimaced. Great. "Yes, I'm fine and yes, I know."

Her words were met with silence. "It was your house, wasn't it?" Valerie finally said.

"Yes."

"Oh my—" A shuddering breath filtered through the line. "Mace, are you okay? What happened? First someone tries to run you off the road, now this? *Why?*"

"My memories have started returning, that's why. It's the only thing that makes sense. Someone doesn't want me to remember that night."

"Come stay with me."

"And possibly put you in danger?" She laughed but there wasn't any humor in it. "No way." She paused. "I've got a police detective helping me. I'm okay right now."

"A detective? Well . . . that's good. I guess."

"Yes, so I think it's better if I just do things this way for now, okay?"

"What if I come stay with you?"

"Val, I don't have a home right now and—"

"We'll get a hotel."

"Val!"

"All right, all right. But text me everything. Let me know you're okay on a regular basis." Her voice cracked. "With David's accident, I just . . ."

Macey closed her eyes and leaned her forehead against the wall. "I know."

Valerie sniffed and cleared her throat. "Okay. I'll be waiting to hear from you."

"Okay. Bye."

"Bye."

Macey hung up and gulped back the tears that wanted to flow. She managed to get her emotions under control and shoved the phone in her back pocket.

"You okay?" Chad asked.

She looked up. He still sat at the table, sipping his coffee, but she had a clear view of him from her position in the den. "I'll be all right and so will Valerie. She's just hypervigilant."

"Understandable."

"Completely."

"And you have to work hard to keep it from making you crazy."

She stared at him then shook her head. "Stop doing that."

He smiled.

"But yes." Macey walked her coffee cup to the kitchen sink. "I appreciate any help you can give me. Just please, watch your back, because I can't take another death on my conscience." She drew in a deep breath. "And now I've got to go. I've got to get ready for my shift."

"You're going to work?"

"I am."

"But someone just tried to kill you."

"And I'm safer in a crowd, don't you think?"

He tilted his head and studied her. "Maybe."

"I've got my uniform and toiletries at the station. I can stay there for now." She paused. "I might be safer in a crowd, but do you think I'll be putting the others who work there at risk?"

He shook his head. "There's no way to know."

She rubbed her eyes. "All right, I'll talk to my boss and see what he says. If he wants me to take some personal time, I will. If he's okay with me working, then that's what I'll do."

She pinched the bridge of her nose and closed her eyes for a second. "After I call my insurance company." She looked down at her bare toes. "I don't suppose you have any shoes I can borrow?"

He grunted. "Those are my sister's clothes. She probably left some flip-flops or something behind. I'll go look."

While he was gone, she called her boss and filled him in that her stalker was targeting her once again. "I don't know what to do. I want to work my shift, but I don't want anyone to be in danger because they're paired up with me."

She heard his sigh come through the line. "I don't have anyone else I can pull at this short notice. Come in and we'll take it one day at a time."

"All right. Thanks."

"Yep." He hung up.

She looked up to see Chad back in the den with a pair of white tennis shoes in his left hand. "No flip-flops, but I found these. Size 7 okay?"

"I'm a 7 and a half, but I'll make do. Thanks."

She slipped them on her feet, her toes curling only slightly.

Chad rubbed his nose. "Want me to escort you to work? Make sure you get there safely?"

She paused. Then gave a slow nod. It would be stupid to say no. "Yes. I'll take you up on that."

"Good."

"I'm going next door to see if my purse survived," she said.

He nodded. "I'll come with you."

She walked out the door with him at her side. Five steps later, she stopped. Standing in his small front yard, she stared at the mess that she had called home and felt the tears well. She held them back and took a deep breath.

Chad's hand came down on her shoulder with a gentle

squeeze. "It looks bad from here, but maybe inside isn't as awful. Come on."

She walked to the front door and pushed it open. "They didn't bother to lock it."

Chad placed a hand over the weapon strapped to his side. "Let me go in first."

"Okay." She stepped back and he swept past her. She followed but quickly came to an abrupt stop. "The fire didn't do this."

Her living area wasn't just scorched and drenched, it was trashed.

He pulled his weapon. "Stay behind me."

She shivered. "You think someone's still here?"

"I don't know."

She fell silent and watched him go to work. He cleared the house with her right on his hip. Every room had been tossed, and her blood pressure skyrocketed with each new find.

When he came full circle back to her living area, his shoulders relaxed slightly. "Well, whoever was here is gone now."

"When did someone have time to do this?"

"After everyone left and while we were sleeping, I guess." He pulled his phone from his pocket and she shook her head.

"Don't." She pressed her palms to her cheeks. "Just . . . don't bother."

"What? I've got to call it in."

She shrugged. "Won't do any good."

"Might get some prints. We can compare them to this ex-boyfriend who just got released from prison."

She nodded. "Fine. I'm going to see if my purse is still here."

"Just don't touch anything else."

"Right."

She'd been so tense, just waiting for someone to pop out from under her bed or out of the closet, that she'd forgotten to look for her purse. She walked into her bedroom and was grateful that it was relatively unscathed—other than every drawer emptied onto the floor and every piece of clothing stripped from the hangers in her closet.

The worst of the bomb and water damage had been done to her den and the roof. Hopefully it wouldn't take long to get it repaired. The rest of the damage had been done by whoever had broken in. Her anger simmered.

She grabbed her purse, which still sat next to the small desk in the corner of her room. She stared at it. So whoever had broken in hadn't been interested in stealing her wallet. She went into the bathroom and, using a washcloth, opened the medicine cabinet. It hadn't been touched. She had a prescription for Lortab she took for the occasional migraine. The bottle was still there, front and center. Which meant it hadn't been someone looking for drugs or money.

So what had the person been after?

EIGHT

After filing the report and talking to the officers who'd responded to his call about the break-in, Chad took Macey to the police station, where she was printed. "Now we can rule out your prints on the note thrown in your window."

She nodded. "Thanks."

"You look tired. Are you sure you shouldn't call in?" She shot him a black look and he held up his hands in surrender. "Forget I asked."

Her expression softened. "I know you're just concerned, but no, I can't call in."

"Okay then. I'll shut up."

"Thank you."

But I won't stop looking out for you. He followed Macey to work. She drove with confidence and precision, the scared, trembling woman from last night replaced by someone who looked forward to going to work. Someone who knew her job, enjoyed it, and was comfortable doing it. He thought about how she'd taken care of his head wound last night. How she'd stayed cool even when she was in danger. How she didn't want to put him in danger by telling him everything, but realizing she needed help, had enough sense to finally ask for it. Yep, he'd want her by his side in an emergency.

When she parked, she raised a hand in thanks and he waved back. "Be careful," he muttered. He watched her walk into the fire station and wished he could stay with her, protect her, watch her back. But he couldn't do that.

What he *could* do was get to his desk and start looking into her past. He wanted to know exactly where Tyler Norwood had been the last three months and where he was in the early morning hours when Macey's house had been bombed.

He pulled away from the curb as one of her coworkers came out to greet her and together the two disappeared behind the steel door that shut them inside.

Chad's head still ached from the hit he'd taken last night, but a sense of urgency drove him. An urgency that warned him he'd better not miss anything. Deep in his gut he knew the clock was ticking for Macey, and it was up to him to beat it.

■ ■ ■

When Macey stepped into the station, two of her coworkers were playing cards while two others worked on paperwork.

And her sister sat on the couch.

Macey's partner, Chelsea James, patted her on the shoulder then walked into the kitchen. Macey appreciated the attempt to give her and Valerie some space to talk.

"Valerie? What are you doing here?"

Valerie rose and crossed the small area to wrap her arms around Macey.

Macey returned the hug with a brief squeeze. "Why aren't you at work? Are Mom and Dad okay?"

Valerie ran a hand over her straight-as-a-stick blond hair. "Yes. They're fine. I was just worried about you. I wanted to see for myself that you're all right."

"I told you I'm fine."

"You said someone is after you because your memories are coming back."

"Yes.

"So stop."

"What?"

Valerie clenched her fists. "Stop trying to remember."

Macey grabbed her sister's arm and pulled her into the conference room. Thankfully it was empty. "Look, Val, I *have* to remember."

"Why? It's all in the past. Let it go."

Macey stared at her. "Let it go? I *can't* let it go. Someone is so concerned about what I might remember that he's willing to kill me to make sure I can't tell anyone what's buried in my brain. And I'm just supposed to let it go?" Through the glass she could see several heads swivel in her direction and realized her voice had risen by several decibels.

Valerie paled and Macey sucked in a calming breath.

"I'm sorry, Val, I didn't mean to yell. I'm just so tired of being unable to move beyond my past." Tears welled up in her eyes. She really didn't want to cry. "And if suffering migraines and dodging bombs and drawing out whoever killed David—because we both know his accident was no accident—is what it takes, then I'm willing to do it."

"Tyler called me," Valerie said, her voice barely there.

Macey recoiled. "What? When?"

"A few days ago."

"What did he want?"

"He was angry you wouldn't talk to him, that you'd taken

311

out a restraining order on him. He wanted me to convince you that it was in your best interests to talk to him."

Macey blinked, unable to believe her ears. "Why are you just now telling me this?"

"Because I was afraid you'd go against all that is common sense and agree to talk to him. I told him you were remembering what happened that night and as soon as you did, the real truth would come out."

"You *told* him that?"

"Yes."

"And you didn't think that might put me in danger? That it might set him off and send him after me?"

"No! Of course not. I told him to leave you alone, that you weren't up to talking to him."

"I can't believe you, Val, sometimes I just truly can't."

Valerie paused and closed her eyes. "He also said something else."

"What?"

"That he wanted what belonged to him and that he was going to get it one way or another."

Macey stilled. Finally her brain started working again. "But I don't have anything."

"He said you have the bag of stolen stuff. He said he shoved it at you the night of the wreck and you disappeared with it. And now he's coming to get it."

A fine rage started to boil within Macey. "And you kept this to yourself? You didn't think I needed to know? Someone has been trying to kill me for the last three days! Actually, it's more likely that they've been planning it since David's death."

"I know that now! But you haven't said a word since the car incident. And I told him I would talk to you, to see if I could get you to meet him. That I would even set it up."

"You told him that?"

"Yes! I mean, I wasn't really going to do it, I was just trying to buy some time."

"Time for what?"

Tears welled in her sister's eyes. "I was trying to protect you. Trying to figure out what to do. I didn't want to tell you about his threat because I was afraid it would send you back into a tailspin of migraines and worry and fear. I've watched you come a long way these last six years, and I just—I'm sorry. I—I was trying to get together the money to pay for a private detective to keep an eye on you."

"What?" Macey could only gape at her sister.

Valerie shrugged. She sniffed and swiped a tear from her cheek.

"A private detective?" Macey asked.

Could Valerie even be serious? Just because Tyler showed up asking about her?

"You should have told me about everything, Macey," Valerie said. "If I had known all the details, I would have done things differently."

Macey bit her tongue on a scathing retort. It wasn't her sister's fault. Not really. Valerie didn't know about Tyler's phone calls from the prison or that he'd shown up at her work. Or that she'd gotten a restraining order on him. A headache started to pound at the base of her neck. "I didn't want to involve you, worry you any more than you already do," she whispered.

"But that's what I'm here for, Macey. I'm your sister, your family. I love you. You have to let people help you."

"I'm working on that issue."

"Well, sounds like you need to work faster. Mom and Dad want to be included, too."

Macey stiffened. "Not them."

Her sister sighed and waved a weary hand. "Work on that issue, too, while you're working on stuff. I'm still trying to find a bodyguard or someone who can watch your back. I'll do whatever I have to do to help you."

"You don't have the money for that kind of thing."

"No, I don't. But I can cash out all of my credit cards and take a second mortgage out on the house. Something. I don't want anything to happen to you."

"I know you don't. I don't either. That's why I'm trying so hard to make sure I take precautions. But I'm not letting this person, Tyler or whoever, get away with this. I'm not letting it go. That's why I'm letting Chad, Detective Latham, help me. I'm following his advice, I promise."

"Good," Valerie whispered.

"And I need to know ASAP if Tyler contacts you again, understand?"

Val nodded. "Fine."

"You look mad."

"I am mad. I'm sad and mad and have all kinds of emotions running through me. I want you to leave this alone. But I guess you're going to do what you're going to do. You always have."

Macey froze. "That was low, Val."

"I know and I didn't mean—" She sighed. "I'm leaving now before I say anything else I'll regret. I'll see you later."

"Where are you going?"

"To work, then to meet a friend for lunch."

Macey narrowed her eyes. "Which friend?"

Val fiddled with the strap of her purse. "Trish. Okay?"

Macey flinched. Why her? "I thought you two weren't that close anymore."

"It's true, we grew apart," Valerie said with a slight shrug. "But recently she came to me and said she missed me and our friendship. She's been amazing—and persistent." At Macey's silence, she sighed. "We've been friends since preschool, Macey, you know that. And when David died, she was right there."

"I know, I saw her at the funeral." From a distance.

"We've gotten together about twice a week since his death. She's understanding and lets me go on and on about how much I miss him."

Macey dropped her chin to her chest. "I know you miss him. Does she"—she looked away—"you know . . . talk about *him*?"

Valerie went still. "No. She doesn't bring him up."

"I guess she's buying?"

"She is, of course. She just got her monthly check and wants to take me out. She knows I have to count my pennies now that David's gone. And I don't argue with her. It's a nice treat in my otherwise dreary existence." Her sister walked to the door. "Do you think it's Tyler who's doing this?"

"I don't know, but I sure can't think of anyone else with a better motive, can you?"

"No." Valerie looked back. "Be careful, please?"

"I will."

Valerie left and Macey stayed where she was for the next few minutes, replaying the conversation in her head. It ended the same way each time, so she finally blinked and moved to find her partner. It was time to get to work. She glanced at the clock. Past time. She'd have to process this new information another time.

"Take the trash out, Adams."

She looked up from her thoughts to find her boss standing in the door. "Okay."

"You all right?"

"Yes." Or she would be at some point in the future. If she wasn't dead.

"You got this stalker thing worked out?"

"No, not since I talked to you this morning."

He nodded. "Let me know if you see him around here. I'll take care of him for you."

"Thanks. I appreciate that."

She went to the rolling trash bin in the corner of the room and pulled the bag from it. She set it on the floor and tied it off then hefted it over her shoulder. She propped the back door open then walked out to the dumpster and heaved the bag over the top. It landed with a thump.

A scraping sound to her right made her freeze. An animal scrounging for food? Did she dare look around the corner of the bin? She took a step back. A shadow fell across the concrete. She turned to bolt toward the door but her upper arm was grasped in a tight hold. She didn't even have the breath to scream.

She spun and lost what little breath she had left. "Tyler," she whispered.

"I need to talk to you." His hard gray eyes bored into hers. "And since you won't give me the time of day, and since your sister is a big liar, we may just have to do this the hard way."

Macey tried to calm her racing heart, but it just beat faster as her fear multiplied. She pulled on her arm and to her surprise, he let her go. She backpedaled toward the door.

"Are you the one who's been threatening me? Trying to kill me?"

His eyes narrowed. "No."

"Don't lie, Tyler. Why are you doing this? How did you know I'd be out here?"

"I've been waiting here for the past two weeks. I figured you would bring the trash out eventually."

Two weeks?

"Did you try to break into my house last night? Did you

throw a bomb through my window?" She kept a tight rein on the hysteria that wanted to burst from her throat. As a result, her words came out low and soft.

"I don't know what you're talking about. All I want is that bag of stuff from the safe. I've been waiting for six years to get my hands on it. And I know it wasn't found. My lawyer kept reassuring me it hadn't been, that the only evidence they had was your testimony. So for six years I've been dreaming of this moment."

"I don't know where it is."

He took a step toward her and she backed up, hand behind her, reaching for the door handle. She couldn't find it, but there was no way she was turning her back on him to locate it.

"Stay away from me." Her arm still throbbed from his initial grip, and she didn't think she could stand the idea of him touching her again.

He stopped and pulled in a deep breath. "I don't want to hurt you. I just want the stuff."

"I don't know where it is, Tyler."

"I gave it to you! You hid it!" His voice rose with each sentence.

Macey stayed frozen to the spot. "We were all hurt that night. It was crazy and cold and—" She pressed a hand to her head, then to her left shoulder. "I don't remember what happened to the bag, and I don't remember who shot me then buried me alive! I don't remember most of that night." Her breaths came in pants, the images flashing again.

She stared up at the person standing over her. "Help me," *she whispered.*

Then she realized the figure had no face. No nose. No *mouth. No eyes. Wait, it had eyes. Two black orbs boring* *holes into her.*

The right arm moved and Macey realized the faceless person was pointing a gun at her.

"You should have stayed home."

She sat up as the person pulled the trigger. The bullet slammed into her left shoulder. Macey screamed and fell back, her right hand reaching to cover the wound. The pain throbbed a fast beat in time with her heart. Then the blackness swept over her once more.

She gasped and blinked. Tyler still stood there, watching her.

"Did you hear me? I said you remembered enough to send me to prison," he hissed and jabbed the air near her face with his forefinger. "Now tell me where it is."

Macey's mind spun. How was she going to get away from him? Her phone was in her pocket. What would he do if she pulled it out? The door behind her was still propped open. Would anyone hear her if she screamed?

"I only told what I saw, Tyler. What I heard. I told the truth. I'm sorry you chose to do what you did, and I'm sorry I had to be the one to testify."

He sneered. "Right. Testifying kept you out of jail. You just wanted to save your own hide."

Anger pulsed inside her. "Was anything I said on that stand a lie?"

His face reddened and his hands clenched. "You're coming with me."

Her heart thudded and she knew the conversation was over. He was going to kidnap her. She started to run, but his hand shot out and gripped her wrist. Macey let out a scream and tried to pull away, but his grip was iron. He dragged her toward the car she just now noticed parked at the edge of the building.

"Help!" She tried to plant her feet, to resist, but he was too strong, too determined. "Someone! Help!"

"Shut up!"

He stopped at the car and she kicked out and caught him in the knee. He screamed and reached into his coat pocket. To grab a weapon? Macey didn't know, didn't care. All she wanted to do was get away. She kicked out again and her foot landed hard against his shin. His hand fell from her wrist and she spun away from him.

"Macey?"

She raced toward the open door. "Chelsea! Call 911!"

She heard Tyler curse and spun back to face him. She only saw his back as he climbed into his car, started the engine, and squealed from the parking lot.

"Mace? You okay?" Chelsea asked.

"No. It was him."

With a trembling hand, she pulled her phone from her pocket and sent a text to Chad. *Tyler found me. Tried to grab me and force me to go with him. But he failed. I'm fine.*

Chelsea was on her phone with 911.

Macey shook her head. "Never mind. Cancel it. They'll never get here in time to catch him."

Chelsea frowned but did as asked. "What happened?"

Macey gave her the thirty-second version of the incident.

"You really should report it."

"I will." Just to Chad, though. He would know what to do with the information. There was no need to get anyone else involved.

Her phone buzzed with a text from Chad. *Are you sure you're all right? Is he still there?*

No. He's gone. And I'm fine. He didn't hurt me.

I'll get his face out there and we'll try to track him down. I'm also requesting a cruiser be sent to sit on the station and keep watch.

Thanks.

She then sent a text to her sister. *Tyler found me. He still thinks I know where the stuff from the safe is. Be careful. He might try to contact you again. Don't talk to him, don't trust him. He's dangerous.*

She shoved her phone back in her pocket and sent up a prayer that God would let someone catch Tyler. She followed Chelsea back into the building and went to find her boss to fill him in.

NINE

The call came in at 4:55 in the afternoon, just as the clouds rolled in and thunder shook the building.

"Let's go, partner."

Chelsea grabbed her jacket, and Macey was right behind her, racing for the ambulance. She scrambled into the seat and clicked the seat belt into place.

A car wreck. A hit-and-run involving a child. Her heart thudded and prayers slipped from her lips. "Please . . ."

"Say one for me, too," Chelsea muttered.

The siren screamed and the radio crackled. Raindrops scattered against the windshield, and Macey kept a tight grip on the door handle while Chelsea expertly navigated the traffic. Six minutes later, they pulled to a stop on I-85.

Macey took in the scene with a practiced eye. Three cars involved. One on the side just ahead, one in the ditch, and one turned sideways in the middle of the highway, stopping traffic. The driver's door to the car blocking the road was open, and she could see a man clutching his bloody head.

Macey climbed from the ambulance and glanced at the darkening sky. The rain had stopped for the moment, but she knew it wouldn't last forever. The deluge was coming. The wind hit her in the face and she shivered, pulling the edges of her coat tighter. She spotted a car seat on the side of the road but no toddler. Then her attention was snagged by the woman sitting on a small hill away from the traffic, holding a child. "I've got them," Macey said.

"I've got the guy in the car." Chelsea took off toward the patient in question while Macey went up the hill about ten yards from the ambulance.

"Hey, are you all right?" Macey let her eyes roam the child clutched in the woman's arms. The little girl looked about two years old, and her brown eyes were wide and curious but not scared—and she didn't appear to be hurt. But she did look cold. Her little chin quivered. Macey looked over her head. "Ma'am? Are you okay?"

The woman's eyes matched the child's. "Yes. I'm okay." She blinked and shook her head. "He came out of nowhere. Was he drunk?"

"I don't know, ma'am. Do you mind if I check your little girl?" The woman nodded and Macey examined the child for any trauma, grateful that she found none. "Was she in her car seat?"

"Of course. I—I just took her out to get away from the traffic."

"She looks good. Where's her coat?"

"In the car."

"I'll get it. What's your name?"

"Sylvia."

"All right, Sylvia. What about you? Any pain?"

"No. I had my seat belt on and he only sideswiped me. I went into a spin but managed to hold the wheel and stop without crashing, but the car that hit us stopped, and it felt like he was just looking at us. Then the other two cars crashed, and he just . . . drove off. I can't believe it."

Macey examined the woman while she talked. A bruised shoulder from the seat belt and a wrenched knee, but nothing broken. She'd been fortunate.

"Okay, hold that thought. I'll be right back." Macey raced down the hill to the car and found the child's coat in the back. She grabbed it, stopped by the ambulance and snagged a blanket, then headed back up the hill.

Her phone buzzed and she glanced at it. Her sister checking on her. Valerie could wait.

She helped the shivering little girl into her coat then wrapped the blanket around the woman.

"I can't believe he just drove off. I can't believe it." Sylvia seemed to take comfort in repeating the phrase.

"Did you get a look at him?"

"No. I mean, I guess it was a guy. The . . . uh . . . windows were tinted. I actually couldn't see the driver."

"Okay, well, I'm sure the police will want to ask you questions and take your statement." Macey needed to move on to the other potential patients. She felt rain hit her face.

"Macey?"

Macey looked up to find Chelsea standing next to the ambulance, a piece of paper in her gloved hand. "Yeah?"

"Come here."

Macey skittered down the hill and over to the ambulance. Law enforcement, fire trucks, EMTs, and paramedics were everywhere. It looked like the scene that had been outside her house in the wee hours of the morning.

"What is it?" she asked.

"It was on the front seat of the ambulance. It has your name on it."

Macey frowned, pulled on the glove she'd removed, and took the envelope. With her other hand, she slid a fingernail under the flap and opened it. She gently grasped the very edge of the card and pulled it out. *We do not remember days, we remember moments*, she read. Fear drummed inside her and she sucked in a deep breath.

"Mace? Why are you being so cautious? What is it?"

"Nothing."

"Something. What's going on?"

"I'm not really sure, Chels."

"Well, how did it get there?"

She looked at the traffic backed up for miles and then the cars slowly passing on the left. The driver's side window was down. Anyone could have tossed the envelope onto the seat. "I don't know that either."

"What *do* you know?"

"That I really need help."

She slid the card back in the envelope and closed her eyes. Someone was watching her, following her. She drew in a steadying breath. Smelled the rain, gasoline, all of the lingering scents left by the wreck.

She had to move, had to get away. The gunshot echoed through the air and the pain took her breath. Or was it the bullet? She looked down to see the blood spreading across her chest, over her fingers . . .

"Macey?"

Chelsea shook her and Macey blinked. "What?"

"Where were you?"

"I'm here. I'm here." She had to think. To do her job. "Sorry, I just . . . sorry. I'm all right." She slid the envelope and the letter into her portfolio. Had it been Tyler who'd left it? "What else do you need me to do?"

"We're transporting to the hospital. Get in."

"Your guy from the Chevy?"

"Yeah."

"I'll drive. You stay with him."

■ ■ ■

Chad scrolled through the information on the screen in front of him while he considered taking a couple more Ibuprofen. Lilly sat across from him, talking on the phone. When she hung up, she turned to face him.

"Anything?" he asked.

"Just that Tyler Norwood was released like Macey said. He's living with his mother and working at a gas station off of Woodruff. He used a credit card at the Walmart and Ace Hardware on Woodruff Road."

"Could have bought the Molotov cocktail stuff there. What about his father?"

"He died of a heart attack two weeks before Tyler got out of prison."

"No way."

"Way."

Chad rubbed his head and let his brain process. "That might be enough to send someone over the edge. So do you think his mother could be behind the attacks on Macey?"

"I don't know. She's still working at the hospital on a full-time basis."

"Was she there last night?"

Lilly looked at him from beneath her lashes. "No."

"Interesting."

"Could be. But get this, I also checked Tyler's phone records while he was in prison. Someone called him three or four times a week while he was there."

"Who? A family member? His mother?"

"No. I can't trace the number. It's a throwaway phone, apparently."

Chad frowned. "That's kind of weird."

"I know."

Chad thought for a moment then shrugged. "You get anything from his mother?"

"No, she didn't answer." His partner tilted her head and studied him like she had something to say.

Sometimes he could read her, sometimes not. "You got an address?" He'd let her bring it up if she wanted to talk about something else.

She focused back on her notes. "Yes, it's in a rather sketchy part of town."

"Wanna pay him a visit?"

"Love to. If he's there." But she didn't move.

"What is it?" he asked.

"She's the one, isn't she?"

He lifted a brow. "Huh?"

"You remember that night we went out for dinner and you told me you were interested in getting to know someone, asking her out on a date, but she wasn't interested in you?"

He felt the heat burn his cheeks. "I said that?"

"You did."

"I don't remember."

"Liar."

He gave her a small smile. "Okay. Yeah, I remember. And yes, she's the one."

Lilly nodded. "Thought so. You ready?"

He was rather shocked she'd decided not to razz him about it any further. Shocked, but grateful. "Yeah. Macey texted and said Tyler showed up at her work."

Lilly frowned. "Is she all right?"

"Yes, he's gone now, but I don't like the fact that he tracked her down. We need to find this guy."

"Then let's do it."

His phone rang and he held up a finger. "Hold that thought. Hello?" He looked at Lilly. "It's one of the police officers who cased the neighborhood last night." Into the phone, he said, "Go ahead."

"We found someone who remembers seeing a figure run across Ms. Adams' yard into the street and climb into a white four-door sedan, a Kia or something. He wasn't sure of the make and model of the vehicle. The neighbor said he was driving home from his second-shift job and had to slam on his brakes to avoid the person."

"He get a look at him?"

"No, he said the guy had on a hoodie with a heavy coat over that."

"Of course he did. What is it with thugs and hoodies?" Chad muttered. "But at least we know it was a white Kia. Maybe. We can work with that. Also a maybe."

"Good luck."

"Thanks." He hung up and nodded to his partner. "Let's go."

They gathered their coats and headed out the door. Chad sent a text to Macey. *You okay?*

Not really. Something strange happened today. Other than Tyler, I mean. I'll explain later. I'm at the hospital right this second.

Adrenaline shot through him. *Hospital?? You hurt? I'm calling you.*

No, don't call. Can't talk yet. Worked a car wreck, dropped off patient, and now doing paperwork.

His pulse slowed. *What happened?*

Will explain later.

I'm coming over. Which hospital?

Greenville Memorial.

"You coming?" Lilly called. She stood with the driver's door open, waiting.

"Yeah. Let's run by Greenville Memorial first, okay?"

"Sure. What's going on?"

He passed her the phone so she could read the conversation. When she finished, she handed it back. "All right, let's go see what she's got for us."

Lilly drove, windshield wipers whipping back and forth, and Chad realized Macey had been all he'd thought of all day. He had other cases that needed his attention, but he had to chase this one while it was hot.

Fifteen minutes later, Lilly pulled into the reserved police parking area and they walked into the hospital. The rain was letting up, and he left his umbrella in the car. Chad flashed his badge to the woman at the desk. The doors that led from the lobby to the waiting area of the Emergency Department opened, and he found Macey standing just inside. "Hey."

She turned. "Hey."

"What happened?"

She opened her portfolio and pulled out a white envelope with her name on the front. "I've already touched it and so has Chelsea, my partner, but we had gloves on. I kept the letter inside the envelope so I didn't have to handle it any more than necessary. Maybe your lab person can get some prints off of it."

He took it by the corner and handed it to Lilly. "Can you get a bag to put this in? I'm sure it's related."

Lilly took it as carefully as her partner. "Sure."

"What does the letter say?" Chad asked.

"'We do not remember days, we remember moments,'" Macey said.

"Another reference to memories."

"I can't figure out if someone *wants* me to remember or *not.*"

"It kind of sounds like they do." He tilted his head and studied her. "So who would actually want you to remember?"

She sighed. "Tyler. He wants the stuff from the safe. I'm the only one who might have an inkling where it is, according to him."

He nodded. "All right. We're getting ready to go talk to him and see what he has to say."

"Thanks." Macey looked at Lilly. "Did they get anything off the letter that was wrapped around my phone?"

Lilly shook her head. "Haven't heard yet, but I'll call once I get this taken care of." She held up the envelope and the letter now safely ensconced in the evidence bag.

Macey nodded. "That would be great. Thank you."

Lilly left.

"Tyler Norwood called my sister," Macey said.

"What? When?"

She shared everything Valerie had told her earlier at the station, and Chad's eyes narrowed as she talked. "Sounds like he could be our guy."

"It does, doesn't it?" She rubbed her eyes. "But we won't know for sure unless he succeeds in killing me or I remember what happened."

"You don't remember anything about him giving you the bag with the stolen goods in it?"

"No. Of course not." She bit her lip then gave a firm nod. "I think I know what I need to do."

Chad tilted his head. "All right, what's that?"

"When David was trying to help me remember what had happened, he wanted to take me back to the site of the accident."

"Did you go?"

She shook her head and her face paled. "I couldn't bring myself to do it. Whenever I thought about it, the nightmares intensified and I had panic attacks. David thought it was because I saw something, experienced something so awful that my brain doesn't want to remember."

"He could be right."

"Could be. But I still think this is the only way to finally put my past to rest, to heal and move on from it."

"When do you want to go?"

"As soon as possible."

TEN

She didn't want to go. With everything in her, she did not want to go. The thought terrified her. And because it did, it also made her angry. Why should she be afraid? What had she seen?

"You should have stayed home."

The voice echoed in her head and she blinked. She knew that voice. Had heard it before. But who? It wasn't Tyler or Collin. She struggled to grasp it, but she couldn't quite snatch it from the recesses of her mind.

"Macey?"

She tuned in to Chad. "Sorry. The memories are coming faster. Each time something happens, it's like the dark curtain is pushed aside a bit more. But even before someone started trying to kill me, I was remembering more, so maybe it doesn't have anything to do with the events." She rubbed her head. "I don't know. I have noticed one thing, though."

"Come on. Let's sit down." He led her to the corner of the waiting room. She sat in the chair next to the wall, and he pulled a chair around to face her and took her hands. "Okay, what have you noticed?"

She could feel his concern in his touch. The comfort. She was so glad he was there. She focused on answering his question. "I'm not getting migraines when I try to remember."

"Well, that's a plus. And you think going to the scene of the wreck will bring everything back?"

She nodded. "I tried it once before and just got a massive headache and no memories."

"When was that?"

"When they were initially investigating the wreck and the murder. I've never been able to go back, but . . ." She closed her eyes for a moment then opened them. Turmoil rolled inside her, but she forced the words through stiff lips. "I think it's time to try again."

"I can take you out there."

She pulled one of her hands from his and pressed it to her head. "I need to finish my shift. I'm off tomorrow night at seven."

"Then we'll go first thing Wednesday morning."

"Let's hope I live that long," she murmured.

He scowled. "Not funny."

She frowned right back at him. "I didn't mean it to be."

He stood and pulled her into a tight hug. "I don't want anything to happen to you, Macey," he whispered against her ear.

"I know. I don't either."

She let him hold her, relished the feeling of just being in his arms and feeling safe. She snuggled closer.

That was how Lilly found them when she came back inside the hospital. Macey caught the woman's eye and tapped Chad on the shoulder. He didn't move. "Ah, Chad?"

"Shh."

"Lilly's here."

"Tell her to go away."

Lilly heard him and rolled her eyes. "I just talked to the lab. No prints on the note or the phone from your kitchen sink."

Chad let Macey go, much to her disappointment. But she couldn't ignore reality any longer. "He wore gloves," she said. Dejection hit her. Would they never catch a break?

Chad squeezed her shoulder. "Hang in there. We'll figure it out."

She nodded but wasn't sure she believed him.

Chelsea came over and Macey introduced them. She tried to picture her friend through Chad's eyes. The African-American woman was pretty with dark eyes that smiled. She had her black hair smoothed back into a ponytail and looked comfortable in her uniform. Chelsea looked at Macey. "Ready to go?"

"Yes." Macey nodded to Chad and Lilly. "Thanks for coming over. I don't expect you to find much on the card, but I appreciate the effort."

Chad shrugged. "You never know. Sometimes you get surprised."

"I guess."

"I've got some friends in high places. You can rest assured someone will be watching your back during your shift. Got it?"

Macey nodded. "I'm not going to argue about it, I'm just going to be thankful for whatever you can do."

"That's a good attitude."

"Or a desperate one." She gave him a tight smile.

"Sometimes desperation can work in your favor."

"Let's hope so."

■ ■ ■

Chad pulled the SUV to a stop in front of Tyler Norwood's most current listed address. His mother's home. He examined the front of the house. "Looks pretty quiet."

Lilly opened her door and stepped out of the SUV. "You want me to take the back?"

"Sure. I'll knock. Let's hope he's feeling cooperative today."

Lilly disappeared around the corner of the house. Chad walked up the porch steps, keeping his eyes on the windows, looking for anything—a flutter of a curtain, the appearance of a weapon. Anything.

And got nothing.

He rapped his knuckles on the green wooden door.

Also nothing.

He rang the doorbell.

Then he tried the knob. It twisted easily in his grasp. He let the door crack open. "Hello? Anyone home?"

When there was no answer, Chad gave the front door a gentle push, and it opened on silent hinges. He called to Lilly, who joined him on the porch a few seconds later. He led the way inside with Lilly at his back.

"Police! Anyone here?"

He stopped walking and just listened. Silence.

He moved into the kitchen. "Garage is out there."

Lilly glanced out the window in the kitchen door. "Hard to see anything. It's too dark."

"That door locked?"

With her left gloved hand, she tried the knob. "Yeah. Locked." She pulled a Maglite from her back pocket and shined it through the glass. "There's a car backed into the garage, but I don't see anything else."

"Okay."

He started moving again and they quickly cleared the den, kitchen, and master bedroom of the small two-bedroom, two-bath home. The door to the second bedroom was shut.

He reached for the gloves he'd tucked into his pocket and

pulled one on. He then grasped the knob, twisted it, and gave the door a soft push.

Lilly stepped around him to sweep the room. He saw her freeze. "He's here."

Chad entered and gave a grunt. A body lay in the bed. "Ugh."

Lilly pulled on gloves and approached the dead man. She leaned in. "Single bullet hole to the left temple."

"Any sign of the weapon?"

She searched the area around the body then went on all fours to look under the bed. "No. At least not that I can see."

"So it's not a suicide."

"No, more like an execution," Lilly said.

Chad pulled his phone from the clip on his belt. "I'll call it in."

Lilly backed away. "Where's his mother? She lives here, too."

His finger hovered over the screen. He looked up. "I don't know. There's no real odor, so he hasn't been dead long. Lots of blood, so he was definitely killed here, though." He checked his phone. "If his mother had found him, she would have called the police. At least I would think so. But there's been no report yet."

"You think she just hasn't been home to find him?"

"Either that or . . ."

"She's dead, too?"

"If she was here when the killer took out Tyler, then yes, she's probably dead too. But where is she?" They'd cleared the house and hadn't found her. His eyes roamed the room. "Closet door is open. There's nowhere to hide a body in there."

"We checked the house. She's definitely not here."

"Let's go through every room one more time."

They did and found nothing.

"Maybe she went away on vacation or something," Lilly said. "It is almost Christmas."

"On vacation without her kid?"

"You never know. Families are weird."

"Don't I know it," he muttered. "Let's try the garage again, then we'll start looking into the family and if Tyler made any enemies in prison."

"You think the person after Macey could have done this?"

"I thought Tyler *was* the person after Macey, so now I just don't know." He paused. "So why go after Norwood?"

"To keep him and Macey from talking?"

"About what? The night of the wreck?"

"Maybe the bag he allegedly gave to her. But she wasn't talking to him," Lilly said. "At least that's the impression I got."

"No, she wasn't. And she didn't have any intention of talking to him either. She also doesn't have any memory of the bag of stolen stuff being in her possession."

"Doesn't mean it wasn't, though. She doesn't remember much of anything about that night."

"True." He motioned for her to follow him back into the kitchen then opened the door that led into the garage.

Lilly shivered. "I'll get the CSU team and medical examiner out here so they can get started on the scene."

"All right."

"Cold enough to hang meat in here," she muttered as she pulled her phone from the clip on her belt.

"Definitely not insulated." He looked around. One of the garage windows was cracked, which didn't help the temperature. He stepped up to the vehicle, an older model red Chevy Impala, probably late seventies. And froze. "Lilly?"

"Yeah?" She looked up from her phone.

"I think I found Mrs. Norwood."

ELEVEN

The rest of Macey's shift passed quickly with no more attempts on her life. She even got a couple hours of sleep without the nightmares haunting her. Still, she was exhausted and couldn't wait to climb into Chelsea's guest bed.

She showered, dried her hair, and changed into a pair of jeans. She pulled a sweatshirt over her head then grabbed her uniform jacket. She hadn't had time to snag her personal jacket when the bomb went off. She'd been too busy running for her life. And she hadn't had time to have her clothes cleaned since the smoke and water damage.

When she walked out of the station at seven o'clock Tuesday evening, she found Chad waiting for her. He was parked with the engine still running. She headed for him and he rolled down the passenger window. She leaned in, drawing in the scents that came with him. She liked them all. Spicy and masculine. "Are you my escort home?"

"I am."

"I'm going to Chelsea's apartment. She took off a little early to see her dad, who's been in the hospital with congestive heart failure, but she said she'd be home in a little while."

He nodded to the bag she had slung over her shoulder. "You have enough clothes?"

"For now. I talked to the insurance company a little while ago, and they've done the assessment. I can go in and get some more clothes whenever I need to. They'll have to be washed, of course."

"That was fast."

"I know. I'm impressed."

"First time for everything, I guess. Is the insurance company sending you a check?"

"Yes. I should be getting that in the next week or so, and I can start putting my house back together."

"Good."

Her stomach rumbled and she gave an embarrassed laugh. "All right, I suppose that means I need something to eat. Do you mind if we swing through a drive-thru?"

He pursed his lips and nodded to the passenger seat. "I can do better than that. Hop in."

She lifted a brow. "All right."

The back of her neck tingled and she looked around, trying to find the source of her unease.

"What is it?" Chad asked.

"Just that creepy feeling of being watched."

He frowned and glanced around. "Get in the car."

She opened the passenger door and slid into the seat. Once she had the door closed, she caught sight of a white Kia sedan pulling out of the parking lot of the restaurant next door.

"Is that him?" she asked.

"What?"

"That white Kia you said was sitting outside my house. Follow it. And hurry! He disappeared around the corner."

Chad put the car in gear and pulled out after the vehicle. "You know it might not be him."

"He was sitting there watching me. It's him."

Chad did his best, she knew he did, but by the time they turned the corner where the Kia had gone, it was no longer in sight.

She let out a breath she hadn't realized she'd been holding. "Great."

"Sorry."

"It's okay. I didn't see him fast enough."

"And it might just be a coincidence."

"I don't believe in coincidences. Whoever was in that car was watching me."

He raised a brow in her direction but didn't argue with her. She silently admitted he could be right.

He drove with practiced ease, his eyes roving from one mirror to the next. "I have some news for you."

She glanced at him. "What?"

"My partner and I went to Tyler Norwood's home to see if we could talk to him, get a feel for whether he was the one threatening you, trying to kill you."

She sucked in a breath. "And?"

"He was dead. Shot in the head in his bed. His mother was also killed execution style."

"What?" she whispered. Pain tore through her. She'd loved Tyler with all of the teenage passion she had in her. And while he'd done a rotten thing, he hadn't deserved to be murdered. Nor had his mother.

She blinked. Her eyes didn't want to stay open. That was the first thing she noticed. Next the pain hit her. Her head, her back, her hip, her legs. There wasn't a square inch on her body that didn't hurt.

She rolled her head to the right and found Tyler staring at her from the front seat. "What did you do?" she whispered.

"I didn't do it! I didn't know he was going to kill him!" Tyler's eyes were wild with fear and shock and pain. His teeth chattered, and Macey clutched her head. She retched up what little she'd eaten that day.

"Shut up," Collin gasped. "Shut up or I'll shoot you, too! Both of you." He lifted his head from the steering wheel and turned to face her. Blood ran down his face, into his eyes, and he groaned even as he lifted the gun.

Tyler opened the passenger door and rolled out of the car and onto the ground.

Somehow they'd landed mostly upright, but all of the windows were gone. Macey crawled through the nearest one. Her legs wouldn't hold her. The damp earth rose up too fast to meet her and she thumped against it with a pained groan.

The driver's door opened. Collin fell out, still clutching his weapon. Again he lifted it. Then his eyes rolled back in his head and he stilled. The gun fell from his limp hand and landed beside him.

"Collin?" She scooted toward him, the pain in her back making her cry out and stop. She clutched the ground, hoping her head would stop spinning and the nausea would ease.

Tyler made his way around to her. She couldn't move. "Ty?" she whispered.

He shoved a bag in her hand. It felt funny. Almost like neoprene, like the material her scuba suit had been made out of when she'd taken lessons two years ago.

She wanted to laugh. Hysterically. She'd just nearly been killed and she was thinking about scuba lessons?

"Go," Tyler said and groaned. "Go. If they don't find the stuff, they won't have any proof. You've got to hide it."

" . . . looks like whoever shot them caught them by surprise. Tyler's mother was in the car, the keys still in the ignition, so she was probably getting ready to go somewhere when the killer shot her first then went and found Tyler in bed—and you're not hearing a word I'm saying, are you?"

"I hear you."

"Then why do you have that very blank stare?"

"Because I remember. Part of it, anyway."

He frowned. "What do you remember?"

"Tyler gave me the bag of stuff from the safe."

"Okay. And?"

"And that's it. He gave me the bag and told me to hide it so the cops wouldn't find it. He said if they couldn't find the stuff, they couldn't prove he and Collin had stolen anything. Or were even at the house."

"So where did you hide it?"

"I—I—" She tried to pull the images back but slammed into a black wall. "I don't know. I think maybe I blacked out at that point."

His fingers gripped hers. "Macey, they never found the bag of stolen goods."

"I know."

"So that means you must have hidden it."

A slow pounding started at the base of her skull once more and she winced.

"Stop," he said.

"What?"

"Stop thinking about it."

She let out a low laugh that held no humor. "How?"

"Ask me what my favorite color is or why I'm not married or something. Just get your mind off of it."

She blinked. Why he wasn't married?

"Never mind," he said. "We're almost there." He turned left onto North Main Street. Traffic was heavy in the downtown area, but it didn't take too long to find a parking spot. "Are you all right with Trio's?"

She finally took in her surroundings as she climbed out of the car. Maybe he was right and she just needed to quit pushing. "Sure. Love this place."

"Great." He waited for her to come around beside him then placed an arm across her shoulders while he glanced behind them.

"So why aren't you married?" she asked.

■ ■ ■

Chad grimaced. Of course she wouldn't go for the favorite color question. Well, he'd opened the box, he might as well deal with it. Lilly would say he'd done it on purpose. And truth was, maybe he had. "I was engaged once."

They entered the restaurant, and he didn't say anything more until they were seated. Macey ordered a glass of water and a Coke. He settled for an iced tea.

"I'll be back with your drinks in a few minutes." The waiter disappeared toward the back, and Chad turned his attention back to Macey.

She looked tired. Worn. Antsy. And definitely curious. "Don't stop there," she said. "You were engaged once . . ."

"Let's decide what we want to eat, and I'll tell you the rest of the sad story while we wait on our food."

A short time later, their drinks arrived and they placed their food order. She then leaned back to listen, her full attention on him.

He drew in a deep breath. "Like I said, I was engaged once. She was a cop as well."

"What happened?"

"She ditched me for another guy—a non-cop." He took a sip of the tea, hoping it would wash away the sudden bad taste in his mouth.

"So she was mentally ill?"

He nearly snorted the tea. Somehow he managed to swallow and gasp in a breath. "No, I . . . um . . . don't think so."

She raised a brow. "If you say so."

"But you just did wonders for my ego."

Her lips curved into a small smile.

He tilted his head. "You look tired."

"Can't say that did much for *my* ego."

"Sorry."

"Don't be. I am tired."

"I know you said you were going to stay with Chelsea, but why don't you stay at my place tonight?"

She blinked a few times. "Huh?"

He held up a hand and felt the heat rise into his cheeks. "Um . . . that didn't come out right. I thought I'd get Lilly to stay there, too. I'm just not comfortable with you in an unprotected environment." He studied her. "And I'm not sure Chelsea would be safe with you under her roof."

The waiter arrived with their meals, and for the next several minutes, they busied themselves getting the food the way they wanted it.

Chad's phone rang, and he rested his utensils on the plate and pulled the device from the clip on his hip. He looked at the screen. "It's Lilly."

"Go ahead and see what she's calling about."

He nodded and lifted the phone to his ear. "Hey."

"Hey," his partner said. "I talked to Shane and ballistics." Shane Stevens, the medical examiner. "They both got to the Tyler Norwood stuff lightning fast."

"Great. What did they find out?"

"Tyler definitely died from a shot to the head."

"What about the bullets?"

"The crime scene unit found both bullets. They pulled one from the bed and one from the backseat of the car. Ballistics said both bullets came from the same weapon and that weapon uses 9mm ammo."

Chad let out a low whistle. "Okay. Good to know. Anything else?"

"No, that's it for now."

"Thanks for the update. I'll fill Macey in." He hung up and nodded at Macey's food. "That looks good."

She used her fork to poke at the pasta. "Yes, and I'm sure it tastes good, too. I just wish I had an appetite."

"Well, eat it anyway."

"Yes, Mom," she teased and popped a noodle into her mouth.

One side of his lips turned up and he cut into the steak he'd been craving for the past three days. A baked potato and broccoli went just fine with the steak.

"So are you going to fill me in?"

He told her what he'd learned from Lilly and she simply nodded.

She took a bite of the pasta. "Mm. That *is* good. I think I got my appetite back. Enough about the case for now. Finish telling me about the crazy chick who dumped you."

He gave a low laugh. "Samantha just had her issues. Like we all do, I suppose. She decided she was better off marrying someone else."

"Like who?"

"Like a partner with Jacoby and Styles law firm."

"Ah."

"Yeah."

She put her fork down and looked him in the eye.

"What?" he asked.

Macey's cheeks turned a bit pink. At least he thought they did. It was a little hard to tell in the dimly lighted restaurant.

"What?" he repeated.

She gave a slight shrug. "She was stupid. You're a great guy. Any woman would be lucky to have your attention."

He felt his cheeks burn and yet his heart rejoiced at her words. Even as confusion drew his brows together. "And yet you wouldn't go out with me."

Macey paused. She picked her fork back up and took another bite. And chewed. Slowly. Finally, she nodded. "I know. But it wasn't because I didn't want to."

He froze, captured by the look in her eyes. "Oh?" The waiter came by and refilled their drinks, allowing him time to gather his scattered thoughts. "So you *did* want to go out with me?"

"Uh huh."

"But you wouldn't."

She sighed. "I'm a trouble magnet, Chad. People who get close to me wind up hurt or dead. Look at what's happened to you ever since you got a little close."

He gave a slow nod and glanced out the window. "Yes, I agree. Trouble is following you, but that's not your fault."

"Of course it is. I wouldn't go out with you because I didn't want that trouble heaped on your poor head—the one that got hit while trying to help me get out of my burning house." Another sigh. "Only now that's exactly what I've done. Without even going out with you."

"See? You should have just gone out with me." She wrinkled her nose at him and he gave a small smile. "What about your sister? You two seem pretty close."

She made a sound low in her throat. "That's because she gives me no choice," she muttered.

He noted the sadness in her voice but his attention was on the car parked outside across the street.

"What is it?" she asked.

"A white car. There. The driver is just sitting in the seat. I think I'll get someone out here to check the plate."

She paled and looked in the direction he'd indicated. Then she stood and threw her napkin down. "Don't bother. I'll get it for you myself."

TWELVE

Macey bolted out of the restaurant and looked both ways before she crossed the street to the white Kia parked nicely against the curb.

"Macey! What are you doing?"

Chad's harsh shout didn't slow her down. The stares of the other patrons from both inside and outside the restaurant didn't faze her either.

She rounded to the back of the vehicle and memorized the plate. Then she walked up to the driver's window and tapped a finger against the glass.

The driver, a twentysomething good-looking man, rolled down the window. He had a Bluetooth in his left ear. "Hold on, will you?" he said to the person on the end of the line. "A pretty lady is trying to get my attention." He grinned at her.

Chad stepped up beside her and gripped her upper arm. The man's smile disappeared.

"Are you following me?" Macey asked. She shook off Chad's grip and stared down the driver of the white car.

His perfectly arched brow lifted. "Following you? You're

pretty, but I'm not desperate. I don't need to follow women. Besides"—he nodded to Chad—"looks like you're taken."

It wasn't him. She didn't think. She nodded. "Sorry, I didn't mean to attack you. It was a case of mistaken identity."

He shrugged. "No problem."

Macey shoved her hands into her coat pockets and turned on her heel. Chad followed her back into the restaurant. She settled herself in the booth once again then peered up at him through her lashes.

"I'm sorry," she whispered.

He reached for her hand. She hesitated then held hers out for him to grasp. When his warm fingers closed over hers, she pressed her lips together to keep them from trembling.

"It's okay, Macey, but going after people like that isn't going to work. What if it had been the guy targeting you? He could have pulled a gun and shot you in the street."

With her free hand, she rubbed her eyes. "I know. I'm sorry."

"I understand you're frustrated and angry and everything else, but you've got to be smart."

"I know! I don't need a lecture." Her throat tightened and tears gathered behind her eyes. She looked down at what was left of her food.

His fingers tightened on hers. "Now it's my turn to apologize. I don't mean to lecture. I just . . . don't want anything to happen to you."

"I'm getting that a lot these days." At his raised eyebrow, she shook her head. "Let's finish our dinner. And . . . if Lilly is willing to spend another night at your place, I'll do the same."

He nodded and the relief on his face touched her. They finished their meal and he escorted her back out to the car.

"Do you need to stop for anything?" he asked.

"No. I had everything I needed in my locker at the station. I brought it with me, including your sister's clothes. I can sleep in them again tonight."

"Nothing from your house?"

She hesitated. "No, not tonight. Like I said, I have a change of clothing for tomorrow. I'm fine for now."

"Okay."

He drove, and she leaned back against the head rest. "Where does your sister live?" she asked.

"In Columbia. She's married and has three kids, ages two, four, and six."

"Boys or girls?"

"All girls."

"Her poor husband."

He laughed. "No kidding."

She fell silent as sleepiness invaded her. She'd been up for over twenty-four hours with only a couple hours of catnapping during that time. Her body craved sleep. Her eyes closed against her will.

The next thing she knew, someone was shaking her shoulder. She drew in a deep breath and opened her eyes. "What?"

"Can you walk or do you want me to carry you?"

That woke her. And she decided she didn't dare answer that question, although the slight smile in his eyes gave away what he was hoping she'd say.

"I've got it, thanks."

He walked around to the passenger back door and opened it. He grabbed her bag from the backseat, and she opened her door to step into the cold of the night. He kept her in front of him, shielding her from anyone who might want to attempt another hit on her. He'd done this all night, ushering her from the car to the restaurant and back. And now to his home.

Lilly's car sat at the curb. "She didn't turn the lights on."

"No, and that's the way we want it."

"It's easier to find your target when they're all lit up, huh?"

"Exactly." But he didn't need any lights. He knew exactly where he was going and led her expertly into the house. She was almost surprised when no one tried to shoot at them. Or bomb them. Or otherwise cause trouble.

Lilly sat on the couch, reading a magazine. She looked up. "Welcome home, kids."

Chad shut the door. "Glad you made yourself at home."

She shot him a smile. "Your place is nicer than mine. I don't mind coming here."

"That's because I spent time fixing my place up. If you ever spent any time at home—"

"My mother's in charge of that, and she's as lousy at it as I am."

Macey shifted her bag to her other shoulder. "I'm going to bed, guys, okay? You can continue this while I snore."

Chad flushed. "Right. Sorry. Come on, I'll show you—"

"I remember where to go, thanks."

"So first thing in the morning we go out there?"

She gave a short nod. "Sure."

She made her way to the room she'd used the night her house had been bombed, set her bag on the bed, and thought about running away. Changing her name, her look, everything. She could do it, couldn't she?

Her phone buzzed. She glanced at the screen and gave a silent groan. To answer or not? She sighed and pressed the green option. "Hi, Valerie."

"Hey." Silence. "Everything okay?"

"Yes."

"I'm just . . . can we meet for breakfast in the morning?"

"I can't, Val. I've . . . got plans."

"Plans you can't change?"

"Yes, why?"

"I just . . . wanted to talk to you about something."

"So talk now."

"No. It can wait. It's just about our parents."

Fear hit her. "They're okay, right? Not sick?"

"No, not at all. They miss you."

Macey froze. "Why do you say that?"

"I talked to Mom today. She said you never call and you don't answer when she calls you and she's just tired of the distance—emotional distance, not just the physical one—between the three of you."

Macey closed her eyes. She couldn't deal with this right now. But . . . "I know. I need to call her and Dad. And I will. It's just that every time I talk to them, I'm riddled with guilt." And afraid that if she spent any time with them at all, she'd just bring more trouble down on their heads.

"Like we talked about before, it's time to put that to rest."

Macey's throat went tight. "That's what I'm trying to do," she managed to squeeze out. She cleared her throat. "They found Tyler Norwood and his mother shot to death today."

"What!"

"I know. They were killed, shot in cold blood."

"But . . . why?"

"That's what I'm trying to find out, Val. But probably because of his association with me." Her sister went quiet. After several seconds passed, Macey frowned. "Val?"

"I'm here. We'll talk about all of this later. Will you call me when you're finished with whatever it is you're doing that you can't change?"

Macey hesitated then decided to be honest. "I'm going to visit the site of the crash, Val. I'm hoping it will stir up the remainder of my memories so I can finally remember what happened and put the past to rest." She paused. "And make peace with Mom and Dad."

"Do you want me to come?"

"No. Chad and Lilly are taking me. I'll call when I can."

"All right. If you're sure." The doorbell rang in the distance. "I've got to go."

Macey tensed. "Are you expecting anyone?"

"Yes, it's Trish. We're going to do a late movie then have a girls' night at her house. She said she'd pick me up so I wouldn't have to drive that clunker I can't afford to replace."

Again the guilt hit Macey. If she hadn't let David help her, he'd still be alive and Valerie wouldn't be worried about money. Or replacing her car. "Don't you have to work in the morning?"

"Don't remind me."

"All right. Well, have a good time with Trish. I guess."

"I will."

And then she was gone, leaving Macey staring at the phone and wondering why Trish wanted to spend so much time with the sister of the woman who was involved—however innocently—in the murder of her husband.

■ ■ ■

Chad rose with the sun Wednesday morning. Lilly still slept on the couch. She must have just dozed off a couple hours before, because when he'd done a perimeter check around three-thirty, she'd still been awake.

He started the coffee, popped open a can of cinnamon rolls he'd found in the back of his refrigerator, spread them on a baking sheet, and stuck them in the oven.

"Hey."

He turned to find his partner sitting up and staring at him with an annoyed look on her face.

"Try to make just a little bit more noise, will you?" she grumbled. He slammed the cabinet door shut and she winced. "Never mind. What are you doing up so early?"

"Couldn't sleep."

"So if you can't sleep, no one does, huh?"

He smirked. "Something like that."

"How's our protectee?"

"Sleeping."

She rolled her eyes and stood. After a stretch that would make a cat proud, she walked into the kitchen. "So . . ."

Chad glanced at her. "I hate it when you start out like that."

It was her turn to smirk. "So . . . what's so special about the girl in your guest room?"

He should have figured she'd bring it up sooner or later. He'd been hoping for later. "I don't know what you're talking about."

She let out a snort that was probably supposed to pass as a laugh. "Come on, we're partners, we tell each other everything. What's drawn you to her?"

He looked at her for a moment then shrugged. "A lot of things, I guess. She needs help. I want to help her."

"So you're the hero, her knight in shining armor?"

"Maybe, but it's more than that. She intrigues me. There's a light in her that wants to shine, but the darkness won't let it. I want to help push the darkness aside so she can find that light again." Even to him, his words sounded cheesy. True, but cheesy. To his surprise, Lilly didn't laugh.

She nodded and gave him a small smile. "She's a lucky woman."

He raised a brow. "Thanks. So what about you?"

"What about me?"

"Any special someone you're interested in?"

"No. No one special."

She was good, he'd give her that. But he knew her too well. There was a subtle darkening of her eyes to let him know he'd hit a nerve.

"I thought we were partners who told each other everything."

This time she let her gaze slide away from his. "My ex is back in town. He wants to see Charlie."

"Are you going to let him?"

"Maybe. Charlie wants to see him. He asks about him every day."

"He misses his dad."

"He does."

"And so do you."

She nodded. "Yes, I do, but that doesn't change the fact that we don't do well married."

"That was four years ago. You've talked a lot since then."

"Yes. We'll see."

"I've got your back whatever you decide."

She smiled. "I know. Thanks. Right back atcha."

He heard the door to his guest room open. "She's awake."

Lilly sniffed. "And those cinnamon rolls are smelling good."

THIRTEEN

Thirty minutes later, after a pot of coffee and a second helping of the cinnamon rolls, they were in Chad's SUV, headed for the site where the accident occurred six years ago.

Macey rode in the front next to Chad while Lilly took the backseat. With her heart in her throat, Macey directed them to the area without any problem, the spot ingrained in her memory as surely as other memories had been wiped out.

It didn't take long to get there. It was just a few minutes outside of Greenville, where the hills weren't mountains yet but could still be deadly to a driver who took the curves too fast. Like Collin had the night of the accident.

"Just a little farther," she said.

Chad put on his blue lights and slowed. Cars passed them, but she barely noticed them as he pulled to the edge of the road. She opened the door and climbed out. Stood at the edge and looked down. Her breath caught. She'd forgotten about the road below that ran parallel to the one she was on now.

"The car hit the guardrail and flipped," she said. "Right here." She ran her hand along the metal that had been replaced long ago. "It landed upright, and Collin was able to guide it down the hill. Only it hit the ditch at the bottom and skidded down the next embankment to crash into the tree. I remember them yelling and my own screams echoing in the night." Her hand went instinctively to her chest. "I didn't have my seat belt on."

"You must have gotten banged up pretty good."

"Yes." The images were coming faster. Why hadn't she done this long ago? Why had she let the fear control her? She climbed over the guardrail.

"I'm going with her," Chad said to Lilly. "You want to move the car and meet us down below?"

"Sure." Lilly took the keys and climbed in. The engine purred to life, but Macey's focus was on the past.

She followed the path down the sloping hill to the road below. It wasn't a hard trek, the hill wasn't very steep, but she remembered tearing down it in the Jeep, the terror that invaded every pore. Then the teeth-rattling stop at the bottom and finally, the skid into the tree.

And the sudden silence.

"I think I passed out for a moment but then woke up fairly quickly. We all managed to get out of the car. Collin was screaming and waving his gun around and then he just passed out." She walked over to the tree that had halted their forward momentum. "He was here. On the ground." She dropped to her knees, ignoring the damp that immediately seeped through her jeans. "I touched him." She reached out, seeing Collin on the ground in front of her.

"Collin," she whispered. She touched his head, but he didn't move. Blood covered his face. The gun lay next to his limp fingers. When she looked down at her hands, they were red. She cried out and wiped them on the ground beside her, but

she couldn't get the blood off. She trembled from the cold, the shock, the loss of her own blood.

And then Collin lifted his head. His eyes focused, his fingers wrapped around the gun, and he lifted it. Pointed it at her. Shoved himself into a sitting position, using the car to hold him up. "Hide it," he whispered even as a keening groan of pain escaped him.

"What?"

"Hide it." The gun moved, swung toward Tyler. "Do it or I'll shoot him."

She blinked back to the present. "Collin grabbed the gun and pointed it at me. Told me to hide the bag or he'd shoot Tyler."

Tyler flinched. "He's right, Macey. If we don't have the stuff on us, they can't put us at the robbery. Hide it."

"Ty?" she whispered.

He shoved a bag in her hand. "Go. If they don't find the stuff, they won't have any proof. You've got to hide it."

Collin's eyes went to half mast. "If you're not back in three minutes, I'll put a bullet in him." Tyler started to move away, but Collin pulled the trigger. Macey screamed, the sound ricocheting through her battered skull. "I'm not kidding. Go."

She rose to her feet, wobbled but stayed upright. She had to hide it. Had to. Had to. At first the neoprene felt cold under her fingers but soon she couldn't feel it. She'd never been so cold. She went to her knees. Smelled the earth, heard the lapping of the water nearby. She got up, fell down again. Over and over until she reached the edge.

"The lake," she whispered.

"What?"

She pushed through the trees, found a small path and followed it. "I think I came this way."

She gripped the evidence. Her fingerprints would be on it. But she didn't care. She couldn't let Collin kill Tyler.

"I threw it in the lake."

"The evidence?"

"Yes. All I could do was follow orders. Collin told me to do it, so I did."

They exited the trees to find themselves standing on the lakeshore. A dock rocked a few feet away. The water was clear and pretty. And deceptive. The man-made lake was large, and during the summer it was a prime vacation spot. Except for this area. Here there was no real beach. Just a small bit of sand that would only take five or six steps to get from the edge of the trees to the water line. And it was private property. The dock belonged to the owners of the land and hadn't been used or kept up in years.

"Did you look inside the bag?"

"No. There wasn't time for that. Only Tyler and Collin knew what was in it. Why?"

"Just thinking. Now that we know it wasn't Tyler after you, I'm starting to see things with a different perspective. Realizing we need to come at everything from a different angle."

She stared at the water. "Do you think it's even possible that it could still be down there?"

He planted his hands on his hips and looked around. "I don't know. Six years is a long time. However, it's not like this is a high traffic area. The dock over there looks abandoned. It's falling apart. So maybe it's possible."

"It could be buried under the mud, or someone else could have found it." She bit her lip. "It's probably a long shot, but that's where the bag was the last time I saw it. It's black with a shoulder strap. I can see it so clearly now." Her head throbbed a steady beat, but at least it didn't feel like the migraine she usually got.

Chad pulled his phone from his pocket. "I'll call it in. We'll get the dive team to search this area."

At the water's edge, she fell. The bag was heavy. She panted from the exertion, the pain, the fear. Sobs wracked her. She couldn't get caught with it. She'd go to jail forever. Her parents would never speak to her again. They'd hate her for sure now. And Collin would shoot Tyler if she didn't get back.

She couldn't pass out. Don't pass out. How had this night gone so horribly wrong? Tyler! Why did you do it? Why? Why had she snuck out? Why had she disobeyed and gone behind her parents' backs? Never again, she promised silently. Get me out of this, God, and I promise, I'll never do anything wrong ever again. Please!

She rolled onto her side, facing the lake, the bag too heavy to lift. She just wanted to stay where she was and go to sleep. Her head felt thick. Too heavy. And the pain . . . she just wanted the pain to stop.

The bag. Its weight pulled her down. She pushed to her knees, used the strap to pull the bag onto her lap, then heaved it into the lake. It just sat there in the shallow water. Not deep enough. She continued to crawl forward and push it. Out, out, out. Until it was finally covered. She stood. Swayed.

So c-c-c-cold. Tremors rocked her, her legs almost gave out, and her eyelids grew heavy, but she hauled herself back to shore, ignoring the pain, the freezing water, the terror—and the knowledge that her life would never be the same.

Tyler. She had to help Tyler. And who else? There was some-one else there, right? Collin. He was going to shoot Tyler.

But why?

She struggled to remember. Her head pounded. She had to get back. Right? But what was the hurry? She could rest for a few minutes, couldn't she?

No. Tyler. She had to help Tyler.

One step at a time, she made her way back to the crash site where Collin still sat, his back against the car. His open eyes stared, and the gun rested on the ground where it had fallen from his hand. "Collin?" She shook him and he fell to the side.

Macey dropped to her knees.

Then looked up into the black faceless creature who reached down and picked up Collin's gun. "You should have stayed home," the voice said.

The gun cracked, and Macey felt the burst of pain even as she fell back against the cold, damp earth.

"I remember it all," she whispered. "All of it."

Her phone rang. She glanced at it and groaned. Valerie. "It's my sister. I'll let it go to voice mail."

"You can answer it."

"No."

She ignored the call while she tried to process the memories that overwhelmed her.

Her phone buzzed again. Valerie. "She's not going to give up until I answer." Macey sighed and slid the bar on the screen. "It's not a good time, Val."

"Don't hang up. I need to know something."

Her sister sounded . . . odd. "What?"

"What kind of bullet killed Tyler and his mother?"

Macey blinked. "Why?"

"Just tell me!"

"A 9mm."

Her sister gave a hitching sob. "I found receipts, Macey, for everything. For the ammunition, for stuff to make one of those Molotov cocktail things. I googled the ingredients and . . . and . . . then there's—" Her voice faded for a moment.

"What, Val? What? Where did you find the receipts? Where are you?"

"I told her where you were going. It's all my fault."

"Told who?"

A muffled pop sounded from behind her. She turned when Chad cried out and dropped to the ground. Blood spread across his left arm.

Macey screamed and the phone fell from her fingers. A hand grasped her ankle and pulled her feet from under her. She landed with a thud and her breath whooshed from her lungs. Another *pop*, and the ground spurted next to her head. "Chad!"

"Stay down. I'm all right," he grunted. "But we're sitting ducks. The bullets are coming from the trees to our left. Head for the other side of the dock." He pulled his weapon and aimed it in the direction the bullets had come from.

She ran for cover, the night of the robbery slamming into her memory with full force. The memories tumbled around in her brain while the terror of being shot again forced her feet to fly across the uneven terrain. Bullets followed them, and she prayed they'd continue to miss.

Chad stayed with her and fired off a shot. They had to reach the dock. If they headed for the woods to the right, there would be way too much open space to cover. They would be easy targets.

"Where's Lilly?" she panted.

"Don't know. As soon as we have cover, I'll call her. And backup."

"I dropped my phone back there." She slipped down the incline to the bottom of the dock. The water rushed into her boots instantly, sending chills over her entire body. She gasped. So cold. Again.

She held on to the slippery post, keeping it between her and the shooter, as the water lapped against her knees.

A bullet zinged past her ear, and Chad pushed her farther

into the water. "Go to the next post. The farther you are, the harder you'll be to hit."

Each step chilled her more. He stayed behind her. She heard him give a hiss of pain. "You okay?" she asked.

"Yeah. One good thing about the cold water, it may stop the bleeding."

She could hear his teeth chattering. Cold or shock from the wound? Probably both. "Do you see the shooter?" she gasped.

"No."

He shoved his gun back into his side holster then held his cell to his ear. "Stay behind this post."

She did, keeping her eyes on the beach area. Waiting for the person to come after them.

Another shot hit the post in front of Chad. He flinched and fumbled the phone. It slipped from his fingers and landed in the water.

FOURTEEN

C had wanted to use words he hadn't used in a long time. He sucked in a breath and went under. The water was only up to his waist. He felt along the bottom of the lake, the muck sliming through his fingers. He opened his eyes but couldn't see a thing in the murky water. He kept feeling until his fingers wrapped around a solid object and he pulled. But it wouldn't move.

He pulled again and it slid up the post. He realized he wasn't holding his phone. His lungs started to strain. He stayed under and let his fingers roam the object. A buckle?

He had to have air. He rose to the surface to find Macey still up against the post next to him.

"Come out or I'm going to keep shooting," a voice called from the woods.

Macey gasped. "I know her. That's Trish," she whispered.

"Who?"

"My sister's best friend. Trish Benjamin. The wife of the man who was killed in the robbery six years ago."

As if to prove her words, Trish fired again. The bullet spat up the water near Macey's waist, and she jerked. This time the shot had come from behind them.

"She's moved." Chad immediately motioned to Macey to slide to the other side of the post. She did, and he pulled his gun again and aimed it in the direction the bullets had come from. But he couldn't see the shooter. And he wasn't shooting blind.

"Come out!" Trish called again. He pointed his weapon toward her voice but still couldn't see her.

"Why are you trying to kill me?" Macey shouted through her shudders. Chad knew she was cold. Dangerously cold. So was he. They were going to have to get out of the water, but it was the only safe place for the moment.

"Because you're remembering."

"Remembering what?" Macey's eyes met his. She swallowed. "That it was you who shot me that night? Then buried me alive in a shallow grave?"

Chad gaped. Rage chased away some of the cold. This woman had buried Macey alive? No wonder she had nightmares.

"My partner will be here soon," Chad called. "She'll have heard the shots!"

A low laugh reached him. "Your partner's not going to be doing any rescue mission, trust me."

His chills multiplied. "What did you do to her?"

"Nothing that I didn't have to do."

She'd shot Lilly. Somehow, this woman had gotten the drop on his partner. Just one more reason to get help here fast.

He lowered himself into the water so that only his head showed. He caught Macey's eyes. "Keep her talking," he whispered. Then he went under.

His shoulder ached, but he'd been right. After the initial lightning-intense, breath-stealing pain when the cold first hit it, the gunshot wound was now almost numb. The fact that he could use his arm said nothing was broken. The bullet had probably passed right through.

He stayed under, swimming slowly toward the shore. The only way he was going to be able to end this was to confront Trish.

He surfaced, his head coming up just enough to let his eyes search the woods beyond.

" . . . did you kill David?" he heard Macey ask. Her words were sluggish. Slowing. Hypothermia.

"He was getting you too close to the truth. To remembering. Are you cold, Macey?" Trish mocked. "You sound funny."

"And you buddied up with my sister so she would tell you everything. Keep you updated with the latest, right?"

"Yes. You're slurring your words, Macey. All I have to do is wait until you pass out and drown, you realize that, right?"

Macey didn't answer. Chad looked back to see her eyes shut, lips a pale purple. She wasn't shivering anymore.

He went back under and was at her side within seconds. She opened her eyes when he touched her face. "Keep talking. Keep moving to keep your blood flowing." His foot hit something and it moved. His phone. "Macey, you hear me?"

"Uh huh. Yes. Okay. I'm fine." She moved her legs and the water sloshed, but at least she was in motion.

"I'm going down again to get my phone. Keep moving." He went under, down to the bottom, his hand outstretched, searching. Finally his fingers closed around the device. *Thank you, Lord.*

When he came back up, Macey was rubbing her hands up and down her face.

"What about your husband?" she called to Trish. "Did you hire Tyler and Collin to kill him?"

"No, that was just an added bonus. He came home from a business meeting early." Trish gave a harsh laugh.

"Sometimes things just have a way of working out. Like now, Macey. You're going to freeze to death and I won't even have to pull the trigger. Yours and the detective's deaths will be ruled a tragic accident."

Chad's jaw tightened and he had to admit she might be right. But what about Lilly? How would Trish explain her death? He kept his lips closed. No need to take her in that direction.

"And Tyler and his mother? You killed them too, didn't you?" Macey shouted. At least he thought she was trying to shout. The words came out sounding like her tongue was too thick for her mouth. But her words made sense, that was a good sign. He motioned for her to go under. She took a breath and he pulled her with him to the next post. Then he stood. Here the water still reached to his waist.

". . . couldn't let Tyler find the contents of the safe. I've been all over this place the past six years, searching. I finally decided it was gone, but then he let it slip that you'd hidden it."

"You . . . um . . . t-talked to him?" Macey asked.

"Of course. I called him on a regular basis while he was in jail. He never knew who I was, though. He just knew I wanted to know what *he* knew about the night of the robbery."

"So you were the throwaway number we found," Chad said. His own shivering had slowed. Drowsiness was beginning to set in. But she had them effectively pinned. If they stayed in the water, they'd eventually die of hypothermia. If he got them to shore, they'd die from a bullet. His brain tried to work, but he found it hard to think clearly.

"Well, I'm not so dumb as to use my home number."

He focused on her words even as his gaze roamed the shore. Where was Lilly? Was she really hurt like Trish said? Was she dead? Desperation tore at him. He had to get her help if there was any chance she was hurt and still alive. He looked at his phone. It was still on. Thank God for LifeProof's waterproof cases. He pressed 911 and lifted the phone to his ear.

"And then Tyler got out," he said to Trish.

"And he was going to go after Macey. I told him to. I told him to get rid of her."

"But he didn't. He wanted her to remember, didn't he?"

"Yes! He was supposed to just kill her, but then I found out what he was doing. He was trying to scare her into remembering."

"So you decided to kill Tyler," Chad said while the phone connected.

"I was afraid she would remember and tell him where the stuff was before I could find it—or kill her."

"911, what's your emergency?"

"10-46, officer needs assistance." He gave the address in a low voice. "Shooter is a white female, name is, uh . . ." He blinked. "Ah . . ." What was her name? "Trish . . ." He shook Macey and she groaned. Blinked. "What's her name, Macey?"

She closed her eyes.

"Is it cold enough for you yet?" Trish called, her tone mocking.

Chad forced his brain to work. "Benjamin," he said, pulling the name from the recesses of his sluggish mind. "Patricia Benjamin." He kept the phone on so the dispatcher could hear. To the woman still hidden in the trees, he shouted, "So you . . . um . . . just decided if you hadn't found it after all these years, no one else would find it either."

"Exactly."

"Only—only—" What was he going to say? Man, he was cold. Oh, right. "Only there was one person who might remember what she did with it—and her memories were returning."

"Yes, I told you all that! You can come out of the water so

I can shoot you, or you can just die a slow death from hypothermia. I'm not going anywhere."

Chad fought the effects of the cold. He had to keep Trish talking until help arrived—or get her to leave so he could get Macey out of the water, because she was fading fast. She was limp against him, her breathing slowing. He felt her pulse and found it steady but slow. His eyes drooped. He was so tired. He jerked. Opened his eyes.

Sirens sounded in the distance. "Help is on the way, Trish," he called. "I still have my phone. All we have to do is wait here for help." Her heard the sluggishness in his own voice, had trouble getting the words past his lips.

He heard a curse, saw the trees move, heard a rustle. Trish had run. That was fine. All he wanted was to get Macey and himself out of the water. He was very close to being sucked into the blackness hovering just on the edge of his consciousness. He headed for the shore, pulling Macey along with him.

"No!" Trish shouted.

He flinched. So she wasn't gone yet. He moved back to the cover of the dock.

More shots sounded. Kicked up the water. How many bullets could she have left? He shook Macey. She lifted her head and opened her eyes. "Fight, Macey." He rubbed her cheeks and massaged the back of her neck. "I need you to stay awake."

"What? Too cold, Chad."

"I know. Trust me, I know."

He moved and three more bullets popped in his direction but didn't come close. Trish was moving away and shooting blind. She was in a hurry now that the sirens were coming closer. He took a chance and moved again.

Nothing.

Taking a deep breath, he pulled Macey out of the water and stumbled onto the shore. He went to his knees, keeping his body between Macey's and the direction of the bullets.

But no more came his way.

Either Trish had left or she'd run out of ammunition. He checked Macey's pulse and found it steady but weak. She needed to warm up. Now.

And he needed to get to Lilly. To make sure she was all right.

He grasped Macey and pulled her close. Then he realized he still had a grip on his weapon. He shoved it into its holster and pulled the phone from his soggy pocket. He lifted it to his ear. "You still there?"

"I'm here. Are you still alive?"

"I think so."

"Officers should be there now."

"I heard them. Shooter's on the run." Now that he was out of the water, he was still almost frozen, but his adrenaline was rushing too. "Tell them to look for a white car. Four-door. Might be a Kia or a car that looks like it. But it's white."

She clicked over to the officers and he knew she was giving them his information.

Two officers cleared the trees and came onto the beach area, weapons drawn. "Police! Don't move! Hands where we can see them!"

Chad lifted his hands and they approached. "My badge is on my belt." He almost didn't have the energy to show them but managed to shove aside his soggy shirt.

"Chad, that you?"

"Mitchell. Yeah." They lowered their weapons and hurried toward him. "She needs an ambulance."

Mitchell stared at his shoulder. "Looks like you could use one too."

Belt. Chad touched his badge then his buckle and looked back out at the dock. "I've still got one more thing to do."

"What?" Mitchell looked at his partner. "Get some blankets out of the car. We'll get her warmed up best we can while we wait on the ambulance."

Chad shook his head. He knew he should still be cold, but right now he wasn't feeling much. "You have a knife?"

Mitchell nodded. "Swiss Army one. Will that work?"

"That'll work." He took it from the officer. "I'll be right back." Chad gathered what strength he had left and forced his leaden legs to carry him back toward the water.

"Hey, what are you doing?"

"Trying to help a friend put her past to rest. Come get me if I go down and don't come back up."

"Chad, you really shouldn't . . ."

"Yeah, I know I shouldn't."

And then he was wading back into the water, pushing his way back out to the dock. He shivered only slightly and knew his body temperature was too low. He didn't plan on this taking long. He opened the knife so the largest blade was out and ready.

He might be wrong, but it was a chance he had to take. He sucked in a deep breath and went under.

FIFTEEN

Macey opened her eyes and pulled in a deep breath. Hospital odors hit her. She blinked again and sat up with a groan. The IV in the crook of her arm pinched, and she grimaced.

"Hey, you okay?"

She looked up. Chad. "Yes. I think so. What happened?"

The question brought another round of déjà vu.

He rubbed his chin. "They got her."

Memories intruded, and she breathed a sigh of relief that she didn't have to struggle to find them. Then grief hit her. "Trish."

He nodded.

"Why was she so determined that I not remember that night? What was it that was such a threat to her?"

"I think I can answer those questions."

"Okay, but first I need water." She pointed to the cup on the bedside table, and he handed it to her. After three long, blessed drags on the straw, she set it down. "Tell me."

"I found the bag of stuff from the safe."

"What? Where? How?"

He gave her a faint smile. "It was caught on one of the posts of the dock. Or pier. Whatever that thing was. There were some jagged edges where the wood was rotting, and the strap was caught. I felt the buckle when I was looking for my phone."

"So you went back out and got it? Are you crazy?"

"I'm sure there was some craziness involved, but yes, I went back out and got it."

"And?"

"I took a good look at the contents."

She took another sip of water. "I remember it being extremely heavy. What was in it?"

"A twenty-five-pound gold bar worth just a little less than half a million dollars. Plus jewelry, about ten thousand in cash, and some personal papers."

"Oh my. Where did George Benjamin get the bar? I wouldn't think those were just floating around—pun not intended—and available to purchase."

"No, not usually. But he got this one legitimately. He bought it at an auction about fifteen years ago, so it's free and clear. The papers that came with it were in the bag, too."

She shook her head. "I can't believe you found it."

"Well, with it being so heavy, it wouldn't travel far even in severe storms that churned the water pretty good."

"And that was so important to Trish that she was willing to kill for it." Macey sighed. "Unbelievable."

"Well, she had a bigger motive than that gold bar."

She frowned. "What?"

"Those papers. And pictures."

"Pictures of what?"

"Her with another man."

Macey's brows rose. "Oh."

"Yeah. And then there was the prenup that she'd signed."

Macey rubbed her face. "A prenup? What did it say?"

"That if it ever came out—even after George's death—that Trish had been unfaithful, all of the assets would revert to one of his charities and she would forfeit everything. Including her very generous monthly allowance."

Macey's jaw dropped. "Oh my. You know, Valerie said something about a monthly check."

"Yes. She knew her husband had put those papers and pictures in the safe, but she didn't have the combination. Collin was eighteen when he was arrested for attempted burglary. His mugshot ended up in the paper, and Trish saw it. She simply did her research and bided her time. He was out on bail when she approached him and offered him the gold bar if he would steal the contents of the safe. All he had to do was give her the papers and the pictures. The gold was his."

"And there was no way he was going to turn down that much money."

"Absolutely not."

"And he talked his best friend, Tyler, into helping," she said. "Probably told him they'd split the money on the sale of the gold."

"Most likely." Chad smoothed his hand down her hair then twirled a stray curl around his finger. "You scared me."

"You scared *me*." Tears gathered before she could stop them. "I thought I was going to lose you." She sniffed. "How's your shoulder?"

"Stiff. It was a through and through. Didn't even need surgery, just cleaning and a round of antibiotics and a few stitches. I was lucky."

"Or God was watching out for you."

He smiled. "Or that."

"Lilly!" Macey gasped. "I can't believe I haven't asked about her. Is she okay?"

"She's fine. Just a bad knock on the head. Apparently when Trish shot at her, it startled her and when she spun, she tripped and hit her head against the front of the car. Knocked herself out cold. Fortunately in her case. Trish thought she'd shot her and didn't have to worry about her anymore."

"I'm so glad she's all right."

"Yeah. Me too."

"What about your family? Did they come to the hospital to check on you?"

"Yes." He gave her a small smile. "And I told them I had someone I wanted them to meet soon."

"I want to meet them. I've seen them come and go from your place but never stopped to introduce myself. I'm sorry about that now." She sighed. "I'm sorry about a lot of things."

He lifted her hand and kissed her knuckles. "No regrets about the past. We have too much to look forward to in the future." He smiled. "Your family is outside."

"Val?"

"And your parents. I told them I'd let them know when you woke up, but I couldn't help being a little selfish and keeping you to myself a while." He moved closer until his face was inches from her.

She felt the heat rise in her cheeks and decided she wasn't cold anymore. "Why would you want me for yourself?"

"Because I don't need an audience to do this."

He closed the gap and placed his warm lips over hers. She stayed still, relishing the feel of him. She raised her arms and slid them around his neck to pull him closer. His kiss was a sweet, gentle exploration. A giving of himself. She gave as good as she got, and when he pulled back, he leaned his forehead against hers.

"Wow," she said.

"Yeah."

"Yes," she said. "I will."

"What?" He tilted his head, his brow furrowed.

"Yes, I'll go out with you."

A slow grin curved his lips. "I haven't asked yet."

"I'm saving you the trouble."

He laughed. "I appreciate that. Where do you want to go?"

"Anywhere. As long as it's with you," she said, all joking aside.

He kissed her again. "Want me to let your family in?"

"Who?" He grinned and she shrugged. "Sure."

He crossed the room to the door and pulled it open. "She's awake."

Val entered first. Her red-rimmed eyes met Macey's. "I'm so sorry," she blurted.

Macey held her arms open. "Come here, sis."

Valerie went in for the hug while her parents stood just inside the door, watching. Macey met her mother's eyes. She saw the tears there and felt her throat tighten in response. Then she looked at her father and his eyes were red, too.

She gave them a wobbly smile. They took that as permission and walked over to add their hugs to Val's.

"We understand we almost lost you again," her father said. His voice was scratchy, like he was having trouble getting the words past his throat.

"Yes, but you didn't. I'm fine."

"Will you stop pushing us away now?" her mother asked softly.

Macey nodded against Valerie's shoulder. "Yes. I will." She looked at them both. "I'm sorry. At first I was just mad. Ashamed of what I'd done and the grief I'd caused you, so I decided to stay away and hope you would just forget it ever happened. And then when David was killed, I connected that to the fact that he was trying to help me. I was afraid if I let you get too close, you would be next."

Chad cleared his throat. "Trish copped to David's death as well. She ran him off the road and tossed the bomb in your house. Tyler only left the notes. The ambulance was a chance thing. He must have been following you, looking for the opportunity to plant the note, and found it that day at the scene. And for the record, Trish drove a white BMW, not a white Kia. But the cars look so similar, it's easy to mistake them."

"So Tyler wanted to scare me into remembering and Trish wanted me dead because I was remembering. Unbelievable."

"Yes. She's the one you saw dressed in black and wearing a mask before she threw the cocktail in your window. She and Tyler must have just missed each other at your house that night by mere seconds."

"That's crazy."

"Definitely. And officers found the receipts your sister called to tell you about. When all is said and done, Trish is going away for a very long time."

"She buried me alive," Macey whispered. Her parents gasped but she was focused on the memories. They came easier this time.

The shot rang out. The pain flashed and she fell backwards into the shallow indention the earth had made. And the darkness came, welcoming, wrapping her in its arms so that she didn't have to feel anymore.

When she woke it was cold, so very cold. She couldn't breathe, couldn't think. Dirt hit her in the face. She thought she heard sirens. Then she noticed a heaviness pressing on her chest. She tried to move and couldn't. Trapped in the darkness, she wanted to scream.

And couldn't.

"I couldn't breathe," Macey said. "I woke up and the dirt was everywhere. I couldn't see, it was so dark and I was so cold." She held a hand out to him.

He grasped her fingers and squeezed. "But they found you, and you lived."

"And you saved me this time. Thank you for everything, Chad."

"You're welcome."

Her father cleared his throat. "Well, I guess we'll head on out of here. Looks like you're in good hands."

Macey wasn't even embarrassed. She looked at Chad. "Yes, I am. The best."

It was his turn to flush and she grinned. Her mother hugged her one last time before they filed out the door. Val gave her a look over her shoulder and a small wave. Macey waved back. Then it was just her and Chad again.

He sat on the bed next to her. "You need anything?"

She thought about it then shook her head. "No." She pulled him in for a hug and rested her cheek against his solid chest. "I have everything I need right here."

He kissed the top of her head then tilted her face up. He pushed her hair behind her ears while he looked straight into her eyes. "It might seem a little soon for this, but I almost lost you today, and I don't want to waste any more precious minutes trying to figure out how you feel, so I'm just going to tell you how I feel."

"Okay," she whispered.

"I love you, Macey."

Her heart thudded. "I love you, too, Chad. I think I have for a long time. You've been a friend when I wouldn't let myself have friends. You were there when no one else was."

"Whether you wanted me there or not."

"I wanted you there."

He smiled. "And I want to be here from now on."

"I think that sounds like a good plan."

"No more letting the past rule the future, right?"

"No. The sins of the past are just that. In the past. As far as the east is from the west. Gone."

"And forgiven."

"Forever."

About the Authors

Dee Henderson is the author of numerous novels, including *Taken, Undetected, Unspoken, Jennifer: An O'Malley Love Story, Full Disclosure*, and the acclaimed O'MALLEY series. Her books have won or been nominated for several prestigious industry awards, such as the RITA Award, the Christy Award, and the ECPA Gold Medallion. Dee is a lifelong resident of Illinois. Learn more at DeeHenderson.com or facebook.com /DeeHendersonBooks.

Dani Pettrey is the acclaimed author of the ALASKAN COURAGE romantic suspense series, which includes her bestselling novels *Submerged, Shattered, Stranded, Silenced*, and *Sabotaged*. Her newest novel, *Cold Shot*, is the first book of her CHESAPEAKE VALOR series. Her books have been honored with the Daphne du Maurier award, two HOLT Medallions, two National Readers' Choice Awards, the Gail Wilson Award of Excellence, and Christian Retailing's Best Award, among others.

She feels blessed to write inspirational romantic suspense

because it incorporates so many things she loves—the thrill of adventure, nail-biting suspense, the deepening of her characters' faith, and plenty of romance. She and her husband reside in Maryland, where they enjoy time with their two daughters, a son-in-law, and a super adorable grandson. You can find her online at www.danipettrey.com.

Lynette Eason is the bestselling author of the WOMEN OF JUSTICE series and the DEADLY REUNIONS series, as well as *No One to Trust*, *Nowhere to Turn*, and *No Place to Hide* in the HIDDEN IDENTITY series. She is a member of American Christian Fiction Writers and Romance Writers of America. She has a master's degree in education from Converse College and she lives in South Carolina. Learn more at www.lynetteeason.com.

If you enjoyed *Sins of the Past*, you may also like . . .